THE TAKING OF JAYLEIA . . .

Alarms wailed.

Jayleia made it to the cockpit as another jolt rocked the little vessel.

Damen sat strapped in at piloting in the U-shaped cockpit. V'kyrri, at navigation, sat beside him. Weapons panel on V'kyrri's right, what looked like a communications panel on Damen's left.

"Are you all right?" Damen asked, tossing a glance at her.

"I won't know that until you return me to the *Sen Ekir*," she said, "which you have no intention of doing, have you?"

The muscles in Damen's jaw bunched.

V'kyrri leaned across the cockpit, reached under the communications panel next to her, pulled out a seat and unfolded it.

"Strap in!" Damen ordered.

Jayleia gaped at him. "You're kidnapping me?"

Berkley Sensation titles by Marcella Burnard

ENEMY WITHIN

ENEMY GAMES

ENEMY GAMES

MARCELLA BURNARD

BERKLEY SENSATION, NEW YORK

THE BERKLEY PUBLISHING GROUP
Published by the Penguin Group
Penguin Group (USA) Inc.
375 Hudson Street, New York, New York 10014, USA
Penguin Group (Canada), 90 Eglinton Avenue East, Suite 700, Toronto, Ontario M4P 2Y3, Canada
(a division of Pearson Penguin Canada Inc.)
Penguin Books Ltd., 80 Strand, London WC2R 0RL, England
Penguin Group Ireland, 25 St. Stephen's Green, Dublin 2, Ireland (a division of Penguin Books Ltd.)
Penguin Group (Australia), 250 Camberwell Road, Camberwell, Victoria 3124, Australia
(a division of Pearson Australia Group Pty. Ltd.)
Penguin Books India Pvt. Ltd., 11 Community Centre, Panchsheel Park, New Delhi—110 017, India
Penguin Group (NZ), 67 Apollo Drive, Rosedale, Auckland 0632, New Zealand
(a division of Pearson New Zealand Ltd.)
Penguin Books (South Africa) (Pty.) Ltd., 24 Sturdee Avenue, Rosebank, Johannesburg 2196,
South Africa

Penguin Books Ltd., Registered Offices: 80 Strand, London WC2R 0RL, England

This book is an original publication of The Berkley Publishing Group.

PRINTING HISTORY
Berkley Sensation trade paperback edition / May 2011

Library of Congress Cataloging-in-Publication Data

Burnard, Marcella.
    Enemy games / Marcella Burnard.—Berkley Sensation trade paperback ed.
        p.   cm.
    ISBN 978-0-425-24090-8 (pbk.)
    I. Title.
    PS3602.U759E6 2011
    813'.6—dc22
                              2010053559

PRINTED IN THE UNITED STATES OF AMERICA

10   9   8   7   6   5   4   3   2   1

ACKNOWLEDGMENTS

Special thanks:

To my beloved husband, Keith, whose patience, faith, and support know no bounds.

To the FF&P members who hang out at the watercooler offering sage advice, strange and wonderful ideas, and good company.

To Jeffe Kennedy for stepping in on an emergency basis to critique what was broken.

To my family for rooting for me, for talking up my book at every turn, and for not disowning me over that faraway look I'd get in my eye whenever a story started playing in my head.

To my longtime friend and cohort, Dr. Kurt "Spuds" Vogel, Lt Col, USAF (ret.) for keeping me rooted if not in the probable then at least in the outer reaches of the vaguely possible.

To Dawn Calvert, Darcy Carson, Carol Dunford, DeeAnna Galbraith, Melinda Rucker Haynes, and Lisa Wanttaja—a great group of writers, mentors and, best of all, friends.

To my editor, Leis Pederson, and to my agent, Emmanuelle Alspaugh, for helping me tell a better story.

To the members of Feline-L whose wide-ranging backgrounds and interests allowed me to ask the most obscure questions and receive cogent answers.

Last but certainly not least, my sincere thanks to Eratosthenes, Autolycus, Cuillean, and Hatshepsut, my feline snoopervisors, lap warmers, keyboard walkers, and reminders that no matter how large looms the deadline, there's always time to play.

CHAPTER

1

THE communications panel trilled, echoing the call in the confines of the tiny cockpit. Damen entered the unlock code.

"*Kawl Fergus*," he said, answering with the name of his fast, little reconnaissance ship.

"Change in plans, Major," his commander's voice rumbled over the com, rolling around and around the cockpit. "Your mission's been shot to the lowest level of Hell."

Damen's chest tightened. "Situation, Admiral?"

"Tagreth Federated accused the director of Intelligence Command of collaborating with the Chekydran," the man said. "He's vanished."

"Spawn of a Myallki bitch," Damen gritted. "Zain Durante isn't a colluder. His cover must have been blown. If there's an extraction plan for him, sir, I'd like to be a part of it."

"He is a colluder, Major. With us. He wasn't providing tactical information to Her Majesty's government with the approval of the Tagreth Federated Council. As for an extraction plan? That presumes we know where he is," his commander replied. "We found out he'd gone underground when the TFC media outlets ran the news bulletin posting the reward for information leading to his arrest."

"We've lost our chance to take down the network of traitors inside TFC, then. Every mercenary in the lanes will be looking for . . ."

"Him, his wife, and his daughter," his commander finished.

Alarm singed the breath in Damen's lungs.

Durante's daughter. Jayleia. Delicate features. Shining black hair. A shy smile and serious brown eyes.

They'd met. He'd helped hijack her science ship. Then the Chekydran had forced them into alliance. She'd barely said two words to him, but he couldn't shake the memory of her gaze on him when she'd believed he wouldn't notice. He could swear he'd seen admiration in the charmed twist of her faint smile.

He'd sensed a wall around the beautiful, dark-eyed xenobiologist, as if she feared what he'd see in her if she dropped her guard. He hoped she still had her defenses online.

The accusation against her father made Jayleia a target for every single one of her father's enemies.

His heart thudded into uneasy rhythm.

"Your orders, sir?" he asked, his tone dead.

"Divert to TFC space. Your objective is Jayleia Durante. She either has the information we need or she is the fulcrum we'll require to pry her father out of hiding," the admiral said.

"Jayleia is still aboard the *Sen Ekir*?"

"Yes."

"Location of the *Sen Ekir*?" Damen asked.

"The ship is on Chemmoxin, where they are responding to an outbreak," the admiral replied. "Captain Idylle tells me the disease isn't airborne, but I expect you to take all reasonable precaution against infection."

"This will end her career as far as TFC is concerned, sir," Damen noted.

"Captain Ari Idylle here, Major," a feminine voice interjected. "I suspect your concern for Jay's loyalties comes a day too late. You're closest, in the ship best equipped to get Jay out of what could turn into a bloodbath. The traitors have put a price on her capture. Four known mercenaries have mobilized. You and I want Jayleia alive more than we want her to like us. Get there first, Sindrivik."

Breath hissed in between his clenched teeth. "Diverting. Top speed."

CHAPTER
2

JAYLEIA checked her sensor boosters, her holo-image generators, and her live traps.

"Temperature forty-point-three degrees and falling at your location," Pietre, several kilometers away on board their space science ship *Sen Ekir*, said.

"It isn't falling fast enough," she replied, panting in the oppressive, dank heat of Chemmoxin's infamous swamps. She'd given up trying to keep sweat out of her stinging, watering eyes about the same time she'd stopped trying to pluck every last hungry bloodworm from her skin.

They'd come to Chemmoxin in response to a flesh-necrotizing illness afflicting the humanoid colonists. The *Sen Ekir*'s crew had traced the infection to the fluffy, arboreal kuorls, which meant observing the creatures and sampling out tissue and blood.

"Signals read green across the board," Pietre replied over the open com line. Sympathy mingled with amusement in his voice. "Your last booster install did the trick. We're recording."

"Get to your blind, Jay, and send me a physical scan," her cousin, Raj, ordered. "You sound squashed."

"Imagine," she retorted, shaking her head. He was right, of course. Most humanoid biology simply hadn't been designed to work for long periods in this combination of excessive heat and humidity. Add a few parasites sucking blood and things turned dangerous fast as the body struggled to maintain a safe internal temperature.

Deep in the bowels of the biggest gnarled, moss-draped, and lichen-deformed qwarfoi tree in the stand, a kuorl coughed and then growled.

Jayleia started. The final trap she'd been setting snapped shut on her hand. "What the Three Hells was that?" she breathed. "Temp reading?"

"Thirty-nine-point-eight."

"Report," their boss, Dr. Linnaeus Idylle, demanded.

Fumbling to free her scraped-up hand from the trap's force fields, she said, "I heard something. Or thought I did."

"Confirm Pietre's temperature reading," he said.

The trap let go. She grabbed her handheld and backed a step away from the moss-shrouded branch holding the kuorl trap.

"Thirty-nine-point-seven," she said, her voice shaking.

"Return to your blind," Dr. Idylle suggested. "Let's get that physical scan. You've been out there in miserable conditions for several hours."

Miserable conditions? He didn't know the half of it. She was drenched with sweat, smeared with stinking mud, kuorl scat, lichen, moss, and assorted creepy, crawly life-forms she doubted anyone had identified, much less quantified the risks of. Jayleia sighed. "My last trap . . ."

"Leave it," Dr. Idylle interrupted. "We'll have plenty of kuorls to study without it."

"You're okay, Jay," Pietre said. "Confirm thirty-nine-point-seven, your location. The kuorls will hibernate until the temperature hits thirty-eight. Even then, you'll have a half an hour or more . . ."

She wouldn't.

Once again, in the primary nest tree, something stirred. She gasped, tabbed her handheld to read bio-signs, and backpedaled. The screen showed knots of bright heat signatures all around her indicative of hibernating kuorls.

Except that the knots were shifting. Moving. Breaking apart. She was in the center of a nest site filled with newly awakened, hungry, cranky, potentially infected kuorls who shouldn't have stirred for another hour at least.

"They're waking," she said.

"What? They can't be!" Pietre protested. "It's too hot!"

"If kuorls can run a fever, would it impact their perception of atmospheric temperatures and thus their hibernation cycle?" she asked, staggering away.

"Aren't circadian rhythms typically independent of internal temperature?" Raj asked.

"No speculation," Dr. Idylle snapped. "We have evidence that these kuorls are either infected or are carriers for the disease impacting the colonists. I want you out of there, Jayleia. Now."

"Acknowledged," she replied, her heart laboring and her lungs burning as she splashed through shallow, slimy, green water to the observation blind Pietre had helped her build. "Entering the blind. Door closed and locked. I am secure."

Unless she counted the new crop of bloodworms crawling up her ankles looking for a relatively clean spot to bite.

"Medical scan, if you please," her boss prompted. "Pietre . . ."

Jay glanced out the leaf-shaded window of her makeshift blind and yelped. "Are we recording? Here they come."

"Got it!" Pietre answered. "Would you look at that? I'll be damned. Their scout's checking the lay of the land. Unbelievable. Temperature thirty-nine-point-seven and holding."

Her blind allowed her to look into the heart of the nest site. The traps were visible where she'd scraped dark lichens from lighter bark so as to firmly seat the equipment. Condensation dotted the window, reducing visibility slightly, but she could still see the opening to the nest through the distortion and the silhouette of the sentry kuorl.

She squinted. There. Movement in the cavity of the largest tree caught her eye. The scout had plucked one of the ubiquitous beetles from the tree bark and stuffed it in his mouth for a truly repulsive breakfast. The rest of the colony was stirring. It would take another half hour for them to emerge.

The kuorls didn't emerge. They erupted, screaming. And began ripping one another to shreds.

Jayleia gaped in horror.

The damned rodents were bad-tempered at the best of times, but these creatures were a roiling mass of flashing claws and bloody teeth. Their soft, ticked, gray pelts were slashed and smeared with gore. Blood spattered the moss- and lichen-encrusted branches. They shrieked and growled in what sounded like rage. She heard her crewmates swearing above the din.

As if the kuorls sensed her equipment didn't belong, they attacked the traps. One kuorl got caught. It would be restrained harmlessly within the confines of the force and containment fields of the device. Anesthesia dosed for the animal's mass would be delivered automatically and the kuorl would never know what had happened. It would go to sleep, she'd take blood and tissue samples, deliver a wake-up drug, and then release the kuorl none the wiser.

Except that it wasn't working. The trap bucked. Either the anesthesia delivery trigger had broken or the drug was having no effect.

The gory mass of enraged kuorls froze for a split second, staring at the moving trap.

Jayleia reeled, deafened in the abrupt quiet.

Then their cries redoubled. The rodents turned on the occupied trap in a seething, self-destructing riot. She clamped a hand over her mouth when the first twitching corpse dropped to the ground. They couldn't have gotten through metal and force fields to the trapped animal. Could they?

That's when she noticed that the ravaged, muddy kuorl on the ground wasn't a corpse. The mangled creature dragged itself back to the tree and up the trunk, then launched from the lowest branch straight at her.

She staggered back against her tiny worktable and croaked. "Twelve Gods, they're attacking the blind!"

It hit the window with a damp-sounding *thunk*, leaving a smear of rotting flesh and fresh blood in its wake as it slid into the brush below.

"Infection status verified," she choked. "They're necrotic."

"Teleport!" Dr. Idylle bellowed. "Now!"

"We're not online!" Pietre cried.

The rest of the kuorls, lathered, lost in bloodlust, flung their bodies, bloodied fangs and claws first, at Jayleia's hideaway.

She flinched, sucking in a sobbing breath at each impact.

The door rattled. Claws scraped and scrabbled at the metal. The scent of putrid, decaying flesh seeped into the blind.

They uttered none of the short, high-pitched barks she'd come to associate with the once-fluffy arboreal omnivores. The creatures wheezed and moaned.

The noise of kuorls trying to peel away her alloy shell jabbed icy terror through her bones.

A pinprick of daylight shone in one corner.

"They're breaking through," she said, sounding as if she hadn't realized these animals would tear her to shreds once they'd ripped through the structure.

The door creaked and bowed.

She threw her back against it.

Mistake.

The door frame had bent. Through the scant crack, claws raked her right deltoid. She yelped, bolted away from the door, shoved the table against it, and realized her body weight and strength wouldn't keep the animals at bay for long.

"Emergency reactor online!" Pietre hollered. "Sixty seconds to teleport, Jay! Hold on!"

She shuddered. The kuorls would break through any second. The hole at the corner of the roofline had grown. The sickly sweet miasma of decay choked her.

Bloodworms, scenting the fresh blood on her arm, hastened up her body to fasten their suckers to the wound.

She could no longer say whether it was sweat, or tears, or both running so freely down her face.

"Belay that, *Sen Ekir*!" a masculine voice ordered via the open channel.

Jayleia's heart jumped. Hope burned through her chest, burgeoning, squeezing out room for breath.

He sounded familiar.

"Firing on the front of the blind, Jayleia. Stand clear," he said.

She heard it then. An atmospheric engine directly overhead. A shuttle? Whose? The colonists didn't have a shuttle. An order. She'd been ordered to stand clear.

"Acknowledged!" she rasped, turned her back, and ducked her head.

She heard the shuttle guns fire. Metal and kuorls shrieked. Heat and the smell of burning, rotted flesh hit her like a fist. Jayleia lost the field ration she'd choked down for breakfast.

Something clattered behind her.

She spun.

The entire front half of the observation blind had been blown away. A rescue harness dangled in the smoldering remains. She dove for it and shoved her feet in the straps. Force fields activated around her chest and hips, holding her to the rescue cables. The invisible harness would keep her in place even if she lost consciousness.

"Go! Go!" It felt like she'd burst her throat shouting.

The line lifted her straight into the air.

The kuorls had been thrown from the building when the wave of weapons' fire had hit. A solitary snarling animal leaped for her as she passed.

She backhanded the thing. It fell out of sight. Relief eased the flood of adrenaline from her body. The shaking began.

"Hang on!" her rescuer ordered. "I'm bringing you up."

How she wanted to do as he said, let him haul her aboard and enclose her safely inside the airborne vehicle. The rescue line wobbled and began reeling her in.

"Negative!" Jayleia yelled, looking up at the belly of the shuttle. "I'm infected!"

The line jerked to a halt.

"Make for the *Sen Ekir*," she directed.

"Jayleia," Dr. Idylle countered, his voice raw and thready. "Get aboard that ship so your cousin can restart my heart. Unless you plan to begin biting people, you aren't contagious."

It surprised her to find that dehydrated, dizzy, and exhausted as she was, she could still smile. "Yes, sir."

The rescue harness lurched into motion again. Her right arm burned. She glanced at the wound on her arm, then looked hastily away from the writhing mass of bloodworms attached to her skin, gorging themselves at her expense. Where a worm couldn't reach her bloody flesh, it bit into one of its own, using its companion as a filter for her blood.

Save for the sharp stabs of pain radiating from the bloodworm-encrusted cuts on her arm, she might have fallen asleep in the sway of the rescue halter. As it was, she'd become light-headed before the shuttle's open doorway blocked out the view of the heat-bleached sky. Hands reached out to haul her aboard.

Jayleia caught a glimpse of a khaki uniform. Her internal alarms fired. What was the Claugh nib Dovvyth military doing inside TFC space? She glanced at the man pulling her to safety.

Damen Sindrivik was taller than she remembered. He'd filled out, broadened, and let his gold-red hair grow since last she'd seen him nearly a year ago.

Beside him, hand steadying the cables, Jay recognized V'kyrri's copper skin, light brown hair, and his easy smile, though the last was noticeably short-lived. Not that she blamed him. Her own good humor had taken a near-fatal hit in that swamp.

As she neared the craft, she realized that fat, gorged bloodworms were detaching from her arm and dropping into the swamp below.

They looked wrong.

She glanced at her arm. Six of the bloodsuckers remained. The pallid creatures should turn first pink, then bright red as they filled with blood. The few still attached were in various stages of feeding. Two were pale, barely pinking up. One, bulging and bloated with blood, looked nearly black.

The winch arm retracted, drawing her into the ship. V'kyrri leaned out, grabbed both cables, and swung her aboard.

Damen spun and entered the release codes to free her from the force fields.

She spilled to the deck, along with a few stiff, black bloodworms that had fallen into the harness rather than into the swamps.

V'kyrri swore and backed away. "Whoa! What the Three Hells are those things? They're all over you!"

CHAPTER
3

"LEAVE them!" Jayleia croaked, cupping her left hand over the last six live bloodworm specimens clinging to her arm.

"Doesn't it hurt?" V'kyrri demanded, his expression tight with distaste.

"Yes, it does," she admitted. Her voice sounded like she'd been gargling gravel. "But these specimens are invaluable. Get me to the *Sen Ekir*."

Damen awarded her an unreadable look. His eyes were the same gray as the storm-tossed northern seas of her mother's world.

"We've got to get you to a sanitizer and then to medical," he directed, nodding toward the bulkhead where he worked. The shower and medi-bay must be on the other side.

An instrument chirped in the bow of the ship. V'kyrri swore. Footsteps pounded away from her as she stumbled into the tiny, gray green medi-bay and grabbed sterile containers.

"Long range," V'kyrri said via the open com.

"Acknowledged," Damen replied, his tone grim.

Did they know she could hear? Did they care?

Though her arm ached and her fingers tingled in response to the pain in her deltoid, Jayleia waited until the last few worms drank their fill. If her hypothesis was correct, and they were draining the infection, she'd give them all the time they needed.

Pain stabbed down her arm. She looked at the bleeding mess that had been the kuorl scratch. The last two worms were withdrawing their jaws and preparing to detach. They were red. Healthy, normal blood, red. She hoped they'd helped remove any infection. That she wasn't yet symptomatic seemed to indicate that they had, but without Raj around to do the testing, she had to assume the worst.

She found a packet of analgesic, opened it, and downed the liquid. The sting in her arm retreated.

Bites covered the deltoid. Blood, thinned by the anticoagulant bloodworms excreted to guarantee their meal, streamed down her arm, dripping to the medi-bay floor. She packed each of the bloodworms into a sterile container and secured them inside the medi-bay's stasis chamber.

The unit's controls weren't familiar and the instructions were rendered in Claughwyth, a language she neither spoke nor read. She'd have to get help, preferably from someone who wouldn't leave muddy fingerprints on the equipment.

Gods. She needed a shower.

"Jayleia?"

Damen. She turned.

Her thought processes and sight fuzzed for a split second as her knees sagged. She cursed. Her voice had dwindled to a hoarse ghost of itself. Dehydration symptoms. She hoped.

Damen's arm around her ribs and the heat of his broad chest against her back brought her forcefully into her body once more. A tingle of awareness rippled through her.

"Are you insane?" she gasped. "One scratch, one tiny abrasion and you'll be infected, too!"

"It's too early in the relationship to let you fall at my feet," he said, the rumble of suppressed laughter in his voice.

She gaped at the far wall. Her brain shorted and rational thought stuttered. They were covered in gore and he was flirting?

Struggling for a rational response, Jayleia shook off mental paralysis by retreating to comfortable, scientific territory. "We'll both require decontamination and testing. For the moment, would you activate the stasis chamber? Then I need a rehydration packet, please."

"Can you stand?" he asked at her ear.

She propped one hip against the diagnostic bed as Damen loosened his grip. "I can lean."

"What possessed Dr. Idylle to allow you into that swamp to begin with?" he grumbled as he searched through cabinets and drawers.

Was that an undercurrent of anger in his voice?

Jayleia's temper woke in response. "It's my job. People on the planet are suffering, Major."

"That trumps your safety?" he demanded.

"Every time."

He turned back and pinned her with a look that rendered her mute. Thunder threatened in the darkened gray of his eyes.

"The teleporters weren't even on standby," he countered, handing her a silver packet. "It's a good way to get a field op killed."

Field operative? The description made her smile. Certainly the kuorls had taken a dim view of her brand of spying. She accepted the rehydration packet and opened it.

"Science ships are all about trade-offs," she said. "Teleporters require power. On the ground, in the middle of an outbreak, we need that power for computers and diagnostic equipment."

"We're both in the business of putting our lives on the line." He shook his head as if the thought disconcerted him. Rounding the table, he gestured at her arm. "How do we stop the bleeding?"

She glanced at the wound, and then at the blood on the floor. "Shower. Bloodworms inject anticlotting agents. It has to be washed out of the wound. I'll . . ."

"Be still," Damen ordered, closing in behind her. "Drink."

"Let me get the blood up . . ." she started.

Damen's hands in her hair stopped her voice. He began untangling the braid she'd put in her hair two days ago when she'd gone into the field. His grazing her skin sent a shiver down her spine.

She drank the packet of water spiked with rehydration salts to distract herself from the sensation. Fire shot up and down her injured arm when she tried to bring the packet straw up to her lips. Breath hissed in between her clenched teeth.

Damen's hands paused.

"Arm," she said.

"How big an emergency is this?"

"I don't know," she replied. "We were investigating the disease and its causes when the kuorls went wrong. In humanoid patients, the infection manifests with fever, headache, and tissue necrosis, which can progress to disfigurement and in some cases, death if left untreated. We suspected sick kuorls were one of the vectors, but we'd never seen anything like what you pulled me from today. I don't know if this is a new manifestation of the illness. I have no idea what impact the bloodworms had on drawing the infection out of my system. I'm sorry. I can't give you a remotely decent answer."

"Damn it. Can anyone besides the *Sen Ekir* treat you?"

Jayleia spun and shoved the empty hydration packet into his chest. "Why will you not take me to my ship?" she snapped. "Beyond my own treatment, I have a job to do. Chemmoxin has to be quarantined before the disease gets off world."

She glanced at her arm. The bleeding had slowed. A little.

"If it hasn't already," she amended. "I'd have said the likelihood of this disease impacting your people was slight, but here I am, potentially infected, and you're wearing my blood."

A hint of a smile touched Damen's full lips, lighting his entire countenance, then he swore, spun, and stalked out of the medi-bay.

As she watched the play of muscles outlined by khaki fatigues, her brain flashed on a memory of a long-toothed Azym casing his territory in the tall, plains grass of the Glenthyk wilderness. The predators were built for speed and agility. They rippled with lithe muscle. Their huge, padded paws sheathed brutal claws. Razor-sharp teeth and strong jaws let them take down prey much larger than themselves.

She pulled in a deep breath, intrigued by the image. A sense of safety tugged at her insides.

Safety? After a fanciful moment spent envisioning him as a deadly predator? Jayleia peeled herself from the diagnostic table and shook her head. She grabbed a towel from beside the tiny washbasin. Mopping blood from her injured arm, she used the cloth to keep from dripping all over the rest of Damen's ship as she followed him down the companionway.

"Through here," he directed, hitting a door-release control and leading her into a cabin. He opened another door. "Shower . . ."

The shipboard alarm blared.

Jay started, her heart knocking hard against her ribs.

"V'k?" Damen touched his ship's badge and yelled above the noise.

The action made her wonder why she hadn't heard a word from her crewmates since Damen and V'kyrri had pulled her aboard. Too far away? Or was her com signal being jammed?

The alarm shut off mid-whoop.

"Short range!" V'kyrri answered. "Erillian Aggressor, no flag, no name. Coming in fast. Shielded. Weapons hot."

Her eyes widened. She knew that ship. Her father used that captain and crew for missions. What were they doing here?

Damen's attention jerked back to her, his gray gaze searching her face.

She choked back a curse. Time to remember she was in enemy hands. She had to guard her reactions.

Instinct whispered that Major Sindrivik would be difficult to mislead, but she had to try. She wasn't willing to compromise TFC's secrets. Not to a spy working for a rival government.

"Why are they after you? Shower!" she commanded, shoving a tendril of fear into her tone as she nodded at the sanitizer. "You're needed up front. I'll wait."

He strode into the unit and cycled on the system.

It gave her a moment to combine the bits of conversation she'd overheard with the ship's accelerating climb through Chemmoxin's atmosphere. She wasn't in a shuttle. That was clear. It looked like a two-man recon ship, exactly what a couple of spies on a mission might use. What would bring them here at the precise moment she most needed divine intervention?

The last time they'd enacted a similar scene with these players, Damen and V'kyrri had been helping their boss hijack the *Sen Ekir*, bringing the Chekydran after them all. If they'd done it again, she'd have reason to start biting and infecting Claugh officers.

She heard the spray of water shut down. After 120 seconds of wishing this were the *Sen Ekir* where he'd have to strip and emerge without a stitch of clothing, she heard the drier cycle off. The door opened.

Damen, fully dressed, left the tiny chamber by stalking straight up to her and glaring down at her, a knot in his jaw.

She couldn't back up or she'd collide with the bed. His bed. Muscles low in her abdomen clenched tight. Confusion rocked her. What had happened to make her react to the man?

She sidled away, circling toward the shower.

He leaned in, his gaze holding hers.

Rational thought evaporated. She stumbled backward into the sanitizer.

"What aren't you telling me?" he murmured, his gaze fixed on her mouth.

The air left her lungs and she struggled to recall that she had no business hoping Damen would make good his implied threat to kiss her. Pressing her lips tight, still trapped by his gaze, she nudged the button to activate the system.

The door shut in his face.

She slumped, able to breathe and think again.

What wasn't she telling him, indeed. What wasn't he telling her?

The spray of water and disinfectants assaulted her. She set speculation aside. Slowly, by forcing her reluctant arm to work, she stripped out of the sodden lab clothes she'd worn into the field, aborted the dry cycle, and went through the wash again, making certain every single red, swollen worm bite got hit with disinfecting spray. She lost count past thirty bites and wondered if she should be concerned about blood loss.

The ship jolted and shimmied sideways.

Cursing, Jayleia spilled to the floor.

She struggled upright and yanked on her clothes as the water recycling system evaporated the excess moisture. The door clicked open.

She made it to the cockpit as another jolt rocked the vessel.

Damen sat strapped in at piloting in the U-shaped cockpit. V'kyrri, at navigation, sat beside him. The weapons panel was on V'kyrri's right, and what looked like a communications panel on Damen's left.

"Are you all right?" Damen asked, tossing a glance at her.

"I won't know that until you return me to the *Sen Ekir*," she said, "which you have no intention of doing, have you?"

The muscles in Damen's jaw bunched.

V'kyrri leaned across the cockpit, reached under the communications panel next to her, pulled out a seat and unfolded it.

Laser fire exploded in front of them, rattling the ship. The flare overwhelmed the view screen filters.

"Strap in!" Damen ordered.

Data coalesced in a flash. A mercenary her father liked to hire showed up at the exact time and place as two Claugh nib Dovvyth officers who, she had to assume, had intended all along to steal her from her ship. Damen asked whether she could be treated anywhere other than the *Sen Ekir*. The Erillian Aggressor had fired on them without doing damage when Jayleia knew damned well that ship had the firepower and the skill to vaporize them. They were being shot at. Not shot. Shot at.

Jayleia gaped at him. "You're kidnapping me?" Squinting against the glare, she stumbled into the seat. "What is it with you people and the women aboard the *Sen Ekir*? Hijacking us a year ago and kidnapping my best friend wasn't enough for you?"

"I'm not"—he stopped short, white lines showing around his full lips.

It made no sense. Why would the Claugh nib Dovvyth kidnap a

xenobiologist? Especially one whose best friend, Ari Idylle, had already defected to that side of the zone? It wasn't as if they didn't have thousands of biologists of their own. Unless it was a political or tactical move. Again, why? What possible advantage could having her in custody . . . she stopped short. It wasn't about her. She represented no specific value, not even from a scientific standpoint. But her dad . . .

"My father," she breathed.

Cold rage settled behind her solar plexus. She glared at Damen. "Tell me."

CHAPTER

4

DAMEN, nonplussed by her accurate leap of logic, shook his head. "Your father has been accused of treason. He's disappeared. We intercepted a message from Gerriny Eudal for you."

"My father's second-in-command? Bring it up," she said. "I see no harm in everyone watching it again."

At her bland tone, Damen awarded her a hard look. Of course he'd memorized every nuance of intonation and expression in the message, had already culled as much information as he could from it. He had a job to do. She didn't have to like it.

Damen turned to bring up the message at the communications station aware that Jayleia represented a new information source. He kept a surreptitious eye on her and trusted that V'kyrri would scan her as well.

The screen flickered to life. A thin-faced man with brown eyes and graying light brown hair appeared on the screen. He sat at a desk and leaned forward into the camera, his posture tense, his hands clasped before him, the knuckles white.

Jayleia leaned back in her chair, her features tight.

V'kyrri shifted, drawing Damen's eye. The telepath grimaced and mentally murmured, *She hates him. Can you feel it?*

I smell it, Damen answered.

Look at her. Barely a hint of what she feels. Without your enhanced senses or my telepathy, you'd never know, V'kyrri marveled.

Damen returned his attention to her. *Control? Or conditioning?*

"Jayleia," the man on the screen said, his tone grave. "By now someone will have told you that some unfortunate accusations have been made against your dad. He's missing."

The man pressed his lips thin, shook his head, then looked into the camera.

The acrid bite of an emotion Damen couldn't easily identify overpowered Jayleia's scent. Hatred? Rage? Not being able to connect a feeling state with the complicated odor unsettled him.

"I'm concerned," Gerriny Eudal said, "for your father and for you. I've done some damage control. As a result, you're considered a victim of your father's deceit rather than a coconspirator. I have our people pulling and preserving every file on your dad they can find. One of our most trusted computer techs says she's found evidence that someone's tampered with the data.

"If it's true, there's a chance your father is innocent. Help me prove it. Call me. Please."

The message ended with the Intelligence Command director's seal.

Damen frowned as another compound altered Jayleia's scent. The volatile smell made his heart pound.

V'kyrri flinched.

Cold terror, the telepath noted.

Damen nodded once, agreeing. Why? He studied her, struggling against the impulse to wrap an arm around her shoulders in comfort.

Her hands clenched in her lap, the only outward sign of the emotions waging chemical warfare within her body.

Laser fire impacted their starboard shield.

Damen spun back to his panel to manage the energy balance in their defense screens.

She knows more than she's letting on, he thought, aiming his silent observation at V'kyrri the way he'd been taught.

His friend sent him a mental agreement. *And she has no reason to trust us.*

Damen blinked. *She knows us. Her best friend . . .*

Changed sides, V'kyrri finished for him. *We're not here for friendship's sake, Damen. We're here to use her to get at her father. Jayleia knows that."*

Aloud, V'kyrri muttered, "That Erillian will not go away."

Damen glanced over his shoulder.

Speculation ran rapid-fire across Jayleia's face.

The impression unfolded within him that Dr. Idylle's soft-spoken xenobiologist masked someone sleek and deadly.

Seeming to feel his regard, Jayleia straightened. Her features settled into the intelligent, shy woman he'd thought he'd met aboard the *Sen Ekir* a year ago. Her gaze was so clear when it focused on his, he almost believed he'd imagined the calculation he'd seen.

"The exact accusation against my dad?" she demanded.

"Collusion with the Chekydran," he said.

She barked a hoarse laugh, then the color drained from her face. Horror stood out in the lines around her eyes and in her quick, audible breath. "Get me a line to the *Sen Ekir*!"

"Leave them out of this," Damen countered.

She spun to face the communications panel, rested her hands on it, but obviously couldn't make out how to activate it.

"Damn it!" he said, concern twisting him as fresh blood tracked a stained path down her injured arm. "It isn't safe and you belong in medical."

"I belong on the *Sen Ekir*!" she retorted, rounding on him. "Do you want Dr. Idylle, Pietre, and Raj dead? Get me a thrice damned line!"

V'kyrri shifted. Looking over his shoulder, the telepath spent a moment studying her before flicking his sea-green gaze to Damen. *She's hiding something. I need more time and fewer people shooting at us to get at it. She is, however, genuinely afraid for her crewmates.*

Damen nodded.

"Opening channel," V'kyrri said aloud.

"Make it fast," Damen growled at her. "You're bleeding."

"And at least one other ship is coming in hot on your aft thrusters. I get it."

Damen leaned past her. Her scent had subsided to her normal rich, creamy cocoa underpinned by lush traces of wine. The smell tainted by the copper of her blood ramped his pulse. He contented himself with breathing her in deep. He watched, fascinated, as goose bumps rose on her bare arms.

Confusion clouded her frown as she pressed back in her chair.

Despite the circumstances and the ship lobbing warning shots at them, he smiled.

Her body reacted to his.

He'd spend his time counting the ways he could turn that to his advantage. Interrogation began to sound like fun. His lower body tightened. Choking back a curse at the sudden discomfort, he opened the channel.

"You're on," he said, straightening.

She faced the panel and seemed to need a moment to gather her thoughts.

"*Sen Ekir, Sen Ekir*!" she said. "Get on the line!"

"*Sen Ekir*," Pietre answered. "Jay? You're ship-wide. What's going on?"

"Lift. Get off the planet. No delay."

She hesitated.

Damen noted she hadn't specified a secure channel. Oversight? Or had she planned it so as to avoid having to give up information to her kidnappers that might lead them to her missing father?

"Go to Kebgra," she said. "Tell Augie my father's been accused of treason and has disappeared."

Three voices competed for the line, peppering her with questions.

"Clear the channel!" Dr. Idylle bellowed. "We'll lift when we have you aboard, Jayleia. You need treatment!"

"I'm being kidnapped," she replied. "I gather Ari hasn't been able to convince the Claugh that I'm no use against my father."

"Sindrivik!" Dr. Idylle snapped. "Tell me my xenobiologist, who has never done so to this point, is overstating her case."

"No, sir," Damen replied. "She isn't."

Silence.

Jayleia turned to stare at him. His regret seemed to drain the strength from her. She paled.

Damen and V'kyrri swore in unison as another mercenary ship registered on long range.

"We will not run when one of my crew . . ." Dr. Idylle began.

Casting quick glances her way, Damen saw Jayleia swing back to the com panel.

She slammed a fist on the console. "This isn't a game! Everyone will put out a grab for the missing director's daughter. You're the last people to know my location. You're in danger! Get off the planet! Raj! Get the *Sen Ekir* and its remaining crew to safety."

Damen shook his head. She'd recovered quickly, efficiently from the shock of her father's disappearance, as if she'd expected and trained for the eventuality. Given her father's occupation, maybe she had.

"I will not be recruited into the family business," her cousin, Raj, bit out.

"Then you'll have a front-row seat when the mercenaries on our tail sheer off to try their luck with Dr. Idylle, Pietre, and you," she said, her tone cold and hard as Isarrite. "Are you off the ground?"

"Atmospherics online and warming," Pietre said.

"Transmitting a safe exit path through the three ships on approach," V'kyrri said.

With her sitting so close behind him, Damen felt her relax.

The ship rocked and skittered sideways, engines whining.

She slid to the floor, and yelped in pain.

"Four ships," V'kyrri corrected, every last drop of good humor drained from his tone. "Transmission complete. Get out of here, *Sen Ekir*. Now. We're taking fire. This ship is fast and agile. We'll outrun them and make sure we draw a lot of attention doing it. Take advantage of it."

"Lifting!" Pietre replied.

"*Kawl Fergus* out."

"What's the weapon recharge rate on that Erillian Aggressor?" Damen demanded of V'kyrri, while keeping an eye on Jayleia.

"How would I know?" V'kyrri snapped.

She sat as if frozen in place, her gaze focused on nothing inside the cockpit of his ship.

"Find out," Damen grated. "Even a few seconds would let me buy the *Sen Ekir* more time."

Come on, Jayleia. I know you know that ship. Give me something to work with. Your friends' lives are at stake.

She swore in an undertone she must have believed he couldn't hear.

Good.

"Erillian Aggressor? No name, no flag?" she repeated, as if confirming the facts.

"Yes." Damen frowned at the lines of stress crinkling the corners of her eyes. Besides the blood oozing down her right arm and the fact that she'd landed in a heap on the deck plating, she looked torn.

He hesitated, wondering for the first time, what doing his job would cost her.

When she began struggling to get her feet beneath her without using her injured arm, he released his restraints and hauled her back into the chair.

"Strap in," he ordered.

"I can't," she snapped.

It occurred to him he was caressing the bare skin of her uninjured arm in mute apology. He met her dark gaze, unprepared for the glimpse of unyielding bitterness there. The urge to gather her into his arms and smooth the tension from her fine-boned face rocked him back on his heels.

She looked away.

He swallowed hard. Admonishing himself to stick to business, he fastened her restraints.

"You might have asked for help," he said.

"Because asking to be returned to my ship for medical treatment has yielded such positive results?" she retorted, her tone so mild that he stared at her for several seconds.

"Weapon recharge rates?" V'kyrri reminded, chuckling.

Damen threw himself into his chair, strapped in, and focused on the computers. He'd let her distract him. After forcing her to acknowledge she knew one of the ships on their tail, he'd let his damnable attraction to her blow the interrogation. He swore, toggled his console awake, and did his best to ignore V'kyrri's knowing grin.

"Their weapons recharge is next to zero," she said. "That Erillian's little more than weapons strapped to engines."

He narrowed his eyes, scanning the sensor readouts. One hand clenched into a white-knuckled fist on his panel.

"How many nonlethal options?" he demanded.

"Two, maybe. They aren't usually hired to take their prey alive."

Meaning her father had used them often enough for her to have become familiar with their spec.

A swiftly changing reading caught Damen's attention. "The Erillian is closing. Looks like they're going to make a grab for us. Shields holding."

"What? No small talk? Whatever happened to romance?" V'kyrri quipped.

Jayleia chuckled.

The sound sent warmth fizzing through Damen's veins, senseless jealousy, too, that it had been V'kyrri who'd elicited her laugh.

"This can't get any worse," Damen muttered.

"It did," V'kyrri grated.

"I see it," Damen said.

"What?" Jayleia demanded.

"The Ykktyryk mercenary's seen the *Sen Ekir*," Damen replied.

CHAPTER

5

FEAR for her friends and family drove ice into Jayleia's chest.

"Bringing weapons online," V'kyrri replied. "Intercept course laid in."

"Locked and executing," Damen said. He shoved the ship into a twisting dive that slammed her against her restraints.

"Take my handheld. Load translation," she said. "I'll cover weapons."

"No time," Damen replied. "I'll talk you through. Weapons are behind you, across the cockpit."

V'kyrri grabbed her chair, hit a control, and spun her 180 to face the panel behind his seat. She realized the cockpit had been designed for them to sit in the corners where they could each reach two stations. Damen piloting and communications, V'kyrri navigation and weapons.

For a moment, she wondered whether she hindered or helped, then the panel beneath her hands lit. She couldn't read the controls, but the permutations of one ship shooting at another had, over time, been rendered as simple as possible. No one wanted to have to think in the middle of a firefight.

"Controls in the middle of the panel," Damen said.

"Yes. Weapons dark, targeting above," she said.

He slanted her a narrow-eyed glance. "I see I'm going to have to have a much closer look at the *Sen Ekir* dossier. You're the second 'scientist' from that unarmed ship to know too damned much about Claugh weapons."

"Skillfully manipulated data can be made to obscure as much truth as it reveals," she said. "Ykktyryk cruiser targeted. Range, forty seconds."

With a mercenary after the *Sen Ekir*, she'd believed the tension couldn't rise any higher. She'd been wrong. It crawled up her spine and wrapped a stranglehold around her neck. She glanced at Damen.

"You're quoting Omorle Lin?" The brush of Damen's velvet tone sent her senses into high alert. Of course. He was the Claugh nib Dovvyth's best computer tech. He would know about TFC's prized computer expert, had likely studied the man's technique.

Did he know that she'd adored Omorle Lin with the whole of her fourteen-year-old heart from the moment she'd met him? Memories of her last seconds with the first man she'd loved burst through her head. Remembered torment clasped a tightening band around her chest and blinded her for a moment.

"Whoa!" V'kyrri exclaimed, slamming upright in his chair. He turned and peered at her. "Jayleia, what the Three Hells? Are you . . ."

Damned telepath. This was undoubtedly why Damen had included V'kyrri on his mission. To extract information by any means possible. Jayleia shoved away pain. Nothing would erase the vision of Omorle's wide-open, dead eyes from her memory, or change the fact that as he'd breathed his last, he'd whispered not her name but the name of the love of his life.

She couldn't hide that kind of emotional memory from a telepath, not even one distracted by racing to the *Sen Ekir*'s rescue.

She'd have to misdirect him, and Damen, who, she noted, watched her far too closely. She was glad she'd moved across the tiny cockpit from him. Maybe he'd have a harder time reading her face while V'kyrri tried to read her mind.

"I knew Lin," she ground out between clenched teeth, enraged by her lack of control and at the two men for intruding into something as painful and intensely private as she wished her childhood crush to remain. "I sat with him, holding his hand as he died. Could we please focus on saving my remaining friends and family?"

Damen blew out an audible breath and spun back to his panel.

"Sorry," V'k said. "I didn't mean . . . That was overwhelming."

Yes. It was. From V'kyrri's clipped words and from the speculation she caught on Damen's face, she knew they weren't going to let it rest. She blinked, cooling the heat gathering in her eyes, and struggled to draw a breath that didn't catch.

The targeting controls under her fingers buzzed. Brilliant scarlet flared beneath the buttons. She had to clear her throat to force out words.

"I have a lock on the cruiser," she said. "Permission to fire?"

"Status on the other three ships," Damen demanded of V'kyrri.

"Two on approach," V'k replied. "No threat until we leave atmosphere. The Erillian is hanging back."

She frowned. "They must have a live capture contract for me and know I'm on board."

"Agreed," Damen said. "Permission to fire, granted. Middle of the panel. Lasers left, missiles right."

"What's the center fire control?"

"Sonic pulse."

A sound weapon for use against a species whose primary sense was auditory. The Chekydran. Jayleia nodded.

"Missiles incoming," V'kyrri announced as sensors and alarms went hot simultaneously. "We have the Ykktyryk's attention."

"Deploy countermeasures!" Damen ordered, throwing the ship sideways in a move that felt like they'd slid off a cliff.

"Where's the control?" Jay yelled.

V'kyrri reached over and hit a flashing amber button in the top left-hand corner of her panel. "It's away!"

"Thanks," she said. "Acquiring target. Locked. Firing lasers."

"Single hit," V'k reported. "Punched through the shield and scorched their hull plate. Get us closer, Sindrivik. We'll drop a load of missiles on their heads."

"Their exhaust," she corrected, glancing at the view screen. The mercenary ship loomed before them, a big, hulking craft, steadily gaining on the *Sen Ekir*. "Isn't that right? Ykktyryk ships don't shield exhaust ports."

"They prefer speed to protection," Damen said.

He was nodding when she glanced over her shoulder at him. His expression, when he looked back, said she was defying known parameters.

Good.

"Something your father told you?"

"Ari."

His face lit with a surprised smile before an explosion rattled their ship. Metal creaked and the plates beneath her feet jumped.

"Countermeasures took out two missiles," V'kyrri said. "One left. We're positioned to take it in the teeth."

"Shields," Damen ordered, pushing the ship into another dive through Chemmoxin's pale sky.

"Got 'em," V'k replied. "We're good."

She watched Damen. He worked his console like a master musician playing a polytonal Taggite organ, minus a Taggite's two extra arms. Concentration put creases in his forehead and at the corner of the one eye she could see. A tick in the fine muscles of his jaw provided evidence of worry.

Jayleia threw another barrage of laser fire at the mercenary, hardly waiting for the targeting indicators to flash red.

The missile impacted their shields and detonated, not on the nose, as V'kyrri had predicted, but amidships, right behind the door where she'd boarded. The impact flung them off course. Lights flashed on the cockpit consoles, bleating and chirping messages she couldn't hope to understand.

"Hull integrity intact. Shields holding. Oh, nice shot!" V'kyrri hollered, punching controls that seemed to help Damen wrestle them into position for another try at the big cruiser.

She looked at the view screen. Their ship spun and swung, flashing the merc ship in and out of the field of view. Blue smoke streamed behind the vessel.

The mercenary fired on the *Sen Ekir*. The science ship rocked, but their shields deflected the weapon's energy.

Giving the mercenary no time for another shot, Jayleia fired the lasers again, followed immediately by an array of missiles.

"That's right," Damen muttered when the big vessel canted their way. "Leave the unarmed craft alone."

"Broadcast another message," V'kyrri suggested. "Make it plain she's aboard. The Ykktyryk came in after the first message to the *Sen Ekir*."

"We've proven that we'll rise to the *Sen Ekir*'s defense," Jay said. "They'll use it as a lure."

Both men swore.

Laser fire sliced through their shields. They shuddered, momentum stalling, and rolled. Alarms tried to wail, then sputtered and died. The lights failed. The atmospheric engine choked and the nose pitched toward the steaming jungles below.

"Spawn of a Myallki bitch," Damen swore. "Where'd they get the power for that shot?"

"Restart!" V'kyrri demanded, unbuckling his restraints.

Damen punched in a rapid-fire command. Nothing happened. "No go!"

V'k threw himself out of his chair and down the companionway. She heard the bang of engine access panels opening as he went.

"Found it! Ten seconds!"

"Why aren't they finishing us?" she muttered, turning back to the view screen. "They've got us dead to rights."

"You nailed them," Damen answered, approval in his voice. He flashed her a brief grin when she glanced at him. He fought his controls, muscles standing out in his arms and shoulders as he struggled to keep the ship airborne. Sweat beaded his temple and trickled down one side of his face. "I got you a shot at their tailpipes and you shoved those missiles straight up their . . ."

"Online!" V'kyrri shouted.

"Get up here!" Damen yelled, punching in the sequence for what she assumed would be a hot start on his atmospheric.

The engine roared to life, pitching the ship in an arc into the atmosphere. Jay heard V'kyrri cursing as he crashed to the deck plating.

"You should have kidnapped Raj if you'd planned on breaking bones," she called down the companionway.

Damen chuckled.

Jayleia's heart warmed at the sound.

"I specifically requested a comedienne," V'k retorted as he limped into the cockpit and took his seat. "Is the *Sen Ekir* safe?"

"They're clear. Transitioning to star drive," Damen said, studying his panels. "And they're away."

Part of her relaxed in response to the relief in Damen's tone. She hadn't gotten the people she cared about killed. When it came to the *Sen Ekir*, at least, it appeared she and her kidnappers were aligned.

She eyed the two men as they worked. They weren't allies, but neither were they enemies, per se. How far could she trust them?

"Why didn't the Erillian make a move while we were disabled?" Damen muttered.

She looked at the screen. Damen had them pointed right at the sleek ship, engine wide open. The blue sky boundary beckoned a few kilometers past the Erillian.

Uneasiness wormed through her chest.

"Does anyone else think playing midair collision games with a known mercenary is a bad idea?" she asked.

"They won't fire on us," Damen said. "Not when they know you're aboard."

"They have tow capability."

"They'd have to disable our engine," he protested.

"Which has already happened once."

"And they didn't lock us down when it did," he countered. "They can't risk killing you."

"No! They can't risk *catching* me. I am not their objective any more than I'm yours. They want my father. They will fire! It'll be to cripple, so that we'll have to declare an emergency and make a run!"

"How could they know we wouldn't run you and them straight to the *Dagger*?" V'kyrri demanded.

"They don't," she replied. "They only have to watch for what happens after you do. Everyone knows that when Admiral Seaghdh interrogates someone, he gets the answers he wants. They're counting on you to do the hard work of finding my father so they can steal him from you once you do."

Damen bit out a curse, his tone grim. "Then they don't get to follow us. Shut down the shields."

He was disabling the defenses? Jayleia boggled. "What?"

"Done," V'kyrri answered.

She glanced between the ruthless expressions on their faces and shuddered. "Look. I'd rather you didn't hand me over to them. The captain of that Erillian Aggressor is messed up. You guys may be kidnapping me, but at least you're sane."

Damen flashed her a feral grin, his gray eyes glittering. "Do you have enough data to support that analysis?"

Her breath stopped in her chest and heat suffused her from head to toe.

He turned away. "They're hailing."

"I've got your answer," V'kyrri replied. "Go."

Her console pinged. She glanced sideways at it and guessed at the significance of the flashing indicators. "They've established a target lock!"

The subtlest vibration beneath her feet warned her that another engine had fired. It shrieked to life. She clapped her hands over her ears. It didn't help. Damen's spy ship leaped for the stars. They screamed over the top of the Erillian Aggressor, so close that every muscle in her body clenched in anticipation of collision. As if it would have made any difference.

"Shields!" Damen yelled.

V'kyrri slammed a control.

Staggering g-forces crushed her to her seat as the ship lurched. She may have blacked out. Pain seared her chest. Her muscles couldn't overcome the stress of gravity weighing on them. She couldn't breathe.

Then she could. Air slid noisily into her burning lungs. It took a moment to realize Damen and V'kyrri had fared little better. She heard them gasping. Slowly, she realized her eyes weren't malfunctioning. They'd left Chemmoxin's atmosphere. Black space, relieved only by distant stars, filled the view screen.

"What the Three Hells was that?" she demanded between gulps of air.

"Data to contradict your sanity assertion," Damen replied.

It irked her that he'd recovered much faster than she.

"You bounced us off their shields?" Jayleia demanded, trembling from a belated flood of epinephrine.

"I blew their defense generator when I did," Damen said.

"Twelve Gods," she muttered. "Isn't that move illegal because it's easier to get yourself blown up than to disable an enemy ship?"

"Yes, it is."

"I thought you needed me alive. My mistake."

"I'd begin an interrogation, but I can see it wasn't that effective a scare tactic." Damen tossed a sly grin over his shoulder at her.

Her heart clenched at the caress of his approving gaze. "Never do it again."

He chuckled.

The contagious sound flushed liquid warmth through her body and she found herself smiling in response. She straightened, wiping the uninvited expression from her face. New aches and assorted bruises rushed to be counted.

They were alive. The *Sen Ekir* was out of harm's way. She sighed and rubbed her face with her hands.

"All right," she said. "Before I can betray my father and my people, I need information."

CHAPTER
6

DAMEN traded a troubled glance with V'kyrri. His gut froze at the no-nonsense tone of Jayleia's voice. He couldn't read the smooth, emotionless mask she'd made of her face.

He studied her and knew that, in his own way, V'kyrri did, too.

"It's not . . ." he began.

"Like that?" she finished for him. "Of course it is. Your commanders didn't order you to kidnap me because they happened to foresee my messy death by kuorl attack."

"No," he replied. "Knowing what kind of death you'd suffer at the hands of the mercenaries brought us to yank you out of harm's way. If it counts for anything, Captain Idylle's first concern was for you."

Mine, too, he didn't say aloud.

She flushed and shifted, but didn't look away. "I'm a means to an end."

"I was ordered to find your father," he said, "and to ascertain the merit of the charges against him. I was not ordered to seduce you into treason."

Her lips twitched. "You could."

Had she meant for him to hear that? Want raked through his gut. Damen held his breath. What the Three Hells was happening to him?

He'd been physically attracted to Jayleia from the moment he'd helped Admiral Seaghdh hijack the *Sen Ekir*. Somewhere in the past year, simple attraction had grown damnably uncomfortable.

He felt V'kyrri's questioning glance. Daring to draw breath again, he forced his mind back to their tactical situation and said, "It looks like we blew more than the Erillian's defense generators when we hit them with our shields."

"They're limping," V'kyrri agreed. "The Ykktyryk set down on the glacial fields in the southern hemisphere. No settlements within a thousand kilometers."

Jayleia shook her head. "Their funeral. What that ice takes, it does not give up. There's a reason the settlements on Chemmoxin are clustered in those miserable swamps."

V'kyrri tossed her a shrewd glance. "The least of the miseries?"

"Very much so."

"All right," Damen said, releasing his restraints. "We're clear and in the lane for Silver City. Let's get you patched up."

She raised her eyebrows. "Silver City? How do we know the mercs won't follow us in?"

"Let them," V'kyrri growled, relish in his voice. "They'll find the Claugh battle cruiser *Queen's Rhapsody* waiting."

She looked between them, sudden awareness, and a tiny, un-guarded smile blooming on her face. Her gaze settled on the telepath. "I see. And I am addressing?"

"Her new captain," Damen supplied.

Jayleia grinned. Her brown eyes lit. "You're leaving the engines for a command chair? Do you even know where to find it? Con-gratulations, Captain."

Damen felt the answering smile on his face and spotted the grin on V'k. She had them in the palm of her hand. Did she know?

Damen cleared his throat.

Jayleia's smile subsided. He thought he could spot the moment she'd brought her defenses back online, but her gaze still sparkled when she turned it on him. He felt her regard as a physical thing, an approving stroke that stirred his blood and sped his heart rate.

He spent a second shoring up his own shields.

"If you load my handheld with a translation routine to interface with your systems," she said, touching the unit attached to her belt, "I'll begin pulling information regarding my father."

Damen studied her.

She'd spoken as if the data pull would be easy for a xenobiologist with no computer tech training.

"Something you learned from Omorle Lin before he died?" Damen asked.

Both from the way V'kyrri stiffened and from the way her expression closed, he knew he'd hit a nerve.

"No, Major," she said. "Science isn't all fieldwork and experiments. I am occasionally expected to do a bit of research."

"Lin was your bodyguard, Jayleia," Damen countered. "For a decade, he guarded you day and night."

Pain spiked in the lines around her mouth.

"Yes, he did. We were aboard the *Balykkal* for the first mission to Ioccal," she said, her tone flat.

He nodded. Six years ago, the Armada battle prowler, *Balykkal*, had escorted the *Sen Ekir* to a world on the edge of TFC space. The world had been colonized early in TFC's expansionist history and then forgotten. When someone on Tagreth had finally uncovered records regarding the colony, the government had mounted an expedition to Ioccal, a habitable moon orbiting a gas giant in the Occaltus system.

Jayleia's records indicated she'd enlisted in the Armada against her parents' wishes just prior to the mission. The expedition, led by Dr. Linnaeus Idylle, had found the colony deserted. During digs meant to determine what had happened to the colonists, the expedition personnel had been struck by a deadly plague.

Of the 217 crewmembers on the mission manifest, five had survived. Dr. Idylle, Ari Idylle, Raj Faraheed, Pietre Ivanovich, and Jayleia Durante.

The scope of the disaster had altered science ship protocols, first contact procedure, and even ship design throughout the known systems. Damen could only imagine what it had done to the survivors.

"When the plague hit, we couldn't leave the victims to die alone and in pain," she said, her face pale and her gaze far away.

"Three Hells," V'kyrri breathed.

The white edges of her lips and the fog of old nightmares in her eyes shook Damen. He'd reached for her before he could conquer the impulse.

Some of the tension left her frame when he settled a hand on her shoulder.

"Ari and I took turns holding the hands of the dying, trading off so we could sleep, though I don't think either of us did. There wasn't much we could do. None of us could, not that we knew at the time and Dr. Idylle and Raj had to try. Two hundred and twelve people died," she said. "I talked to the ones I sat with, got them to talk to me. I wanted to know who they were, what had been lost."

A piece at a time, Jayleia returned from her corpse-lined past. Sorrow lingered in the bleak set of her features, but Damen knew she saw him when the color began returning to her face.

She turned her gaze from his. "Omorle Lin, my bodyguard, was the twenty-second person to die on my watch."

"Didn't he tell you he was your father's best computer espionage agent? Didn't he teach you before you went to work for your father?" Damen pressed. He felt the shimmer of anger in the muscles beneath his hand.

"Of course I've worked with my father and his personnel," she snapped. "In the course of our research aboard the *Sen Ekir*, we gather significant data on the Chekydran that might one day be of tactical use. Even the plagues . . ."

"You send your father copies of research data?" he interrupted.

She blinked. "What else would I send?"

He bared his teeth, enjoying the hunt. It distinctly wasn't a smile. He saw her register that fact when she glanced into his face.

Her scent changed, giving away her ire.

"You're telling the truth, as far as it goes, but there's more."

"It's all the truth you're going to get, Major," she countered, her features a study in neutrality.

"How much did your father have Lin teach you about cyber-espionage?" he prodded. "Have I been chasing you through the Claugh nib Dovvyth's computer systems for the past . . ."

"Stop it," V'kyrri demanded aloud, closing a hand around Damen's arm.

Jayleia shifted out from beneath Damen's touch.

V'kyrri's mental voice sounded in his head. *What are you doing?*

Damen glanced at his friend's hand, still on his arm, and mentally answered. *My job. Between what we suspect we'll find in the Silver City data store and the information Jayleia's father could bring us we . . .*

V'kyrri's expression hardened. *Damn it, Sindrivik, this is Jayleia. Not a tool. Not something you can use and toss aside. You've seen the signs. Someone has done a number on her. Conditioning, blocks, walls . . .*

. . . and the defenses she's erected lock us out and cut her off from her heart, Damen finished for him. *If I can't pry her free, V'k, I'll have to break her open.*

You want to shatter her, V'kyrri accused, his face and mental presence twisting with rage, *just to see the pieces fly apart.*

Did he? The predator at his core stirred, intrigued at the prospect. His heartbeat stumbled at the thought. No. Not like that. Too bad. This was war. He had a job to do.

If you have something I can use, let me hear it. Otherwise, I'll use every weapon at my disposal to get at her.

V'kyrri peered at him, hard.

Damen's head felt too full for a split second. He met his friend's probing gaze without flinching, letting him read the resolve and determination that he'd do whatever it took to protect the Empire.

V'k's grip on his arm relaxed. *She's afraid to feel.*

Damen nodded once.

You know her past. Take the time to gain her trust, Sindrivik, to unlock her. I like Jayleia, he warned. *Do permanent damage, you'll answer to me.*

Damen held his eye for several seconds. *Which is why the admiral assigned her to me. Not you.*

Maybe, but I hear that voice in your head saying you're the last person in the universe she can trust. Don't make me tell Seaghdh he's made a mistake, V'kyrri replied. His eyes narrowed and he smiled without humor. *Or do you not know what you feel?*

Damen yanked out of V'kyrri's hold, his lips curling in a silent snarl. He didn't feel. He wouldn't. None of them could afford it.

And Jayleia had watched the entire, silent byplay with the fascination of a child handed a new toy.

How much had she guessed? He'd made a mistake in letting V'kyrri read him.

"That was amazing," she breathed. "You were arguing. Weren't you?"

She glanced at V'kyrri. "You go away. Did you know? Your body was sitting here, but you weren't in it."

V'k blinked, looking startled by Jayleia's observation.

"You." She turned her keen scientist's eye on Damen.

Awareness jolted him. *Keep emotion at bay with science and logic? Oh, no. I won't allow that.*

"What?" he urged, putting the slightest grit of want into the tone.

As he'd intended, the sound abraded her nerves, disrupting what she'd meant to say. Her scent changed again, the stir of arousal overpowering the lingering traces of anger.

"I—Your presence in the cockpit," she fumbled, "intensified. As if . . ." She broke off, shrugged, and looked away, flushing.

Don't rescue her, Damen commanded mentally as V'kyrri shifted beside him. "As if?"

"You sensed something?" V'kyrri prodded.

She looked between the two of them, visibly gathered her resolve, lifted her chin and said, "It felt as if Major Sindrivik was everywhere all at once, almost a palpable pressure in the cabin."

Damen smothered a smile at her attempt to distance herself from him—and what she'd felt—with formality. Maybe getting at her soft underbelly wouldn't be difficult after all. The heady bouquet of her nascent desire and her obvious discomfort with her body's yearnings suggested he had a potent weapon at his disposal.

Convenient.

Fun.

Locking a knife-edged gaze on her, he allowed himself a tiny smile and a nod of acknowledgment.

She raised an eyebrow, putting faint creases in her forehead.

How long to break her control? The scent of want, tinged by the first tang of fear lingered in the cockpit. Yet, she let him see none of it in her face, eyes, or body. The impassive ones usually shattered into the smallest pieces. All it took was skill and time.

Unfastening his restraints, he rose, wondering how many layers he'd have to peel back to get to her. He extended a hand. "Let me take care of that arm."

She hesitated, tilting her head as if the perspective change would help her comprehend the shift from officer to predator and back again.

Damen couldn't be certain what she saw in his face, but her lips curled in an alarmingly good parody of his smile that hadn't been a smile.

His people had a saying. "The hunter's existence is justified by one worthy adversary."

Staring into Jayleia's dark brown eyes, Damen's heart stumbled. Elation tipped into his blood.

He'd just found his.

CHAPTER

7

JAYLEIA recognized that Damen had been trying to force her to admit Lin had taught her. It irked her that he'd been succeeding.

Thank the Gods for V'kyrri's save. Much more and she might have punched the major in the nose.

Besides the fact that she'd hate to destroy a nose as straight and nice as his, she suspected he'd consider the blow little more than a love tap and an invitation to play. She'd never survive his notion of play.

Heat suffused her abdomen.

She bolted to her feet, ignoring his proffered hand.

The knowing smile grew on his face.

Jayleia swallowed a curse. She'd avoided his touch for her own peace of mind, and thereby handed him yet another weapon to wield against her. She had no business being affected by him at all.

She turned on her heel and strode out of the cockpit into the medi-bay.

He followed. Crossing his arms, he leaned against the door frame. His eyes followed every move she made.

She turned her back on him. Gathering medical supplies from

the dull green cabinets lining the gray walls, she listened to her pulse thundering in her ears.

The game of hiztap and tezwoul in the cockpit had provided behavioral confirmation that Damen's species, the Autken, had long ago evolved from a clawed and fanged predator. Their exact history remained unknown. Legend suggested the race had fled a planet orbiting a dying sun.

Over the generations, hybridization had produced the modern version of the species, a rough-and-tumble, violent people with a love for sniffing out mineral deposits on some of the most forsaken asteroids and planets in the known systems. The Autken had founded Silver City and the mining guild, but over the years, citizens from worlds scattered across space had found the station's frontier, anything-goes way of life to their liking.

At last count, the Autken members in the United Mining and Ore Processing Guild were outnumbered nearly two to one by other species. Not that it mattered to guild politics. None of the other races represented in the guild had yet managed to form enough of a coalition to wrest power from the Autken guild mistress, Kannoi, and her council.

Predatory mannerisms remained ingrained in the species. Those who joined the UMOPG learned and adopted them, or they didn't survive.

Jayleia turning her back on Damen in the midst of a battle of wills was either a display of trust or a deadly insult. Either way, she'd told Damen she didn't count him a threat. Which was a lie. Why was he hunting her? Hadn't he already captured her? If he wanted to know where her father was, why not just ask?

"You need information," he said.

The dangerous, velvet quality of his voice had vanished. He spoke once more with the musical cant of a Claughwyth speaker using a non-tonal language like Tagrethian.

Momentary truce for the good of the mission?

"Yes. Was anyone other than my dad accused or arrested?" she asked.

She heard him shift.

"You think this move against your father might be a major power grab?"

"I won't know until . . ."

"Until you have a list of who was arrested," he mused, his tone all business.

"And a report about what's happened to anyone who was picked up in the sweep. If that's what this was," she said. "Source that from our governments, the UMOPG, and the Citizen's Rights Uprising."

"The CRU?"

"Sensationalist though they may be, my parents believe they have access to information the rest of us don't." Concern sliced through her and she turned to him. "My mother. Has she been contacted?"

Damen frowned. "We'll find out."

"I trust her people will protect her," she said. "If I can speak to her, she may be able to provide insight I lack."

Damen's gaze weighed heavy and his smile felt like it could cut. "Why are you cooperating?"

She rubbed her forehead. "You saved my friends and you aren't currently using them as leverage against me. Isn't that reason enough?"

She couldn't begin to interpret the wordless sound he offered in answer. Acknowledgment? Sympathy? An exhortation to prepare for siege?

"Where is your father?" he asked, the smooth, velvet quality in his voice again.

Siege. And her, with so few remaining resources.

"I don't know," she replied, schooling her voice to mimic the hint of danger in his. "Beyond that, be careful how you pursue your prey, Major. I bite. Right now, that'll get you infected."

He whispered a curse.

She paused in her search among the medical supplies to look at him.

The muscles in his jaw flexed. He met her gaze.

"Your father has identified the traitors internal to Tagreth Federated," he gritted. "He may have been trying to neutralize them when someone made him."

"I'd come to that conclusion," she said. "That he'd gotten too close."

Damen crossed the bay in a single stride, closed gentle hands around her wrists, and drew her around to face him.

Electricity flashed across her senses.

She heard him draw a ragged-sounding breath and stared at him, transfixed by the serious light in his eyes.

"Help me find your father and let's finish what he started," he urged, his fingers resting on her pulse points.

The sensation of her blood pounding through her veins in response seemed to soothe him. His shoulders relaxed and he leaned closer. "We could end this war with the Chekydran."

Longing wound around her heart. She could so easily be seduced by his offer to make her part of his team. Because of him? Or because of the goal?

Or was she victim of a masterful interrogation?

She shook her head.

Damen released her.

Instantly, she missed the contact of his skin on hers.

"Would Tagreth Federated still be Tagreth Federated? Or would it end up consumed by the Claugh nib Dovvyth Empire?" she whispered.

"Does it matter?" Damen asked. "We're losing, Jayleia. The Chekydran are grinding down our defenses. We lose more ground every day. If our kind are wiped from known space, what difference will our allegiances make?"

She closed her eyes at the pain that cut through her chest. Gods. How could her father have dropped his mess into her lap and disappeared? She had to find him. If only so she could kill him herself.

"I'm sorry," Damen murmured. He sounded sincere.

She opened her eyes.

Concern lined his forehead.

"You've had a hell of a day," he said, stepping back.

His understatement surprised a smile from her. "I won't break. And I appreciate your honesty as well as the straightforward interrogation."

The tension in his face eased.

"Someone once suggested that when I wanted to know something, I ought to simply ask," he said, his tone challenging her to identify the quote.

Surprised to hear her best friend's words coming from him, she lifted an eyebrow. "Ari's tolerance for games ends at the edge of the dueling floor grid."

"And you?" he asked, his voice a caress that brought blood to the surface of her skin. A gleam of enjoyment showed in his eyes at her blush. "What games do you enjoy?"

"Ones to which I understand the rules," she gasped, fighting the urge to cover her burning cheeks.

"Some of the best games have no rules," he countered.

Jay's heart thumped hard at the innuendo. She could think of no response, and that appeared to please him. At a loss, she returned to hunting for medical supplies.

From the sound of his footsteps, she gathered that Damen returned to the doorway.

"When you last spoke to your father," he finally said, "did he give any indication that anything was wrong?"

Jayleia hesitated. She closed her hand on a regeneration unit and then faced him. "Not per se. It was what he didn't include in his last message."

Damen frowned. "Explain."

"He encodes his communications to me with content of no interest to anyone but me."

"Such as?"

"Lania's second baby is a girl," she said, as she dumped the medications and gear on the diagnostic table.

Damen made a distressed sound in the back of his throat before gesturing at her right side. "Is your arm supposed to be that size?"

She started and glanced down. Uttering a laugh, she rounded the diagnostic bed and handed him a bottle of spray medication. "The antihistamine will help. Press this button. Cover all the bites."

"Lania's second baby is a girl," Damen repeated, raising his eyebrows. "Was it supposed to mean anything?"

"Only that my cousin's child was a girl. Or do you mean something beyond my dad encoding a message that inane simply to force me to practice decryption? He's my father. He has never explained himself to me," she groused.

A faint smile lightened his features, the first she'd seen unclouded by ulterior motive. That she knew the difference so readily jolted her.

He nodded and sprayed medication over the swelling, blood-crusted wound.

It felt like acid. She flinched and squeezed her eyes shut, gritting her teeth to keep from swearing.

"Why didn't you have me numb this first?" he rasped, anger in his voice. "Where is it?"

"I took pain medication when I came aboard," she retorted, opening watering eyes. "Put regen in place, directly atop the wound. The discomfort will diminish . . ."

Damen slapped the antihistamine down on the table. Pinning her with a pointed glare, he found the anesthetic spray and coated her arm.

Jayleia slumped in relief.

Damen caught her, brushed the collection of medical supplies to one side, and then lifted her to sit on the table, pressing his way between her knees so that her thighs bracketed his hips. He smoothed the hair from her face.

Jayleia choked on her breath at the hormones assaulting her system. The heat of him against her legs scorched her, scattering her ability to form rational thought.

"No more stoicism," he commanded. "I do not like causing you pain."

Intimating that he could and would? Jayleia stared into his face and swallowed hard. Why didn't the implied threat scare her?

He smoothed all hint of feeling from his face and brushed his fingertips against her cheekbone.

She flushed at the tingle following the path of his touch. No. His threat didn't frighten her. Her response to him did. She had to refocus him. Pain was easier to bear than whatever he was doing to her.

"Y-you don't wish to be accused of torture?" she asked.

"Pain is a poor motivator," he murmured. "Pleasure is far more effective."

Jayleia laughed to quash the liquid fire rushing through her veins.

He raised his eyebrows.

"I'm dehydrated, exhausted, hungry, and waiting to see whether or not I'll develop a grotesque infection," she said.

Not to mention that he'd somehow seen or sensed her body's response to his touch and turned it into a weapon he skillfully wielded against her. She wished knowing that rational fact made it easier to resist.

"Your options for making good your innuendo are limitless. I don't know where to beg you to begin," she said.

His full lips quirked into a tempting smile and humor sparked in the depths of his eyes. "Let's get you healed up. Hold the begging in reserve for a better time and place."

"You're attempting to manipulate me."

His smile deepened as he leaned into her to pick up the regeneration unit to affix to her injured arm.

She held her breath as the move slammed her senses.

"Is it working?"

Refusing to retreat, she met his eye and challenged, "Ask your questions and see." Her voice sounded damnably husky to her ears.

He shook his head, and activated the device he'd strapped into place, the first glimmer of trouble in his eyes. "I don't want to interrogate you."

She barely caught back her snort of derision in time. *But you've been having so much fun doing it.* The thought continued unbidden. *Maybe I have, too.*

"What do you want?"

Her question seemed to startle him. He stared, unmoving.

"This war over," he finally said, his voice muted. "The people I care about, you, Dr. Idylle, Raj, and Pietre, safe. If anything in your father's last communication can help . . ."

She blinked. He cared? "My father didn't encode his last message. First time ever."

Damen had to have known that she and her father had played cipher games. Most kids did, assigning numbers to letters and leaving one another secret messages. Few children had a father who could teach them the real thing, much less who demanded they stay practiced at deciphering anything thrown at them.

Her father had handed her more and more complicated ciphers as she'd grown. Until his last message, when he'd handed her silence.

"Until now, I couldn't make anything of the lack."

He stepped back, frowning. "Now?"

She shook her head. "At what point does no message become a message? How am I supposed to decipher something that wasn't there?"

"It wasn't a prearranged signal?"

"Not that I knew." Even she heard the frustration in her tone.

He rubbed the back of his neck, his look contemplative, his tone easygoing and full of just-trying-to-help goodwill. "Yet, it sounds like you and your dad are close."

"Come right out and tell me you don't believe I don't know where my father is."

He met her glare with a lazy smile and hooded eyes.

Jayleia struggled to quash the heat flooding her belly.

"Major Sindrivik!" V'kyrri bellowed from the cockpit.

Damen and Jayleia both jumped. They seemed to realize at the same moment that there'd been no proximity alarm. It wasn't a ship approaching with all guns firing. They traded a baffled glance.

"Are you going to feed your guest or go on badgering her while she's wounded and weary?" V'kyrri demanded.

Jayleia chuckled.

"Can't you at least pretend you aren't eavesdropping?" Damen hollered back, irritation mingling with guilt in his tone.

"On this tiny boat?" V'k retorted. "I'd have to be breathing vacuum."

"Don't tempt me," Damen grumbled.

Grinning, Jayleia slid off the diagnostic table.

He shot her a warning look. "Was I unclear about your penchant for stoicism?"

"You're bucking cultural conditioning, Major. You know TFC values."

He grimaced. "Yes. Go forth and conquer or die trying. Tagrethians are so perverse."

"Says the man who has done little more than kidnap Tagrethian women for the past year," she retorted, smiling at his sour expression. "Look, the swelling is nearly gone. I can bend my arm."

"And stand upright," he said, as he turned to a control panel on the wall. "Do you need another rehydration packet?"

"Just water and lunch, if it's still on offer."

"Recon ships don't rate fancy commissary units," he warned over his shoulder.

She lifted an eyebrow at him. "Your notion of manipulating me with pleasure includes disclaimers?"

He laughed outright, a rich, vibrant sound that enfolded her and tempted her to join in. She wondered how something as simple as his amusement could reach so far inside and make her forget he'd pushed her perilously close to the edge of her control in the cockpit.

"Go on. I'll bring a tray," he said. "I was too busy getting us to Chemmoxin to manage breakfast and V'kyrri was too hungover."

She laughed all the way into the cockpit.

V'kyrri glanced over his shoulder, a long-suffering look on his face.

"I'm never going to live that party down, am I?" he grumbled.

She dropped into the seat behind him.

"People make captain and get drunk all the time," Jayleia said. "I suspect your recovery rate is at issue."

He shrugged. "I slept it off."

"Most humanoids require twenty-four to forty-eight hours to process the effects of alcohol," she replied. "And they suffer from headache and nausea the entire time. Your body must detoxify the metabolites differently than other races."

Damen strode in bearing a tray laden with sandwiches and drinks.

"The good-natured ribbing you will endure is called 'masking the barb of envy in humor,'" she told V'kyrri.

"Speaking of masking, did you avoid asking for painkillers on purpose?" V'kyrri asked in a nonchalant tone.

As he secured the tray in such a way that all three of them could reach, Damen shot a speculative look between V'kyrri and Jayleia, but said nothing.

"Why?" she asked, sudden caution warning her to choose her words carefully.

"If you had, it would mean you were deliberately using pain to keep me from reading you," V'kyrri replied without looking at her. He snagged a sandwich from the stack on the tray.

Surprise stopped her in mid-reach. She blinked, aware that, if she admitted to blocking him, the telepath would have reason to really go digging through her head. Great. Tag-team interrogation. Never answer what you could question.

"That works? Using pain?"

Damen chuckled. "Never did for me."

She didn't like the sardonic ring, much less the distress in V'k's face at Damen's statement.

"Just this once," V'kyrri said, meeting her gaze. "I can force my way past a pain shield if necessary. Is it?"

"No," she said, picking up a sandwich of dense bread and what looked like a shelf-stable protein substitute. Simple fare, but nutritionally complete. It had the added bonus of offending as few dietary restrictions among the known humanoid species as possible. She hoped neither of the men noticed that her hand shook. "You must have picked up what I felt to have interrupted Major Sindrivik's interrogation."

She glanced at Damen.

He looked not the least discomfited by her classification of their conversation in medical.

V'kyrri nodded. "As it happens, that burst of anger and frustration aimed at your father was the first clear impression I'd gotten from you since we picked you up."

"It can't be. You reacted when I flinched at the mention of Omorle Lin."

"You didn't flinch. You jumped like you'd been burned. Anyone would have reacted to that, telepath or no," he countered. "Even Sindrivik felt that, though he might not be able to tell you why."

"I can," Damen said, his gaze intent, as if he expected to catch her at something.

It shook her confidence. She struggled for something to say.

"You speak of me reading you as if I could open you like a file," V'kyrri went on, his tone saying he'd gotten down to business. "It isn't that easy. My crewmates train to work with me on a nonverbal level. Developing openness and trust takes time."

Understanding dawned. "You need to build a baseline?"

"Something like that," V'kyrri allowed. "Telepathy is a layered ability. At the very top is awareness of the conscious minds around me. I have an innate knowledge of where everyone is in spatial relation to me."

"You really do have a sixth sense," she mused, then took a bite of her sandwich. The rich, hearty flavor startled her.

Damen's gray eyes danced with suppressed mirth at her murmur of appreciation.

She awarded him a bland look. Of course she valued the motivational power of pleasure. Especially after the swamps of Chemmoxin. What he didn't seem to comprehend was that as her morale improved, his chances of winning information from her diminished. Did he think feeding and healing her would put them on even footing?

"If I pay attention," V'kyrri went on, yanking her back to the fact that the resident telepath had admitted he had a bead on her, "I can pick up emotion. In most cases, it has to be strong, primal stuff. Subtler feelings require more work."

"You're working up to tell me about diminishing returns versus escalating resource costs," Jayleia said.

V'kyrri's sea-green eyes widened in surprise before he laughed.

"I'd never thought of myself as a resource with a price," he said, grinning, "but yes. To access someone's thoughts, I have to shut out everything else. It isn't as useful as you might think."

"I imagine your greatest utility is as a lie detector."

"Even then," V'k said after he'd eaten half his sandwich in two bites. "I don't look for a lie. Emotions conflicting with words are usually enough."

She nodded. "When I said I didn't know where my father was, I wasn't conflicted."

"You weren't, but it was hard to get a clear read through the noise of your physical pain."

"Go count your medical stores. You'll find a packet of painkiller missing because I drank it. I didn't use physical pain on purpose," she said, then picked up and downed a container of water. "I'd heard of the technique, but I had no reason to expect it would work."

"Because TFC member races don't produce telepaths even as mutations," V'kyrri said, sounding like he might be quoting someone.

"Right."

"Why is no one aboard the *Sen Ekir* afraid of him?" Damen asked.

Jayleia snagged another container of water and shrugged. "We fear on a much smaller scale."

V'kyrri's grin widened.

Damen nodded. "Microscopic."

"Precisely. Watching people die radically adjusts one's phobias."

The communications panel chimed a tri-tone.

Jayleia noticed that Damen and V'kyrri both stared at the board as if it had sprouted horns. Buttons lit up, three different colors, one for each note. The sequence repeated.

Damen touched a control.

Claughwyth, rendered in script she couldn't decipher, ran across the holo-display.

"*Queen's Rhapsody* hailing," Damen said.

"What?" V'kyrri asked, concern and surprise in his tone.

Damen opened the channel. The background hiss of interstellar radiation filled the cockpit as the audio systems went live.

A woman's voice speaking Claughwyth broke across the static. Damen replied in kind. Jayleia caught only the name of the ship. *Kawl Fergus*.

V'kyrri faced the communications panel, tension in the set of his shoulders. "Commander Parqe, this is Captain V'kyrri," he said in Jay's language, "are you comfortable speaking Tagrethian?"

"Yes, sir," the woman responded, her words accented and musical.

"We're twenty hours from rendezvous at Silver City's space dock," Damen said.

"My apologies, Major," the commander replied. "We've received new orders and are on intercept to your location."

"Report," V'k interrupted, frowning.

"A cloaked contingent of Chekydran broke through the defense lines and attacked the *Dagger*," the commander said.

V'kyrri flinched.

Damen's hand clenched on the panel.

Alarm rocketed through Jayleia. Her heart rate picked up speed, making her aware of the headache building behind her eyes.

"They're alive," the commander said, "but the *Dagger* is disabled. Captain Idylle spotted the ambush just before it hit. The body count is low because of that fact. Our orders are to pick you up, Captain V'kyrri, and return to the front lines with all haste to protect the *Dagger*'s flank while the crew affects repairs."

V'kyrri sat upright, rage lighting a fire in his sea-green eyes. "The Chekydran?"

"One destroyed, two made a run for it. They got away. Last known course has them headed into United Mining and Ore Processing Guild space."

Jayleia frowned. An attack on the UMOPG would cripple fuel supplies for the Claugh and TFC militaries.

Uneasiness fired against the inside of her skin. Had Damen been right? Was she better off betraying her father and her people to the Claugh in order to save them from the Chekydran?

"Increasing our speed to maximum," V'kyrri said. "We'll be in teleport range within the hour. I'll transfer to the *Rhapsody* . . ."

Jayleia's attention jerked to the conversation. She gaped at V'kyrri. "Absolutely not."

"Stand down," V'kyrri ordered, awarding her a hard glare. "Her Majesty is in danger. I have a job to do."

"So do I," she said. "You're on a plague ship, Captain. I'll be damned before I let you teleport out of here to infect your entire command, much less your queen."

CHAPTER

8

SILENCE. Except for the pounding in Jayleia's head keeping time with her pulse.

Damen and V'kyrri stared.

"Two things," she said into the weighted quiet. "First, *Queen's Rhapsody*, do you have a quarantine advisory for this vessel? The flag would have come across the alliance pipeline. Second, does the *Kawl Fergus* have the capacity to initiate teleport as well as receive?"

The men blinked in unison.

"Both ships must be able to initiate teleport for the biofilters to work in synchronous and thereby detect infection," Jay pointed out.

"Identify," the commander said.

"Jayleia Durante of the TFC science ship *Sen Ekir*," she replied.

"Stand by."

Damen closed a hand around hers.

Awareness lit every nerve. She met his gaze.

"The *Kawl Fergus* has teleport," he said. "Why would we be quarantined?"

Ah, military personnel, so intoxicated with guns and warships, they never considered the power of a pathogen or of a single-minded scientist to bring them to their knees.

She shrugged. "Depending on how pissed off Dr. Idylle is, he may have flagged us."

V'kyrri examined her with disbelief in his face. His brows lowered. "You're serious."

"Very," she replied.

Damen swore, then pinned her with a look that said he'd caught her lying. "He wouldn't endanger you."

"To prevent an epidemic, he would," she countered. "Stop looking at me like I'm speaking Chekydran. Even if he has issued a quarantine alert, it will be a 'detain and treat.' We won't be shot out of the sky."

"*Kawl Fergus*?" the woman's voice interrupted. "We have no quarantine alerts linked to your vessel ID. May I request a status summary?"

"We've been exposed to a blood-borne pathogen, Commander Parqe," Damen replied, releasing Jayleia and running his hand down his face as he paused for thought. "Without adequate medical personnel aboard, we cannot verify infection status."

"Blood-borne?" the commander echoed, her tone stating she didn't see the problem.

Weary, Jayleia rubbed her aching forehead. "He fails to mention that I bled all over his ship and all over him. I can't take chances, Commander. The health of Claugh nib Dovvyth personnel is of vital concern to Tagreth Federated and to me personally."

The commander snorted. "If only because we're fighting the war for you. This is one group baxt'k of an alliance."

V'kyrri's eyes widened at his commander's comment.

"I'm a scientist," Jayleia said, keeping her tone even. "Not a politician. As such, it's not my job to give a damn what you think of the alliance. It's my job to keep you alive to fight that unbalanced war and to protect my friends aboard the *Dagger*. With that established, how recent are the biofilters aboard these two ships?"

V'kyrri pinched the bridge of his nose as if pained. "Biofilters for all vessels in the fleet are updated via broad dispersal burst on an as-needed basis. The only delimiter is distance and the speed of the carrier wave. Since the *Rhapsody* was recently in contact with the *Dagger*, the filters should be no more than a few hours . . ."

"Thirteen hours, sir," Parqe interjected.

"Excellent," Jayleia said, relief easing the tension gathering in her shoulders. "The markers for the Chemmoxin pathogen were released a month or more ago. The *Rhapsody* should have them. We'll synch the biofilters and teleport you to your ship, then, Captain."

"If he's infected the teleport won't go through?" Damen guessed. He matched her nod. "Then we each teleport."

"What?" V'kyrri demanded. His cautious tone and the way he eyed her told Jay he'd picked up her hesitation.

"Primary symptoms are setting in," she said. "I doubt I'll teleport."

The muscles of Damen's jaw knotted. "We'll try."

"We could decontaminate the ship the way we did aboard the *Sen Ekir* last year," V'kyrri suggested. "Wouldn't a radiation bath work? The *Kawl Fergus* would handle a slingshot."

"Undoubtedly, on both counts, but we wouldn't have the pre-exposure vaccine to shield us. We'd take a full dose of radiation," she said. "You'd both be sterile, even after months of gene therapy."

They cringed.

"The *Rhapsody* could send three doses . . ." V'k began.

"It's radioactive," she said.

"Then it won't teleport," Damen concluded, his tone grim.

"Captain, if I may?" Commander Parqe interjected.

"Go ahead, Commander," V'k said.

"I've taken the liberty of briefing our medical officer," she said. "Jowun suggests stasis for your infected passenger."

Something dark and cold gripped Jayleia's chest. She couldn't draw a full breath. She didn't comprehend the sensation and grappled for control of her runaway heart rate and blurred vision. When her eyesight cleared, she found herself on her feet, staring at the companionway outside the cockpit door.

Confusion and deep uneasiness swept her.

She drew a slow, purposeful breath, just to be certain she could. Air slid easily in and out. Frowning, she turned back.

Damen half stood, one hand braced on the back of his chair, the other on his panel, as if she'd caught him in the act of rising. He eyed her, his gaze searching. Whatever he saw drew him to her side.

He slipped an arm around her waist, pulling her against him.

"Easy," he murmured. "It's okay."

Was it? Resting against the solid warmth of Damen's chest, she relaxed. The last remnants of cold fled her body. A sense of safety crept over her and she sighed.

"What happened?" Jayleia asked. Her voice sounded thin and scared. She focused on V'kyrri's dazed expression. "Did you do that?"

He turned his head toward her, though his eyes didn't quite focus.

"He didn't do anything," Damen said. "What happened?"

Panic spiked into her chest. Her vision hazed.

"Breathe," he commanded at her ear, tightening his arm around her. "I've got you. You're safe. Breathe, Jayleia."

She sucked in a ragged breath.

Her vision cleared in time for her to see V'kyrri grimace.

"Are you sure you aren't trained in telepathic ambush, Jay?" he grumbled. "Cause that hurt."

She gaped at the telepath. The pounding in her head made her queasy. "What? No. You did something. Are you telekinetic? Or did you influence me mentally? Take over and drive me out of the cockpit? Why would you do that?"

"Explain this if you can," Damen said to V'kyrri as he led her to her chair. "Or I'll refuse you painkillers for that headache you're broadcasting."

V'kyrri sat upright. "Am I broadcasting? Sorry." His gaze turned inward.

"Sit down," Damen urged, his voice pitched to soothe and reassure.

It worked. She obeyed, embarrassed by how badly she'd needed his arms around her.

"Thanks."

"Is that better?" V'kyrri asked.

The ache in Jay's head had diminished. She blinked. How could she, a non-telepath, have been picking up V'kyrri's physical pain?

She wished his ability accounted for the entirety of her discomfort. She distracted herself from the throb in her head by mentally cataloging a set of experiments to define how much a non-telepath could sense from a telepath. Could she pick up other physical sensations? What about thoughts? Or feelings?

"I'm sorry, Jayleia," V'kyrri said, calling her attention back to her aching body. "I had nothing to do with your run from the cockpit. As far as I can tell, you reacted to the suggestion of stasis . . ."

"Stasis?" she interrupted, startled. "No."

"It certainly seemed to be the trigger," he hedged.

"It isn't stasis specifically. I don't like dark, enclosed places," she admitted, ignoring the sour bite of fear on her tongue.

Damen and V'kyrri traded a doubting look.

"You blasted me with a bolt of pure little kid, middle-of-the-night, terror," V'kyrri said.

Had she?

Concern stood out in the tightness of Damen's lips.

"One thing at a time," he said. "We're minutes from teleport range. Let's get V'k aboard his ship and en route to protecting the *Dagger*."

Jay nodded, relieved as much by the change of subject as by the logic of the suggested course of action.

"Agreed," she said, forcing herself to shift out of a reactive, feeling state and into cool, rational thought.

The best way to conquer an unfounded fear was to face it. With her pulse hammering in her temples, she forced herself to ask, "I assume the *Kawl Fergus* has a stasis chamber?"

"It won't be necessary," he said. "We'll route straight to the *Dagger* . . ."

"Negative, Major," Commander Parqe replied. "Admiral Seaghdh asked me to relay the following: 'Silver City objective critical.' He said you'd understand."

"Message received and understood," Damen said. He glanced at

Jayleia, disquiet in the depths of his eyes. "I'll push our pace. Silver City medical will treat you."

"It doesn't sterilize the ship," she said. Had her mindless reaction been so disturbing?

Rubbing her aching forehead, she sighed. He didn't have to be logical. She did.

"While stasis cannot cure me, it would slow the infection," she said. "You could teleport to the *Rhapsody* after V'kyrri, and blow the airlock remotely while I'm under sedation in stasis."

Damen grinned without a hint of humor in his face. "Leave the TFC spymaster's daughter alone aboard my ship?"

She gaped at him. "What do you expect me to do while I'm in a medically induced coma, locked inside a thrice-damned, airtight coffin?"

Amusement glittered in his gray eyes. "Did you know one of the Autken's primary senses is scent? I don't need V'k to be my lie detector. I won't leave you alone aboard my boat."

Three Hells. Could he really smell a lie? What about omission? She blew out a shallow breath. That both explained and complicated everything. It also reinforced her determination to escape Major Sindrivik's custody. Once she'd found her father, or could prove his innocence or lack thereof, she could offer her dad the option of using the Claugh nib Dovvyth in an end-game maneuver. Assuming that's where his plans were and not locked in stasis of another kind.

"Is there reason to resort to drastic measures for something curable?" Damen asked.

"The pneumonia outbreak last year," Jayleia said.

Damen frowned. "When the plague the Chekydran had seeded in Captain Idylle went hot."

"You didn't even get a sore throat," she said. "V'kyrri nearly died."

"How happy I am to remember so little of that stay in the *Dagger*'s medi-bay," V'kyrri interjected before fixing her with a keen eye. "You're afraid of finding a race susceptible to this disease?"

"Every race has adapted to handle different illnesses. The danger is combining a low-risk illness with a population that has no natural defense to it. You'd be horrified, assuming you survived, by how swiftly a benign disease with low morbidity can change its stripes and become a killer. How many species live and work on the *Queen's Rhapsody*? Or on Silver City for that matter?" she asked.

"If you're treated, and the ship sterilized upon docking, what's our exposure?" Damen asked, frustration darkening his expression.

"With this disease, minimal," Jay replied, "but greater than zero."

He blew out an audible breath, shot a glance at V'kyrri, and said, "Given the admiral's message, my decision stands."

V'kyrri nodded.

"Stand by to teleport," Damen ordered.

"Medical personnel standing by," Commander Parqe said over the open com line. "Biofilters confirmed online."

"Initiating teleporter diagnostic," Damen replied. "System online. Biofilter compatibility confirmed."

"Acknowledged."

"System is warmed and ready, Captain," Damen said to his friend. "Let's get you to your ship."

V'kyrri strode out of the cockpit, down the companionway, and into the bay with the door where Jayleia had entered.

She turned her chair to watch.

V'kyrri glanced at Damen's back, then grinned at her and mouthed, "Good luck."

That he seemed to feel she needed it troubled her. She bit back the urge to plead with him to stay. She didn't know how long she could withstand the full-on assault of Damen's persuasion.

Considering the determination she'd seen in Damen to complete his missions, he wouldn't find out until too late that breaking her wouldn't help him locate her father.

"On your mark, Commander," Damen said.

"On my mark, aye," Commander Parqe said. "Three, two, one, mark."

"Mark, aye," Damen replied. "Teleport in progress."

She felt the *Kawl Fergus* slow and could only guess at the immense power required to blink a person from one point in space/time to another. One moment V'kyrri stood in the entry bay, the next he vanished as if winked out of existence. The engines surged.

Good. V'kyrri was safe.

"Teleport complete," Damen said behind her. "Confirm you have Captain V'kyrri aboard."

"Confirmed," V'kyrri replied over the com. "Nice job. Jay? Your turn."

She levered herself to her feet, ignoring the pounding in her head and the trickle of sweat tracking a chilly path down her spine. Great. Fever. Another symptom. She stumbled to the point where she'd watched V'kyrri disappear then turned to face the cockpit door.

Damen's gaze tracked her, his features set in tense lines.

"Ready," he said, misgiving in his face and in his voice.

"Three, two, one, mark."

"Mark, aye. Teleporting."

Alarms erupted.

The noise touched off a wave of dizziness. Jay folded her knees and sat where she'd been standing.

The alarms went silent.

"Jayleia's down," Damen said.

"Standing by," V'kyrri replied.

The fever heightened her senses. She caught a whiff of rain and green, growing things before Damen crouched beside her and drew her against his side. Rather than exacerbating the pain in her head, the odor seemed to mitigate the symptoms.

His scent?

"I don't want to put you in stasis," Damen said in a voice pitched only for her ears and rough in a way she'd never heard before.

"I have reason not to open the ship to vacuum, but if it's the only way to keep you safe, I will."

A moment of clarity burst through her. Of course. It wasn't concern for her nameless fear. He was running more than one mission at a time.

CHAPTER
9

EVEN with a fever addling her brain, Jayleia realized that if she was merely a distraction from Damen's true mission in this part of space, her options for escape broke wide open. Once she was well.

Damen was a spy with a job to do. Possibly several. At least one of which precluded using vacuum to sterilize the ship. That meant cargo that could be damaged or killed without atmosphere and heat.

By confiding that detail to her, he'd offered her a good-faith gesture. She'd return the favor.

"Another option," Jay breathed. "I'll sleep. Eighteen to forty-eight hours. You won't be able to wake me."

He shook his head, the portion of his face she could see clouded by wariness. His voice sounded tight, terse. "Explain."

She closed her eyes. Conditioning against disclosing more information than necessary argued with her desire to ease the troubled lines from Damen's face. If only momentarily.

And that wasn't rational.

"It's a racial ability," she whispered before she'd reached the conscious decision to do it anyway. "I'll go into a healing trance. Think of it as a voluntary coma, save that it isn't, strictly speaking, a coma. Body functions slow, allowing for reallocation of resources to immune system activity. While I'm under, my immune system will mount a massive assault on the infection. Unlike stasis, which would freeze me and the illness in time, when I wake from the healing trance, I'll be cured."

It felt as if every muscle in his body tightened.

"I know a little bit about your mother's people," he said, his tone considering. "Your file makes it clear you didn't complete your training with the Swovjiti Temple."

That part of her personnel file was public, perhaps because the circumstances behind her expulsion from the program had been humiliating. Jayleia opened her eyes and shrugged.

He sucked in an audible breath that sounded as if she'd given him the missing piece of a vital puzzle. "Claugh data on the Swovjiti healing trance are so sparse that we assumed the technique was the pinnacle of Temple training. If it isn't, what is?"

"I won't answer that. Help me to the medi-bay?"

"No," he said, tucking an arm around her waist, pulling her to her feet, and then down the companionway. "Come on. The cabin. The diagnostic bed is suited for torture, not for sleeping."

"I'll keep that in mind," she murmured as the cabin door opened and he ushered her into the tiny room.

He swept the covers from the bed and eased her to sitting.

The throb behind her eyes subsided when she sank onto the edge to kick off her shoes.

"Teleport," she said.

Damen studied her, his expression set in patently noncommittal lines.

"I can't sleep until you do," she ground from between clenched teeth, her breath coming in short rasps. "Your health is my job. Open the room com so I can hear, then lock me in. If you teleport out and then right back, I won't have time to hijack or sabotage your thrice-damned ship."

"All right," Damen said. His tone, pitched to placate, didn't quite mask his amusement. "You win."

"You lie badly."

He chuckled.

She smiled, knowing he'd realized she wasn't a threat in her present condition. Too bad it was true. She heard Damen move, then the musical cadence of a piece of equipment activating.

What did it mean that the Claugh valued the beauty of music even in the most utilitarian applications? Not even TFC luxury liners were equipped with gear that switched on with anything more than a click.

"Com is live," Damen said. "Stand by to teleport, V'k. This will be a rapid shot. Out and back, confirming infection status only."

"Understood. Resetting teleporter to the *Kawl Fergus* cockpit. Synch your biofilter over to match, please," V'kyrri's voice replied over the open link. "Standing by."

Damen strode out of the room.

"Biofilter synch confirmed. On your mark, Captain." Damen's words echoed, coming both through the open cabin door and via the open com link.

"On my mark, aye," V'kyrri said. "Three, two, one, mark."

"Teleporting."

Ship's speed lagged. Jayleia collapsed back into the bed in relief. No alarms. Damen was safe. The engines ramped, then slowed and revved again.

"Gods," Damen grumbled. "Give me a systems failure any day over disease. Best speed, *Queen's Rhapsody*. My regards to Her Majesty. *Kawl Fergus* out."

He strode into the room and into her limited line of sight. His chest expanded as he drew a deep breath. Tension mounted in the set of his shoulders.

"Thank you," she murmured.

"You'll heal now?"

"Yes. You're safe."

That brought a surprised and pleased smile to his face.

"You'll be more comfortable without this." He unclipped her equipment belt, draping it over his arm. "I'll pull data on your father and load it on your handheld while you sleep. Translation, too."

Jay settled deeper onto the mattress. It responded to her weight and heat, conforming to her body. Even before she began the trance triggers she'd been taught from childhood, her eyes closed.

Damen pulled the blankets over her. With the bed and covers saturated with his scent, she couldn't keep her imagination from enclosing her in Damen's arms. Had he intended that? The uncomfortable pounding of her heart eased. She thought she smiled as she sighed and snuggled into the bed.

He smoothed hair away from her face. Warm lips lingered on her forehead.

"Get better," he murmured. "I need you."

JAYLEIA woke to the distinctive *snick* of a neural cuff closing around her left wrist. She tried to frown and realized she felt like someone had neural-locked her entire body. What was going on? Where was she?

Mental processes sputtered, stalled, then kicked and restarted. Ah. She was coming out of a healing trance. Memory provided a rapid-fire replay of events. Chemmoxin. Infected kuorls. Her rescue/kidnapping courtesy of the Claugh nib Dovvyth. Damen. Safe. Her father. Missing.

Anxiety sat on her chest. Her dad. What more had come apart while she'd slept off her infection?

Her respiration rate increased and by virtue of memory, she knew where she was, aboard the *Kawl Fergus*, in Damen's cabin. In his bed.

While she was conscious, it would take her several minutes of concentrated effort to regain control of her body. She resented the cuffs, even though she hadn't heard them activated.

She groaned.

"Jay?"

Damen. Sounding uncertain. Off balance.

"Can you hear me?"

Of course she could. She simply couldn't answer.

"Damn it," he grumbled. "I hope this means you're waking." He closed the other cuff around her right wrist, but he didn't secure it.

Why not?

"I'm taking you to the station medical facility," he said, "so the cleaning team can get aboard."

Jay realized she didn't feel or hear the engines. Apparently, they'd made Silver City. What had Damen said? They'd been twenty hours out when the *Rhapsody* had intercepted them?

Twenty hours of healing trance. Good. The infection had barely established a foothold in her system, then. She'd be up and causing trouble in short order.

"Station authorities require that you be secured for transport," he said. "If you're cured, and you'd better be, it's a needless precaution. You've been so amenable since I picked you up, and I can't work out why. I kidnapped you with the intent of using you to flush your father from hiding."

He paused, whispered a curse in a language she didn't recognize, and shifted.

"In your place," he went on, "I'd have cooperated long enough to get to Silver City, knowing it represented the perfect opportunity for escape."

How fortunate. She didn't have enough physical control yet to laugh at his oh-so-accurate calculation. Or, more troubling, to indulge her growing inclination to warn him that he'd made a mistake in not cuffing her properly.

His compassion and her attraction were going to get both of them into trouble.

Damen lifted Jayleia from the bed and eased her onto the stretcher he'd found in the *Kawl Fergus*'s medi-bay. Long strands of shiny black hair spilled over the edge. He tucked it up beside her and found he had to resist stroking the silky tresses.

He studied the exotic cream and chocolate cast of her complexion and searched for any further sign that she might be waking. She had warned him he wouldn't be able to rouse her. It hadn't troubled him the first few times he'd looked in on her. The fourth time, and every time thereafter, it had.

To distract himself, he'd pulled up the log files of her most recent conversations with her parents, hoping to catch a hint of what had happened to her dad.

Since he'd helped Pietre break an IntCom lockdown of the *Sen Ekir* last year, he'd had a back door into the ship's systems. That they hadn't detected him, much less shut him out, made him uncomfortable. He couldn't decide if the scientists were simply too trusting, or if he was somehow betraying the friendships he'd developed with them.

It didn't matter. Admiral Seaghdh recognized the strategic importance of the unassuming science ship. He'd ordered the surveillance.

Damen had loaded and run Jay's last message from her father. He detected a pinched look at the corners of Zain Durante's hazel eyes.

"I want you off that ship," Jayleia's father had said. "You promised you'd come back. You're a fine scientist. Any research facility would be glad to have you. Come home."

In the video, she'd stared at him before shaking her head. "I'm flattered, Dad. What home were you referring to? Yours? Mom's? I've carved out a life of my own and you want me to give it up?"

"Your mother had you most of your childhood and I didn't interfere," her father had replied.

Jayleia's bitter-sounding laugh made Damen resolve to pull up her file again.

"I'd like a turn at knowing the person you've become, Jayleia," her father had noted. "Take some time. Think about it. Your mother won't like that I've asked you to return to Tagreth, but you're an adult now. I know you'll make the right decision. The *Sen Ekir* was pulled from the Ioccal project and repurposed as an outbreak first response vessel. What kind of future are you building out there?"

"My own," she'd said.

He'd shaken his head as if disappointed. "I love you. I want you to be happy. You can't be happy if you don't lay the framework for it. Come home. I'll help you examine your options, maybe open a few doors that would otherwise be closed to you," he'd said before signing off.

A message from her mother had followed. Margol Durante, a slender woman with delicate features and skin a shade darker than her daughter's sat rigid before her camera, rage etched in the lines around her mouth.

"Your father had no right to say what he did to you," her mother had said. "You grew up here, surrounded by family, trained in the ways of our people. You've shirked your responsibilities to the Temple and to the people who love you long enough. When you enlisted against my wishes, I said little."

In the log replay, Jayleia propped an elbow on her panel and rested her forehead in her hand.

"Young women deserve to make their own way in life for a little while before the dictates of duty and obligation weigh upon them," her mother had continued. "I wanted that experience for you, even if I disapproved of your decision to endanger your life to get it. You've made remarkable contributions to the people of Tagreth Federated and to the war effort, Jayleia. It is time to pass that burden to a new generation. All I have to offer is my love and the adoration of your extended family. Come. Take your place . . ."

"Mother," Jayleia had finally burst out. "I was exiled!"

"You would give up so easily?" the woman had asked. "That misunderstanding can be remedied with a tactful apology. Or is this your way of telling me your father has won you away from me with promises I cannot hope to match?"

Suspecting that Jayleia's official file didn't tell the real story regarding her banishment and disturbed by the emotional blackmail her mother employed, Damen had finally shut off the replay. While he'd seen signs of strain in both of Jayleia's parents, he hadn't seen or heard anything to help him find Zain Durante.

He'd gone to look in on Jay yet again. He'd lost count of which peek at her it had been, but he'd realized that the subtle, sickly scent of decomposing flesh he'd smelled when she'd collapsed had vanished.

That had been hours ago. Why wouldn't she regain consciousness?

He craved another shot at her defenses. Shoving aside a surge of anticipation, he activated the stretcher's anti-grav unit and reminded himself he didn't have time to indulge his appetites. His first order of business would be verifying her cure.

The sooner she was healthy, the sooner he could strip her defenses and find out what she didn't want him to know. And get to her father.

The makeshift bed, bearing Jayleia, rose to his hip. Damen took the head of the unit and steered the stretcher out of the *Kawl Fergus*'s cargo door, out of the docking bay he'd been assigned, and through the halls. Miners and stationers passed with little more than a glance at his passenger. A turn into a main corridor leading to the station hub meant more noise and more people. Jayleia didn't flinch.

He frowned, concerned, and sped his steps.

"Hold the lift!" he commanded a group of four miners as they piled into the elevator.

They ignored him.

"Medical priority, damn it," he shouted, sprinting the last distance. He stuck a foot into the closing door, drew his gun, and shoved it into the closest gap-toothed grin.

"Baxt'kal. Medical. Priority," he gritted.

The doors opened. Damen gestured. "Out."

The men glowered at him. "You got balls of solid Isarrite, boy," one of them grumbled.

Damen didn't bother answering. He backed into the lift, his gun still trained to ensure their safe passage. The lift doors closed on the miners' anger-reddened faces. Only then did Damen relax, punch in a destination, and turn to his prisoner.

"Jayleia?" he murmured, holstering his gun. "Please tell me you're awake."

She opened her eyes, and squinted, discomfort in the crinkles in her forehead. Her eyes closed again.

"Jayleia?" he said, leaning closer, and brushing her hair from her face.

She drew an audible breath and turned into his hand, a faint smile on her lips.

Heat skittered down his body. He froze, caught off guard by the strength of the response. He cleared his throat and dismissed his taut nerves as nothing more than concern for his prisoner's well-being.

"I need you to wake up," he said, opening the cuff he'd never locked, and smoothing the skin of her right wrist.

She sighed in response to his touch.

Twelve Gods he needed her to regain consciousness, to remember that he was the enemy, and to erect her defenses between them, again. Every breath he drew flooded him with her intoxicating wine and chocolate scent—no longer tainted by any hint of illness.

He hadn't had anything like professional detachment regarding Jayleia Durante from the moment, a year ago, that he'd surprised her prepping experiments in the shadow of the *Sen Ekir* and taken her prisoner. Her crewmates had been angry and scared. She'd done an impressive job of masking her fury. She'd studied the team of four men who'd taken the ship as if making plans to take them all on single-handedly. She'd looked like a Myallki bitch poised to protect her spawn, all shining black hair and supple beauty, but hiding poisonous fangs.

Damen smiled at the memory.

Her eyes opened. As her gaze focused on him, she frowned. She lifted a hand, hesitating for a split second as the neural cuff dangling from her left wrist caught her eye.

Confusion clouded her expression.

"To pacify security," he said.

Her gaze returned to his face and concern etched lines into the corners of her mouth. She laid her fingers against the ridge of bunched muscles in his jaw.

Electricity raced along his nerves. Soothing him, he realized. She'd barely awakened and she was trying to offer him comfort?

Her brown eyes darkened and she smoothed the skin of his jaw. The faint rasp of his whiskers slowed the stroke.

White-hot desire shot straight through him. His heart rate took off at supralight. Biology. Nothing more than hormones and the six long months since he'd taken anyone.

Damen choked back a groan.

"You're still half out of it, aren't you?" he asked, his voice gruff to his ears.

Her gaze lowered to his mouth as her beautiful lips parted. Slipping her hand around his neck, she urged him closer.

Longing raked his insides. He resisted for a moment, then gave in. It would build rapport. Might even make her believe they were on the same side. It had nothing to do with his need to taste her.

"Jayleia," he murmured against her lips.

She arched into the kiss.

Damen's nerve endings lit from head to toe.

She wrapped her left hand around the back of his neck.

The pressure of the free cuff cupped in her palm spilled cold awareness down Damen's spine. Reality wrenched him out of the fog shrouding his brain and body.

He'd let the spymaster's daughter get the drop on him. He broke contact.

"Jay. Don't . . ." he growled as her right hand found the restraint control at his hip.

She hit the switch. The neural disruptor fired. A bolt of pain shot up the base of his skull straight to the top of his head. Damen blacked out.

CHAPTER

10

CURSING, Jayleia tried to catch Damen as the neural disruption field interrupted signal processing between the brain and the spinal column. He slumped unconscious across her body and spilled to the floor.

Heart pounding, she sat up, jumped to her feet, and then fumbled for the restraint control so she could restore feeling to her left arm. That done and the cuff removed, she checked him. Respiration regular and even, color good, pulse slightly elevated. Relief flooded her. He'd wake soon. She didn't have much time.

Tucking his gun into the waistband of her trousers, Jayleia rose to examine the elevator controls. They weren't just going up or down. The lift was cutting across a central station hub. To medical, he'd said.

She wanted the docks. Damen had taken her handheld as she'd entered trance, she recalled. With any luck, he'd loaded translation, as well as data regarding her father's disappearance. Once she had access to the *Kawl Fergus*'s control panels via her handheld, chances were, she could steal the fast, little spy ship.

She eyed the elevator panel lock and automatically reached for the wrench she'd used assembling kuorl cages on Chemmoxin. Her tool belt was gone. Of course. Damen had removed it so she could sleep, just as sometime during the past twenty hours, she realized, he'd removed the regen unit from her now-healed right arm. He'd put her expedition boots back on her feet, but he hadn't restored her belt.

Fine.

One well-aimed kick and the elevator panel swung open. She tripped the emergency stop. The compartment skidded, stopped, and slipped a few meters before the brakes caught and held. An obnoxious alarm blared. Hull breach survival masks dropped from a panel beside her.

She ignored them. Kneeling on the wobbly stretcher, Jay used the anti-grav unit to lift her to the escape panel in the ceiling. It refused. Overrides kicked in with the stretcher one and a half meters from the floor.

Cursing, she reached up, pushed the removable ceiling panel out of the way, and gingerly rose to her feet. As she got her arms and shoulders through the opening, the stretcher shot out from under her. She came down hard on the support bars with the undersides of her arms. It wrung a cry of pain from her as she dangled, feet kicking in midair.

It took a moment before she could get her hands positioned to hoist herself into the emergency-red-lit lift tunnel.

Damen groaned.

Panic spiked through the guilt gnawing at her. More to slow down pursuit than to prevent it, she dropped the ceiling panel back in place. No one would be fooled. She just didn't like the notion of a hole at her back, a hole through which, she imagined, a pissed off and headachy Damen Sindrivik was going to emerge shortly.

Picking a direction, she climbed onto the narrow maintenance walkway and took off jogging. Someone shut down the audible alarm and she heard tezwoule squeal below her. One hoary specimen, his long, scaly tail gleaming in the emergency light, leaped from the middle of the walkway into the tunnel depths as she ran past. The furry creature shrilled harsh cries of reproach in her wake. Anyone in these tunnels would be able to mark her passing by the chiding tezwoule, if not by the racket she made running.

Jayleia slowed, trying to quiet her footfalls while still making time and distance. A rush of wind against her face and the impression of fluttering wings suggested that arets inhabited the rank tunnel system. She wondered what the winged mammals fed on, insects presumably. The thought made her snap her mouth shut and slow her pace further.

She hit a junction, where several tunnels converged on a central traffic exchange core. It was there that she discovered what ate the tezwoule and arets.

A sickly, pale bug twitched in midair in the center of the walkway. As she approached, she realized that the "bug" was actually a lure dropped on a translucent appendage by an ooze. This one looked well fed, judging from the sizeable splay of its pod made up of proteins, polysaccharides, and what looked like lift grease.

She edged around the lure. Oozes used venom-laden stinging cells to incapacitate their pray. Like she'd sucker-stunned Damen. She shoved away guilt.

Still, some oozes had venom that could paralyze to the point of suffocation. She didn't want to find out the hard way that this was one of them.

Picking up her pace again, she kept a sharp eye out. She couldn't afford to blunder into the nematocysts of a hungry ooze. It would hurt if it didn't kill her, and if it did kill her, she was too heavy for the ooze to reel her in as a snack. She hated that kind of waste.

She scanned the tunnel juncture. If the mining station followed standard protocols, they would shut down the lift tunnels surrounding the emergency stop site. Computers would route traffic around the stuck compartment. If she could find her way out of the emergency buffer zone, she could hop another compartment, or she could pry open a set of lift doors and walk away into the crowds.

No matter which she picked, she'd need to move quickly and

hope that security teams hadn't yet made it to every single lift door. Sure, she had Damen's gun, but she had no desire to hurt anyone unlucky enough to be in her way.

What she wouldn't give for her handheld so she could access the station system. She needed a schematic. She had no idea how to get to the docks.

Stop it and think.

Given: she was lost in the bowels of Silver City. In any deep space station, however, atmospheric controls, power generation, water processing, and medical bays clustered at the core of the structure. Docks lined the exterior rims where malfunctioning ship thrusters and breakaway cargo containers couldn't collide with the station and destroy vital functions.

The core and the docks would be most heavily guarded. Could she find her way back to the *Kawl Fergus*'s docking bay by retracing Damen's path with the stretcher in reverse? Almost. She could almost trace her way back, save for the time spent in the lift when she couldn't be sure how many decks or sections they'd traversed. Damn.

She could give up on stealing the *Kawl Fergus* and find living quarters where she could hide unnoticed for days. Population and traffic levels would be lower. From what she knew of the station, drifters and itinerants were common and unremarked. It would take longer to find legitimate transport off station that way, but it would attract far less attention than stealing a Claugh spy ship.

She hated the idea. In the search for her father, she'd already lost twenty-six hours. Since she'd just added the Claugh nib Dovvyth major to her growing list of problems, she suspected time was on his side, not hers. If she couldn't steal the *Kawl Fergus*, she'd find another ship, but she had to get off station. *Now.*

She dodged a few more ooze lures before noticing trash on the walkways, signs that squatters inhabited the tunnels. The walkway narrowed and she blundered into a boy hunting tezwoule with a makeshift sling. He'd already killed three and carried them by draping their scaly tails over one shoulder.

He yelped, dropped his catch, and sprinted down the walkway.

"Wait a minute!" she yelled. "I just . . ." She broke off and sighed. "I just want directions."

Several meters down the walkway he vaulted over the railing and dropped out of sight. He screamed, the sound high and scared.

Jayleia's breath froze in her chest.

The sound of a body dropping to the deck echoed down the tunnel.

She gritted her teeth. *Leave it, Jay. It's an extortion scam. You know it is.*

She should mind her own business. First unwritten, but well-known rule for "How to Survive Silver City." She should keep going. From his clothes and his presence in the tunnels, she could assume the kid was a native. He could take care of himself. Right?

"Damn."

She tore down the walkway and peered over the railing.

He'd fallen so that she could see only one out-flung hand. His sling lay in a jumble.

Resisting the urge to pound her forehead against the metal railing in frustration, Jay climbed over and dropped to the deck plating three meters below.

Something sticky and wet struck her right cheek. She yelped in surprise and stumbled back, her hand automatically coming up to wipe the slime away.

An ooze.

She huffed out a breath. It had tried to sting her and failed, meaning it had stung someone within the past few minutes.

She offered the uncaring ooze a dirty look before kneeling beside the child. Dark brown hair tangled on his damp forehead.

Her heart squeezed tight. The boy was sweating. His respiration was rapid, audible, and shallow. She could see the sting site, an angry, red bull's-eye, the flesh swelling as she watched.

She rubbed her cheek where the ooze had tagged her. What kind of luck was it that she'd scared the life out of a little kid, he'd run right into an ooze, and then turned out to be allergic?

If this had started as a bid to collect a payoff, it had turned deadly.

Jay blew out a shaky breath. Even if the boy had intended to guilt her out of money she didn't have, he'd gotten more than he'd bargained for. His reaction would kill him unless he got treatment. Fast. Even then . . . she stopped the thought, shook her head, and scooped him into her arms.

She jogged for the docks. Any ship with medical facilities aboard couldn't legally deny her emergency access. Of course, on Silver City, "legal" didn't often play well unless it benefitted the Mining Guild.

A figure dropped into Jay's path, gun in hand, pointed right at her. "Hold it! Put the kid down!"

Jayleia paused.

A young woman, rage overlaying fear in her eyes, faced her. Curly hair poked out from under a filthy cap. A lush figure filled out her motley assortment of spacer's coveralls, a threadbare vest from the long-disbanded Gaustoron Space Force, and mismatched shoes.

"If I put him down, he'll die," Jayleia said.

The rage heightened in the woman's face. "What did you do to him?"

"He's having a reaction to ooze venom. I don't have time for twenty questions. Do you have access to antihistamines?"

"Ooze?" The muzzle of the gun drooped. "Show me."

Jay eased sideways, turning so the woman could see the puffy red mark on the boy's neck.

She swore, then eyed Jayleia's cheek. "You were chasing him. The ooze got him, and then tried to hit you."

"I startled him," Jay corrected. "Do you have meds or not?"

The woman pressed pretty, sculpted lips tight. "Do I look like I got the credits for drugs? No. Where were you taking him?"

"Docks."

"What ship?"

"I don't care. Any ship in the lanes will respond to a medical emergency," Jay replied.

The child groaned.

The woman tucked her gun into a holster concealed by her too-long vest. Fear won out. It sounded shrill in her voice. "You ain't in the lanes. They won't help."

"And this child is dying while we do nothing," Jayleia shot, striding past.

The woman ran to catch up.

"Give him to me!" she demanded, grabbing Jayleia's arm.

Swearing, Jay swung around, her teeth bared in rage.

Tears flooded the woman's eyes. "He's mine. My son. I heard him scream . . ."

From so far away? Jayleia snorted. More likely, she was his control and afraid she wouldn't get her cut if the kid serviced a customer without her knowing.

"The delay is killing him," Jayleia ground out.

"You Myallki bitch, he's my baby!" the woman shrieked.

"Fine. Here." Jayleia placed the boy in her arms. "Good luck. I hope . . ."

"You did this. You fix it! Come on!" Her wild curls bobbed as she pelted down the walkway.

Dropping her chin to her chest, Jayleia unclenched her fists one finger at a time and struggled for a breath not constricted by the desire to murder the curly-haired woman. *Stop it.* The child was in grave danger because of her. She shook her head and sprinted in their wake.

The woman pulled up short, shot out a hand to stop her, and tossed an assessing glance her way. "Can you hop a lift?"

"Yes."

Air pressure built in the tunnel and she could hear the whine of anti-grav turbos activating below them.

"Right here. On three. One. Two. Jump!"

Her brain balked at jumping into empty space. Jayleia ignored it and forced her body into motion. They hit the roof of the lift compartment. The young woman dropped to her knees in an effort to keep a grip on the boy. Jay grabbed her arm, stabilizing her.

"Vala," the woman said, leaning in close as if afraid someone else might hear. "My name's Vala. This is Bellin."

"Jayleia. Or Jay."

"What ship did you come in on, Jay?" Vala asked.

"Claugh ship. The *Kawl Fergus*."

"I know it. This lift will take us up, and then loop. Your ship is four hops from this next one." She fell silent as the lift slowed and stopped.

It surprised her to find she couldn't hear anyone within the lift. Jay felt the compartment shift as people came and went, but she heard nothing.

"Shielded?" she whispered.

Vala nodded, but she didn't speak again until the unit lurched into motion. "Secrets equal profit. The station shields the lifts. Gets them a monopoly on what's said inside. The guild don't like competitors."

CHAPTER
11

"WHO'S after you, Jay?" Vala asked.

Jayleia smiled at the woman's casual tone. This was Silver City. Someone was always after you when you stepped aboard the labyrinthine hulk. "The guy who owns the ship."

The woman tried and failed to hide the spark of interest in her eyes. "Will he call security?"

"I doubt it. I made it personal. He'll settle this on his own."

That was true, Jayleia realized. She'd scored a momentary hit to Damen's ego. He'd hunt her, but he'd do it alone and if he found her, he'd give no quarter.

"This is us."

Jay jumped from the top of the compartment when it paused. Vala handed Bellin to her and swung off the lift. The woman hesitated, then shook her head when Jayleia tried to offer him back to her.

"Gotta open the dock door," she said. As the compartment sped away, Vala trotted back the way they'd come.

Jay followed, slowed by Bellin's weight and the fact that she hadn't had anything to eat or drink for twenty hours while she slept off a flesh-rotting disease. By the time she reached the correct dock door, Vala had it open and waved her through, grinning.

Jayleia pulled up short. The ship sat, ramp down, hatch open. Inviting.

She'd expected—something, if only the clean team. Yet there the *Kawl Fergus* sat. Empty, wide open. It added up to one very attractive lure.

Like Damen Sindrivik.

Bellin groaned and she shook off hesitancy. Save the child's life first. Worry second.

They pounded up the ramp.

Vala shut the door after them.

Jay went straight to the tiny medi-bay and settled her charge on the exam table. His weight triggered instrument readouts she couldn't understand. Dodging out to the cockpit, she held her breath, hoping Damen had left her handheld in plain sight and had kept his word about loading translation. If he hadn't, her decision to treat the child aboard the *Kawl Fergus* rather than running him to the Silver City hospital could cost him his life.

Her breath went out in a rush. The handheld sat tucked into a holder on the piloting panel, still connected to the ship's systems. Her belt sat in a heap in the nav chair. She grabbed it, secured it around her waist, then picked up the handheld and initiated a rapid check.

"Twelve Gods, Damen, I love you," Jay muttered as Claughwyth systems messages morphed into Tagrethian. He'd kept his promise.

Time to keep hers.

Linking into the medical systems as she strode from the cockpit into the medi-bay, a more aware part of her brain informed her that a clean team had been aboard the *Kawl Fergus*. Spots of her blood no longer stained the deck plating.

She frowned and grabbed a dehydration packet. Mighty fast sterilization.

Shaking off doubt, Jayleia hurriedly drank, then returned to Bellin's side, checked his vitals via the diagnostic bed readouts, and fought back fear. His condition was deteriorating.

Vala, her expression pinched with worry, watched. She petted one of Bellin's puffy hands as if not conscious of what she did.

Jay spent a moment sampling out blood and placing it into the reader. Once the analyzer beeped "done," the medi-computer concurred with her. Histamine levels dangerously high, organ damage mounting, and blood oxygen levels declining. The screen before her lit up with a list of recommended treatments based on Bellin's body mass and condition.

She dove for the cabinets and drawers lining the medi-bay walls. Translation on her handheld didn't mean she could read the Claughwyth script indentifying which medical supplies lived in which storage spots. She had to look at the individual packets of medicine.

Medical supplies the galaxy over came with pictorial representations of their uses. She'd never pointed out to anyone that the pictures presupposed that every species in the galaxy could see, much less used vision as their primary sensory input.

It didn't matter. For her purposes, the pictures worked, allowing her to identify vials of medication regardless of the color-coded Claugh text in which the names of the drugs were rendered.

Jay went step-by-step through the prioritized list, putting an oxygen generator on the child first. A series of injected meds went in next, slower than she would have liked as she double- and triple-checked the dosages she'd prepped against the computer's recommendations for the child's body weight. Finally, she spread antivenom ointment on the sting site and placed a regeneration unit on it.

By the time she'd finished, Bellin's color had improved and the swelling in his extremities had visibly lessened. Breathing a sigh of relief, she looked for Vala.

The woman stood in the doorway, the gun Jayleia had taken from Damen in her hand, her own still in its holster.

Jay froze and pressed her lips tight to keep from swearing at her stupidity.

"He looks better," Vala observed.

Jayleia studied the woman. Granted, Vala had both guns. Jay had reason to read hostility in her stance, but she didn't comprehend the edge of agitation in Vala's voice.

Jayleia nodded. "He is better."

"You going to let us go?"

"You do have the guns," Jay said. "What's it going to be? You turn me in, now that he's okay?"

Vala's lip curled and anger flashed through her eyes. "I could."

"Yes."

The woman's gaze turned inward. Mistake. Jay purposefully let the opportunity to take both weapons from the woman pass because she swore to almost all the Gods that she saw jealousy in Vala's hazel eyes.

Of what?

The woman focused on Jay again, a resolute set to her lips. "I won't." Vala stuffed the gun into her coat, strode to where the handheld rested on the counter, and spent a moment inputting a data string. "Use that on the hatch once we leave. It's a lockout station security has never been able to breach."

Not meeting Jayleia's gaze, she slipped past and took Bellin in her arms.

He opened his eyes and rasped, "Vala?"

"Hey, kid. Take it easy. You had a busy day."

The boy wrapped his arms around the woman's neck, snuggled close, and shut his eyes.

"He doesn't need this anymore," Jay said, removing the oxygen generator. "He'll be sleepy and weak for a few days. Take this."

She put a container of liquid medication in Vala's vest pocket. "It's an antihistamine. If he's stung again, he'll need it. The directions for using it are on the chip attached to the vial."

"Thanks," Vala said. "If you come back . . ."

"A child injured in the tunnels?" she asked, feigning surprise. "Are you telling me you don't secure your maintenance ways?"

"Never trust someone else to lie for you," she said. "I owe you the kid's life. You come back; look us up. We'll watch for you."

Considering the dislike sharpening every sweet word falling from Vala's tongue? It'd be a chilly holiday in the hottest level of Hell before she trusted anything the woman said or did. "Thanks. Hold on a second. With a sick child, you're going to need some things."

Jay raided the emergency stores and draped a pack of food and basic first-aid supplies over Vala's shoulders. "That'll hold you for a few days."

"You don't have to do that."

Jayleia grinned. "Giving's easy when it's not your stuff."

"Get out of here before the guy catches you," Vala ordered as she angled down the companionway.

Jay hit the hatch release.

Bearing the sleepy boy, the woman trotted down the ramp.

Jay closed and locked the door, using her code from the *Sen Ekir* to complete the task.

Never trust someone to lie for you. Never trust someone else's lockout. Especially when that someone looked like she'd rather shoot you than help you.

Jay shook her head. Now all she had to do was break into the command console of a ship locked down by the Claugh nib Dovvyth's foremost computer expert.

Rolling her eyes at the flutter of desire the thought of Damen fired off, she grabbed food and water, then ran for the cockpit, flung herself into Damen's chair, and hesitated, staring at her handheld screen.

She was out of her depth.

Omorle Lin had refused to teach her computer espionage. He hadn't wanted her trapped by the lure of needing to prove her skills superior to everyone else's.

Still. He had shown her a few tricks. Little things, he'd said, that might come in handy. She hoped so.

She requested a check of life-support systems, the one thing any ship would do whether she had unlock codes or not. The console complied, running through a set of preconfigured diagnostics.

Racing into the companionway, Jayleia yanked back engine covers, looking for the auxiliary engineering console. It was tucked against the bulkhead near the centerline of the ship. So was the evidence that Damen's clean team hadn't sterilized the ship. Splotches of blood marred the undersides of the deck plates.

Swearing, she connected to the auxiliary console and waited for the translation protocol to make sense of the Claughwyth command trees.

TFC built emergency override codes into all of their ships, codes designed to grant limited access to the computers in the event of an atmospheric emergency. Presumably, so did most other militaries, including the Claugh. She smiled as familiar code rolled across her handheld screen.

They did.

She tunneled into the heart of the ship's system using a trick no one knew she knew. Except for the man who'd taught it to her while she'd been little more than a gawky teenager.

Once the emergency override system kicked in and offered her the structure trees for life support and rudimentary engine function, the tunnel provided access, not to command codes—those were too protected—but to the actual physical control core of the ship. From there, Jay could reprogram the entire ship if need be, save that she lacked the ability to do so. She did know enough to find, pull, and read the authorization codes into the handheld. With those, she could bring ship's systems online and start the engines.

Then she had a choice. Initiate a hard-core hack to extract the actual command code that would unlock steering and let her hijack Damen's ship for a change, or input a code Ari Idylle had given her that would lock the ship on an automatic course to Ari aboard the *Dagger*.

She closed out of the emergency override system and changed the default lock so no one could do to her what she'd done. A twinge of conscience gnawed at her as she rose and returned to the cockpit. At least each time the Claugh had hijacked *Sen Ekir* personnel they hadn't marooned anyone.

She ignored the prod of guilt. Plenty of commercial passenger liners hit the station. Damen wouldn't be stuck for long.

With the codes she'd brought over to the handheld, ships' systems came up without hesitation. Jayleia started the checklist and began an automated panel routine to brute force the command code file. It was sloppy and inefficient, but it was all she had.

Something chirped. She started and swore. Thrice damned access violations. Hands shaking and heart pounding loud in her ears, she watched her program running through panel control combinations. She didn't have all the time in the world. Someone would eventually come knocking.

A hand appeared from over her shoulder. Jayleia bit back a shriek of fright. It emerged as a squeak.

"Going somewhere?" Damen asked at her ear, sending a shiver of awareness down her spine. With swift, graceful commands entered on the panel, he secured the *Kawl Fergus*'s computers, locking her out.

CHAPTER
12

Transfixed by the heat that rushed through him as his chest brushed her back, Damen swallowed a curse. Damn it. He had to find a way to keep his body from lighting up like a glow-in-the-dark fral-fly in mating season whenever she was near. He needed his anger. He couldn't keep his aching head clear without it.

He choked off the second question he wanted to ask. Whether her kiss in the elevator had started as a bid for freedom had no bearing on their situation. And neither of them had the time for his notion of revenge. Or fun, depending on her answer. His lower body tightened at the thought. Hell of a way to ease a headache.

Ignoring discomfort, he brought up a sonic shield. He'd allowed the Silver City cleaning crew aboard. Of course they'd planted listening devices. He had no intention of giving the guild anything to use against them.

Jayleia glanced at him as the subtle hum came online, her expression troubled.

"We have a problem," she said.

"Several," he agreed, staring down at her.

His intent to exact retribution registered in the surge of apprehension in her face and in the flicker of her gaze fleeing his.

Good.

He studied the panel she'd been working. A bitter laugh escaped him, cutting off her indrawn breath.

"All systems but steering online," he said. "For someone whose file suggests she's had no programming training, that's damned impressive. Would it have been as easy had I not loaded translation on your handheld?"

Her smile looked brittle and didn't reach her eyes. "Had it been easy, you wouldn't be aboard."

"Where were you going?"

"To look for my father."

"You do know where he is," he noted, modulating his tone to sound as if he had all the time in the world to stalk her.

"No, I'm going to look, not to find," she countered.

He hadn't withdrawn his hand from the panel, pinning her in close contact. He felt a single tremor move through her body.

"Where?" he snapped.

She balled her hands into fists. "You understand I can't answer that."

The whip in his tone had been a mistake. Someone had taught her to stonewall interrogation. Who? Why? The urge to wrap her in his arms sideswiped him. He straightened. "You understand I can't accept that answer."

"You aren't asking me to give up my father," she said. Only the rasp in her voice offered evidence of agitation. "You're after the director of IntCom. Without specific orders from him, I will not compromise the security of my people."

Damen stared at her. "Not even to save him?"

She tossed him a pained glance that sent his heart thudding against his ribs.

It took his breath.

"Not even to save you," she rasped. "Or me."

Stunned, he sank into the chair beside hers. He tried to keep his words light, but they emerged thick and choked sounding. "You'd save me?"

Her gaze touched his face and the lines of pain around her mouth deepened for a moment. Then the conflict died in her eyes and her expression warmed. "If you ever find yourself in the middle of a nest of infected kuorls, don't hesitate to call."

His chuckle sounded strained.

She turned away, but not before he detected the edge of vulnerability in her eyes.

"Do you know what an insult it is among my kind that you work so hard to contain what you feel while in my company?" he asked.

She started, then peered at him as if waiting for what he'd said to sink in and make sense.

He suppressed a smile as he watched her mentally scramble for safe footing.

He leaned in, until he saw uneasiness spike in the white-knuckled grip of her hands on the arms of her chair. He could indulge in toying with her a little. It was the least he deserved after taking a neural disruptor to the head.

Pressing back in her chair, she shook her head.

"Why is it an insult?" she burst out, every bit of her attention on his face, her gaze keen, penetrating, seeing too much.

He faltered.

She edged forward, studying him. "You said it was an insult that I control what I feel in your company."

"It is." On impulse, he put a hand on hers, felt her shiver, and scented the cascade of hormones that dumped into her system, altering her body's fragrance. His pulse turned thready and erratic.

"Emotional safety is paramount among my kind," he said. "Slamming your shields up in my face tells me that you believe I'd willingly hurt you, that I can't be trusted."

Blowing out an unsteady breath, she sat back. "You do work for the enemy, Major."

He flashed a grin at her. "We're allied."

"I lured you into a kiss, then knocked you unconscious."

"Until the loss of consciousness, I enjoyed every sexy moment," he replied.

She flushed an alluring shade of crimson, but he swore he saw her struggling to contain a smile.

His heart lifted and he shifted closer to wrap his hands around her bare arms. "I've gauged your defenses."

"By weaponizing sex?" she said. "I am aware."

"I'm a Claugh nib Dovvyth officer. I am trained to break past a rival agent's conditioning by any means available."

She frowned. "It isn't all that's available."

"No, but it is the most fun."

The glimmer he'd begun to think might be a breach in her shields winked out in her brown eyes.

He bit back a curse. Second mistake. Someone in her past had used sex to hurt her. Why wasn't that in her file? A light went on in his brain. It wasn't in her file because she was a spymaster's daughter. Chances were good that the file he'd committed to memory wasn't real. Time to go digging where TFC and IntCom didn't want him.

"I appreciate your honesty," she said, her tone dead.

"Do you?" He choked back a haze of rage aimed at an enemy he couldn't see or fight. "Jayleia, the last time I saw shields as brittle and as overwhelmed by what they contained rather than by what they fended off, it was on a woman who'd survived three months of torture by the Chekydran."

Her lip curled. "I'm nothing like Ari."

"Aren't you?"

"She survived something I couldn't have. She's brave and smart and tough and . . ."

"Twelve Gods, Jayleia," he said. "You face deadly diseases every day. When I came to kidnap you, you were fighting off bloody, fanged, furry, prey animals. Your father is missing. Yet, you had the presence of mind while sick and feverish to formulate a brilliant escape. How can you pretend you aren't your friend's equal?"

"I'm not Ari," she snapped.

It was intoxicating, experiencing the surge and pulse of her feelings struggling to break through her defenses.

"No, you aren't Ari. As much as I like and admire Captain Idylle, it's you I want." The vehemence in his voice startled them both.

She stared at him. The disbelief hovering behind her eyes tore at him.

He leaned closer still, close enough to detect the upswing in her heart rate by the flutter of her pulse beneath her jaw. He wouldn't kiss her. No matter how much desire ripped his gut, that move was hers. If he couldn't coax her out from behind her defenses, he deserved to suffer.

"Yes, you knocked me cold after lighting me up with that kiss. First blood to you. I will have revenge in my own time," he whispered, his gaze on her mouth.

She sucked in a ragged-sounding breath.

"I won't hurt you," he assured her, struggling against the heat and tightness in his lower body. "When I take second blood from you, we will both enjoy it. Eventually."

"Three Hells," she breathed. "I'm enjoying it now."

Elation and want nearly paralyzed him. Vulnerability stood out in her wide, brown eyes, luring him. He whispered a curse.

Her gaze dropped to his lips.

No way would he be able to keep his promise. It didn't matter anymore who made the next move. Did it? He needed to taste her one more time. And not be knocked unconscious before he'd had his fill.

The com panel chirped.

Damen closed his eyes, frustration lending claws to the pain in his head.

Jayleia cursed in a language he didn't recognize. Her mother's tongue?

The disappointment in her tone made him chuckle. Opening his eyes, Damen rose, crossed the cockpit, and tapped open the channel—incoming text-only message.

Jayleia savored the warm tide of desire washing her bloodstream.

A species that valued emotional over physical safety. Twelve Gods. It was a promise worth switching sides for.

Maybe at this point, it didn't matter. Her escape had failed. She had to find her father, regardless. Couldn't she modify her plans and use Damen and the Claugh nib Dovvyth the same way they intended to use her? After all, They'd volunteered.

Sifting her options, she picked up her handheld, still connected to the *Kawl Fergus*'s systems.

"Come," scrolled across the screen. "Bring your friend."

Damen's breath hissed between his teeth. She caught the tight set of his lips from her peripheral vision.

"I can't compromise you," Damen typed.

Hard to read tone into two lines of text, but she thought she sensed amusement in the reply.

"Not your call, hizzett. I'm waiting."

Damen cut the line more violently than strictly necessary.

Jay put her handheld into place on her belt and forced her desire-shrouded brain into action as Damen glanced at her.

Evidence suggested Damen had a relationship with someone on station, a relationship close enough or contentious enough to include pet names. Damen's nickname "hizzett" was a Tagrethian word for infant mammalian predators valued for their propensity to hunt vermin. Someone who'd fallen victim to the same impression she had of Damen as a long-toothed Azym, but who obviously didn't feel at all threatened by the man?

The man in question pressed the heel of one hand against the center of his forehead. "I need a dose of painkiller."

Guilt stirred in her chest.

"Don't you dare say you're sorry," he warned.

Stung, she retorted, "Only that I failed to escape."

He eyed her, approval in his gaze and a sly smile on his full lips. "Will it require another shot to my head to get you to kiss me again?"

She flushed, discomfited by the irrational desire to answer with a demonstration to the contrary. He needed medication. She needed to get far away from the disturbing pressure he exerted against her crumbling self-control.

"Medi-bay," she choked out, then fled.

His chuckle trailed in her wake. He followed and leaned against the medi-bay door frame.

With his gaze upon her, Jayleia felt naked. Shoring up her defenses, she wondered how he'd managed to see through them. So few people bothered.

What did it mean that he'd invested the time and effort to get around her walls? He'd said he wanted her. When he looked at her, something in his eyes made her believe he saw her, Jayleia. Not the scientist. Not the warrior. He seemed to see past her protective masks, past her repeatedly broken heart, and genuinely desired her. How much longer could she resist that? A sore spot opened in her chest in answer.

Stop it, Jay. You've been down the path of believing someone wanted you. It got you exiled. Stick to business.

"We have some issues complicating our next move," she essayed as she rummaged through cabinets. "First, the ship isn't sterile. The clean team did a cursory mop up. Any one of them could be infected."

"I doubt it," Damen replied. "They may have cheated me out of a few Imperials, but the quest for easy credit comes second only to self-preservation on this station. What else?"

"I gave most of your medical and emergency stores to a woman named Vala."

Damen straightened, frowning.

A packet of medication in hand, Jayleia stopped a double arms' length away from him. Given the tingle in her nerves, even that was too close. She held up the medicine. "Here. It's not liquid, but it's all that's left."

"I don't bite," he grumbled, taking the medication and swallowing it dry. "Unless you beg."

That surprised a smile from her.

The lines of tension and discomfort in his forehead eased.

Had winning a smile from her done that? The medicine certainly hadn't had time to work yet. Pleasure glided through her at the possibility.

"Why give my stores to Vala?" he asked, nothing more than curiosity in his tone.

"Her son, Bellin. At least she claimed he was her son," she hedged.

"He is."

Jayleia eyed him, suspicion rolling through her at his calm assurance. "They were bait to catch me?"

His admiring smile made her grit her teeth. "If you keep seeing through them, I'll run through my repertoire of dirty tricks in no time."

"Your dirty trick nearly killed that boy," she bit out. "He's allergic to ooze venom."

"Most of us are," he said. "This is my territory you're playing in, Jayleia. The rules are complex and as alien to you as if they were written in Chekydran. Don't judge Bellin, or me, by what you think you know. This is Silver City."

And his species base wasn't the same as hers. That implied different moral constructs, cultural mores that wouldn't make sense to her primate-derived brain.

She cursed. She'd been making the mistake every rookie science student made, trying to fit the evidence to her preconceived hypothesis rather than following the data to its inevitable conclusion.

"Most people would have left him and escaped," Damen said, studying her.

That he believed her capable of leaving the child to die cut to her core. Jay stalked past him, then stopped short.

"Your advice goes both ways," she said, facing him.

He turned to study her, a shrewd light in his eyes.

"I am the product of a complex culture bound by rules alien to you."

"I can't judge your willingness to forgo escape in favor of saving Bellin's life by the standards of my kind?" he finished for her.

"No."

He frowned and his gray eyes darkened.

Transfixed by the gathering emotion in his expression, her heart skipped a beat when he cupped her face in his hand. "Can we forget rules and judging long enough for me to say thank you for saving my son?"

Shock stole the breath from her lungs. *His son?* And Vala was his mother. No wonder she'd seen jealousy in the woman's eyes.

He smiled. "I'll take that as a yes."

Leaning close, he brushed his lips against hers.

Sparks flashed across every nerve ending.

"Thank you," he whispered.

CHAPTER

13

DAMEN was right on one vital point: Jayleia didn't understand Silver City or its people. Certainly, she didn't comprehend the man so successfully dissecting her defenses.

"M-my pleasure," she stammered, and then flushed. His kiss *was* her pleasure. Bellin and his mother notwithstanding.

He'd said he wanted her.

Did that mean he no longer wanted his son's mother?

Confusion chilled her. She pulled out of Damen's grasp.

He let her go, his keen gaze undoubtedly catching every thought, fear, and doubt plodding across her face.

Feeling raw and exposed, she retreated to the cabin. She cycled through the shower, letting the warm ultrasonic cleansers wash away feelings of defeat. While she wasn't beaten yet, she also wasn't up to regrouping. She hadn't identified a fallback position other than capitulating to imprisonment and someone else's plan for finding her father.

As the drying system activated, she combed and braided her hair for the first time since leaving Chemmoxin. She put back on her dark brown trousers and her tough, comfortable expedition shoes. The shirt, colorless and sleeveless for wear in the heat of the swamp, wasn't warm enough on station.

Jay raided Damen's closet. If he protested, she'd quote alien rules to him again. At least he wouldn't likely kiss her for stealing his clothes. At the back, behind the uniforms, she found a soft, dark green button-down. It was too big, but she loved the feel of the fabric against her skin. His scent in the fabric didn't hurt, either. She put on her sleeveless lab shirt, tucked it in, donned Damen's shirt on top, and then slung her gear belt around her waist.

When she stepped out of the cabin, Damen had the engine covers pulled back. He'd descended into the space between the deck plates and the hull.

She'd thought the engines had been shut down. She'd been wrong.

Bright, yellow light illuminated Damen's face as he worked on something out of her line of sight. He glanced up as she approached the edge of the open deck plates.

He sucked in an audible breath, hunger in the set of his lips, and his gaze smoldering as he eased away from the silent engine. He raked her with a look that sent reaction, hot and damp, fluttering down her belly.

She cleared her throat and ignored her body.

Focusing on the splotches of dried, flaking blood on the undersides of the deck plates, she said, "Careful, the . . ."

"I appreciate your concern for my welfare," he murmured, his eyes half lidded.

As Jay once again fumbled for something to say, she glimpsed a hint of predator surfacing in the way Damen's muscles tensed when he leaned her way. He reminded her of the adult version of a hizzett, minus the tail and whiskers, considering whether or not to pounce on a toy.

"My lucky shirt," he said, eyeing her up and down. "I never dreamed I'd be lucky enough to see you in it."

Blood rushed hot to her face.

He smiled and turned back to the light pulsing on the interstellar engine.

She took a deep breath.

"You were right," Jayleia said.

His eyebrows climbed.

"We're allies and we're friends," she said, doing her damnedest not to stumble over the last word. She did not want to discuss friendship when she spent most of her time in his company feeling like he was hunting her. "I don't mean to insult you or your culture, Damen, it sounds very seductive, entrusting my emotional safety to someone, but that's never gone well for me. I can't . . ."

"Honesty, then," he said.

She contemplated that. "Can you promise it in return?"

He looked startled.

"Manipulating me doesn't result in honesty," she said.

"Unless you're enjoying it," he countered, "then I get the real you."

She stared at him. Patently not true. Was it? He couldn't have found a way in. If he had, she'd lost. She'd be at his mercy. Entirely. Could she handle that?

Her heart whispered *yes*. He wanted her. She wanted him.

Her rational mind rolled uneasily. What if he was just doing a job? Using her to get to her father. She knew what that was like being used. Could she take that chance?

If she were the only one taking the risk, maybe. But she wasn't. She'd be gambling her father's life as well.

"No."

He flashed that devastating grin her way. "Jayleia. Scientist. Swovjiti trainee. Your father's fledgling spy. How do I work my way past the many facets to get to your heart?"

Her head spun. How many more faces could she carve out of her body and soul? Was there enough of her left over for him? Or for herself?

Something snapped inside, it felt like the ties binding her so carefully compartmentalized life.

"Your question presupposes I have a heart," she replied, unable to press the rough edges out of the admission.

Shaking her head, Jayleia waved off the alarm in his expression. "There's a time and place for the kind of psychology you're suggesting. This isn't it."

"You asked for honesty," she said. "I can offer this: I guarantee mercenaries are on station already. I'll lay credits on agents being here as well. The mercs we know and understand. They're out to collect paychecks. The agents will be harder. Some will be my father's people, legitimately trying to contact him and get back in play."

"The rest will belong to the traitors who sent your father into hiding in the first place," he finished, his expression tight. "We'll have no way to tell them apart."

"That sums it up," she said. "We're in a race for my father's life."

"I don't think so," he countered.

Surprise rocked her.

"Based on what Admiral Seaghdh and Captain Idylle have said about your father and how he operates," he said, "he's secure. He'd have made sure he could rise to fight another day."

She shuffled Damen's appraisal into her still-developing hypotheses and nodded. "Yes. That makes sense. But Dad's no longer at IntCom's helm, which leaves the traitors free to do . . . what?"

"I don't know. That's where you and I come in," Damen said, looking pleased by her quick acceptance of his version of the situation.

"Then why are we still standing on this Gods-forsaken station?" she demanded.

"I've tracked indications of UMOPG involvement in the traitors' network to this station. More important, I found a file on your father in the Silver City data store," he said. "I couldn't get in before counter intrusion fired."

She nodded. "What?"

Movement at the edge of her vision yanked her attention to the engine well.

"Get out of there!" she yelped.

Damen dropped his tools, vaulted out of the engine compartment, and followed her horrified gaze.

Two bloodworms, pale, hungry, and looking for a meal, crawled across the hull straight for where she crouched on the deck plating.

"What the Three Hells?" he rasped.

"Damn it," Jay muttered, racing for the medical bay. She grabbed a sample container and a lid before returning to the edge of the open compartment.

"Are you bitten?" she demanded.

He shook his head. "I don't think so."

"Strip," she countered. "Bloodworms excrete a numbing agent. You wouldn't necessarily feel them."

He unsealed and kicked off his boots.

"You could hit the shower," she said.

"And miss an opportunity to see you blush?" he retorted. He stood and dropped his trousers. "Everything?"

"Shouldn't be necessary," she replied, ignoring the burn of her cheeks as she searched for marks on his legs. "They'd bite . . ."

Long, lean muscle, pale skin, and gold-red hairs invited her touch. She curled her fingers into her palms, pressing the nails into the flesh to distract her wayward imagination. Forget bloodworms biting him. She wanted to.

"Turn," she instructed, cringing at the catch in her voice.

Jayleia didn't need to look at his face to know he wore a self-satisfied smile. He exuded male conceit and she was merely examining his ankles. And calves. With an occasional glance at strong, cut thighs. She was too much of a professional to satisfy puerile curiosity about the rest of his body.

She scooted closer, her eye caught by matching scars around his ankles.

"My hand on your ankle," she said and traced the even band of old scar tissue.

He jumped as if burned.

"Sorry," Jayleia gasped. "Does that hurt? I . . ."

"No bites?" he demanded, his tone clipped, rough. He stepped into his trousers, jerked them up as if suddenly embarrassed by his partial nudity.

"No," she said, uncertain. She thought she'd understood enough about Damen's people to know that they had no nudity taboo. She frowned. What had happened?

"Where did the bloodworms come from? You put them in stasis," he said, the agitation diminishing in his voice as he turned to face her.

"I put the ones from my arm in stasis," she corrected, crouching at the edge of the engine well to get a bead on the free-roaming creatures. "I suspect these had been caught in the rescue harness when you hauled me up. I'd assumed they were dead. Twelve Gods, the cleaning crew could have been bitten and they would never have known."

Damen pointed. "There they are. How do we handle the cleaning crew?"

"I have to assume the disease is on station," Jay said, following his direction. She spotted the pair of wriggling, obviously sniffing worms and hopped into the compartment. "If I can get a secure message to the *Sen Ekir*, Raj can send the treatment protocols to the station clinic. Got you, you little—whoa!"

As she bent to scoop the creatures into the container, one of them managed to latch on to the outside of the container and head for her hand. Jayleia let go. The container and bloodworm tumbled to the hull.

Damen dropped into the well, grabbed her around the waist, and tossed her up onto the deck.

She squeaked in surprise and then in pain when her backside landed so hard on the plating that her teeth clacked together.

"What are you doing?" she gasped. "Damen! Get out of . . . wait. Look."

He paused in boosting himself out of the engine well. His gaze followed her nod.

The worms hesitated, the front halves of their bodies upright and waving back and forth as if trying to catch a whiff of something.

More to the point, they weren't at all interested in Damen standing right next to them. Why not?

"Would you look at that?" she breathed. "I wonder. Is that reaction unique to you? Or do you suppose they can detect the difference between the blood of primate-based species and non-primate-based species? The *Sen Ekir*'s going to need a blood sample, Major, if you're willing."

"You're going to win second blood, too?" he asked, his voice rich with humor. "Do you know what a debt you're piling up?"

Laughing, she edged her way around to the side opposite Damen. Jay kept her attention on the confused invertebrates. "I don't need blood this instant. Let's see if my theory bears out. Do me a favor? Keep your eyes peeled for more of them."

She dropped into the engine compartment.

"Jayleia. Kill them."

Damen's terse warning sounded sharp, worried.

"I'll be okay if none of them sneak up on me. Besides, I've slept the disease off once, already," she reminded him as the worms subsided to the hull surface and turned in her direction.

"If we don't know what the traitors are planning, we might not have time for that."

"I am aware," she said, not taking her eyes from the bloodworms. Waiting until they'd come within arm's length, she changed tactics. Instead of trying to scoop them up, she dropped the container on top of them.

"Got them! If you detect any others, feel free to vaporize them," she said, using the lid to coax the creatures into the sample container, and then sealed it. "These guys are going into stasis. They were black and stiff with infected blood when I came aboard. Look at them."

She held up the clear container for examination.

"Like nothing ever happened," Jayleia marveled. "The little blood-suckers could be the missing piece of the epidemiological puzzle. Good for Chemmoxin. Bad for Silver City."

Damen rounded the engine, stepped closer than necessary, and wrapped his hand around hers.

Electricity danced along her nerves as he tilted the container, studying the pallid worms.

He shook his head.

"I don't like knowing we can be hunted by something I could crush beneath my heel," he said, a hint of distress in his tone.

"It can't be comfortable for a predator to realize he can become prey," she answered. A thought made her frown and Jay examined Damen.

Primate-based species had evolved as prey and still had brain structures that triggered the chemicals that helped the body respond in the face of threat. Wouldn't the brains of a species that had evolved from predators differ? She didn't care so much what that looked like in the way of physical brain structures, she'd rather know what it felt like. How would Damen's body experience perceived danger? Could she set up a test to find out?

"Would you consent to brain imaging, too?"

Threatening annoyance melted in his face when his gaze met hers. Humor glinted in his eyes. "Should I be concerned that at some point you're going to want to dissect me?"

His teasing bumped Jayleia back to the *Kawl Fergus*'s engine compartment and the man holding her hand in his while he smiled down at her.

She grinned. "Biology elucidates behavior."

"There are better paths to understanding." His smile deepened, the clear gray of his eyes going inexplicably smoky.

Her smile faltered.

"Truce?" he offered. "We're a good team. If the sickness has escaped containment, along with everything else we have on our plates, the people of this station will need us."

She backed away, reclaiming her hand from his warm, unsettling grasp.

"Damn it," she sighed. "I should have gone into stasis and had you vacuum this ship."

"And deprive me of leverage? Our goals align, Jayleia. Even if the details don't. Work with me."

Did he have any notion what truce meant to her mother's people? To her? Did she have any choice but to show him?

The memory of the infected kuorls on Chemmoxin ripping one another to shreds filled her vision for a moment. Jayleia shuddered. No. She didn't have a choice. Not if sick stationers began turning up.

She blew out a shaky breath and nodded. "Truce. And all that entails."

CHAPTER
14

JAYLEIA smiled at Damen's raised eyebrow. She gestured with the container of bloodworms and climbed out of the engine compartment. "Stasis."

He nodded.

She stowed the specimens. Despite his assurance that Jay wouldn't understand the rules of Damen's turf, when she found behavior inexplicable, like she did with the citizens of the UMOPG, she studied. She thought she knew more about his cultural mores than he gave her credit for.

Among his kind, she knew the trading of blood formalized treaties and agreements, though usually it was blood won in a ritualized fight. Since Damen had gone on about her having "won first blood," did it make sense to return the favor? Could she show him that she understood some part of his culture? Why not? If blood was the coin by which bargains were struck, she'd honor that tradition.

Battling back uncertainty and ridiculous fear, she found the medical leech and snapped a sample vial in place. She leaned against the diagnostic bed. Heart pounding like she'd run a long way, she activated the unit against her forearm. The device hummed for a moment, then beeped. She extracted the sample vial, and put the leech back in its drawer.

Gripping the vial in her fist, she returned to the open engine compartment and crouched at the edge where Damen stood.

A crystal sat in contact with the matter feeders. It pulsed in time with the subtle thrum of the injector.

She frowned. "The reason you didn't want to open the ship to vacuum, I presume. What is it?"

"I don't know," he replied. He traded his handheld for a screwdriver and loosened the clamps on the crystal. "I can tell you it's crystalline. Our geology labs claim to have quantified the makeup and structure."

"'Claim'?" she echoed.

He lifted the crystal from its bed. The glow died. The stone paled until it gleamed, milky and opaque, in his palm.

Jayleia raised her eyebrows. "Geology is not my strong suit, but I don't think crystal is supposed to phase between translucent and opaque. You believe the matrix is altered when it's in contact with the matter feeders?"

He tucked the broad, double-terminated stone into a metal canister, which he sealed and locked. "It behaves differently depending on the energy source. The matter feeders are the only one that causes the crystal to clear and fluoresce. It also boosts engine efficiency when in contact with the injectors."

"Energy in restructures the crystal, changed energy emerges," she said as Damen climbed out of the hole and closed the covers. "Something more than a high-tech light source, then."

"Come on," he said, rising and holding out a hand. "We're going to see someone who will have more information."

She accepted the assist with her free hand, dismissing the thrill that wanted to shoot through her at the contact.

He touched a series of controls beside the door.

The sonic shield died.

She'd forgotten about the barely audible hum guarding their words until it fell silent.

Damen opened the door and ordered the ramp down. On the threshold, he paused and turned sideways to peer at her.

"What's it going to be this time?" he asked. "A game of hiztap and tezwoul through the station corridors? Or do I turn away at the wrong moment and take a blow to the back of the head?"

Jay tucked her hands behind her back, her grip on the vial tightening. "We have declared a truce. For the duration of that alliance, or until you break faith, you are under my protection."

His eyes widened. He stilled, not even breathing as far as she could tell. Emotions she couldn't identify flashed across his frozen countenance. He finally sucked in a sharp breath and the sly, feral gleam returned to his eye. His heated gaze fell on her like a caress.

She flushed head to toe.

Did Damen know that when he didn't know how to respond to a situation he turned straight to sex?

"Your protection," he repeated, lingering on the words as if tasting them.

It hit her. She'd offered to protect a predator. Her smile felt grim. "I meant only that you are safe from me."

He went on studying her with a gaze that felt like he'd gotten inside her skin.

"No one said anything about you being safe from me," he noted.

Her head spun and her body heated. *No, damn it.* She had a job to do. They both did. Forcing the haze from her brain, she gathered her courage and stepped up to face him. "Fair enough."

Damen detected the sharp, smoky bite of anger and the faint salt tang of fear.

The bottom dropped out of his stomach. Had he finally frightened her? How? And why did he feel no hint of triumph?

She tucked something warm into his hand. "Here."

Damen glanced at the vial.

Blood. Her blood.

Staggered, he stared. Did she have any idea what she'd done? He glanced at her.

Uncertainty fired her eyes while uneasiness drained the color from her face.

No. She thought she understood what she'd done and even her limited understanding filled her with dread. She had no idea what a gift freely given blood was among his kind. Nor did she realize what it implied.

A mating offer. He blinked back dizziness. His first. And all wrong. She was supposed to have offered her blood to him in the throes of passion. He shouldn't be holding a vial of her blood extracted by a cold, unfeeling medical leech that couldn't taste the desire and devotion in her blood, that couldn't gauge the thunder of her heart as it trembled in awe at the risk.

He sucked in a ragged-sounding breath, dismayed to find that it didn't matter how she'd offered her blood. Only that she had. His own heart beat so hard against his ribs, he wondered if Jayleia could detect the noise.

He closed the precious vial in his fist. His head spun, and he imagined he could detect her body heat still radiating from the container.

Every drop of blood he'd ever had in his past, he'd had to take. Even if she didn't grasp the magnitude, the gift cut straight to his heart. Here he was holding her blood in his hand. Had she known she'd make him bleed with her gesture?

"Thank you." He could barely squeeze the words past the burning knot in his chest.

Alarm touched her perfect features, the flutter of hope in her eyes crashed.

She wants to please me. The awareness arrowed through him. And now, she either couldn't read how she'd stunned him or she was misinterpreting what she saw.

Brushing her cheek with his free hand, he brought the fist clutching the vial to his chest and willed her to see how her gesture had moved him.

She met his gaze. Relief swept her features; tension melted from her body.

He smiled, reveling in both the gift and at her flattering desire to delight him.

"This way," Damen directed, slipping the vial into his pocket until he could store it properly. "Public areas are safe at this volume. Say nothing in lifts. Keep an eye out for anyone watching or following."

"Understood." She stiffened her spine and glanced down the ramp. All business.

He led her out of the bay, into the public corridor and straight to a lift. Two Jjurtak natives, both in glaring, iridescent yellow freighter uniforms, slid into the lift with them and went on chattering at one another in their language of nasal hums, audible puffs of air from their cheek pouches, and gestures of their three-fingered hands.

Damen pulled his sleek, military-issue handheld from his belt and activated it.

Frowning, Jayleia retrieved her unit and turned it on. When nothing came up on her screen, she glanced at him, one eyebrow raised.

He met her gaze and stifled a grin at the covetous gleam in the look she shot at his handheld. Her unit had been designed and customized to maintain contact with the *Sen Ekir* as long as she remained within a few hundred planetary kilometers of her ship. From the speculation in her face, he could see her guessing that his handheld ignored the stringent rules governing what the devices could do.

He concentrated on linking his unit with hers.

Her screen went active. She scanned it and nodded. He'd been locking down the *Kawl Fergus*. She apparently approved of the precaution.

A symbol glowed in one corner of his screen. Incoming transmission. He accepted the message.

"Safe?" it said. He glanced at Jayleia.

She lifted her thumbs from the front of her pad as if asking, "Well, is it?"

"Safe and ironic," he replied via the handheld. They couldn't speak in the transport without fear of being recorded. Yet, handhelds were everywhere. Attempting to intercept a specific data stream would be akin to trying to grab a single proton from a beam of light. The Mining Guild wasn't the only government that found it easier and cheaper to simply bug the elevators in an effort to capture secrets.

Jay smiled without reservation at her screen. "I wonder if the guild has a translation routine for Jjurtakish."

"As popular as the race is for freighter work? I'm certain they do," he responded.

The Jjurtak were slow, methodical people with an uncanny appreciation for minutia. Special adhesion patches in their three-fingered hands, six-toed feet, and body fur allowed them to cling to vertical surfaces, making them much sought-after cargo masters.

Damen linked back to Jayleia's handheld, curious about what had her working her pad so steadily. She'd initiated a grab of public source data regarding her father.

"News?" he typed, overriding the transmission protocol so his query appeared directly on her screen. "Reply. I'll see as you type."

She froze for a moment, then slanted a narrow-eyed, envious glance at his unit.

He suppressed a grin.

"Traitors playing it close to the cuff," she responded. "Few files mention my dad."

"Good."

"He's alive and free or they'd saturate the media."

"Agreed. Stand by."

"Here we go," Damen said aloud.

The lift slowed and stopped. They stepped past the two freighter crewmembers and out into the pandemonium of the market ring.

Damen felt Jay tense and freeze. He turned.

Her gaze darted around the ring. White lines edged her lips and she flinched at the roar of stationers rooting for what looked like a low-gravity Hazkyt match that had devolved from a game of "get the puck from the other teams' nets" into an all-out brawl.

Damen took her arm and detected the too-fast beat of her heart. "What's wrong?"

"The kuorls sounded like this," she murmured. Her brow furrowed, but the wild light eased in her eyes. "Something else, too. The smell . . ."

"So many different species all in one place," he agreed, sniffing the familiar odor. "It gets ripe."

"I'm being flooded with adrenaline," she replied. "I'm surprised that on a station as multiculturally and ethnically diverse as this that some part of my biology recognizes the scent of a predatory race by smell. I wonder . . ."

"Experiment later," he said, steering her through the throng of people. "Walk now. I'll give you a tour."

She tossed him a look filled with reproach, but nodded.

"Market ring," he said at her ear, deliberately dropping his tone into a suggestive purr. "Every vice and illicit thrill Federated Credits, Claugh Imperials, or precious metal can buy."

Jayleia shivered at the electricity dancing in her blood in response to his innuendo. She settled a quelling glare on him.

He smiled, a lazy twist of gorgeous, full lips.

"Anything you want," he continued, his pitch dropping close to a growl. "Anything at all, can be had."

She sucked in a damnably audible breath at the rush of heat into her core. He was not talking about the junk piled in the crowded shops or on the cobbled-together vendor carts strewn haphazardly around the deck.

He chuckled.

"I can't afford the price, Major."

"But you are in the market," he said, a self-satisfied smile on his handsome face.

She tried to ignore the buzz rippling along her nerves. "Did your files on me fail to mention that I am bound by an oath of celibacy until my twenty-sixth birthday?"

Damen jerked upright. "What?"

CHAPTER

15

JAYLEIA smiled at the horrified expression on Damen's face. She'd take that as a no.

Apparently, she hadn't lowered her voice enough. Heads turned in their direction. It struck her as she cataloged the knowing grins and appraising stares. Every single person surrounding her, with the exception of Damen, bore scars. The younger the individual, the fewer scars and the more likely the person was to have all of his or her appendages intact. The older people laughing, pushing, and carousing through the colorful crowd had multiple scars, many of them indicative of major injury, including missing fingers, hands, arms, legs, and eyes in a few cases.

Damen ushered her out of the crowd, down a narrow corridor and into another lift already occupied by a snoring and, judging by the smell, drunken miner stretched out along the back wall.

"What happened to these people?" she asked. "I know you said emotional safety is more important than physical safety but this . . ."

"Mining."

She frowned. He'd said it as if being maimed by one's profession made complete sense.

Feeling Damen's gaze intent upon her, Jayleia glanced at him.

"You took the Temple's oath of celibacy?"

"Yes." She met his eye and had to swallow the urge to smile at his disconcerted scowl. She had no intention of telling him she'd turn twenty-six within the week.

Was that anger she detected in his eye?

The lift stopped.

He stalked out, his features tight.

She followed and opened her mouth to tease him again about trusting incomplete data.

He pulled her to his side before a door. It was violet, a hue so saturated, it vibrated as if the color had been created for a species with photoreceptive sensory organs tuned to a different spectrum than her own.

The door pinged and opened.

Damen led her into the cool, dim interior.

A man with short hair dyed bright green sat in a wheelchair, his back to them, before an array of holo-screens and computer consoles.

Jay stopped, brought up short by the pressure building in her chest, and by the blaring sense of familiarity with the layout of the displays.

The man grabbed the wheels of his chair and turned around.

Stunned, she rocked back on her heels. Her breath died.

"Tahem," she choked.

Tahem Acquival. Olive complexion, lively, light brown eyes marred by a hint of petulance, and a beautifully sculpted chest and torso. He'd been the love of Omorle Lin's life and a fixture in Jayleia's until Omorle's death.

A dizzy sense of displacement assailed her.

What was he doing on Silver City and how did he know Damen well enough to have given him a pet name?

"Jay, sweetheart," Tahem said, a sly smile on his handsome face. "I can't tell you how pleased I am to see you. It's been what? Four years?"

"You know . . ." Damen began, looking between them, then broke off. He rubbed a hand down his face. "Of course you know one another."

Tahem chuckled, the sound sharp and bitter. "Your girlfriend adored the man I loved, hizzett. We all but adopted her while she was still a gawky and hopeless teenager. Speaking of which, breathe, Jayleia. I've denied station medical personnel access to my quarters for years. I won't change that even for you. Don't pass out."

Jayleia pulled in a badly needed breath, fumbled to a chair, and dropped into it. She scowled and realized why the computer config felt so familiar. It was Omorle's code-running layout. A part of her heard his smooth, rich voice saying, "I'm going in. Watch my back."

She hadn't heard that voice or those words in more than six years.

Swallowing hard, she spun her chair away from the displays, her eyes and chest burning.

Damen shifted.

She glanced at him. Concern stood out in the faint lines in his forehead.

Tahem looked between them, then held a hand out to Damen. "We'll take care of business, shall we?"

Nodding, Damen gave him the metal canister containing the crystal.

"Coded to you," Damen said.

Tahem grunted, unlocked and opened the tube. "Radioactivity?"

"Not native in this state."

"You found this at the coordinates I gave you?" Tahem asked.

"Yes."

"What else?"

Damen shot a look at her.

Tahem laughed. "Hizzett, Jay is family, even if it takes her father's disappearance to bring her to visit me."

She jerked upright. He knew about her father? How? And what specifically did he know?

"We found indications of a base or a research station," Damen said.

Scowling, she forced her attention to the conversation and to the man in the wheelchair debriefing a Claugh agent while examining the crystal, a crystal he'd sent Damen after. Had the United Mining and Ore Processing Guild developed its own spy program? And co-opted a Claugh agent in the process? Or had the Claugh co-opted a UMOPG agent?

"A station? Under whose auspices?" Tahem demanded.

"We didn't have time to find out."

"What is that?" she asked, nodding at the crystal.

Tahem pressed his lips tight, glanced at her, and shook his head. "A death sentence."

A moment of fear knifed through her sternum. "For whom?"

"That remains to be seen," he replied, his tone grim.

It made her look closer. Studying Tahem, she realized he'd abandoned his masks. Interest lined his face. Professional, intent curiosity focused his attention on the crystal before him.

He'd let his bitter, sullen cover slip. It would be deadly in front of an enemy. Something, she realized, she could all too easily be.

"You're showing," Jay said, repeating the phrase her father had used whenever his spies blew their covers.

Tahem muttered, "Baxt'k."

Damen eased into the chair beside hers and looked between the pair as if studying a new life-form.

Tahem glared. The hard set of his features eased and he nodded once, acknowledging her warning. He arranged his features into the familiar, practiced pout he'd worn until derailed by professional interest.

Two spies trading advice, save he had yet to offer any.

"What happened, Tahem," she asked, "that you're in that chair?"

"Do you know," he began in a falsely conversational tone, setting the crystal in his lap and crossing his forearms, his elbows propped on the arms of his chair. "When Omorle was assigned to guard you, he said he'd always wanted a daughter and that no matter what, if something happened to one of us, the other could take comfort in you. How can I do that? How? You're nothing like him!"

She wilted and looked away. "No. I don't suppose I am."

"You loved him," Tahem said, his accusation sounding muted by too many conflicting emotions.

"I still do." She shrugged. "So do you. I was a child, Tahem."

Jayleia gathered her courage to meet his eye. "You were the first people to treat me like me. Not like my father's daughter. Of course I adored Omorle. I even harbored a crush on you for a while. Or didn't you know?"

A surprised smile touched his face. "You've never been an easy read, sweetheart."

He picked up the crystal and shook it at her, grinning. "Omorle would have yelled his head off at me about this chair. The fact that I'm in it is my own damned fault."

"Let me get you an anti-grav . . ."

"No," he said, his tone final. "I want to remember every time I move that I did this to myself. I want the sores that come from planting my paralyzed butt in this contraption day after day."

Jay blinked at Damen. She had no idea where she stood with her mentor's widowed lover. She hoped Damen had a better read on him.

The light in Damen's gray eyes captured her, and she found the heat rising through her body. She frowned.

"You," Tahem said into the silence.

Shaking off the tug of sensual awareness, she locked on to Tahem in time to see him studying the pair of them, a thoughtful—and was that pained—look on his face.

He pointed at Damen.

"Something's shifted in you," Tahem said.

"What?" Damen demanded. His tone said that Damen felt the truth of Tahem's observation, but didn't know what it signified.

Jayleia's heart stuttered. Had he been bitten and infected after all? "What are you detecting?"

"You're the xenobiologist." Tahem jerked his chin at her, chuckled, turned his chair, and drove straight for the space between them. "You figure it out."

Scowling, she lifted a foot and locked it on his left wheel. Tahem's chair stopped. The one-sided braking turned him to face her.

"Go ahead. Come between us," she challenged. Gods. He couldn't hide the longing in his eyes. Tahem had fallen for Damen.

Were they really here again? Competing for the affections of one man?

Jay started. Was she? Really?

Apparently, her cover had slipped, too.

Tahem laughed outright at whatever he saw in her face. "You were always hopeless when it came to men."

"Men?" she echoed. It occurred to her. He wasn't talking about Damen, which meant he knew the true reason she'd been exiled from her mother's world. Mortification hit her in a rush. "How did . . ."

Tahem waved off the question. "It was Omorle's business to know, sweetheart. Neither of us bought the story explaining your expulsion from the Temple. We dug up the truth for ourselves."

Jayleia glanced at Damen's patently neutral expression and suppressed a groan. "Thanks for challenging him to go digging through my past again."

Tahem chuckled.

She blew out a short puff of breath. The man was distracting them. Both of them. She scowled at Tahem.

"You have a crystal specimen you sent the Claugh to find. You have information about my father. Yet rather than tell us what's going on, you're diverting me with the past and with hints about Damen's changing biology. You're wasting time. Why?"

Tahem's grin was beatific. "Because, dear girl. Omorle trusted you with the one thing he never gave me, a trip into one of his missions. He could never love you in a romantic sense. I knew that. But he gave you a part of himself he refused to give me. Did you know how he adored you? He was your damned bodyguard and he fancied himself your surrogate father. Idiot.

"Yes, I'm stalling, keeping you here to no purpose because it is a wasted day that brings no profit. I sold you out."

CHAPTER
16

SENSING the hurt underpinning the spite in Tahem's voice, Jayleia swore.

Damen growled.

She shoved Tahem's chair away, leaped to her feet, and charged across the room.

The door burst open. She skidded to a halt, hands shoulder height, and stared up the barrels of a trio of laser pistols.

"Hold it! Hands where I can see them!" a gruff male voice barked. The lead pistol barrel gestured at Damen. "Get up. Nice and easy."

Looked like Tahem had overcome his crush on Damen.

"Nothing personal, sweetheart," Tahem said. "Don't waste your anger on me."

Breath coming in short, angry gusts, Jay glanced at Tahem. What had he seen to make him use that specific phrase? Not "don't be mad." Not "anger is useless."

Tahem's words suggested that she should, in fact, nurse her rage and, that if applied correctly, it might change the game in her favor.

She'd loved him once. She'd thought he'd cared about her.

"When Omorle claimed he couldn't keep time to save his life," she said, choking on the acrid taste of his betrayal, "you taught me to dance."

Tahem pinned her with a stare, the masks gone, the petulance erased as if it had never existed.

Jayleia wondered how much she really knew about her beloved bodyguard's partner.

"I will again, sweetheart," he said. "Don't let the past get in the way of what you could become."

That was a coded message, if ever she'd heard one. How many games was Tahem playing, and where did she and Damen fit in?

Above all, what was it supposed to mean?

Damen, wary and deliberate, stepped in beside her, his hands up, mirroring hers.

"Search 'em," the gruff-voiced security guard ordered.

"Get out," Tahem ordered, turning his chair to face the computer screens.

The bulky guard stretched thick lips into a placating grin. "You got your cut. Let us handle . . ."

"Get out!" Tahem bellowed.

The guard's com badge beeped. Growling, the guard gestured them out the door.

"All right, all right," he snarled. "You heard him. Out."

Three guards, two male, one female. The leader, the one Jayleia thought of as "Thick-lips," showed signs of wanting to show off. The woman with close-cropped, pale orange hair, looked half amused, half bored. The greatest danger, Jay judged, was the youngest guard. The thin, dark-haired man looked as jittery as he did watchful. He'd be unpredictable.

"How about we take our time getting back to lock up?" Thick-lips said, leering. "I'll find me a quiet spot hereabouts so this pretty, little gal can resist arrest."

Rage gathered in her chest, scorching her from the inside out, setting her senses to high alert.

"Nah," the woman drawled. "She's gonna be put up for merc auction."

"Mercenaries won't care about her condition," the man retorted.

"Orders are clear," the youngest guard piped, his voice high and reedy for an older adolescent male. "Someone's saving her for something special."

With her body systems ramping to overdrive, Jay imagined she felt the subtle uptick in Damen's body heat beside her. She heard the sharp intake of his breath. Anger? She hoped so.

"Got no orders on pretty boy, though." The thick-lipped guard sneered.

The youngest sniggered. "He'll get sold to the sex trade again. Want to have fun with him, go ahead. Didn't think he was your type. He'll fight back."

Jayleia stopped dead. Her heart and mind froze in horror as the words replayed over and over in her head "sold to the sex trade *again.*"

Damen?

Fury and pain burst into flame within her. She could hardly draw breath.

"Hey." The bulky guard behind her pushed her right shoulder.

She remained still.

A few paces ahead, Damen and the young man at his back hesitated, and then turned to look.

The woman trailed them, caught halfway between Jayleia and the young guard.

Jay met Damen's gaze knowing she couldn't communicate her ire or her intent.

His gray eyes widened. His lips thinned.

Maybe she could.

"Move it!" her guard growled. The edge of increased effort in his voice alerted her to another, more forceful shove. Observation and his own words suggested he'd enjoy sending her sprawling.

Years of training gripped her. She sidestepped his blow, grabbed the arm and shoulder that passed her when he missed, and using his already off-balance body weight against him, Jayleia slammed the guard chest-first into the wall.

The impact knocked his breath out of him in an audible *whoosh*. His face hit. Blood erupted from his broken nose.

He rebounded.

She did not release him. Jay turned so that his semiconscious, still-on-remote-control body stood between her and his companions. The woman took a step toward them before she thought better of it and drew her gun.

Her indecision gave Jayleia all the time in the world. Driving her victim with the last remnants of momentum, she planted him in the woman's arms. She had to shoot him, sidestep him, or catch him. In the heat of the moment, Jay saw panic spike in the guard's brown eyes.

She tried to catch her coworker with one arm and angle her weapon around for a shot.

A well-placed kick to the back of the man's left knee bore both guards to the floor. Jay pounced, stomping on the woman's gun hand, sending the weapon skittering down the corridor and wringing a muffled cry of pain from her.

Damen roared a warning.

Jayleia dropped to the floor. A bolt of light and heat sizzled over her head. Rolling away from the two bodies on the floor, she bounded to her feet and, already sprinting for him, shot a glance at Damen's young guard.

The kid dangled several centimeters from the floor.

Damen held him aloft, one fist wrapped around the wrist of the boy's gun hand. Growling, Damen cocked back and knocked him senseless. He plucked the gun from the kid's limp hand and tossed him aside.

Jayleia heard the telltale beep of a com badge activate.

The woman.

"Prisoners," the woman gasped, her voice tinged with pain and effort, "escap—"

Jayleia shoved the unconscious guard off the woman, yanked

the com badge from the guard's uniform and pulled the woman to sitting.

The guard stared past Jayleia, blanching.

Damen moved in beside Jay, pistol in hand. He pulled the trigger.

The woman collapsed.

The muted whine of the weapon registered after the fact. Jay nodded.

He'd stunned the guard, not killed.

Wishing for access to an airlock port, Jay glanced at the com badge in her hand. She settled for a trash chute.

"Catch me if you can," she growled at the still-transmitting badge, before lobbing it into the garbage.

Damen joined her and held out a pistol. "Take it."

"No." She strode down the vacant corridor, aware they had precious little time to clear the area before backup arrived. The lack of gawkers fired her instincts and she began cataloging escape routes and lines of possible attack.

"Jay, you'll need it," Damen persisted. "Take the gun."

"I can't shoot," she confessed, glancing at him as he kept pace beside her.

His brow furrowed. "Temple dictate?"

She flushed. "No. I mean I can't hit the broad side of the *Sen Ekir* standing ten paces from it."

That earned a surprised grin from him. "Do you know how to use a gun?"

"Do you imagine I could live and work with Ari for six years and not?" she retorted, flashing him an annoyed look.

His grin deepened. "Then take it. No one else needs to know you'd empty the cartridge before you hit something important."

She accepted the weapon. "I'd be more effective using it as a club."

Stifling a laugh, he turned eyes dancing with mirth upon her. "You were damned efficient empty-handed. I thought you'd given up Temple training."

"I tried."

"What happened?"

"My family," she said, shaking off the bitter memory of her expulsion. "They rallied to convince me that staying in top physical condition would augment my performance and endurance for fieldwork. Masterful piece of familial love and manipulation. The galling part is they were right."

"Families are the same across cultures, then," he noted, still grinning. "Mine . . ."

"Twelve Gods, Damen, no they aren't." A chill crawled into her gut. "Your family sold you into slavery."

"My mother," he corrected.

She blinked at his matter-of-fact tone. "That's family."

"No."

"What?" She stopped dead in the middle of the corridor.

"Tahem is my family. The people I've recruited and trained, they're family," he said, taking her elbow and tugging her alongside him. "Admiral Seaghdh, since he recruited and trained me."

"What do you call blood relations, then?"

"Kin. Or blood."

"And you maintain no bond, no ties of loyalty to your kin? Or they to you?" she marveled.

"You do?" he asked, the glance he flicked her keen with interest.

"Definitely. Among my people, your mother would go to prison for selling you, especially into the sex trade. It's such a gross betrayal . . ."

He started. "Betrayal? Those who don't work the trade are pitied and ridiculed."

The defensive tone in his voice bumped her out of her gathering sense of injustice. She peered at his unsettled expression. "How old were you?"

"Eleven." The lines of trouble around his mouth deepened when all she managed was a squeal of rage in response. "We reach sexual maturity faster than most species. The sex trade is a practical solution to the problem of having adolescents at home with infants."

She sucked in a sharp breath. "Of course. The female of most predatory species can only provide for one or two infants at a time.

Your people drive away the adolescents in order to safely breed again. The adolescents band together for mutual protection."

From a biological standpoint, it made sense, but the image of eleven-year-old Damen, his world sundered and his heart savaged, made her blood run cold.

She felt Damen's searching gaze on her and met his eye. His smile looked pained.

"Thanks," he muttered.

"For what?"

He shrugged. "No one's ever understood before."

"I don't," she said. "I'm taking refuge in science to pretend that the thought of you abandoned as a child doesn't shred my heart."

His grip on her elbow tightened and he looked unsettled, as if he didn't know how to handle the fact that she hurt on his behalf.

"Why did you leave your training and your family? Will you tell me? The real reason?"

Shame scalded the inside of her skin. Jayleia opened her mouth, but could find no words to give him.

People stepped into the corridor.

She saw the guns first, yanked out of Damen's grasp, and reached for her weapon.

Damen swore.

CHAPTER

17

DAMEN ground frustration between clenched teeth. So close. He'd been so close to getting her to confide in him.

A man with thick, black hair, indigo eyes, and a face as cold and hard as Isarrite blocked the corridor. At his right shoulder, a shapely, grinning woman with flaming red hair stood, feet splayed to brace against the recoil of the tricked-out Autolyte 49-G assault rifle in her hands.

Mercenaries.

Damen eased a step ahead of Jayleia to shield the weapon in her grasp from casual view.

"Ms. Durante," the man noted. His tone contained no hint of warmth or of compassion.

Damen growled, his pulse thundering in warning. First salvo.

"Captain Trente," Jayleia acknowledged, edging into the open.

Stifling the urge to shove her behind him, Damen instead followed her gaze when it flicked to the woman.

"Edie," she said, her tone so neutral that Damen tensed ready to spring. "Good to see you."

"Hey, Jay," the woman said, her words oddly flattened by an accent he didn't recognize.

"I see you have everything under control," Trente said, peering down the hallway behind them.

"At the moment," Jayleia said.

"Reinforcements en route," Edie said, her eyes moving as if reading something.

Damen spotted the sensory enhancement module she wore. Granted, they were mercenaries and as such, not wholly concerned with legalities. If, as evidence suggested, the woman was reading the station security net, Damen could count at least eight laws shattered in the past few seconds, half of them by his hands.

"Four minutes," she concluded.

Trente nodded once, then turned and gestured as if to invite Jayleia to walk with him.

Damen put himself between them. "Jayleia Durante is under the protection of the Claugh nib Dovvyth Empire. If you intend . . ."

The man looked at him for a long moment. Damen felt a predatory smile growing on his lips at the challenge in the man's dark blue eyes.

Jayleia closed a hand around his wrist.

Damen swallowed another growl and forced his taut muscles to relax slightly. Message received and understood. Wait and watch. No attack. Not yet. He had to unclench his hands.

"I exist to plague Her Royal Pain-in-the-Ass and the Empire as a whole," the man said.

Damen heard the first hint of emotion in his voice and cataloged the man's name and description for later research. His animosity and suppressed rage were directed at the queen of the Claugh nib Dovvyth. Damen would be certain he gave Admiral Seaghdh an exhaustive file on the man and the threat he represented.

"Killing me to get to Jayleia would be a minor inconvenience to Her Majesty," Damen replied.

"Three minutes," Jayleia said, tension in her voice.

Edie snickered and slung her rifle over one shoulder. "Two parties. Using the lifts fore and aft with orders to take Jay alive."

Damen glanced at Jayleia's placid expression. Only the hard, watchful glitter of her eyes gave away her willingness to do battle if need be.

"I owe your parents my life," Trente finally said to Jayleia, his words a monotone.

Damen felt her start and studied Captain Trente again. Did he? Given a good computer link, Damen expected he could find out why within three days' time.

"Consider this a down payment on the debt." The man held out a pack. "Your uniform. From your mother, along with a message. She says, 'Put it on. Live up to my faith in you. Prove him innocent.'"

"No pressure," Edie added.

Jayleia choked back a laugh, released Damen, and took the pack. "Thank you."

"Did Mrs. Durante survive questioning?" Damen demanded.

"My parents have been trying and failing to destroy one another for two decades," Jayleia answered. "Both of my parents are damned hard to kill."

"I see," Damen said. "Your mother summoned Captain Trente and is matching or beating the price the traitors put on your capture."

Edie laughed. "Cute and smart! I like him, Jay. What'll you give me to take him off your hands?"

Damen bared his teeth. "You're confused about who is whose prisoner."

The woman tucked her chin to look over her SEM lenses between Damen and Jayleia. "Am I?"

"Not helping, Edie," Jay sang from between clenched teeth.

He stifled a grin.

"Get out of here," Trente ordered. "We'll cover your back."

Gambling that the sour expression on Trente's face shored up Damen's supposition that the man had double-crossed an employer, Damen asked, "Whose paycheck won't you be collecting?"

Jayleia resumed her quick pace down the corridor, shoulder to shoulder with Edie. Trente dropped in behind her at Damen's side.

"IntCom," Trente replied, the first inkling of respect in his gaze.

"Baxt'k," Damen grumbled. "IntCom is compromised."

Trente's look sharpened. His smile turned glacial. "Spoken like a Murbaasch Tu agent."

"Guilty," Damen replied. Let the man chew on the fact that he'd been tagged by a Claugh agent.

Jayleia shot a pained look at the man.

Trente offered her a message chip. "Gerriny Eudal recorded this for you."

"Is this the 'I'm concerned and there's a chance he's innocent' while Eudal sits in my father's office and uses his official seal message?" Jay asked, looking at it but not taking it.

The mercenary's blue eyes lit with amusement for a moment. "The same."

"Seen it. Not his best performance. And I'm willing to bet it's being traced."

"Your father's second-in-command is a Carozziel slime-bat," Edie said.

"Painfully aware," Jay said in such a way that Damen's hackles went up.

Apparently, so did Edie's. The woman studied Jayleia for a moment. "History between you?"

"Not that I know. He worked for my dad when I was a kid, but it didn't last long. Dad fired him by the time I was five. Four years ago, Durgot appointed Eudal to IntCom's second seat over my father's protest," Jayleia said.

"A plant," Edie surmised.

Jayleia shrugged. "Supposition. Dealing with him fires off the same alarms as dealing with the Chekydran when they'd call the *Sen Ekir* to quiz us about our research each time we stopped on Ioccal."

Meaning she counted the man an enemy, even if she couldn't say why, Damen noted.

"How much would it take to have you hit him?" Jay tossed, her tone half-joking and a troubled light in her eyes when she glanced back at Trente.

"I'd arrange his accident and count myself well paid if I got to watch him die," the mercenary grumbled. "But I gave up a lifetime's association with Tagreth Federated to repay my debt to your folks. My crew and I will never see that side of the zone again. Sorry."

Damen and Jayleia swore in unison.

"You've already been accused of treason for helping me?" Jay demanded.

"Will be by the time we leave station," Trente answered as if it mattered not at all.

"Got a preferred destination, Jay?" Edie asked, her tone neutral.

Jayleia glanced at Damen, her look of misgiving deepening.

"Tahem's office," he said. "Third Level of Hell."

"Third Level . . ." Edie choked back whatever she'd meant to say and landed a flustered look on Jayleia.

"Yes, he was in the sex trade, and he's a Claugh agent," Jayleia said. "He hasn't hurt me, Edie."

"I won't," Damen swore.

The mercenary blinked, then tossed a look tainted by old scars at him.

He met her gaze. Someone, somewhere, had brutalized Jayleia's friend.

"Down here," Edie directed, looking away. "This hall is from an old radioactive waste hauler. Station instruments can't get a clear shot through the shielded alloy."

"They'll have a cordon on the exit," Damen warned.

"Don't have to go that far," Edie replied. "Maintenance tunnels will take you to the core and down to the vice decks."

Ragged women and children patrolled the hallway, sizing up the band, either as potential marks or as customers. Perhaps they were cowed by the number of visible guns on the four of them. No one approached with whispered enticements.

"Wish I could co-opt your talent with explosives, Edie. I'll undoubtedly wish for your expertise at some point, but mission parameters are still gelling," Jayleia said, a feral grin on her face.

Damen's blood quickened in anticipation of hunting at her side.

"Here." Trente spent a second unlocking an access panel.

Damen frowned. "Hasn't anyone worked out that the surveillance in the maintenance tunnels is state of the art? Trust is a dangerous game."

Jayleia snorted.

"Desperation is worse," Trente replied.

The men stared at one another again, no longer sizing up, preparing for combat. This was realization. They each knew too much about the kinds of pain suffered in this shielded hallway where the most sordid aspects of the sex trade flourished.

"I appreciate your assistance, Captain Trente," Damen said.

"You're delusional," Trente retorted. "You took off running and lost us in this filthy dung-hole. Next time I spot either of you, I won't hesitate to drop you."

"You won't see us." Damen slipped into the maintenance tunnel.

"Keep your eyes open," Trente ordered, looking at Jayleia. "Eudal has people on station. So does your dad. Wish I had better intel for you."

Jayleia nodded. "I appreciate it."

"I mean what I said to your man. Next go, I'll redeem myself in the eyes of a corrupt government and collect IntCom's paycheck."

Your man. Damen smiled, slipped his hand into his pocket, and closed his fingers on the vial she'd given him. Little did they know.

Jayleia sidled through the already closing door, stuck her pistol to her utility belt, and brought out her handheld.

Damen tugged Jay out of sight of the doorway and saw she'd brought up a schematic of the station from the public data point.

"What a group baxt'k," she breathed, examining the diagram.

Damen nodded. Most space stations had been designed and built to suit a specific purpose. Not Silver City. It had evolved. Messy. Organic. As much a living thing as the diverse guild members and their customers taking refuge within it.

Nearly a century ago, the nascent Mining Guild had taken over the abandoned deep space outpost, revamped it, and then had begun haphazardly hooking in salvaged ships, aged ore processing derricks, and space debris. As myriad different species flocked to the station, lured by the promise of freedom and mineral riches, they'd brought craft suited to their varying body configurations. Those had been co-opted and added into the expanding station.

Damen suspected the UMOPG kept the whole thing running via a dark pact with all Three Hells.

He shook his head. Jayleia's diagram would be of limited use. The maintenance tunnels weren't part of the public . . . he blinked and swore as the station security seal appeared, then disappeared from her handheld screen.

"Spawn of a Myallki bitch," he ground out. "That would have taken me twice as long to break."

Her face, illuminated by the screen of her unit, showed him the pained glance she flicked his way.

"A trick Omorle taught me," she said. "It doesn't always work, but on a station like this, cobbled together from so many technologies, one or two of them are bound to use default pass-codes."

A simple and obvious ploy exploiting humanoid forgetfulness, not a sophisticated hack. Damen subsided.

He'd backed her into a corner filled with hard memories. Maybe he hadn't hurt her physically, but by his count, he'd landed more emotional hits than she let on. In the sex trade, he'd have used physical stimulation to lay bare her emotions. As an agent of the Claugh Empire, he should use her emotions to expose her secrets. He couldn't.

How silly was it to want her to offer him her secrets and her heart like she'd offered her blood?

"This way," he ordered, urging her down the walkway. "This section is self-contained."

"Meaning?"

"Haul your butts," a sharp, feminine voice urged from the walkway behind them. "Before security decides to vacuum the tunnels."

"Vala," Damen said.

"Run," Vala snapped, elbowing her way past.

Jayleia, mouth set in a hard line, slung her pack strap over her head and shoulder.

"Vacuum the tunnels?" Jayleia demanded.

Lights flashed below the walkway.

"There go the airtights!" Vala yelled.

Alarm spiked through his blood. With each footfall, Damen felt vibration rumbling through the soles of his boots. Security had ordered the airtight bulkheads closed in preparation for decompressing the tunnel.

Vala sprinted for an open access hatch.

Jay dove, tucking and rolling to her feet on the other side as Damen shoved his broad shoulders through sideways. The door slammed shut behind them.

They were back in the market ring. It had originally been designed as open space, a park for the people living in the surrounding quarters. That had lasted until the guild had commandeered the structure. Vendor carts, greasy pubs, and at least one fly-by-night drug outlet populated the bottom ring where trees and greenery had once grown.

Overhead, twelve levels up, a transparent layer of alloy glass provided a view of the mineral-rich asteroid belt that had drawn miners in the first place, and the vivid orange, red, and yellow-striped gas giant that Silver City used as a kind of gravitational anchor.

"They can't open those tunnels to space!" Jayleia gritted. "There are people in there!"

"Station security calls it 'vermin control,'" Vala replied.

Jayleia cursed.

"Security saw us exit the tunnel. They won't bother," Damen assured her. "We're headed to that lift and going six stops. If we get separated, don't go to the *Kawl Fergus*. There's an ore freighter."

He grabbed his handheld and shunted a code string and location to her unit. "That's the lock code. The station techs can't break it."

She nodded, her gaze busy scanning the crowd.

"No. You are not taking her to the office," Vala protested, darting around in front of him and stopping him with a hand to his chest. "Not her. Not there. You're mine!"

Damen stiffened and snarled.

Stationers who had been brushing past, growling or cursing at them, suddenly gave the stationary trio a wide berth.

Jayleia looked between them, her eyes wide.

He glanced pointedly down at Vala's hand, then met her angry gaze.

She snatched her hand back to her side and caught an audible breath as if realizing what she'd said. Lips trembling and eyes filling, Vala bowed her head.

Damen took Jayleia's elbow, directed her around Vala, and walked away.

Behind them, he heard Vala begin to weep.

Jayleia looked over her shoulder, frowning, and slowed.

"Don't," Damen said. "She challenged. She lost."

"She's jealous, Damen," Jayleia countered. "She's in love with you. What gives you the right to break her heart?"

CHAPTER
18

"YOU don't understand," he snapped.

"Then explain it," she said.

For a moment, she thought he'd refuse. His lips tightened into an angry line. Then he glanced at her.

She offered him her best in-the-interest-of-science face.

"Tahem is the station Sex Master," he said. "He recruits, trains, and runs the workers. He recruited me. I was good, but I was better at computer espionage."

"He's been using the sex trade as a cover to cultivate and train his own spy force?" she surmised.

Damen turned an approving look upon her. He nodded. "When I surpassed Tahem's ability, he saw to it that Admiral Seaghdh found me. Don't worry. The admiral knows."

Jay swallowed her frown. "Vala?"

"Tahem made me responsible for finding, training, and protecting a network of spies on station. Vala is one. If I allow her to challenge my control, I can't protect her. I made the mistake once. I won't do it again."

The suppressed rage and sorrow in his voice shriveled her courage to ask what had happened. Given the hurt radiating from him, Jay could guess.

"Is it possible that Vala wanted proof that she's more than a job to you?"

He blinked as they entered the crowded lift and stared down at her, dawning awareness in his eyes, as well as speculation.

Jayleia found she couldn't meet his gaze. Her question had made it plain that she was familiar with feeling like something to be checked off a list.

"Nah, I told him Zambol'd kill him faster than flash ice . . ." the woman squeezed in next to Jayleia said. She and her companion laughed.

". . . off to join the war effort. Stupid kid," a man behind Jay grumbled. "Told her sex work on station could be just as exciting . . ."

". . . new plague hitting Folran outstation. Big troop depot," another voice from the back of the lift said.

Jayleia's head came up as she tried to zero in on the conversation, her heart constricting.

"Ain't a frontline world," the voice went on saying, "but sure sounds like a Chekydran plague. Course, the media's keeping it all hushed . . ."

Damen touched her hand.

She sucked in a sharp breath. Blood thundered in her ears. An outbreak? On a troop depot? Gods, she had to end this and get back aboard the *Sen Ekir*.

Damen pressed his lips tight in warning, took her hand, and led her out of the lift.

One lone whistle followed. "Don't know which of you kids is luckier!"

The lift door closed on laughter.

Jayleia drew up short, all question of outbreaks shunted aside.

Thick black carpet, soft beneath her boots, covered the floor. Shimmering, translucent drapes shielded the walkways from what looked like a lounge in the center of the large octagonal room. A trick of the filtered light showed her people in various stages of repose on the couches, tables, and luxurious-looking armchairs.

On Jayleia's side of the curtains, doors lined the outer wall of the octagon. Smell registered; the faint, sweet scent of alcohol underpinned by a mingling of musk and blood that made her heart race. Then she heard the cries. Moans. Screams. Male. Female.

Damen squeezed her hand and urged her into motion. "Recorded and piped in."

His whispered assurance startled her. Had she looked that bad? Squaring her shoulders, she followed him a third of the way around the room.

He palmed open a door and led her through. The door shut behind them, and he loosed her long enough to code lock them in.

"I hadn't expected your sympathy for Vala," he said. "You sound well acquainted with jealousy."

She turned away to survey the room. "My best friend is a blond bombshell with energy-blade medals draped around her neck and captain attached to her name. I've lived with that for six years. Of course I understand envy."

More diaphanous curtains, a couch, easy chairs, a desk, and along the back wall, another door.

He strode to the door and opened it. Creases lined his forehead, but he didn't quite frown. Still. He wouldn't meet her gaze. "In here."

Curious as to what could so unsettle him, she marched into the other room.

Computer display screens formed a semicircle in the center of the room, but it was the rack pushed against the wall to her right that grabbed and held her attention. It was equipped with leather ankle and wrist straps that told her instantly where Damen had come by the scars on his ankles.

The bottom dropped out of her stomach.

A row of whips, sex toys, and devices she had no wish to contemplate too closely lined the opposite wall.

She felt the blood drain from her head. What the Three Hells did the Claugh nib Dovvyth want with someone who knew what all this stuff was, much less how to use it? As a former sex worker, he'd know wouldn't he?

With a start, she realized Damen stood at her side, watching her shock, her fears, and probably the damned illicit thrill worming its way unwanted through her blood.

"You'd be surprised what sort of information a competent sex worker can stumble over when a client is in the throes of his or her chosen ecstasy," he said, as if reading her thoughts.

She wrinkled her nose. "It smells."

He breathed in the scent and nodded. "I like it. It's a history of desire, blood, pain, want, and satisfaction. Need. Everyone has needs. They're all different."

The wistful note in his tone transfixed her and Jayleia stilled, watching the faraway light in his eyes.

"What do you need?" She hadn't meant to ask the question aloud, but realized she had when she saw the words slam into him broadside.

He froze, lips parted on the verge of saying something. Finally, he looked away, his gray eyes bleak.

"Something I can't have." He stalked to the computer setup and began powering up the systems.

She battled back the urge to wrap her arms around him and warm the chill out of his eyes. She wanted to assure him he could have anything he wanted, but how could she? She couldn't guarantee it, not for him, not even for herself.

The man had grown up in the sex trades. She'd grown up pampered. Protected. Shielded by her parents, her bodyguards, and by the priestesses teaching her in the Temple. Jayleia didn't know how to handle feelings, not her own, much less his. She dealt in facts. Logic. Trying to offer comfort to a man complicated by a past like his would be patronizing at best.

Knowing she couldn't trust her voice, she turned her attention to the computers. He'd included two chairs in front of the panels and a virtual-immersion-feed headset just like the one Omorle used the few times he'd taken her on a mission with him.

She picked it up and shook her head. "I can't go in with you. I am not a tech. I know a few simple games. Omorle refused to teach me . . ."

"Keep watch," Damen interrupted. "It's what you did for him. Will you do it for me?"

She blinked. It's what Omorle had asked of her the three times he'd taken her on his missions. How had Damen known?

"Are you sure you want me guarding your exit?" she asked. She was in what amounted to a sexual torture chamber, no matter that clients paid dearly, in more ways than one, to be . . . serviced by the man entrusting his life to her. How in the names of the Twelve Gods had she ended up in this situation?

He turned an eager, enticing smile on her that jolted every nerve. "With you running the code path beside me, I could steal the Gods' own data bank."

Her heart picked up speed and she choked on a laugh. It hit her that she wanted to be the reason his gray eyes lit up so brightly. She needed to ease the lines of tension in his face.

Before she could think, she smoothed trembling fingers across his forehead.

He wrapped his arms around her waist, closed his eyes, and sighed.

Hope and a sense of power swelled in her chest. "Okay."

Damen hugged her tight, opened his eyes, and ushered her into a chair.

Using her handheld, she isolated the virtual-immersion-headset feed and changed the default security code. The last bit of advice Omorle had given her. Never leave an unlocked back door.

Damen sat down next to Jayleia and felt the quiver running through her muscles where her thigh brushed his.

She picked up her VI set and put it on, as much, he suspected, to keep him from seeing the memory haunting her as to prep for the run.

"Easy, Jay," he urged. "Slow down. We've got a little time."

"Cravuul-dung. Getting here was too easy," she countered, her voice tight.

"That's why you're keeping watch," he assured her. "I'm going to tether you to me. Keep an eye on this feed. It's station security alerts. If they detect us, you'll know."

"Understood."

"Inserting into the code layer," he said as he slipped into the station's internal computer systems.

She shifted.

He glanced at her, but couldn't see her eyes. "The VI headset allows you to process this foray into the computers as if you were walking through it. It may be disorienting. If it's too much . . ."

"Incoming," she said.

Damen slammed his attention back to the code and nodded to mask the exhilaration twining through him. He'd been right to bring her with him.

A snooper, a snippet of code designed specifically to identify intruders and report back to station security, came their way. It hadn't detected them yet.

Jayleia had sensed the danger before the wandering program could alert out.

His fingers moved on his panel. The spy code withered and died.

No wonder her bodyguard had drafted her for lookout duty.

"Did you love Omorle Lin?" Damen asked, then choked back a bitter laugh. They were thigh-deep in the peripheral data systems adjoining Silver City's heart. What she'd once felt, what she might still feel for her dead friend, had no bearing on their situation. He couldn't let it. Still. He didn't comprehend the burn in his chest.

"Yes," she said, her voice flat. "I loved him. I still do. Always will, I suppose. His being dead these six years hasn't seemed to have had much impact on that."

"Because he was the first man to treat you like you, not like your father's daughter? Which is what I've done."

She sat frozen in silence for a moment, before she tilted her head and sighed.

"In all fairness," she said, "I've kept so many secrets over the years that I don't know who or what I am anymore. You can hardly be blamed for falling back to my last known good identity."

Damen chuckled. He felt her relax. The soreness around his heart eased and his breath came more easily.

"Here we go," he said. "It's going to take some time to get through this lock."

"What is that?" she asked, forestalling him. She directed his attention to a tiny pinprick of unmoving data. The information flowing past it left eddies in the stream.

He scowled.

Imminent data-stream failure from a leak in the sending and receiving structures? Or spyware he'd not seen until now? Uneasiness swept him.

He directed a few queries at it, then blew out a frustrated breath. "It's not sending or receiving. I don't know what it is."

Jayleia nodded. "I have the oddest feeling we're being watched."

The skin between his shoulder blades tingled as if waiting for the impact of a shot. He shook off the impression.

"How's the security feed look?" he asked, directing her attention away from the bit of frozen data.

"Brawl on market four," she said.

He grinned. "Let's break this code lock."

"Wouldn't it be easier to find the key?" she asked.

"You might not know how to run code, but you know what questions to ask. You fight. And you're a scientist?" he marveled.

"Did the Claugh assign you to recruiting, too?" she asked, humor in her voice.

"Are you suggesting you can be turned?"

"Don't you have enough TFC personnel on your side of the zone?" she countered, a smile in her voice.

His heart lifted.

CHAPTER

19

JAYLEIA glanced at Damen.

He played the lockout programs with the same concentration and virtuosity he'd displayed at the controls of the *Kawl Fergus*. He was easily as good as Lin had been. Maybe better.

She'd had years of watching TFC's star computer-espionage expert, yet she found herself admiring Damen's skill. It looked like Tahem had been a good teacher.

Jay straightened. "Damen? What are the chances that this lock is Tahem's handiwork?"

"Why do you think I asked you to follow me in?" he asked, tensing beside her when the lock code flared in response to his tinkering. "Damn it! The man taught me everything he knew about running code. What the Hells is his key phrase? I can't get into the heart of Silver City's data store unless I can break this lock."

"The heart?" she echoed, frowning. A niggling buzz at the back of her head caught her attention. "Try Ioccal."

Damen went dead still beside her and breathed a laugh. "Based on the notion that this phrase is the key to Tahem's heart? Nice."

It didn't work.

Jayleia breathed a curse and checked the security feed. Nothing. And that felt wrong. Surely it wouldn't take any great brainpower to work out where they were holed up.

"It's a good theory," Damen said. "Try again."

"Omorle Lin."

A security breach alert buzzed under her hand. She jumped, shut it off, and said, "Security's on the way."

Another failure. The code lock glow intensified. The glare looked threatening.

"Jayleia Durante," Damen typed.

Her heart lurched to think she'd be the key to breaking Tahem's heart, but she nodded. It made sense.

It, too, failed.

In her VI headset, it looked like the lock exploded. She knew it was nothing more than the defense mechanism alerting out, notifying security of the intruders attempting to break into the system. The visual assault hit before she could shut her eyes.

Damen felt Jayleia flinch, heard her pained gasp, and slammed a fist down on her panel, cutting her link.

She cried out. Her hands clutched at the headset, then fell limp as she crumpled in her seat.

Damen severed his connection by yanking the power supplies to each of the console systems.

"Jay?"

He removed the VI set.

She groaned.

"On your feet," he said, dragging her upright. "We've got a few minutes, but we have to get moving."

That snapped her out of her daze enough that she rasped, "Erase your system."

"What?"

"Power your boxes up and fry them so that no one can trace you."

"No time," he countered. "Get out of here. Go to the ore freighter. It looks dead. It isn't. Get off station."

"I'm not leaving you to face espionage charges," Jayleia snapped, her eyes clearing as she rubbed her forehead. "And I'm not leaving without that file on my father."

"How are you going to get it without the key?" he demanded.

"Never let what you are frame your data," she quoted. "Omorle said that. If you can't download it, I'll steal the hardware."

Steal the data by brute force? He blinked. Had he really come to identify himself so thoroughly as Admiral Seaghdh's computer expert that he'd blinded himself to all other means of data retrieval?

Jay twisted out of his grasp, grabbed the power cores, and slammed them into place. "Stow the argument and boot the damned systems. Your culture isn't the only one with rules, Major."

He glared. Rules? She wanted to throw rules in his face? After lecturing him about Vala?

Growling, he brought the nearest systems to life.

"You requested the truce. You're under my protection," she said as he worked the waking panels. "Not while it's convenient. Not until I'm in danger. You made your safety my responsibility up to and including my death. Don't like it? Don't ask for a truce from a Swovjiti. Want someone to follow orders blindly? Pick another damned scientist."

Ire drained out of him. She'd die to shield him? The burn in his chest intensified until he shifted, trying to break free of the discomfort.

"Done," he said, straightening. "Simple data destruct cascade."

Damen touched her cheek.

Her gaze searched his face.

He didn't know what he saw, but her expression softened, the tension and anger draining away.

"Thank you," he said, forcing the words past the boulder lodged in the spot where his heart should be. "I'm not accustomed to being protected."

She smiled wryly. "Our cultures seem specifically designed to offend one another."

"I don't give a damn about your culture," he murmured. "Just you. I have no practice in accepting care with grace. Help me."

Her smile died. She cupped his cheek in her hand, her brown eyes darkening. Uncertainty fired in her eyes, but she battled it down and pressed her lips against his.

Damen fought back the urge to yank her to him and consume her. In time. Time.

He pulled away. "We have to go."

Nodding, she asked, "Which way?"

"We split up and give security two targets to chase," he said. "You'll go out the back door. I'll go out the front."

She grimaced and her hold on him tightened. "I can't protect you if we're separated."

Her reluctance to leave him sent a rush of pleasure through him. Savoring the sensation, he replied, "And I can't protect you unless we do."

She eyed him, her face drawn in grim calculation. She nodded.

"Trade me," she said. "I've seen the lay of the deck out the front door. If I can get out without being shot, I'll be invisible in short order."

"Done. Make for the ore freighter."

She ran to the door.

Damen followed and opened it. In the outer room, he flattened himself against the inside wall and decoded the door lock.

It opened.

Nothing happened.

Jayleia threw him a troubled look. "Be careful," she muttered, then she strode into the corridor.

The door shut.

Was it a shout he'd heard as the door sealed and locked? Heart in his throat, he returned to his office, knowing something had gone wrong. That security hadn't been positioned in the corridor meant they'd come up with a plan he hadn't foreseen. He glanced at the secret door Tahem had built into the back room decades ago. He'd said that a spy always had more than one exit.

Damen suspected he'd had more than the few Damen knew about.

Pushing aside the rack of whips and other implements, he cursed in a steady monotone. He'd failed to steal the data store. He'd risked Jayleia and turned her loose on a hostile station. He brought out his handheld, tapped it to life, and unlocked his escape hatch.

Time to begin sorting the mess and see what could be salvaged. He stepped into an empty, dark shuttle bay.

The hair at the back of his neck stirred.

The barrel of a gun pressed against his temple. Lights flared.

Damen squinted, hands raised, and hackles up. He knew the scent of the woman standing before him.

"Guild Mistress," he said.

"Dear, sweet Damen," a sultry, feminine voice drawled. "Members of your own family came to me with tales of your spying and sabotage aboard this station."

Damen knew better than to answer the charge.

"Sindrivik," the chief of security said, locking a set of neural cuffs on first one of his wrists, then the other. He activated them.

Damen's arms went dead.

"You're under arrest for treason."

"You've betrayed your own kind," the guild mistress said, "and endangered every man, woman, and child on station. Get him out of my sight."

CHAPTER
20

JAYLEIA examined the dead-looking hulk from the shadows and shifted, not at all comfortable with how simple it had been to give station security forces the slip.

Either they were laughably understaffed and undertrained, or she and Damen had miscalculated. Badly. Sitting alone in a freezing-cold docking bay with few working lights, no running water, and from the smell, no sanitary pump out, an oily tendril of fear slid into her gut.

Shaking, she crossed to the freighter, went up the stairs to the personnel door, and used the unlock Damen had given her.

A click and whir and the door cracked open. Jay slipped in, then closed and locked it.

"Damen?" Vala called, footsteps coming closer. They stopped with a clump on the deck plating. "You! You weren't . . . Where's Damen?"

Jayleia's breath constricted as her head completed Vala's sentence. "You weren't supposed to make it." She spun on the woman, ice stabbing into her chest. "Damen left the same time I did. Find him."

Vala caught in an audible gulp of air. "Which door did he take?"

"Back."

"No!" Vala rasped. "No! It wasn't supposed to happen like that! You were supposed to use that door! It's the rules!"

Jayleia stared at Vala, her heart hammering against her ribs. "What have you done?"

Vala choked back a sob. "He'll think . . . oh, Gods." She sank to the floor, her hands clenching fists full of her curly hair.

"Where is he?"

"Nothing you can do."

"Where!" Jayleia shouted, turning her back on the woman and sprinting for the cockpit.

Vala followed.

Boots clumped down the companionway in their wake.

"Station lockup. It's secure," Vala whispered. "The guild will accuse him of treason. They'll kill him."

"How?" Jay demanded.

Vala's tears ran faster. "They space traitors."

A surge of horror struck Jay to silence. She dropped into the pilot's seat.

"No," she grated and realized her denial was likely true. *Think, Jayleia.* "They won't kill him right away. They'd want every scrap of information they could rip from him first."

Bellin skidded to a halt inside the cockpit door and stared at Jay, then at Vala.

"Vala?" he quavered, looking back and forth between the two women. "What's wrong?"

"Damen's in trouble," Jayleia answered in Vala's stead.

"I know you," Bellin said as Jay connected her handheld into the ship's systems, and began trying to find a way into the station's prison computers.

"My mission was to find you and lead you to him," the kid said, "wasn't supposed to get stung."

Jayleia blinked at the turn of phrase "my mission," then recalled Damen's statement that he'd been recruiting spies from among the station's populace. She glanced at the boy. Damen's gray eyes peered back at her. She smiled. "Does Major Sindrivik have you run missions for him often?"

"All the time," Bellin said, pride in his voice. "When I'm old enough, he's going to recruit me. Here. I'm supposed to give this to you."

He held out a metal tube.

Jayleia took it, recognizing the container that Damen had given to Tahem with the crystal inside. She frowned. "Who gave this to you?"

"Not supposed to tell," the boy said. "He said, 'You're going to need it. It's the key.'"

Jayleia stared at the tube. Damen had given it to Tahem, who had obviously given it to Bellin. Was the crystal the key? Or was Tahem delivering yet another coded message?

She tried to open the tube. Locked. Damen had coded the mechanism to Tahem. Who would Tahem code the lock to? Her heart stumbled.

Of course.

She input the unlock code Damen had given her for the freighter. The tube opened, spilling the crystal into her hand.

Damen.

The key to Tahem's heart and the key to the Silver City data store.

"You going to help him? Damen, I mean?" Bellin demanded.

Jayleia tried to breathe around the sting in her chest and straightened. "Yes."

"I wanna help," Bellin declared.

"Me, too," Vala said, her voice thick. Isarrite-bound determination underlay her words. "I can get you into the lockup via video and audio feeds."

"Do it," Jay ordered, rising.

"I tried to get you killed. You're going to trust me?" Vala challenged.

"You love him," Jayleia countered. "I trust that."

Scrubbing tears from her face with her sleeve, Vala took the copilot's chair, and glanced at her son.

Jay followed her gaze.

"Gather the family," Vala instructed. "It's an emergency."

Bellin didn't respond. He paled and sprinted for the door.

Once the door closed behind the boy, Jay waved off Vala's attempt to lock it.

"Find Damen," she instructed, code locking the door.

Vala spent a few minutes that felt like a lifetime accessing the feeds.

"You were right," the woman said. "Couldn't find him in a cell. They have him . . ."

Video connected on the holo-display in front of them.

"In an interrogation room," Jayleia finished and flinched.

Damen sat with both wrists cuffed to a chair.

She couldn't tell if they'd activated the neural lock, or if Damen had gone as still and expressionless as Isarrite out of rage.

They'd searched him. His equipment littered the table behind him.

A woman with short-cropped gray hair and an old, jagged scar marring her jaw stood barring the door, arms crossed over her gray and black uniform.

The freighter's personnel door cycled.

Jay looked over her shoulder.

"Vala? Bellin said it's an emergency," a young, male voice called as the door shut and locked. "What's going on?"

A scrawny, adolescent male with dark hair and hazel eyes appeared in the cockpit doorway. He glanced at the screen and blanched.

"Baxt'kal Twelve Gods. Is that Damen?"

"Jay, this is Kebbin, Damen's second-in-command," Vala said.

Startled, Jayleia cast a surreptitious look between them. She'd assumed Vala was Damen's right hand on Silver City.

Vala wouldn't meet her gaze.

"Who's that in the room with Damen?" Jay asked.

"The woman at the door is Calmin," Vala said, her face turned to the screen, "head of operations."

Leaning in to stare at the scene, Jay said, "She's not asking questions or . . ."

The woman straightened as the door opened.

Two men entered.

"Acquival is not on station," the thick-set man, also in gray and black, with thinning straw colored hair and a square face said into the silent room.

"Janka, chief of security," Kebbin said. "The skeletal guy in the green medi coat is Altu."

Jayleia frowned. "He's not chief medical officer?"

Kebbin shook his head. "The C.M.O. is too old-fashioned for interrogation."

"He refuses to hurt people," Vala clarified.

Abruptly sick, Jay shot to her feet. "How do I get in there?"

"You don't!" Kebbin gritted, grabbing her arm.

She snarled at him.

He yanked his hand back as if burned. "That place is a fortress. Blunder in there, you'll both die."

"You've run a trace on Master Acquival?" another voice, one that tripped every alarm in Jayleia's system, said.

Peering at the screen, she sank into her chair.

The man had his back to the camera. He stood out in his navy uniform. Thinning and graying light brown hair suggested she should recognize him.

"The trace came up empty," Janka said.

Meaning they'd had a locator on Tahem. Had he known?

"I trust your people are combing this station for Jayleia Durante," the man in blue said.

Jay knew him then. Gerriny Eudal, her father's former second-in-command. He'd come after her himself? What had her father said or done to have rousted Eudal out from behind the scenes where, her father liked to complain, he pulled all sorts of strings?

"Three squads," Janka replied.

Head spinning, Jayleia sucked in a ragged-sounding breath.

"Change the access code on that door!" she barked, gesturing over her shoulder in the direction of the freighter's personnel door.

"On it," Kebbin said, pouncing on a workstation.

"Until you acquire that particular point of persuasion," Gerriny said, turning to poke at Damen's possessions where they sat arrayed on the table, "may I suggest that you locate the woman Vala and her son? My sources indicate they are a weak spot in the major's armor."

Janka grinned and activated his com badge.

Vala, Kebbin, and Jayleia swore over the drone of orders being issued.

"Bring Bellin in," Jayleia said.

Vala bent to her station, sending out a recall code for her son.

"I've got to get Damen out of there," Jayleia said. "I don't know what Eudal is capable of."

"The slimy one in blue?" Kebbin clarified. "Who is he?"

"Acting director of the Tagreth Federated Council's Intelligence Command," she replied, her tone grim. "The spawn of a Myallki bitch went after my dad. Now he's after me."

"Then you can't go in there!" Vala protested.

"No, I can't," Jay said. "You were right. I'd get us both killed. I need an alternative plan. Help me out here."

Kebbin and Vala awarded her blank stares.

Jayleia choked back a curse, and flogging her brain for a workable plan, turned back to the screen.

Janka spun on Damen and snapped, "You were ordered to take your passenger to medical."

"So you could sell her to the highest bidder?" Damen growled.

Janka shrugged. "She isn't one of us. Why would you care what happened to her? You disobeyed a direct order and endangered your people."

"That does make the accusations of treason ring true," Eudal noted.

"Tahem Acquival is my master on this station," Damen retorted. "He summoned me and ordered me to bring Ms. Durante."

"Why?" Janka demanded.

"He knew her."

"Of course he did," Eudal said. "His life partner was her bodyguard for years. I daresay he considers her family."

"You were arrested exiting Acquival's office on the vice deck after an aborted attack on this station's systems," Janka growled. "My investigators found your biomarkers all over your master's office. Hers, too."

The muscles in Damen's jaw bunched. "I'm his favorite. She's a new recruit."

Kebbin uttered a harsh-sounding laugh and leaned his head in her direction. "Welcome to the family."

Jay gaped at him, her thought processes shorted, tangled, and presented her with recall of the sex toys lining one wall of the room where she'd kept watch while Damen had tried to steal Silver City's data.

Hot blood rushed to her face. "What? No! I took an oath . . ."

"You're attempting to protect Jayleia Durante, Major Sindrivik. I commend your sense of duty and loyalty," Gerriny Eudal said, holding something between thumb and forefinger as he lifted it to the light for inspection. "Given what I've found here in your belongings, however, I suggest your devotion to the young lady may be misplaced."

Jay propped her forehead on her clenched fists and glared at the screen trying to make out what the man held. "Shut up, you Carozziel slime-bat!"

"Blood," Eudal mused.

Realization hit her like a meteor impacting atmosphere.

The vial of blood she'd given Damen.

"You took first blood?" Janka grated, the look he turned upon Damen approving. "Huh. Didn't think you had the drive."

"A sample vial," Gerriny corrected. "A sterile, dispassionate way for a predator to claim a victim. Or a mate."

Jay's breath stopped in her chest. *Mate?*

"He didn't take this blood," the man went on. "She did and undoubtedly offered it up with pretty words. It was a cold, calculated move from a frigid, conniving young woman. Or did you not know that her own people exiled her when she seduced and attempted to murder a rival warrior's brother?"

Rage exploded through her.

"That is *not* what . . ." she wheezed.

"You gave him your baxt'kal blood?" Vala breathed from beside Jayleia.

She glanced between Vala and Kebbin.

The amazed disbelief in their faces shot deep uneasiness through her.

"T-to seal a truce," she stuttered.

Pity rushed into their faces.

Ice flushed her veins.

"Don't doubt for a moment that she knew exactly what she was doing to you, my friend," Gerriny Eudal said.

Staring at the screen, Jayleia saw Damen flinch. Her heart tore. She squeezed her burning eyes shut.

"Altu." The woman's voice broke the stillness that had fallen. "Major Sindrivik was ordered to bring the prisoner to medical for verification of her infection status."

"Yes, Officer Calmin," the medi replied. "That did not take place."

"Is the woman a danger to this station?"

"The disease is blood-borne," Altu said. "The major claims the subject has recovered from the illness and is no longer contagious. Even if that assertion is false, the young lady would have to spill her own blood in order to infect another."

Jay opened her eyes in time to see Calmin shoot the man an annoyed look. "How many Autken are aboard this station?"

The round-faced, beige-skinned medi blinked.

The head of operations uncrossed her arms, scowling. "Predators every one, perfectly capable of drawing her blood, thereby spreading a messy disease all over Silver City."

"This blood must be tested, then," Eudal said, closing his fist around the vial.

"Agreed." Altu nodded and held out a hand. "I will return to medical . . ."

"Nonsense," Eudal said. "You have the perfect test case right here."

He looked at Damen and extended the vial to the medi.

Jayleia scrambled to her feet.

"No!" Damen shouted, straining against the bindings holding him.

Grinning, Altu took the vial.

Behind him, Janka shifted, his face and his posture telling Jay how uncomfortable he was with the situation. She'd use that. Somehow.

The medi set his kit on the table before rummaging through it. He snapped the vial of her blood into a wicked-looking device and faced Damen.

"Fastest results possible?" the medi inquired, his tone avid.

"I suggest that's wise," Eudal said, smiling.

Sweat stood out on Damen's face. From the motion of his chest, Jay detected the change in his respiration from measured to rapid and shallow.

She stared at the contraption in the medi's grasp. Her blood ran cold. "That's a needle. A barbaric antique! He can't . . ."

Altu slammed the needle into Damen's chest, slightly left of center.

Damen uttered a strangled cry and convulsed.

Vala's breath hissed in between her teeth and she whimpered.

"Baxt'k," Kebbin growled.

Jay's heart beat so hard, it hurt. She had to get him out of there. No matter the cost. She glanced over her shoulder at the pack holding her uniform.

The medi withdrew the needle and returned to his gear.

Jayleia's throat constricted at the sight of Damen limp in the chair. It took several seconds of watching to realize he was still breathing.

Damen groaned.

Gerriny Eudal laughed, a high-pitched, unhinged giggle that raised the hair at the back of Jayleia's neck.

"There you are," Eudal said, rubbing his hands together. "A marriage made in Hell. Her blood is your blood and if it's not infected, you'll live your entire life mated to a woman whose only intent has been to use you."

"Marriage?" Jayleia burst out. "I meant to seal a truce and ended up proposing?"

Vala lifted her tear-streaked face from her hands. "You didn't know?"

"Twelve Gods," Kebbin rasped. "You read a file or some dusty research report about Autken traditions, didn't you?"

"And assumed I understood them," Jay gulped, shame raking the inside of her skin. What had she done?

Indulging her childish attraction to him and believing that intellect would never lead her astray, she'd endangered Damen as surely as if she'd dropped him into a nest of infected kuorls.

"If it's her heart you want," Eudal offered on-screen, "I'll give it to you."

Jay sneered at the man's image. "I may deserve a place in the lowest level of Hell, Eudal, but if I'm going, I'm taking you with me."

She stalked to the bag she'd dropped against the bulkhead. "I'm going in . . ." She broke off as her brain presented her with a memory from her training.

The Swovjiti had rules.

Good ones like never attack directly that which can be diminished with a thousand tiny cuts. And that gave her an idea.

She spun on Vala and Kebbin. "How many people does Damen claim as his?"

"Including dependents?" Kebbin asked.

"Yes."

"Just over forty," Vala answered.

"I can't do this alone," Jay said. "Muster everyone you can trust with Damen's safety. The rest, I need on this boat. We're leaving the station the moment he's free."

Eyeing the doubting expressions on Vala's and Kebbin's faces, she said, "If I can't go in and get him, I have to make them want to let him go."

"How?" Kebbin demanded.

"Didn't they say Tahem had left Silver City?"

Kebbin and Vala traded a confused look, but the young man shook his head. "Yes, but . . ."

Jayleia waved off the protest. "I know. It's supposition, given that they have no proof of his departure, only proof that they can't find a man who's become a spymaster in his own right. Am I correct in thinking he's also the Silver City computer-security expert?"

Kebbin's hazel eyes lit. He grinned. "Why, yes, he is. And now he's vanished."

"What an unfortunate time for an attack on the station's system, then," Jayleia said, shoving her handheld at Vala. "I need the items on this list within the hour. Who's your best code runner?"

The pair traded an uncertain look, but Kebbin lifted a finger.

Jay nodded. "You're going to hack Silver City."

"Objective?"

"Twofold. One, make them send Damen in to stop you because, two, . . ."

"I'm going after every last one of the guild's secrets?" Kebbin finished for her. He sounded eager.

"Yes."

"You're sure this will work?" Vala asked.

"No," Jay replied, "but I'm certain we have to try. Now. Who knows how to milk oozes for their venom without getting stung?"

"Bring him around," Gerriny Eudal said from the screen, his tone laden with pleasure. "I'd like to put a few questions to our handsome, young guest."

CHAPTER

21

DAMEN sat still, letting agony drain from his body.

"Neural enhancers," Gerriny Eudal noted, as he set down the control unit. "Medical devices, useful, I'm told, for quelling the pain of surgery. Unless, of course, someone breaks the security protocols . . ."

"And modifies the design spec to cause pain, make it feel as if surgical lasers were dissecting him from the inside out," Damen growled, muscles trembling and sweat drenching his shirt. "I'm familiar with the hack."

The man smirked. "Major Damen Sindrivik, loyal soldier of the Claugh nib Dovvyth, liege man to Admiral Cullin Seaghdh, assigned to Colonel Kirthin Turrel's command, you've had Jayleia Durante in custody for nearly two days. Don't tell me you've failed to break her in that time."

"She broke me."

Janka barked a laugh. "Did that gal of his really seduce a man then try to kill him?"

"Yes."

The security chief chuckled and met Damen's eye.

Damen smiled.

"You finally met your match, son?" Janka asked, grinning.

"Doesn't matter, does it?" Damen replied, then jerked his chin at Eudal. "This plant-eater mated me to her."

Janka sobered, a troubled gleam in his eyes.

The blare of intrusion alarms jolted the room.

Janka stalked to the com panel and silenced the noise. "Report!"

"Station core under attack!" Calmin's voice responded via the com.

"Show me," Janka ordered.

A holo-image lit one brushed-silver wall.

Damen studied the orange-lit, skeletal walkways punctuated by conduits and cables.

"Replay from six minutes ago," Calmin said. "Security cordon Core-716."

For several seconds nothing happened at the guarded checkpoint designed to restrict access to the life support functions of the station.

Then a black and crimson shape dropped in front of the camera eye. It landed and resolved into human form. Lithe. Agile. Female.

The guards started. Before they could snap to attention, much less draw weapons, the woman rushed the cordon, leaped from the walkway to the top of the six-foot-high security barricade, and kicked one guard square in the jaw. His head jerked to one side before he fell like a bag of sand. The other guard stumbled back, struggling to draw his gun. It cleared the holster and he began firing as he brought the weapon to bear on the woman perched atop the barricade.

She wasn't there anymore.

She'd executed some kind of flip that carried her up and over the guard, his shots following her arc in bright flashes until she landed behind him and struck, kicking his legs out from under him, and then pouncing. The barricade and cordon control panel blocked the camera eye. Damen couldn't see what she did, but the audible crunch followed by silence drove ice through his chest.

The woman stood. Recognition and realization swamped Damen. Jayleia.

She'd dressed in snug black fatigues. The trousers, padded at the joints and thighs, were supple-looking hide, stitched in scarlet. The garment made no sound as she moved. The top outlined every curve of her nimble body with what looked like buttery-soft, black Skeppanda silk.

The tiny, wiry, sentient Skeppanda created strands that when woven into fabric displayed ballistic properties matched only by military-grade armor. They never sold their silk, but they did occasionally award it when someone met with their favor. Something Jayleia must have done to merit a Swovjiti warrior's uniform woven from the precious threads.

She stepped up to the control panel and accessed it. Not a stray wisp of hair, not a sliver of skin showed through the black and crimson cloth covering her. Only dark eyes rendered colorless by the camera glinted in the wan light.

Jayleia looked into the camera eye, lifted her right hand, touched the fingers to her forehead, and flicked them out in a sort of ironic salute before she ordered the camera off-line.

The screen went dead.

Pride swelled in Damen's chest. He made certain it didn't show on his face.

"Get it back!" Janka commanded.

"We're trying," Calmin snapped. "Neither Ops nor your sec teams can access that panel or that surveillance feed."

Another alarm wailed.

The security chief snarled. "What?"

"Market ring!" Calmin responded. She pounded a panel. The alarm died. "Losing atmosphere! Power to the vice decks off-line! Gods baxt'kal damned freeloading space jockeys!"

Damen could guess that ships were blowing dock en masse. Gods knew that if he could get to the *Kawl Fergus*, he'd do the same. But not yet. Not until he'd done his best by the woman who'd just hijacked Silver City.

"These are tricks," Damen said. "Distractions."

Eudal whispered a curse. "Jayleia Durante."

Damen glanced at him. What did it mean that Eudal recognized her almost as readily as Damen did?

The man stood, stiff with tension. He stank of fear and rage.

Janka spun, fists clenched.

Shards of glass dug at Damen's nerves. Manipulating Gerriny Eudal, a man without enhanced Autken senses, was one thing. Playing the station's security specialist was another.

"Explain," the big man snarled.

Damen shrugged. He and Admiral Seaghdh had learned a hard lesson a year ago when they'd hijacked the *Sen Ekir*. The guild was on track to learn the hard way, too.

Never underestimate a righteously pissed off scientist.

He had no intention of warning the guild.

"She attacked the cordon to clear a path to the core," Damen said.

"Obvious," Janka said.

"She's controlling environmental systems," Damen pressed. "Inciting panic, creating so much havoc that you won't realize until too late that she's after the Silver City data store."

"Unless," Damen hedged, sliding his gaze sideways to IntCom's second-in-command, "he has agents running a decoy while his personnel steal Guild secrets."

Janka's nose wrinkled, and Damen knew he scented the man's biting worry.

Gerriny Eudal started and laughed. "He's Murbaasch Tu. A Claugh spy!"

"And you're a turncoat from Tagreth Federated," Janka mused, his lip curling. "A spy crazy enough to think he can cut a deal with the Chekydran while stabbing his chain of command in the back."

"All true," Eudal said, his tone oily. "But it is for the betterment of Tagreth Federated and of your people, should my discussions with the guild mistress bear out."

"His aren't the only agents on station," Damen tossed into the silence.

Janka glared at him.

"Director Durante's people are here," Damen said. Spiteful satisfaction crawled through his chest at the sour expression on Eudal's face at the mention of Jayleia's father. "If they have a location on the director, they may be attempting contact using Silver City resources."

"Source?" Janka demanded.

"A mercenary betrayed IntCom to render Ms. Durante aid," Damen answered as if he didn't care in the least.

He thought he heard Eudal growl. The burnt rubber smell of the man's rage heightened.

Captain Trente and Edie had seemed capable of looking out for their own interests. Damen trusted they'd left station hours ago.

Over the open com channel, another alarm claxon blared.

Growling deep in his throat, Janka spun and stomped to his panel. The claxon fell silent.

"Janka, here."

"Looks like Sindrivik called it!" Calmin's gravelly voice responded. "Someone's in our systems! Counter-intrusion measures . . ."

"Access point!" Janka barked.

"We don't know. Trace routines are being diverted all over the station!"

That piqued Damen's interest. Jayleia wouldn't know how to do that. Would she? He frowned. *Jay, what are you doing, and how are you doing it?*

"This is it," he said. "This is the grab."

"How do we stop it?" Calmin demanded.

Janka uttered a strangled sound.

"You can't," Damen said. "This is an organized attack by either IntCom or Murbaasch Tu agents. No offense, but if Tahem really has left station, you don't have the skill to shut down a full-on data grab."

"But you do?" Eudal sneered.

Janka studied Damen, then strode across the room and unlocked the neural cuffs.

"Are you mad?" Eudal protested. "This man . . ."

"Has family on this station," Janka retorted. "He's got no reason to protect us, but he will protect them."

Damen levered himself to his feet, nodding.

"Stop them," Janka commanded. "Or I'll hunt down every man, woman, and child in your organization."

"Understood."

"Call the guild mistress," Eudal demanded. "She would never permit . . ."

"Permission to teleport to my office, Mistress?" Janka said to the room at large. "The panels here aren't enabled for this kind of work."

"Permission granted. Teleport the lieutenant director to my location." The guild mistress's voice flowed over the room com, sounding amused. "We don't expect you to understand us or our ways, Lieutenant Director Eudal, the major won't break faith. He can no longer afford the price. Lock him into the office with you, Janka."

"Acknowledged."

"We'll be watching, Major," the guild mistress said. "Every move. Every thought."

Teleport distortion saved him from giving away the shock and the first tendril of hope ripping open his insides. He'd expected to die in Janka's prison.

Jayleia had gotten him out. It shouldn't have been possible.

Damn if he hadn't underestimated her. Again.

Biting back a grin, he strode for the chair beside Janka's as the security chief shot him a wary look.

"Send a team to that core panel you can't recover," Damen said as he sat down.

"Done. It was rigged with a handheld running a feeder loop," Janka said.

"ID on the unit?" Damen asked as he accessed the computer system under Janka's watchful eye.

"Wiped."

Damen nodded, unable to suppress a smile.

Someone had been thorough.

"All right," Damen said. "They aren't smash and grabbers. That shores up my theory that we're dealing with trained agents. The question is whose? What about your other cordons?"

"Secure. Guarded and monitored."

"Like the one on video?" Damen asked.

Janka shook his head and keyed in his authorization code, before waving a hand at the display and stepping back.

Damen watched alerts and commands scrolling past before he dove into the code, aiming for the system's heart. He could guess what was being done and he could guess how.

How had she broken through the lock on the station's core?

Behind him, Janka ordered the mobilization of three security teams. He sent them to manually check each of the security cordons.

"Nothing on monitors, sir," a young security officer protested.

"You know for a fact we still own those cameras, Chiekal?" Janka demanded.

Damen dropped into the station's system programming and faltered. She wasn't there. No one was there. He blinked. The hard way, then. He came up out of the system operating code. The counter-intrusion alerts were still firing off rapid-pace.

Working quickly, Damen picked up one of the trace-back routines. It was a clunky piece of code, but it gave him a glimpse of someone's real-time input before the trace was shunted into an infinite loop. He grimaced.

Looked like Jayleia had recruited half of his trainees on station, most of them inexperienced code-runners. It was their first major mistake, one that could end their party before it had started.

"How do I shut down counter-intrusion?" Damen demanded.

"What?" Janka yelped. "You can't!"

"I'd better. Whoever's handling this attack is about to crash the entire station by routing your counter-intrusion assaults into infinite feedback loops. It's overloading your array."

"Baxt'k!" Janka growled. "Guild Mistress?"

"Do it." Kannoi's voice filtered over room speakers. "It will not leave us entirely defenseless."

Janka charged to Damen's side, activated another panel, and entered an override code.

Access alerts continued to fire from points all over the station. Damen thought he'd begun to detect a pattern. If he was right, the team was pulling the station's complete data set. No handheld could handle files of that magnitude.

Damen smiled and straightened.

"What is it?" Janka said.

"I know where they are."

CHAPTER

22

DAMEN met Janka's searching gaze. "Send your people to the central processing core. It will be booby-trapped. Expect those traps to be lethal."

Janka's expression tightened into a grim mask. "This button here. Direct com line to my badge code. You tell me when." He turned and, shouting orders for guns and officers, sprinted out the door. It auto-locked behind him.

Damen could break the code lock if he could find a way to disable the room monitors. After he'd found Jayleia. He forged a path through the data trees, looking for the branch he wanted. He shifted. He should have found it already. Swearing, he backtracked. The marker code had been changed. Damen shook his head. If the access code had been changed, Jayleia might get away with her brash robbery, and he'd never have the chance to tell her how crippled he'd be without her. How much he admired her. How much he needed her now that her blood was his.

Heart pounding, Damen input the code he'd supplied to Jayleia so many hours ago. He waited, hands shaking. The tree lock flashed from red to green. He sucked in a deep breath and rushed from the station computers into the system aboard the mothballed ore freighter.

"Twelve Gods," he muttered at the control panel. The data tree ended in another lock. One he hadn't put in place. It flashed "ident" over and over.

Interesting.

No one used identity locks anymore. They were a relic too easy to defeat, but damned deadly in the wrong hands. The code was simple enough. It checked an entered identity against an existing list. If your ID was listed, you were in. If it wasn't, you were kicked out. If you had on a SEM, you were tossed out in the worst and most fatal way possible. Without a SEM, the feedback surge could easily blow out a panel.

Damen hesitated. Who'd written this file and how pissed off was he or she?

"Ident."

He keyed in his name and waited. File-check loops were notoriously . . . the lock code vanished. He sat at a blinking cursor. Nothing happened.

"Jay? Let me help," he typed in Claughwyth, knowing the computer on board the ship had a translator. He'd put it there himself.

No response. He kicked himself mentally. Of course she wouldn't be aboard the ship. She'd have his family there where they'd be safe if Janka's team managed to suddenly work it all out.

"Secure station?" someone aboard the freighter typed.

"Janka's," he replied.

"Monitored."

"Not text. Disabled at root."

"Com capability?"

"No," he replied. "Room monitored."

"Damn it. Need to hear your voice."

He hid his grin from the room camera, his heart in his throat. "I need far more than that from you, Jayleia Durante."

"Sorry it took so long. I kept waiting for you to call on me for rescue."

He hid a grin. "They weren't infected kuorls."

"I beg to differ."

"Let's finish this. Command me."

"Issue the recall order," she typed. "Data pull at ninety-two percent. By the time everyone assembles on board, we'll be clear."

Data pull at ninety-two percent? He reeled.

"How'd you get through the data lock?" he typed.

"Bellin gave me the key."

Damen stilled, frowned, and rubbed his forehead. "What was it?"

"You."

He blinked.

"'Tahem loves you,'" she typed. "Your name was the key."

Proximity claxons wailed through the station.

"Problem."

"I hear," Jayleia answered.

"Stand by."

"Acknowledged."

Damen spun to another station, opened a com channel, and said, "Operations? What the Three Hells is going on?"

Shouted obscenities overrode the alarm before it fell silent. "Incoming, unidentified craft!"

"What is it?" the security chief bellowed over his com badge.

"Get me a visual!" Damen ordered, bringing a monitor to life.

He keyed in to station communications as the operations people directed external feeds to his monitor.

"No ID!" Damen yelled and scanned the visual field outside the station.

"I've got three, no—five marks, coming in hot!" the ops head hollered.

"Ships? Get me an ID!" Janka demanded.

"Got two!" Damen replied. "Chekydran cruisers! Nothing on the other marks. Get station weapons online!"

Another alarm warbled through the operations center and Janka's office. Collision warning.

Damen swore.

"No response to hail!" a young woman bellowed. "No voice contact!"

"Biomech soldiers," Damen said, digging into the proximity sensors for a coded glimpse of the single-occupancy fighters. "It's a dual attack! Look for a mother ship! The fighters will land or 'port the occupants in! Stand by to repel boarders!"

"Chekydran and biomech soldiers attacking my station?" the guild mistress bellowed, her voice ringing over the room com. "This is your demonstration of goodwill, Eudal?"

"I am not so stupid that I would order an attack while I was on station," Gerriny Eudal snapped in reply.

"Collision! Two-minute warning!" Calmin yelled. "Current course, central docks."

Cold rage swept Damen. "Can we teleport the pilots out and use guns to deflect the ships?"

"Negative, Major!" the head of operations replied. "I'm reading a 'port jammer."

"Baxt'k," Damen and Janka said in unison.

"Damen?" flashed on his screen.

"Chekydran. And biomechs, like Kebgra."

"Why?" she typed.

"Don't know."

"Issue the recall. Let's get off this accursed station."

"How?"

"Here. Parameters set." She sent him into a file tree.

Damen studied the short program. It was an emergency transmission routine he'd set up when the guild had first locked down the freighter.

"Executing."

"Janka?" Damen said aloud. "The biomechs are Chekydran made."

"I have the file," the security man growled. "You gave it to me eight months ago."

"Face shots. They're landing."

"Secure my data banks!" the guild mistress commanded.

"I've got their ringleader backed into a corner," Damen replied. "And it's not the core, Janka. Stand by."

The deck beneath Damen's feet vibrated as station weapons came to life.

"Can you get to your ship?" Jayleia asked.

"What's your destination?"

"Safer if you don't know."

"Have to make it look like I'm working against you. Beating you."

"Lock me out of station. Blow dock clamps."

"Engines not powered?"

"Not yet."

Station guns fired. The consoles rattled.

"I'll find you. I love you." Grinning, not caring who saw, Damen dropped out of the ship system, back into the station tree before Jayleia could respond. He prayed with all his heart she'd responded. And would again when he met her on her mother's world. Where else would she go with an ore freighter full of his family?

He entered a swift clip of code, tucked it into the station security parameters, and executed the change. The computer access alerts ceased.

"Got them!" Damen crowed. "Going in for the kill."

The station guns fired again.

"Collision warning!" Calmin cried from ops. "All hands brace!"

"Recall, Janka! Recall. I've isolated the hackers. They're on the docks," Damen yelled.

The guild mistress and Janka began issuing demands and commands at the same time.

"Clear the com!" Damen bellowed over them. "They are locked out of your systems. I'm isolating them now. Let me do my job."

Silence.

"Of course, Major," the guild mistress said, her tone placating. "You have assured my faith in the alliance between the UMOPG and the Claugh nib Dovvyth."

"Assuming I'm not still under arrest, I'll be certain to tell Her Majesty so," he retorted as he surreptitiously flipped on the video feed monitoring the freighter. He could see Jayleia in her black and crimson uniform. That she waited at the hatch for the rest of his people to heed the retreat orders, he could guess.

As he watched, three teens scrambled up a rise, dragging a fourth, larger form between them. Damen bit back a curse.

Vala was down.

Jayleia bolted from the hatchway, swept the woman into her arms.

The teens sprinted into the ship. At the hatch, Jay lowered Vala to the decking.

Damen could see that Jayleia crouched beside Vala, but with her back to the camera, he couldn't tell what she'd done.

She rose slowly. Bent as if curled in upon herself, she turned and stumbled down the stairs, her arms wrapped tight around her middle.

Damen's heart stuttered.

Vala was dead.

Jayleia sat down hard on the dock floor and buried her masked face in her hands.

He ached to wrap her in his arms, to offer comfort, and to take comfort.

She looked up, shoving herself to unsteady feet as her head moved as if following something overhead. Leaving the shelter of the freighter, she spent several seconds fiddling with something out of camera range.

Damen bit his lip to keep from shouting at her to get back aboard.

She straightened, glanced back the way the kids had come, and ran for the hatch. Pausing half in, half out of the door, she slumped for a moment, then looked into the camera eye, brought the fingers of her right hand up, not to her forehead in mocking salute. Not this time. Instead, they stopped where her lips were hidden behind her mask. Then she tipped her fingers out, pointed at the camera.

Damen leaned in. Where had he seen that gesture . . . he remembered and warmed. She'd blown him a kiss.

Just before she pulled a gun and took three shots to blow out the camera.

"Baxt'k." Damen blinked, momentarily blinded by the flash.

"We've got them cornered!" Janka called.

"Aboard that dump of an ore freighter," Damen said. "I know. And your mystery woman, the one who attacked your security cordon is on board. If you have troops in the vicinity, pull them back."

"Not on your life!"

"I watched her arm a trap, Janka! Pull back! Now!"

"Sol! Fall back! Fall back!" Janka shouted.

"Intruder alert! Intruder alert!" Calmin screamed. "Weapons fire reported on dock ring D-sixty-four, C-eighty-two D . . ."

"Acknowledged! Acknowledged!" Janka shouted. "Seal the docks! Evacuate civilians! All available personnel! Full armor! Face shots only!"

Damen's heart kicked hard. The soldiers were on station. He had to get Jayleia off.

His vision cleared piecemeal, but he couldn't wait. He keyed deep into the system again, jockeying his way to docking control. Via Janka's open com channel, Damen heard something pop. Someone screamed. Another pop and a second voice joined in, shrill and terrified.

Damen began swearing in a steady stream. His pulse thundered in his ears and his breath came in shallow rasps. She hadn't killed anyone unnecessarily, had she? She wouldn't start now. She wouldn't.

On the other hand, Jay would give him ample reason to blow the dock locks, release the clamps, and make a show of assuming the freighter would simply float free in space until the UMOPG sent tugs to get it.

The station jerked and shuddered.

That felt like a direct hit on a station gun. One down, untold dead, five more guns to go.

For a split second, artificial gravity cut out and it felt like the station and everyone on it fell through the endless reaches of space.

Fire alarms wailed, sounding far away.

"Damage-assessment teams! Report to . . ."

Gravity slammed on.

He shut out the audio feed broadcasting fire, casualty, and damage reports. He didn't have time.

He redoubled his efforts. Jayleia and the remaining people who looked to him for protection were counting on him. The locks holding the freighter in place let go. Damen activated the emergency dock release. Charges fired simultaneously at each clamp, sending the dead-looking freighter away from the station.

"Gotcha," Damen said aloud for the benefit of his audience. "Do I send security tugs after them? Or do we blow them out of the sky with the remaining guns?"

"I want those thieves," Kannoi snarled, "begging for death in my interrogation room."

"Who the Hells are these people?" Janka ground out. "Medi team! Docking bay E-six. Three officers down! Ooze venom."

Ooze venom? Damen bit back a curse. Jay had turned a racial allergy into a weapon? No wonder she'd waited to the last minute to arm and spring that trap.

"They're neutralized and isolated aboard that freighter," Damen said to the room at large. "You can recover them at your leisure. Change your primary access codes to secure your systems from me."

"Thank you," Guild Mistress Kannoi said. "I am pleased."

"Ops to Major Sindrivik!" a trembling female voice rasped.

"Sindrivik, go ahead," he replied.

"The freighter has fired engines!"

CHAPTER
23

DAMEN bolted to standing, his hands flat on the panel. "You've had that ship in dock for months and you didn't deactivate the engines?"

"It was the first thing we did!" Janka protested.

"What the Three Hells is going on?" Damen demanded.

The guild mistress growled a curse. "Janka! Where are Vala and her brat? They will be my guests until Damen returns with those agents in custody."

"We're a little too busy to search the tunnels!" Janka retorted.

Damen closed his eyes to hide the emotion surging through him. Elation because his family wasn't on station to be held over his head any longer. Sorrow and regret at Vala's death. He hadn't loved her. He'd believed she hadn't loved him, even though she'd always welcomed him into her bed when he was on station. Until this trip. Until Jayleia had seen what he couldn't.

She'd rescued him and the people he'd sworn to protect.

He opened his eyes.

The guild had no idea what had been done to them.

He clenched his teeth and his hands to battle back the ingrained conditioning whispering to him that his loyalties were inextricably bound to his people and to this station.

No.

Not. Anymore.

Jayleia's blood ran in his veins now.

Damen forced a passably civil tone on his tongue. "How do you propose I retrieve them for you, Guild Mistress?"

"Your ship," she snapped. "Alert your commanders that you have been released from UMOPG custody, Major. I will not have it said that this government broke faith with a signed, sealed treaty."

Now that the Chekydran were pummeling the station? Convenient.

"Understood," he said, pulse hammering against the confines of his skin. "The *Kawl Fergus* has tow capacity. If I am required to blow their engines, I have teleport on board as well."

"Go," she ordered. "Should it occur to you to cross me, remember, when you report to your Empire, that the guild gives up nothing without gaining something in return. Your transfer to the Claugh nib Dovvyth came through me. Ask yourself what I profit by having insinuated you into their ranks. Bring the spies back alive and I'll trade you. Full disclosure for their rotting corpses in Janka's prison."

Chill fingers ripped through Damen's heart. Did that mean she had a data transmitter embedded in him somewhere? He'd seen one before, in Captain Ari Idylle. If TFC could plant listening devices inside a soldier's head, why couldn't his people do the same?

The hand he lifted to punch the com button for ops shook. "Sindrivik to ops."

"Ops! All due respect, Major," Calmin said, "I've got a real cravuul-dung storm here."

"Guild mistress's orders," he replied. "Single teleport to the cockpit of the *Kawl Fergus* and emergency clearance for immediate departure, please."

"Major . . ."

"Do it!" Kannoi snapped.

"Stand by to teleport," the ops head said.

"On your mark," Damen replied.

"On my mark, aye. Three, two, one, mark."

A moment's disorientation and Damen stood trembling in the cockpit of his ship. He leaped for the controls, slamming a sonic shield to life before unlocking his panels and firing his engines.

The com chirped.

"Ops to *Kawl Fergus*."

"*Kawl Fergus,* go ahead," Damen said.

"You are cleared for immediate departure. Transmitting tracking data on the freighter."

"Acknowledged. I am receiving."

"Clear skies, Major," Calmin replied.

The line died.

Depressurization warning lights flashed in the bay. Damen nudged his engine output. The *Kawl Fergus* rose.

The dock doors parted. It took every ounce of his control to keep from slamming through the slow moving barrier.

The lights flashing in the bay died. Clear skies. Except for two Chekydran and a biomech mother ship out there lurking behind who knew which moon or asteroid.

Engines to thirty.

The *Kawl Fergus* slipped out of Silver City and into space.

Damen brought up the tracking data for the ore freighter, set his shields to maximum, and throttled up. He couldn't follow Jay too closely without the risk of leading mercenaries and agents after her.

So many other captains had blown free of the station, the lanes were clogged with traffic. He had a legitimate excuse to power back and weave through the other vessels. Anyone trying to get a bead on him would have a difficult time keeping track of one small craft among the hundreds littering the lanes.

It took an hour of maneuvering, ramping speed, cutting back, dodging here, and ducking there, before he hit the outer beacon. The automated navigational buoy pinged his com.

He opened a line.

"Final tracking information, Major," Janka said. "Get those bastards and do it now."

Damen fired his interstellar drive in answer. The shrill of the warming engine drowned out anything more Janka might have said.

Damen forced himself to double-check his navigational data. The nav system chimed. Course laid and locked.

He engaged the drive.

He was free.

Because of Jayleia.

Because of her foolish gesture with a vial of blood and because of her warrior's heart that wouldn't let her leave his family behind.

Except for Vala. Whose fault was it that she was dead? His? Vala's? Certainly not Jayleia's.

Damen engaged the autopilot, surged to his feet, and stumbled to his cabin.

He should be searching for and eliminating the listening devices the guild had planted aboard his ship. He needed to report in and warn his commanders that per the guild mistress's own words, he might be compromised.

Instead, queasy with emotions he couldn't name digging their jagged hooks into his flesh and pulling, he went straight to the shower, turned on the unit, and slumped as the cleansers sluiced over him.

CHAPTER
24

JAYLEIA strode into the Temple's official audience hall, kicking the diaphanous layers of her gem-encrusted, silver skirt out of her way. Ceremonial robes had always been her least favorite Temple attire.

Early morning sunlight washed the rough stone and polished wood of the room in gold.

"You're late," the high priestess of the Temple noted in a sharp voice.

"I had good reason," Jay said, slinging a bag strap from her shoulder. She set the bag at the foot of the dais where Tiassale, the high priestess, sat wrapped in the silver blue robes of her office, her long brown hair twisted into intricate braids piled high atop her head.

The contents of the pack clanked.

The woman lifted an eyebrow. "Good reason? So you've always said, yet your excuses have always been found wanting."

"Only by you," Jay shot.

"Given that I speak with the voice of the Temple in all things," Tiassale said, a hint of a sneer in her tone, "my opinion is the only one that matters. Give me one good reason not to have you executed."

Jayleia pulled her lips back into the smile that wasn't a smile, the one Damen had taught her. "You'd break my mother's heart and destroy her legacy."

Tiassale smirked. "You've never been slow to cash in on your mother's good name and hard work."

"And you've never hesitated to flat-out lie in your quest to rob my mother of her rightful place as high priestess of this Temple," Jayleia retorted, fists clenched.

Biting back a curse, she rubbed her forehead. A single day on Temple grounds and she'd reverted to acting like an angry, wronged teenager. After six years away, couldn't she at least pretend she could identify a lost cause when she had her nose rubbed in it?

"Enough," she grumbled. Was there an opposite of homesickness? What should she call the pinching sensation telling her she simply didn't fit into her mother's world anymore? Had she ever? "You have the position you wanted so badly. Say whether the Temple will give refuge to the people I brought."

Tiassale sat back in her chair, her rage-twisted expression smoothing out a piece at time. "This Temple exiled you for your crimes six years ago."

Jayleia snorted in derision, but did it softly. She had nothing to gain by pointing out she hadn't been the only guilty one six years ago. "Yes, it did."

"What possessed you to return clad in the uniform you were forbidden to wear?"

Jayleia threw her arms wide. The bells tied to the ends of her hair chimed. "Two governments and a network of traitors seem to think I'm the key to finding my father. In the midst of their agents and mercenaries trying to capture or kill me, I ended up with a ship full of abused men, women, and children. Where else could I take them where they would be accepted, welcomed, and nurtured?"

"It didn't matter to you that by our laws you could be executed for returning?" Tiassale pressed.

"Of course it mattered," she retorted. "The UMOPG intended to

use those people as leverage in the interrogation of a spy. I didn't
have the luxury of saving my skin at the expense of their lives."

"No. I don't suppose you did," Tiassale mused, studying her for
several seconds, before she gestured at the bag on the floor between
them. "What is that?"

"Silver City's data store," Jay replied. "There's indication that the
guild is building a standing military."

"What?"

Jay nodded. "The Claugh nib Dovvyth sent an agent to retrieve
the data. I assume they want to understand what a UMOPG mobilization means, as it appears to predate the war with the Chekydran.
Their agent was captured. I completed the mission in his stead."

"You believe the information you carry impacts the war with
the Chekydran as well as detailing the UMOPG's true motivations?"
Tiassale guessed, a troubled light in her eyes. "If you are correct,
danger follows your prize."

"Agreed. If you will accept the refugees, I will transport the data
off planet until I can safely entrust it to my father and the leader of
the Murbaasch Tu."

Tiassale shot her a sharp look. "You truly have no idea where
your father is?"

"I have ideas," Jayleia said, "but I'm watched too closely to act
on them. I wish I could. I'd have my life back."

"I wonder."

Jayleia snapped to attention, dismay flooding her at the grim tone
of Tiassale's voice.

The priestess met her eye. "First, I have no further information
regarding your father. Your files are as up to date as my own. This
bodes well."

"He hasn't been captured," Jay concluded, relief easing a fraction
of her concern.

"Precisely. Second, a representative of the Claugh nib Dovvyth
government has arrived on planet with clearances granted by someone within TFC. He comes flying an alliance flag."

Jay swallowed a curse.

TFC and the Claugh nib Dovvyth boasted a marginal alliance. But that was for the war against the Chekydran. The concept of working together was too new, too unsettling for the alliance to mean anything more than sharing a few wartime dispatches and enemy positions.

"They believe they can infiltrate the Temple so easily?" Jayleia growled.

Tiassale smiled. "Your concern for the sanctity of the Temple is heartening. You'll be relieved to hear I can't kill you."

Jayleia lifted her brows.

"You stand relieved of duty to the lives you pledged to protect. The Temple has offered asylum to the refugees you brought to safety," she said. "We will train them."

Relief burned through Jay, weakening her limbs, and setting prickles at the backs of her eyes. She could put down that particular burden. "Thank you. Most of these people are Autken. They don't define family via bloodlines, like we do. They split along lines of alliance and loyalty."

"And they mature sexually far earlier than our species. We will adapt. So will they."

"High Priestess?" Jayleia recognized her mother's voice behind her.

"Ah. Margol. Come in," Tiassale commanded, straightening.

Heart lifting, Jay turned as her mother strode into the hall. The silver-haired woman took her hand in greeting.

"Mother." She kissed her mother's hand, wondering how she'd missed noticing how frail the woman had begun to look.

Jayleia saw the khaki uniform in the doorway before a tendril of awareness wrapped around her. Her heart and respiration rate increased. She imagined she could detect a hint of green growing things and fresh spring rain. Heat rushed into the center of her body.

"High Priestess, Jayleia," Margol said, "may I present Major Damen Sindrivik?"

Jubilation fired through Jayleia, head to toe. Dizzy with fierce, ridiculous hope, she spun. He'd said he loved her. She knew, logically, that it was because of her blood. He'd had no choice in the matter, had he?

Her heart didn't seem to care. It pounded against the inside of her ribs. Maybe she should be mortified by how desperately she wanted his "I love you" to be true.

A cool, remote Claugh nib Dovvyth officer stalked the Temple floor. He drew even with her and nodded to Tiassale.

"High Priestess," he said. "Her Majesty, Queen Eilod Saoyrse extends her compliments and thanks you for your gracious hospitality in receiving her duly appointed representative. I, personally, thank you for the care you've given my family."

"You're the agent TFC tried to plant on Swovjiti?" Jay marveled, swallowing a laugh.

Damen turned a frankly appraising and appreciative stare her way. He drew a deep breath as if scenting her.

"Jayleia, Twelve Gods, you are beautiful," he murmured.

The assault on her senses redoubled. She stiffened her spine and tamped down on the powerful impulse to throw herself into his arms.

Tiassale's gaze moved between them, her eyes narrowed. "I am interested in knowing which branch of our government dared offer you a diplomatic clearance, Major."

Damen returned his attention to the priestess. "My commanders wondered the same thing, madam. Our people are at work untangling the encrypted file origination tracers."

"My money is on Gerriny Eudal," Jayleia muttered.

Tiassale shifted, drawing Jay's gaze. "Do not make the mistake of believing the lieutenant director of Intelligence Command is your sole, or even your worst, enemy."

"Too many empire-building games are being played by too many people, too highly placed within the government," Jayleia's mother agreed. "Gerriny Eudal is a psychopath, but he may simply be the most visible of our worries."

"Major Damen Sindrivik," Tiassale said, "what is your purpose on Swovjiti?"

"A twofold recovery mission, madam," he replied. "Her Majesty requests Jayleia Durante's presence, along with the data store taken from Silver City."

"Am I under arrest?" Jayleia inquired. Her blood ran hot at the avid smile Damen turned upon her.

"Are you fond of neural cuffs, then?" he asked.

"I recall that ended badly for you," she said, grinning.

"I learn from my mistakes."

"I perceive that the Temple need not extend an offer of sanctuary to Jayleia," Tiassale noted, her tone sour. "However, three matters of interest to the Temple remain."

Alarms fired off in Jayleia's head, yanking her attention back to the woman on the dais.

"The accolade of the Temple is yours by right of battle," the high priestess said, her expression stony and her gaze focused over Jayleia's head.

Her mother gasped.

Jayleia gaped. She'd have rank in the Temple, a voice among her mother's people once more. She'd have the right to wear the uniform she'd put on to save Damen's life. Why would the priestess even consider. . . "Tiassale, I thought you hated me."

"I do. You are a thief, a harlot, a half-breed . . ."

"That didn't take long."

". . . and a disgrace to this Temple. But your mother is a much valued elder whose worth to the people is beyond measure. Nor can I overlook the fact that you have single-handedly brought over fifty abused and malnourished men, women, and mostly children to sanctuary," Tiassale said.

"It was hardly single-handed. Their rescue was an intricate plan with many pieces," Jayleia countered.

Tiassale awarded her a hard stare. "Do you deny that the plans had been in place for months prior to your arrival? Or that you took it upon yourself to alter those plans because of the immediate threat?"

"No." Jay blinked, taken aback both by Tiassale's knowledge of circumstances and by her judgment. She gathered that Damen's people had been talking her up.

She also noted that Damen watched her, pride glowing in his face. His admiration reached something deep inside her. She'd spent so many years refusing to strive for anyone's approval, yet she'd won his esteem merely by acting on her convictions.

The priestess looked away. "Perhaps, then, you have learned something of worth in exile."

Fortified by Damen's regard, Jayleia studied the woman. "More than you believe. Tiassale Gorn, I pledge my service as one of the trained to the precepts of the Temple and to the directives of their appointed guardian."

Her mother laughed in pleased surprise and squeezed her hand.

"Well played," Damen murmured for her ears only.

The stunned light in Tiassale's eye heartened Jay. One should always endeavor to surprise the enemy and regardless of the civility of the conversation, she knew full well Tiassale would rather knife her in the back than offer up the accolades of the Temple. That she had done the latter led Jayleia to believe they could at least work together.

"Three things you said, High Priestess?" Jayleia prompted, feeling more at ease in the Temple than she could ever remember.

"The woman Vala," Tiassale said, looking uncertain.

Sorrow bumped Jayleia out of her euphoria.

"She died while under your command."

"Yes."

Her mother's hand tightened on hers to the point of pain.

"Then, by the law of the Temple," Tiassale said, "the child, Bellin, is your responsibility, your son-by-right."

"What?" Damen snapped.

"No," Jayleia said.

Tiassale's eyes widened.

"You refuse . . ." her mother gritted.

"No!" Jayleia exclaimed, her voice ringing through the room. "Major Sindrivik is Bellin's father."

She turned to face Damen, tugging free of her mother's grasp. The pain shadowing his eyes wrung her heart dry.

"It's our way," she said. "When a warrior falls in battle, her commander adopts her children, sees to their welfare and their training. I'd be honored to do this for Bellin, for Vala, and for you, but he is your blood kin. I don't have the right."

She heard her mother catch a trembling breath.

Damen's gaze darted over her shoulder at her mother. He frowned, the lines of conflicted feeling deepening around his mouth.

"My heart has ached for a grandchild," her mother breathed, tears in her voice. She stepped in beside Jayleia to face him. "But not like this, never at the expense of a woman's life. Bellin is your son, Major. What arrangements would you make for his care?"

Damen met Jayleia's gaze, grief and confusion fighting for dominance in his face. As if on impulse, he brushed her cheek.

Jay tried to steel herself. It didn't work. She leaned into the stroke and the air rushed from her lungs. One of the ridiculous bells in her hair chimed.

Damen's troubled expression eased. "Bellin aspires to a career with the Murbaasch Tu."

"Wise child. Intelligence Command is an unhealthy career choice at present," Margol observed.

"You would entrust him to Madam Durante's care?" he asked, offering Jayleia a tremulous smile.

Her heart started beating again. "Yes."

He nodded. "Until my life would no longer endanger his, it would please me to have him sheltered in your family. He should have the opportunity to grow up as strong and as honorable as you have."

Honorable? Pleasure twined around her heart.

"Mother? Will you train Bellin?"

Her mother froze for a moment, not even breathing. When she spoke, her words were thick with emotion. "It would be my honor. I will guard Bellin with my life."

Jay closed her burning eyes and smiled.

CHAPTER
25

Jayleia's mother clapped her hands. "It is your birthday, my dear, yet it is you and Major Sindrivik who give me the greatest of gifts. Dare I hope for another?"

"What?" Jayleia squawked, eyes snapping open. She'd known her birthday was imminent, but with diseased kuorl, healing trances, and plotting an exit off of Silver City, she'd managed to lose track of the exact day of the week.

"I perceive the Keeping of the Calendar isn't among your devotions," Tiassale said. "Remedy that."

Her twenty-sixth birthday, the day her oath of celibacy expired and the day her mother's people expected her to pick a man to father the next generation of warriors. After all these years away, after so much careful planning to be on the opposite side of the galaxy on her birthday, preferably elbow deep in some deadly outbreak somewhere, she'd ended up where she had least wanted to be. And she had no one to blame but herself.

"This brings us to the third and final matter of interest to the Temple," Tiassale said. "You are bound, by your duty to the Temple and to your Lady Mother. Is this man your choice?"

She could admit to herself that she wanted him. Badly. But he deserved the chance to make his own choice.

"Major Sindrivik doesn't understand our . . ."

"My brother then," she said, her tone arch.

"Over my dead body," Jayleia growled.

Tiassale smiled, the first Jay had ever seen on her face that overtook her entire countenance. "Something that could be so easily arranged. Or did you mean to betray your oath of loyalty so soon after uttering it?"

Damen's lazy smile when he looked at her sent a ripple of heat down Jayleia's spine.

He traced a hand down her bare arm. "Your oath of celibacy ends today, doesn't it? Your mother made a point of telling me."

"Twelve Gods," she groaned, recalling his comment aboard the *Kawl Fergus* about not being safe from him. Could she admit she'd gotten damned tired of safe?

"You do have a choice in this," she said.

"But you don't," he surmised.

"No."

Damen's expression hardened to cold Isarrite as he looked between the high priestess and Jayleia. "She would give you her brother? The one who raped you seven years ago?"

She gaped at him, heart in her throat. "W-what?"

He took her by the shoulders. "You are a smart, strong, lethal woman. Why would you let someone hurt you?"

Tiassale laughed, spite turning her voice shrill.

Damen snarled.

The woman fell silent.

"I was young and naïve." Jayleia choked on humiliation. She had to clear her throat to continue. "I'd been using my training to steal things."

"No," Damen said. "I broke the sealed file your high priestess hid so carefully. Your males take items of value from the women they wish to bed and ransom those items for sex. Recovering what someone else had stolen doesn't make you a thief."

Some of the shame cleared Jay's system. She blinked up at him.

He nodded encouragement, his bracing touch warming her courage.

"Say it," he urged. "Tell me you were raped."

"I wasn't," she said. "Call it extortion, maybe. Tiassale's brother realized what I was doing. I let him convince me that he wanted me, that if I slept with him, everything would be forgotten. I'd give up recovering stolen items. He'd forget he'd ever seen anything incriminating and no one ever need know."

"He raped you and then turned you in anyway?" Damen rumbled, baring his teeth.

"It wasn't pleasant," she confessed, "but I upheld my part of the bargain. When I found him bragging that he'd turned me into his whore, I broke his nose and one leg. Mother lost her position in the Temple and her title. I was exiled."

Damen's breath went out in a rush. "I'll kill him for you."

"He fights like a girl," Jayleia said. His outrage on her behalf felt like a shield, something protecting her. "Not worth your time."

"That—" Tiassale began.

"You have said enough on this subject over the years!" Margol thundered.

Shock froze Jayleia's breath. Why hadn't her mother risen to her defense before now? Her mother would have retained her position, her title—Jayleia's thoughts skidded to a halt. She eyed her mother, suspicion chilling her. If she'd spoken in Jayleia's defense six years ago, she'd have remained weighed down by her responsibilities as the Temple's high priestess.

"Jayleia isn't the first warrior with the entrepreneurial spirit to misuse her ability. She won't be the last. You haven't exiled the others," her mother noted.

Tiassale drew herself up, eyes flashing. "She was banished because . . ."

"Your brother earned his results, and you're a bigot?" Jayleia offered.

"No. She's afraid. Of you," Damen countered, his head cocked and his nostrils flaring as if testing the air.

Jayleia blinked. *Afraid?* That made no sense. Hate, yes. Afraid? She shook off the chill seeping through her gut. Hate made people nasty. Fear made them vicious.

She glanced at her mother. "You could have said something like this before I was exiled, Mother."

Her mother returned her gaze with a placid expression and unreadable smile. "I had my reasons."

"Care to share them?"

"No."

"You used me? Thanks."

Her mother chuckled.

Amusement threaded through Damen's voice. "I thought Autken mating rituals were strange. I blundered into a trap, didn't I?"

Jayleia met his gaze. "Yes."

He eyed her up and down, humor crinkling the corners of his heated gray eyes. "Given the bait, who can blame me? I accept."

Jayleia's heart squeezed hard.

Damen wrapped her hand in his.

"One final question," Jayleia's mother said. "The council of elders has interviewed the evacuees."

Jay nodded.

Her mother raised a silver eyebrow. "Have you destroyed the threat to their lives as is your duty?"

"That's my job," Damen countered.

Jayleia bared her teeth in a bloodthirsty parody of a grin. "Too late. I've already begun the process."

Interest and a spark of amusement lit her mother's dark brown eyes.

Alarms rent the morning.

"Report!" Tiassale shouted into her wrist com.

A shriek of engines cleaving the atmosphere rose above the Planetary Defense alarms. Jayleia recognized the sound. The distant thunderclap of weapons' fire made it clear.

Swovjiti was under attack.

"Biomechs," Jay bit out, her voice shaking with equal parts rage and fear. "How many ships?"

"Unknown! Reports are still arriving," the high priestess replied. "You know these attackers?"

"The massacre on Kebgra," Jayleia answered.

Tiassale shot her a glare filled with accusation and loathing. "You dare bring those abominations upon us?"

"Get us off planet," Damen said. "The traitors obviously know Jayleia is here."

Jay's heart leaped to her throat and she spun for the doorway.

"It is a ruse to flush you from the Temple," her mother said. "The people working against your father cannot reach you within the walls of the Temple. They know this and must resort to butchery in hopes of driving you into the open."

Breathing hard, trembling with the rush of fight-or-flight chemicals, Jay stared at her mother. Who seemed to know more than she'd let on about who might be working against her father.

"It's damned effective!" Jayleia said. "The vows you drilled into my head all my life don't permit me to sit in safety while innocents are threatened or killed."

"Jayleia!" Damen snapped. "Reunion when you aren't a target! Where'd you hide the data?"

She growled at him.

He grinned. "Hold that thought."

Her knees went weak. Gritting her teeth, she turned and grabbed the pack of data chips.

"Get us out of here," Damen commanded. "I won't have it said that the Claugh nib Dovvyth handed Swovjiti's high priestess and her council to the traitors."

"We'll need teleport!" Jay hollered.

"Teleport from here to where?" Tiassale demanded.

"The *Kawl Fergus*!" Damen said. "Swovjiti Space Port."

"Mother!" Jayleia said. "Teleport home. When we reach the *Kawl Fergus*, I'll establish a com link with you . . ."

"I am watched here, Jayleia, by agents I can't identify! My lines aren't secure." She pulled up short, eyeing the resolute expression Jay could feel on her face. "You're counting on that, aren't you? Very well. Tiassale? Will you authorize my teleport?"

"Planetary Defense is standing by," the high priestess replied. "Go."

"I have the data," Jayleia said to Damen as teleport distortion warped the sound waves in the room.

Her mother vanished. The space between Jayleia's shoulder blades itched as if expecting laser fire to rip through the hall at any moment. She hadn't heard another flyby. Did the relative quiet mean soldiers were already on the ground murdering people in an effort to find her?

"Inform all personnel that the soldiers can be destroyed by shots to the face!" Damen instructed the priestess.

Another buzzer shrilled through the stone hall.

Jayleia jumped. The Temple had been targeted.

Tiassale, pale, her lips tight with rage, shouted, "Teleport! Remove these monstrosities from my planet!"

Damen leaped up the dais and yanked Tiassale down beside Jayleia.

The priestess yelped.

He grabbed her wrist and shouted into her com, "The high priestess is in danger! She teleports with us! Three plus equipment to teleport! Now!"

An explosion rocked the Temple.

Teleport distortion grabbed Jayleia as the stone and wood above her head erupted in a shower of sparks and deadly bolts of plasma. Then it vanished along with all sensation.

She winked back into existence and fell flat on her face, black hair pooling in her line of sight, the bag of data chips a hard lump beneath her ribs.

A shout and the sound of weapons whipped from holsters brought her rolling to her feet, her ceremonial skirts tangling momentarily around her legs. She flung hair out of her face, bells chiming.

"Release the priestess!" a man commanded.

"Hold!" Tiassale countered, her voice shaking. She climbed to her feet with Damen's assistance. Her braids had come loose. Three drooped over one ear. She seemed not to notice. "The major saved my life."

Damen opened his hands, freeing Tiassale.

The Planetary Defense staff lowered their weapons.

"Complete teleport," Tiassale ordered.

The soldiers scrambled to their stations. "High Priestess? If you will step out of the incident field?"

Tiassale rounded the control panel. "Clear skies, Major. Jayleia."

At least the second wave of teleport distortion didn't drop her on her face. They materialized in the entry corridor of the *Kawl Fergus*.

"Secure the data!" Damen dashed for the cockpit. "This jump is going to be hard, fast, and dirty."

"Never had a better offer," she quipped.

It sounded like Damen choked on a laugh as he woke the systems.

"Open a channel to my mother!" she yelled, stifling a grin.

"Connecting," he replied, then said, "Madam Durante? You have Bellin in your care?"

"I do," Jay heard her mother reply, sounding tinny over the com connection.

Jayleia pounced on a familiar-looking pack lying against the door. Someone had teleported her belongings.

"May I speak with him?" Damen asked.

"Go ahead. You will have to do the talking," her mother said. "The child has not spoken a word since . . ."

"I understand," Damen interrupted. "Bellin, it's Damen. Major Sindrivik."

"Are you coming to get me?" Bellin demanded.

Jayleia rolled her eyes as the engines grumbled to life beneath her feet. Of course the boy would speak to Damen. They were family.

She fished through her pack for the metal crystal tube Bellin had given her aboard Silver City, leaped to her feet, and ran for the cockpit.

"It isn't safe," Damen answered. "We're under attack and I have a mission for you."

Jay collapsed into the navigation seat and planted the bag of data chips between her feet.

"A mission? Sir?"

"Do you remember the Shollen Family Mission?"

"Yeah!"

"Can you do it again, here?" Damen asked.

"Yes, sir!"

"Good man. I'll expect your report when I see you next."

Smiling, Damen cast Jayleia a glance. He muted the com line when she lifted an eyebrow at him.

"Bellin has a nose for spies," he said. "He'll ID every mole on Swovjiti if your mother will let him."

"They'll make a good team," she said, smiling.

At her nod, he opened the channel again.

Yanking restraints into place, she addressed the open com line. "Mother, we're lifting."

"We have word of attacks in every major Temple city. Casualties are mounting, but the creatures are being driven back under the combined force of Planetary Defense and Swovjiti Temple ranks. Tell no one your destination. Seek refuge someplace that knows how to deal with these monsters. It's what your father would want," her mother said, her words hurried.

Jayleia sat bolt upright. Another coded message? Tahem had said, "Don't let the past dictate what you could become." Now her mother?

Jay shook her head. She couldn't work out what any of it meant.

CHAPTER
26

DAMEN glanced at Jayleia's nonplussed expression and frowned.

"What is it?" he murmured.

She shook her head, the lost light in her eyes driving apprehension through his chest. "I think my mother just tried to tell me where my father is and I have no idea . . ."

Alarms rang through the cockpit.

Swearing, he closed the com line and silenced the proximity warning. Lights flashed across the panels.

Jayleia turned to the weapons station. "They're on us. We're in their sights."

"I see it," he replied, scanning the takeoff instructions coming in from Planetary Defense. "Hang on. I'm being instructed to burn off planet."

Jay met his glance, her eyes wide.

The *Kawl Fergus*'s interstellar drive would fry anyone or anything within one hundred meters of the ship's exhaust port and leave a trail of radioactive particles in the atmosphere. For that reason alone, it was illegal throughout the known systems except in extreme emergencies.

"Planetary Defense authorized that?" she marveled.

"I'll aim for a few biomech fighters as we fire out." Damen slammed the atmospherics to full power, eyeing the swarm of fighters speeding for their position.

The *Kawl Fergus* lurched into the sky.

Fighting the g-forces mashing him into his seat, he waited for the brief lull indicating they'd maxed out acceleration with the atmospherics. He activated the shields and hit the emergency start on his interstellar drive.

The plates beneath his feet shuddered and the drive shrilled awake with bone-rattling force.

Weapons fire jolted the ship. The view screen flared as the plasma bolts went wide.

Damen bared his teeth in a feral grin.

The *Kawl Fergus* slammed through the sound barrier. Heat built in the cabin as the friction of atmosphere resisting their ascent tested the integrity of the reentry shielding. Excruciating weight crushed the breath from Damen's chest. He didn't black out, but for a few long seconds, he wished he could.

The biomech fighters on their tail kept pace, but couldn't close the distance. With the fighters at or near the limit of their weapons' range, Damen had no trouble throwing the *Kawl Fergus* out of the way of the few shots aimed at them.

Gradually, the pressure eased, the cockpit cooled, and he could move again. They'd left Swovjiti behind, but not the fighters.

Damen hissed and wondered how far the little ships could follow. No one knew enough about the hybrid TFC/Chekydran tech to have range information on the vessels. At least they'd stopped firing. Conserving energy?

Someone had changed the rules of the game by sending the Chekydran-built soldiers after Jayleia. He gathered that she'd been reclassified from information source to deadly threat. Why?

Had she recognized the shift?

He glanced at her. She returned his grim look, released her re-

ENEMY GAMES 197

straints, and pushed herself to standing. "Need my handheld. I can't read the panels."

He watched her stride out of the cockpit into the corridor, her glittering skirts swaying. She was his. All he needed was open sky, no one shooting, and the leisure to show her in detail. His pulse sped.

She returned wearing an oxygen generator.

"Jay?"

"My physiology doesn't handle the stresses of takeoff as easily as yours," she said as she sat. "Minor hypoxia. It won't take long to clear my system."

She'd already activated her handheld and linked into the weapons panel.

"Mother ship on long range," she said.

The claxon warbled. Damen swore and shut it off. "Keep your eyes on. Given the size of the attack force on planet, I'd expect more. They may try to box us in."

"We can't outrun them?"

"Damn it. I need that crystal," he muttered, scanning for potential hiding places.

Jayleia shot him a penetrating look and tucked hair behind one ear as she scanned the floor. She scooped up a metal tube and presented it to him.

"Tahem gave it back," she said. "Coded to you."

He took it and spared a glance at his panels. The clump of fighters had managed to close by a few kilometers. One mother ship registered at the edge of long range, along with a few commercial freighters.

He opened the tube. The milky, opaque crystal slid into his palm. He frowned. "Why?"

"Tahem gave it to Bellin," Jay replied, staring at the crystal, her brow furrowed as if in concentration. "He'd said, 'You're going to need this.'"

She frowned. "He had to have given the crystal to Bellin after he had us arrested."

"Which makes you think he counted on our escape," Damen said.

"He'd provided intel on the crystals. Admiral Seaghdh had me run a joint mission, me on recon and recovery, Tahem on analysis."

We must have been compromised and the games to mislead us in his cabin were his way of mitigating damage."

"I don't see how," Jayleia grumbled.

Damen stared at her. "He knew you, knew what you could do."

"He also knew I'd been kicked out of the Temple seven years ago," she protested. "He had no way of knowing I'd stayed in practice. He gambled your life on me."

Elation filled his chest, crowding out breath. "You said he loves me."

"He does."

"Would he have gambled with my life unless he'd looked in your eyes and decided it was a very safe bet?"

She blinked, looking stunned as a tremulous smile spread on her face.

Damen grinned.

"No need to look so smug," she said, "there's still the question of how Trente and Edie knew where to find us."

"You think Tahem told them?"

She shook her head. "He would have to have known that they were on our side. He'd have to have known they'd come from my mother . . ."

"He already knew about your father's disappearance."

"I know. What the Hells is going on?"

"We're getting out of here so we can find out without getting shot out of the sky," Damen replied, jumping to his feet, and tearing for the engine. He tossed engine covers open and dropped into the compartment.

"Second mother ship!" Jayleia yelled.

The proximity alarm fired. Damen heard a sound like a fist landing on a panel. The alarm died.

"Much closer! She was using the Lunar Agro Platform for cover."

Growling low in his throat, Damen set the crystal into place, grabbed a screwdriver from the tool set in the compartment to tighten it down, then yanked his handheld from his belt with one hand and put the screwdriver back with the other. It took interminable seconds to initialize his handheld and link into the engine interface.

Damen routed the plasma flow through the crystal.

The stone cleared and flared to gleaming life.

The *Kawl Fergus* surged.

In the cockpit, Jayleia whooped. "Ha! Cross everyone but mother two off the 'on our tail' list."

"Distance?"

"Twenty-six thousand kilometers and closing," she called. "Coming in on a trajectory intersecting ours."

"On my way!" he yelled.

Something buzzed in the cockpit. Target warning. The mother ship was lining them up for a shot. From so far away?

He barreled into the cockpit and threw himself into his chair.

"Changing course to match," he said. "Watch the distance."

The star field swung.

"Run us off a few degrees," Jayleia advised.

He nodded. So the mother ship couldn't drive them straight into a waiting trap. A few degrees off course translated to hundreds of kilometers over distance. It would give them time to react.

"Too bad I can't get a crystal like that integrated with sensors," she quipped, removing her oxygen generator and dropping it into the equipment pouch on her chair. "Or weapons. Or the onboard computers. If that crystal could boost processing and data storage the way it boosts engines . . ."

Scientists.

"Jay. Distance?"

She shook her head. The bells tied to her braids chimed. "We've put a thousand kilometers on them. That's all."

He glanced at his handheld, then back at her. "V'kyrri recommended keeping particle flow through the crystal at a trickle. He had concerns about the structural integrity of the stone and the damage it would do to the *Kawl Fergus* if it blew in contact with the engine feed."

The proximity alert fired again.

They spun to their respective panels. Two more mother ships.

"Twelve Gods!" Jayleia yelled. She slammed a fist down on the button to silence the alarm. "How many ships do they have out here trying to murder one person? Unless . . ."

He cast quick looks at her face, uneasiness boiling up within his gut.

"This is it," she said, her tone dead. "What if this was Eudal's plan? Neutralize and discredit my dad. Then eradicate the Swovjiti warriors, the last remaining dedicated force within the confederation with the will and the unswerving loyalty to rise up and oppose the overthrow of the Tagreth Federated Council. The soldiers weren't after me. They were sent to destroy the Temple."

"They were failing," Damen said, closing a hand around her arm. "Your mother said they were being driven back. We pulled an entire squadron and three mother ships away from the planet."

"Increase the power to that crystal," she instructed. "If we survive, make for the *Dagger*. The traitors believe I'm a threat worth killing for? Let's find out why. Maybe Ari and Seaghdh can think of something I haven't."

Damen released her and altered course again, diving out of the snare set for them.

The ships opened fire.

He bared his teeth in a silent snarl. *Ah. Didn't like that move? Desperation from their tormenters, at last? Good.*

The *Kawl Fergus* bounced as energy bolts sprayed past.

"Increasing particle flow by five percent," he said.

The engine pitch changed.

"Distance to mother two still twenty-seven thousand kilometers. No. Twenty-seven five."

Another barrage of slow-moving weapons fire rattled the ship.

"Distance to the noose, twenty-nine thousand kilometers," Jayleia said.

"Another five percent?"

"Being vaporized by a plasma burst would be better than ending up in Chekydran captivity," she countered.

Damen couldn't smile at her dry tone. He'd seen firsthand the horrific damage the Chekydran did to the humanoids they captured. She was right. He nudged the particle flow.

The interstellar drive howled. Consoles shook. The deck plates clattered. Damen's teeth vibrated in sympathy with his ship. Adrenaline flooded his blood, shooting his heart rate to a painful gallop. Too fast. The *Kawl Fergus* couldn't handle the stress.

He stabbed at his handheld. Miss. Concentrating, he poised to try again.

Jayleia caught his wrist in her hand.

He glanced at her and squinted. It didn't help. She seemed to be synced to a different vibration frequency than he was. That she held up her other hand in a command to wait a moment, he could make out.

Most disconcerting to him was that she seemed not to be troubled by the energy trying to shake the *Kawl Fergus* apart.

"Now!" she shouted, releasing him. The sound distorted as if her voice couldn't find a place to fit into the cabin air.

Damen tried to hit his handheld and failed.

Jay turned, watched him for a split second, then latched on to his wrist to guide him.

Hull stress chimes sounded as if from very far away.

He shut his eyes.

She pushed.

He obeyed. His fingertips connected with the handheld screen. Already entering the power down commands, Damen opened his eyes.

The *Kawl Fergus* dropped out of the odd asynchronous vibration. Metal creaked and popped. The engine quieted. The hull stress alarm cut off mid-chime.

Jayleia, breathing as if she'd run a race, stared at him, elation in her wide, sparkling eyes. "Over two and a half times your engine's top speed rating."

"What?" Damen whispered, staggered.

A grin grew on her face. She nodded. "Forget about being followed or tracked, much less captured."

He pounced on his panel. "Changing course. Give me a long-range report. Where are we?"

"Nothing on long range," Jayleia replied. "We don't seem to be near the commercial traffic lanes. No buoys or aids to navigation."

"We'd been running for the border zone when mother two tried to intercept," he said, working the navigation console. He whistled. "We flat covered some space. I have a fix. Fifty-seven hours, give or take, we'll be in Claugh space."

"With or without tapping the crystal again?" she asked.

Damen shook his head and eyed her. "Without. I don't want to find out at what point the *Kawl Fergus* will break apart. That distortion didn't bother you?"

"It didn't seem to impact me the way it did you. Different species, different abilities," she said with a shrug. "We're still running faster than spec. Good. Even if we blunder into someone, we'd be gone before they could bring weapons to bear."

"Setting shields to standby," Damen said. "Enabling long-range alerts and engaging autopilot. We've earned some downtime."

CHAPTER

27

Downtime? Jayleia closed her eyes and propped her elbows on her knees, hands hanging, letting her hair fall, bells tinkling, to shield her from Damen's gaze. She had to resist the urge to grit her teeth.

"Jayleia. What's wrong?"

"It's all questions and no answers," she grumbled. "I have two code phrases that sound exactly like something my father would hand me to decrypt. Tahem saying, 'Don't let the past dictate what I could become' and my mother telling me to 'Go someplace that knows how to deal with these monsters.' Neither makes sense. I feel like I'm in the middle of an enormous puzzle with a pattern that keeps morphing and shifting under my feet. I can't help my father. I don't know what made me think I could.

"We have a crystal jammed into the matter injector on your engine, and granted, it saved our asses, but we don't even know what it is!"

"Jayleia," Damen said, wrapping his hands around her wrists. "Look at me."

She met his hooded gaze.

"How do you resolve roadblocks when you're working research aboard the *Sen Ekir*?"

"I train."

His eyes lit with interest. "Train?"

She shrugged. "My aunt, Raj's mother, sent me training holos. She insisted I wouldn't be exiled forever."

A dead sexy smile touched his lips. "You require physical distraction to give your brain the time to fit puzzle pieces together?"

"I suppo—" she began and froze.

Twelve Gods.

He was stalking her.

Hot blood fluttered low in her abdomen. She broke eye contact. Not that it helped. She found herself staring at his luscious smile.

He fingered one of the bells tied into her hair.

Jay caught in a breath at the electric sensation and at the look of transfixed delight on his face.

"You picked me," he noted. The combination of teasing and deadly velvet in his voice shot a heady mix of hormones into her belly. "Why?"

"You won. I can admit that you make me feel things I didn't know were possible for humanoid physiology," she breathed, knowing she was handing him a potent weapon. Her heart raced. She wanted to know sooner rather than later whether he intended to use it against her.

He growled. In a blinding move that left her dizzy, he scooped her out of her chair into his lap.

Blood thundering in her ears, she struggled against his hold only to realize that's all it was. She wasn't trapped.

"You're mine. We both win. Let me show you." He stroked her hair.

She squeezed her eyes shut. Heat rippled through her.

Damen wrapped his arms around her, and tucked her head beneath his chin. Warmth radiated from his body, urging her to relax.

"You aren't as contact shy as Captain Idylle was after she'd been released by the Chekydran," he noted, splaying his fingers over the skin bared at her waist by her dress. "But you mistrust what you feel as much as she ever did."

Heat suffused Jay at the pressure of his nails drawn tauntingly over her flank. She gasped.

"We'll work on that," he promised. He hooked an arm under her knees and rose.

"No!" she rasped, stiffening.

He met her gaze with eyebrows raised as he carried her out of the cockpit and down the corridor to his cabin.

"No?" he challenged.

Jayleia thumped the heel of her hand to the center of his chest.

He grunted and chuckled.

"No! I don't want to be a job, or a toy to be used and broken. Not again."

She caught in a sharp breath, trying to call back the words she'd never meant to say.

"You are my heart," he whispered at her ear, sending a shiver of longing through her, "my blood. I can't break my own heart."

"Damen, you had my blood forced on you!" she gasped, struggling to free herself from his grasp. "In the worst possible way. If I take advantage of that . . ."

The cabin door opened.

"Don't trouble yourself on that point," he said. "I intend to take every advantage you'll afford me. And maybe a few you won't."

He tossed her on the bed.

She barely had time to register her backside contacting the mattress.

He pounced, pinning her with the weight of his hips against hers, his feet hooked over her shins. A self-satisfied smile on his face, desire smoldering in his eyes, he smoothed the hair from her face and caressed a line down the center of her chest.

"Why did you give me your blood?" he murmured.

He pressed a heated kiss against the pulse point in her neck. His lips twitched against her skin as her already too-fast pulse rate ramped.

"To seal our truce," she gasped.

He lifted his head to look her in the eye.

"You're holding out on me. Why did you give me your blood?" He traced the base of one breast through the silky fabric of her dress.

Her entire body tightened in response.

"Y-you kept on about first blood," she stuttered, barely able to breathe. "It seemed important to you. I wanted you to have something I thought you'd value. I didn't want you to forget me."

"Ah," he breathed, rewarding her by closing his hand on her breast and playing his thumb over the taut peak.

She bit back a moan.

"One more question," he said, moving so that his mouth hovered above her breast. His warm breath seeped through the thin fabric.

Suddenly, she wanted—needed—nothing more than his mouth on her.

"With your skill, you could have taken me out any time and escaped. Why didn't you?"

She stroked his cheekbone to draw his gaze to hers, fear colliding with desire in her bloodstream.

He looked at her, lines between his eyebrows. "Was I right? You enjoy being my prisoner?"

"Back to neural cuffs again?" she asked, tracing the arch of his brows with her fingertips. "I never wanted to hurt you."

He trembled beneath her caress. "I'm tougher than I look."

"That's why I can't hurt you," she replied, threading her fingers through his hair. "Not like that."

He smiled and lowered his head to her breast, teasing her through the silky dress.

She couldn't suppress the moan the attention wrung from her throat.

"Let me show you what your first experience . . ." Damen began, running a hand along the line of her belt.

"And last," she interjected, needing him to understand.

His idle exploration froze.

"You've had no one for seven years?"

Jay uttered the ghost of a laugh at the disbelief in his voice.

"Plague left me in the company of a man who is like a father to me, my cousin, and Pietre," she said.

"And because Pietre prefers men, he's celibate as well," Damen surmised.

"He'd change that for you," she said.

Damen raised his head and propped himself on one elbow, anticipation in the set of his smile. "What about you?"

His question startled her into meeting his gaze. "What?"

A wicked gleam in his eye, he bent to trail his lips along the scooped neck of her dress.

She clenched a fist in his hair, trying to dissuade him, but with her muscles weakened by delight, she failed.

"Will you change being celibate for me?" he murmured against her skin. He shifted his weight, until he rested between her legs, the evidence of his arousal scorching her.

"Gods!" she gasped, arching into his kisses. "You don't play fair!"

His chuckle vibrated throughout her body and he returned to take her mouth in a ruthless assault on her senses.

Potent, primitive chemicals flooded her, shooting hot blood straight to every taut, greedy nerve in her body.

He pulled away, his breathing ragged, and murmured, "No. I don't. I don't fight fair, either. I'm desperate for you, but I won't do this without your permission."

Her heart fluttered. He had her backed into a corner. He could so easily make her beg him to take her. Instead, he offered her a choice when no one and nothing else in her life had.

Unfamiliar emotion swelled in her chest, twining through her skin and bone and blood. Damen had been used, and she gathered, abused. Still, he'd risen to her rescue, offering himself up for use yet again, rather than leaving her to the less than tender mercy of the Temple.

She owed him a modicum of courage. She longed to experience the kind of love his touch and his smile seemed to promise.

"You're not accustomed to being protected," she whispered against his lips. "I'm not used to . . ."

"Being cherished," he finished, his hand at her breast again, tantalizing her with brushes of his fingers. "Loved. You can learn. Let me teach you."

"Yes," she gasped, tightening her arms around him. "Please. Now."

"Begging so soon?" he teased, rocking his pelvis against hers. "I hadn't planned for that until much later."

Anticipation and pleasure zinged through her. Daring to turn Damen's technique against him, she kissed the pulse point in his throat, savoring the life beating against the tip of her tongue.

The breath he drew sounded ragged.

Smiling, she kissed her way up his jaw to nuzzle his ear and whisper, "I won't be the only one begging."

Damen closed his teeth on her earlobe and half growled, half chuckled.

Her heart, and anatomy significantly lower, clenched tight in response. She tripped the release on his uniform shirt and slid her palms over the supple muscles of his chest, easing the fabric from his shoulders.

He unhooked her belt, rolled away from her, snaked an arm under the small of her back, and lifted her hips. He swept her skirt to the floor, planting a kiss in the center of her belly.

She moaned.

He released her, perching on the edge of the bed to rid himself of his shirt.

She sat up. Faint red lines marred the pale skin of his back. Scooting close, she laid an exploratory finger above one of the aged scars.

He flinched.

"Does it hurt?"

"Not physically." A whisper of tension touched his voice.

Like the marks on his ankles, she gathered. Jayleia choked back the urge to ask how he'd come by them. But that part of his past seemed to trouble him and she could guess. She smoothed a palm over his back and instead pressed a kiss against the highest mark.

The rigid set of his shoulders eased and he sighed when she moved to the next line and then the next. He tipped his chin to his chest, his eyes closed.

Pleased by the uneven catch of his breath whenever her lips touched his skin, she kissed her way down each mark until the band of his trousers halted her.

Uttering a sound of disappointment, she splayed her hands wide against the small of his back and followed the line of his waistband until her arms circled him.

He shuddered.

"Don't stop," he pleaded in a whisper.

"Never," she rasped, releasing him only long enough to sit up, shrug out of her top, and press her naked chest against his back. Wrapping her legs around him, she slid her hands over his skin.

Leaning his head back against her collarbone, he combed her hair over his shoulders, and then slid her shoes from her feet. His deft hands kneaded the muscles of her bare calves, then up to her thighs until she could barely draw breath.

Following the line of muscle down the center of his belly, she ran her fingertips over the release for his trousers. "Coded to me?" she breathed into his ear.

He shook with a silent laugh, unhooked her legs, and surged off the bed, kicking his boots across the tiny cabin and shedding his pants while his gaze touched every part of her.

Flushed, she subsided into the mattress when he prowled up her body, glorious, passionate, male. She reveled in discovering every inch of him. When her trembling fingers brushed the heated length of his arousal, he sucked in a shuddering breath before shifting out of her reach and dropping his mouth to lavish kisses on her breasts.

Sensation exploded through her, wringing a groan from her throat.

Damen kissed and teased, touched, licked, and nibbled until the pressure of need drove her to the edge of reason.

"Now!" she implored. "Damen, please."

Resting his forehead against hers, he eased into her as if afraid she'd break.

She whimpered.

He stilled and gasped, "Hang on. You won't hurt me, even if you draw blood."

"No!" she choked, smoothing her hands over the hard muscles of his backside, deliberately relaxing her grip.

"Still protecting me?"

"Until the day I die," she swore in a ragged whisper.

He drew a breath that sounded like a sob and surged the last distance into her.

She cried out at the intoxicating blend of need, pleasure, and exhilaration. Arching into him, her body silently begged for completion.

He responded with a possessive, rough growl and claimed her mind, body, and soul until the volatile compound of sensation and emotion they'd brewed exploded. She felt the cry wrung from her throat, then Damen groaned, convulsed, and collapsed against her.

Breathless, reeling, she collected the scattered pieces of herself only to find her heart no longer where she'd left it. She knew where to find it, though.

Damen rolled them to their sides.

Jayleia pressed her lips against his chest and brushed scar tissue. She leaned back to get a better look.

The faint tracing of veins showed through his pale skin. Curls of golden hair drew her fingers to explore the silky texture. She found the pink, shiny spot she'd felt. It sat directly over his heart.

"Where your blood was introduced to my system," Damen rumbled, a look of deep contentment and peace in his eyes.

She traced the pattern and frowned. "Was it my blood that made you want me?"

He picked up one of the bells still tied in her hair. "Your blood came a year too late to make me want you. It sensitized me to you. You're my mate. I am not whole unless I'm with you."

She stared into his face, her heart trembling. "You're saying I have an unfair advantage?"

He laughed. "I am indeed coded to you. Now. Let me teach you about the rapid recharge rate of my species base."

She knew.

Academically.

When Damen's people had turned their prey drive from hunting humanoids to hunting ore, the exposure to radioactive minerals and toxic chemicals had negatively impacted fertility rates. Adaptation had taken over.

The species reached sexual maturity much earlier than primate-based species.

And as Damen proved in the most engrossing way possible, the males of the species required very little recharge time.

CHAPTER

28

WHEN Damen emerged from the shower, Jayleia had already dressed and left the cabin. He stood in the center of the room, closed his eyes, and drew in a slow breath, savoring the scent of her presence and of her pleasure, amazed by the sense of contentment wrapped around his heart.

He'd kidnapped her with every intention of seducing her if he could. Never had he imagined that she'd turn the tables with her vow to protect him until the day she died.

It made him dizzy. He had to pause in pulling on his fatigues. After a lifetime of fending for himself and of protecting others, fierce, sweet Jayleia had waltzed right past his defenses, scooped his heart out of his chest, and cradled it.

Now, he need only hear her say that she loved him.

He grinned and tucked in his shirt. Given her numerous sensitive spots, he suspected they'd both enjoy having him coax the admission from her.

Once the cabin door opened, he spotted her.

She sat at the edge of the open engine compartment, her knees drawn up to her chest and her forehead resting on her knees. Tension stood out in the set of her shoulders.

He froze opposite her, the gap of the open engine compartment yawning wide between them. His heart skidded into an uneasy rhythm. "What's wrong?"

She glanced up, disbelief in her too-wide eyes.

"Wrong?" she echoed, an edge in her voice that stabbed fear through him. "I've done what I swore I'd never do. Gods. How could I be so stupid?"

"You slept with the enemy," he concluded for her, clenching his hands. He'd pushed her too hard, rushed her.

She huffed out a desolate-sounding laugh. "Why not add that to the list, too? No. I'm falling for someone I can't have just like my mother did."

Shock and delight crashed through him. He felt the grin on his face, but didn't care. Reeling, he lowered himself to sit on the edge of the open compartment.

"Falling?" he croaked.

The white edges around her lips faded. She met his gaze, the corners of her eyes lined with confusion.

He dropped into the engine compartment and closed the distance between them.

She straightened, letting her legs dangle over the side.

He insinuated himself between her knees and wrapped his arms around her. "You have me. I'm yours. Nothing can change or get in the way of that."

She sighed and wove her fingers through his hair.

He closed his eyes, reveling in her touch.

"You can give up being Claugh to join us aboard the *Sen Ekir*? Or am I to abandon the innocent men, women, and children of Tagreth Federated to the traitors who seem bent on handing the known worlds to the Chekydran?"

Her questions drove a shard of ice through his chest. "We belong to one another."

"It may not be enough," she countered. "It wasn't for my parents.

How do you know I'm capable of love? I want to be, but I wouldn't know love if it bit me."

He took her hand and pressed a kiss against her fingers, then bit one knuckle gently.

She was already shaking her head and pulling out of his grasp. "No," she said. "You can't love me. You don't know me."

"I know what's important, Jayleia."

"You know a façade!" she protested.

"Your camouflage as a mild-mannered scientist?" he said, grinning. "What kind of predator would I be if I hadn't isolated that parameter right away?"

"Your mixed predatory and computer-tech metaphors are giving me a headache," she groused.

He laughed and swept her into his arms.

"You can run," he said, his lips against her ear. "You can try to evade me, but you're mine."

The breath she drew sounded like a sob. She tried to extricate herself from his grasp.

He ignored the attempt.

"I'll only hurt you," she protested.

"I can take it."

"I can't."

The despair in her voice pierced his heart.

"I won't give up on you, Jayleia," he swore, running a hand down the thick braid she'd put in her hair.

She quivered beneath his touch.

Her response soothed the anxiety gnawing him. She needed time. Despite her doubts, her body recognized his claim. He'd use that.

She eased out of his grasp and darted a glance at him. The blush staining her cheeks seemed to rob her of words.

"I don't want you to give up," she murmured.

He shifted as the fit of his trousers tightened at her muted confession. Seducing her had turned into a damned uncomfortable double-edged blade.

She looked away to stare at the glowing crystal. "Right now, I think I should show you what I've found."

Something in her tone dumped ice down his back. Discomfort forgotten, he straightened. This didn't sound like Jayleia taking refuge in logic.

She sounded rattled.

He nodded.

She poked her handheld. A flood of data filled the screen.

"What is that?" he demanded.

Jayleia worked her handheld's interface for several seconds. "Your crystal."

"What?"

"The light it emits flickers," she said. "It looked like a pattern, so I applied what amounts to a few tests for life and came up with a partial data stream. But look at this."

Staring at the yellow glow in his engine compartment, he accepted her handheld. "You're saying that thing is alive?"

"No," she said, wrapping a hand around his arm. "Look at the handheld."

He did. And started. "The eye."

"Like the one you tagged in the Silver City data stream," she affirmed. "Yes. I think we can conclude it wasn't a leak of any kind, and neither is this. Damen, where did you get this crystal?"

"A rocky, hostile, uninhabitable planet at the edge of Chekydran space," he said. "Admiral Seaghdh got wind of an UMOPG outpost on the planet."

"Was that wind named Tahem?" she asked, her tone and her expression mild. "Vala mentioned he'd been feeding intel to you. And to IntCom."

"IntCom?" Damen gritted, disbelief chilling him.

She nodded. "I don't know who Tahem's contact was at IntCom. It could have been my father, or it could have been any other agent. We have to assume that Gerriny Eudal has the same information you do."

Rubbing his forehead, Damen swore, then sighed. "Your father was working with us."

She went unnaturally still.

"Not for," he emphasized. "With. He had agents inside the network of traitors working with the Chekydran. He hinted that he had a complete identity list and that it implicated people close to Her Majesty."

Jay's frozen expression thawed, turned considering. "Knowing my dad, he had a plan to take out the moles inside TFC. He'd expect Admiral Seaghdh to handle Claugh personnel. Dad would have used Dr. Idylle to pass the intel to Ari."

"Yes," Damen said, watching calculation run rapid-fire behind her brown eyes. "Before your father could hand off the identification file, he vanished."

"One of his agents blew a critical cover then," she said, sounding grim. "If you troll the data you grabbed from Swovjiti . . ."

"What makes you think I stole data while under a diplomatic flag?"

She awarded him a bland look that made him grin.

"You professed a desire to steal the Gods' own database," she pointed out. "You couldn't help yourself. The rest of your people hunt riches. You hunt knowledge."

He felt the impact of her offhand observation clear to the center of his being.

"You asked me whether the crystal was alive," she said. "It isn't, but it shows signs of having been made or altered by sentient life-forms."

Damen clenched his fists. "What life-forms?"

"What lives on that rocky, uninhabitable world you took this from?"

"Nothing," Damen replied. "The only signs of life were concentrated in a facility below the surface. No more than a few hundred."

"ID?"

"It was a smash-and-grab," he said. "I snuck in, snagged the crystal, and ran. I picked up energy signatures from at least three other ships on planet. I cleared out before they could lift. Their power curves didn't match known vessels."

Jayleia frowned. "UMOPG's military base?"

"So far off the beaten path?" he countered. "We'll pass within sensor range of the planet in a few hours. Maybe it's time to get an indent."

She nodded.

He studied the crystal glowing and flickering as if sending coded transmissions via light pulse. His brain stumbled. "Twelve Gods," he wheezed.

"What?" Jayleia's question sounded alarmed.

"It's a data store," he said. "You said it yourself. The crystal matrix changes in contact with energy. That means the physical, atomic structure has to shift and realign, which means energy discharge."

"The light."

He nodded. "It could be the equivalent of the data stream we're accustomed to."

She stared at the snapshot of information she'd frozen on her handheld and shook her head. "How do you read it? This is a deluge and I suspect I'm only picking up one tiny piece of what's coming off that rock."

Damen hauled himself to his feet and held out a hand. "Come on," he said. "Cockpit. We'll come at it another way. Above all, I think we'd better determine whether or not that crystal is broadcasting."

Five hours later, Damen knew three things. One: he'd turned his entire ship into a pulsating beacon to whatever species had created the crystal. Two: the clamps holding the crystal in place had fused. Shutting down the broadcast would require stopping his power core and blowing it into space. Three: he adored Jayleia Durante. She'd attacked the problem of the fused clamps with imagination, determination, and a vocabulary every bit as off-color as his.

She tossed her wrench back in the tool bag and shook her head when he brought a stack of sandwiches. Jayleia boosted herself out of the engine compartment and crossed to medical to wash her hands.

"What now?" she asked.

"We eat."

"I appreciate the application of pleasurable motivation, though I now consider the bar raised significantly higher than protein replacement sandwiches and water," she said, the glimmer of humor in her eye belying the solemn expression on her face. She followed him into the cockpit.

"I take full responsibility," Damen replied, leering over his shoulder at her, his pulse speeding. Would she let him show her how much fun a cramped cockpit could be?

She smiled, checked the readings on her handheld, then shook her head.

"I suppose we could power down the interstellar drive," she mused, dropping into second seat.

With effort, Damen yanked his wayward attention back to business.

"Run atmospherics only?" he said. "I'm not opposed to spending the next forty years alone with you, but shudder to think you'd accuse me of torture after a few months of nothing but sandwiches."

She replied with a wry laugh. "No one can live by protein substitute alone. You, least of all."

"Supplements," he said, and popped a pill into his mouth before picking up a sandwich.

Jayleia took a sandwich and studied him, a calculating light in her brown eyes. "What's our fuel store for atmospherics?"

Proximity alarms wailed.

Jayleia started and spun to her station.

The tray of sandwiches Damen hadn't gotten around to securing, crashed to the deck.

"What the Three Hells?" he yelled. "What is it? Who got past the long range?"

Jayleia silenced the alarm. "Chekydran?"

"No!" he said. "The entire Empire runs the *Sen Ekir*'s ion scans. If this is cloaking, it's technology other than Chekydran."

"Where are we?" she demanded. "I've got a solar system at the edge . . ."

"Damn," Damen breathed. "The uninhabitable rock? That's the system. Those energy signatures I couldn't identify? Three on approach, coming in hot."

Without a word, she brought up shields and primed weapons.

Damen grabbed his handheld and lowered the energy flow through the crystal. It would slow them down, but he wanted the extra power for shields.

The targeting warning buzzed.

"Damn it," Jayleia said. "I can't see anything out there!"

The ship rocked.

"Taking fire!" he said.

"Where the Hells is it coming from?" she demanded.

Damen scanned his panels, then his screen. "Not registering . . . Wait!"

The ship jolted again.

"They become visible when they fire! By the Gods, they look like UMOPG ore scouts!"

"I see them!" she countered. "Targeting last-known location. Pour on the particle flow! Get us out of here!"

"Can't! We'll lose shields."

Two shots hit the ship at once. The panel above communications blew out. Smoking-hot debris rained over the cockpit.

Jayleia yelped.

The acrid smell of an electrical fire made Damen cough. He swore, heart pounding, calculated their odds, and slammed communications to life in spite of the result. "Broadcasting a distress call on all Claugh frequencies. This isn't a warn-off. They're executing a destroy-on-sight order."

CHAPTER

29

DAMEN shot a glance at Jayleia.

She met his gaze with eyes watering. Hundreds of red pinprick burns showed on the backs of her hands and on one side of her face. Despite the lines of pain in her forehead, she turned back to weapons and fired a barrage at the last place they'd seen a ship.

The laser sprayed harmlessly through empty space.

"A kill order? Why? Try hailing!" she demanded.

"I have been," Damen countered. "No response. I can't offer to trade myself for your safety."

She shot him a wide-eyed look. "I'd intended to trade me for you. But that is a good point. We don't even know which of us they're after."

"Or if they even know who we are."

"Then what the Three Hells have we stumbled over?" she shrilled.

Another flash of ore scout.

She hit the fire control.

"The crystal?" he grumbled, shaking his head.

Missiles streaked away from the *Kawl Fergus*, headed for the visible ship.

The scout fired and vanished.

"Is that it?" she asked. "Are they reading the crystal? Read the *Kawl Fergus*'s energy signature! Does it match theirs?"

"Or do you suppose this is revenge for the fact that I put a contagion alert out for Silver City?"

"You did what?" Damen squawked, stunned. A contagion alert on Silver City would bring the station to its economic knees. Was that what Jay had meant when she'd told Tiassale she was in the process of destroying the people responsible for harming his family?

Jayleia smiled. It looked grim.

Their missiles reached maximum cruise range and destructed.

She swore.

"How did UMOPG get cloak capacity?" she choked.

"Or that kind of power for weapons," Damen responded. "Ore scouts are supposed to be set up for station keeping and sample grabbing. Would you look at that! You called it."

"What?"

"Our energy reading," he said. "It isn't an exact match, but it's close."

"Damn. I can't target them, much less hit them," she groused.

Another explosion rocked the *Kawl Fergus*. They'd hit something vital that time. The power to the shield flickered and died.

The proximity alarm whined to life again. They started and stared at the view screen.

Damen sucked in a sharp breath, something cold and slimy wriggling through his gut.

He looked at Jayleia.

Staring at the ships visible on their screen, she paled.

"Chekydran," Damen confirmed, his voice sounding dead to his ear.

The UMOPG ships all fired at once, undoubtedly meaning to finish them. He hoped they would.

Beside him, Jayleia drew an audibly ragged breath. "I can't protect either of us from Chekydran."

He clenched suddenly burning eyes tightly shut for a moment, then forced them open. Shooting her a glance as he banked the ship hard to avoid the shots from the scouts, he said, "Medical. Tranqs. Massive doses. I won't let the Chekydran have you."

The hard shine in her eyes hurt him.

She shook her head. "I gave everything to Vala. Unless you resupplied the ship, I can't even make you sleepy."

"Baxt'kal Twelve Gods."

With so much power gone, he couldn't wrest the *Kawl Fergus* out of the line of fire. He watched the Chekydran cruisers fire on the three UMOPG ships, the cloaking that confounded his instruments no apparent impediment to them.

The first UMOPG shot took the *Kawl Fergus* amidships and blew out life support. The second exploded the view screen.

Damen flung himself to one side as part of the panel blew inward.

Jayleia cried out.

Something struck the right side of his face. Agony seared him. He couldn't see, couldn't feel the blood, but he tasted its metallic bite on his tongue.

The ship shimmied.

Guidance beam?

UMOPG ships didn't have guidance.

One last thought arrowed through Damen's awareness before pain and darkness claimed him.

The Chekydran had them both.

There would be more excruciating pain between them and their eventual deaths.

COLOR. *So much color. It surrounded her, engulfed her. She breathed it, tasted it. She heard it. Cascading, swirling, humming. More color than had ever existed. Some couldn't be seen, only experienced via all the other sensory inputs, several of which, she was painfully aware she did not possess.*

"Come to us," the color whispered. "Help us. Save us. We will save you."

Jayleia woke from the odd dream a tiny piece at a time. Smell registered first. The scent of sun-warmed soil, and the sharp, green-sweet tang of plants throwing off volatile oil compounds with abandon wafted past her face on a warm breeze. Her ears picked up the chur of insect and wildlife mating songs.

She sighed. Her side and neck hurt. Her feet had gone numb. When had she gone to sleep? Why was she strapped to her seat?

Gasping, Jay tried to straighten and had to bite back a groan. Muscles cramped. How long had she been hanging slack in her restraints?

Stirring her brain to sluggish life, she forced her eyes open and frowned.

Dark. Not a glimmer of light from the panels, no star field on the view screen. The only light filtering into the cockpit came from behind her.

She managed to trigger the release to her restraints and slid sideways out of her chair onto the debris-strewn deck.

Debris? What?

Her heart bumped hard against the inside of her ribs.

They'd been attacked.

Where was Damen?

She peered at his chair. In the bluish light penetrating the cockpit, the pilot's chair seemed wrong. Planting her hands, she levered herself to sitting. Pieces of charred detritus crunched beneath her palms. She propped her back against the base of the nav console.

Damen's chair looked like some giant creature had taken a bite out of the backrest. The first tremor of fear walked down her spine.

Sweat prickled her forehead. She shrugged out of the long-sleeved shirt, tugging it free of her equipment belt and dropping it beside her. That helped.

Get it together, Jayleia.

She recalled three UMOPG ore scouts she hadn't been able to see until they'd fired weapons. And fire they had.

Remembering the pain of hundreds of tiny molten bits of electrical panel branding her skin, she touched her cheek.

No pain. No scars.

Two more ships had appeared on-screen, she recalled. They'd fired, but not upon the *Kawl Fergus*.

A tendril of ice slipped into her belly. She'd known the ship configuration before Damen had said the word.

Chekydran.

She shuddered, tamping down a quiver of panic. She wasn't in a prison cell and couldn't hear or feel the hum of hundreds of Chekydran enclosed on a ship.

Where was Damen?

Why was she alive and still in the *Kawl Fergus*?

She buried her head in her hands and wracked her brain. As far as she knew, the Chekydran ships hadn't fired upon them. Only the guild ships had.

Their last volley had taken out the *Kawl Fergus*'s view panel. She'd ducked as it had exploded. Shrapnel had hit her shoulder blade with such force, she must have blacked out.

No further images or impressions responded to her prodding the memories.

She tested both shoulders. Had she dreamed the injury? Frowning, she retrieved the shirt and held it up to the weak light.

No. A tattered, bloodstained rip in the back of the shirt validated her recall. She'd been in a healing trance, then. How long?

No motion or vibration under her tailbone. Had they made planetfall? Were they prisoners?

Where the Three Hells was Damen?

She accessed the emergency panel set into the base of the pilot's chair, ripped open a packet of chewy, tasteless field rations and forced it down, followed by the contents of a hydration packet.

She found and activated an emergency light.

The beam lit the brown, flaking remnants of a pool of blood.

Jayleia's heart stumbled and she stared, unable to draw breath, as she played the light over the trail leading out the cockpit door into the corridor.

Someone, or something, had dragged Damen, injured and bleeding, out of the cockpit.

Jayleia's brain and body kicked into gear. She yanked the rest of the rations out of the compartment and stuffed them in her empty handheld holster. The remaining hydration packets fit into a pouch that had so long ago held laser triggers for kuorl traps. The woefully inadequate-looking first-aid kit attached directly to her belt.

She climbed to her feet. Energy and resolve surged within her as the calorie- and nutrient-dense field ration hit her system. Sweeping the weapons panel with the light, Jay shook her head.

If the damage to the rest of the ship matched the destruction in the cockpit, the *Kawl Fergus* would never fly again. The thought opened a sore spot in her chest.

She tried to swallow the lump in her throat as she retrieved her handheld from beneath the pile of blackened rubble that had blown out of the panel above the weapons station.

Jayleia hit the power on her abused device. It flickered to life. A hairline crack ran diagonally across the screen and pocks marked where hot debris had melted portions of the casing.

Hands and heart trembling, she switched the unit to read bio-signs.

One humanoid life sign. Hers.

Whispering a curse, she forced herself to follow the trail of smeared blood out of the cockpit and down the corridor where she stopped short.

They'd landed.

The *Kawl Fergus*'s door stood open, the ramp down. Diffuse blue light shone through the open hatch.

The dwindling trail of blood led to the open door and disappeared. Jayleia studied that final print.

Another pool of blood had dried in the doorway, smaller than the one in the cockpit. Rivulets had dried in lines all going the same way as if blown by strong wind. Prints she couldn't identify tracked the blood a few steps down the ramp.

Her handheld still registered no sign of humanoid life. She blinked hard against the fear burning her.

A warm breeze blew past her, dusty smelling. Negative ions and a coming rainstorm? Or was this planetary morning and dewfall?

She peeked out the open hatch.

The *Kawl Fergus* sat on the edge of a massive plain. Ochre and brown soil smeared with green stretched as far as she could see. Hundreds of low, fuzzy-looking yellow mounds dotted the ground. Smooth, black rock outcroppings broke up the plain. Bits of spiky yellow, green, and red foliage poked up, as high as her shoulder. The plant life looked sharp-edged and malevolent.

She glanced at the sky. Thick, striated blue and gray clouds obscured the planet's sun. Given the warmth, she had reason to be grateful for the cloud cover.

Nothing moved save the breeze. She could still hear the buzz of insects or animals, but hadn't yet spotted any of them.

Wishing she had the gun Damen had given her on Silver City, Jay edged out of the shelter of the *Kawl Fergus*, down the ramp, and into the faint shadow cast by the ship and stared into a deep, forested canyon.

Another meter to starboard during landing and the ship would have fallen into the kilometer-deep gorge.

An updraft brought a whiff of cooler, moist air, colored by a hint of unfamiliar spice. The faint echo of animal life hooting and calling drifted up.

She turned back to survey the plain and to walk to the nearest fuzzy, yellow mound. The yellow fluff looked like thin filaments of . . . something. A web of some kind? Plant life? She studied the regular placement of the mounds and frowned. A crop? Or burrows?

Her handheld beeped. It sounded disturbingly off pitch. She glanced at it.

Life.

Humanoid.

Right on top of her.

CHAPTER

30

JAYLEIA spun.

Damen crouched atop the dented, scorched hull of his ship.

Giddy and grinning with relief, she stumbled in his direction.

He jumped from the ship, landing no more than two meters in front of her. The breeze stirred at her back, lifting his hair from his face.

She squeaked, then clapped her hands over her mouth in horror.

A deep, jagged cut on the right side of his face ran forehead to cheekbone. It had destroyed his right eye. The ruined socket was dark with crusted blood.

Her breath coming in dry, wracking sobs, she stood frozen as Damen paced back and forth in front of her. He lifted his head as if searching for a scent.

"Damen?"

He ranged closer, apparently oblivious to his injury. Why didn't he seem to recognize her?

Awful instinct whispered within her. *Infected.* Drawing her hands from her mouth, she clenched her fists. What made her think that?

The facial expressions that denoted conscious thought processes had evaporated from his face and body. He moved in the rangy, sinewy way she recognized from observing wild predators. When he paused, he crouched, tipping his head first one way, then the other, studying her.

Sweat beaded his forehead.

Fever?

She activated her handheld, accessing medical readings. Yes. Fever. Increased respiration. Blood pressure higher than normal, indicative of pain response.

Her heart slid into an uneasy rhythm.

"Damen? Let me . . ."

His head came up, tension and purpose in every line of his posture. He smiled, pure feral intent.

Despite the worry for him consuming her, liquid heat rushed into her belly. She stomped on the urge to rush into his arms.

Jayleia admired the coordination, the loose-limbed stride, the flow of red gold hair, even as he stalked her. He coiled and sprang, trapping her in contact with him. He wrapped his arms hard around her and fastened his mouth on hers before she could blink.

Her handheld dropped.

She tensed, expecting the metallic bite of blood on his lips, or the sour tang of illness. She sensed neither. He tasted clean, like spring rain, warm and sweet, filled with promise. Still, she clenched her teeth when he sought to push into her mouth.

Because it wasn't Damen kissing her. Some vital piece of him was absent. She was being assaulted by a puppet wearing his face.

Jayleia stiffened her spine. When trying to loosen his grip had no effect, she changed tactics, leaning closer, pressing tight, wrapping her arms around him.

He shuddered at the touch of her hands.

And for a moment, she heard it.

Humming.

She'd heard it before. Her pulse beat loud in her head.

Chekydran.

It sounded so like the dream she'd woken from, Jayleia strained to listen. She started when it resolved into something comprehensible.

". . . no harm. Have no fear. Help us."

Her heart squeezed hard.

Damen was infected, somehow, if her medical readings could be trusted, and had been reduced to serving as a vector.

Someone needed her infected.

Why?

With what?

Had her healing trance prevented them from infecting her the same way they'd infected Damen?

"Help us."

Damen gained access to her mouth and invaded.

She'd expected him to release her the moment he'd achieved his objective. He didn't. Neither did his attack ease, but the tenor shifted. No longer concerned with transferring a pathogen to her, it felt like someone relinquished control of him. He was present, arms tightening, mouth demanding a response from her.

Something about that perceptible shift, as if he'd suddenly been given back control of his body, touched off a superheated chemical reaction in her blood.

Until the pain hit, taking her breath.

Damen broke the kiss, but refused to release her.

Hurt sliced through her body.

"Gods!" she yelled. "Does nothing have an incubation period? Ow!"

The illness ripped apart her insides, shaking vital bits of her out, and rearranging them. The impression of being remade stabbed violent nausea through her middle.

Damen clasped her to his chest, running his hands over her back as if she were a child in need of soothing.

Maybe she was.

The nausea and discomfort eased.

She breathed a sigh of relief and leaned back to look him in the face.

He closed the gap and took her mouth again. The gentle strokes of his lips against hers felt like an apology.

The hum intensified. She heard it and sensed it vibrating through her body. Coming from him? Or from her? Approval. Encouragement.

Desire gathered at her core, burgeoning, eroding thought and identity until it erupted.

She gasped and shuddered.

Damen gasped and shuddered.

They broke apart and collapsed in unison.

JAYLEIA came to, warm and comfortable. She felt sinfully good. Hell of a kiss if it could—memory kicked her in the gut. It hadn't been the kiss.

Chekydran.

She knew of at least one other case wherein the Chekydran aural network, the hum the insectoid creatures used to connect to one another, had excited sexual responses from human prisoners. Up to now, she hadn't thought the Chekydran had known they could affect humanoids in that fashion.

There'd never been any indication that the Chekydran cared how they affected other species.

She forced her eyes open and tried to banish the glow still shimmering through her veins.

Where was she?

Alone. Wrapped in pale yellow strands of—what was this stuff?— web? Light bled through layer upon layer of strands wrapped around her.

Too tight.

Too close.

Fright wrapped around her chest. The air grew heavy in her lungs and her vision hazed.

Heart racing, she thrashed against her bonds. The web loosened and gave as she fought, easing her initial burst of panic at the enclosed space. She struggled for a deep breath, found she could get it, and that the air felt fresh.

She gasped, momentarily spent. It took a long time for her runaway pulse to approach normal.

Comfortable, and not confined, or at least not bound. This did not mesh with what she thought she knew about Chekydran prisons.

She couldn't feel the vibration, but Jayleia caught a strain of hum. Chekydran.

Check that. They were prisoners.

Memory handed her a snippet of tactile sensation, Damen's mouth, hot and demanding on hers, and a hum. She'd imagined she'd understood that nonverbal, low-level vibration. "Help us," it had said.

Think, Jayleia.

Given: Chekydran cruisers that didn't fire upon the *Kawl Fergus*, even though the Chekydran and the Claugh were at war. She was captive on a planet rather than aboard a war cruiser. The Chekydran seemed to know they affected humanoid emotional and physical responses via their aural network. A warm, cozy cell made of webbing that gave way as she moved. What if she and Damen weren't prisoners per se?

If they weren't prisoners, it followed that she wasn't in a prison cell.

She was in a cocoon.

Intrigued by the possibility, she picked a spot where the incoming light seemed brightest, drew her knees to her chest, and kicked. The web compressed. As she watched, the strands adhered to one another and coalesced into a sheer, shell-like layer.

She kicked again.

The shell fractured. Light bled through the cracks, bright but diffused.

She coiled to deliver another blow.

Someone, or something, outside grabbed hold of one of the cracked pieces and pulled. The shell snapped. The individual came back to wrench away another piece and this time Jay saw what reached in to help her.

A tentacle.

Terror flooded her. Her heart raced. Her hands shook and she broke out in a cold sweat, but she refused to retreat.

Another segment of shell broke away.

She could hear and feel the hum of the aural net, now. It sounded muted; nowhere near as mind numbing as she'd been led to believe it ought to be.

A shadow fell across her. She looked up.

A Chekydran, or at least the head of the creature, extended into the cocoon, sweeping back and forth as if unable to see her. The creature issued a short, inquisitive burst of sound. Apparently satisfied, it drew back and reached for her with two tentacles.

Jayleia braced herself, but they never made contact. Looking again, she saw the tips curling in an unmistakable "come here" gesture. An offer to help her out of the cocoon?

How civilized.

Not an adjective ever attached to descriptions of Chekydran behavior.

She frowned and paused in reaching for those tentacles. How could she know with such assurance what the gesture indicated? Body language didn't always translate from one species to the next. More to the point, how could a species with only rudimentary visual capability possibly know that crooked "come with me" appendage motion?

She couldn't still her quaking, so she straightened her spine and forced herself to grab hold of the offered tentacles. She'd expected slimy or sticky. The creature's skin was cool and dry and soft, despite the faintly sticky segments under her hands.

The Chekydran pulled Jayleia out of the thing she'd thought of as a cocoon.

The creature holding her aloft didn't look like any Chekydran she'd seen on a view screen. The head had the familiar three rows of vestigial eyes, though they gleamed with iridescent rainbows like polished Novastone. The precious few people who'd survived Chekydran captivity hadn't mentioned that detail.

This Chekydran had wings. Another detail never before mentioned. Jay tipped her head, studying the play of light on the glossy, finely veined wings lying along the creature's back. Cocoons. Did that mean the species' body form varied based on life stage?

It lowered her until her feet touched ground and her legs agreed to hold.

She glanced around. They stood on ochre plain marked by the low, yellow-webbed mounds dotting the ground as far as Jay could see.

Cocoons. The plain was a nursery.

Several more Chekydran, all identical to the one that had freed her, scuttled about on the plain. They shuttled items back and forth, pausing once in a while to dig into the webbing and push whatever they carried deep before covering it.

She frowned, watching the other Chekydran. They spared her not a glance. Only the creature beside her hovered, keeping an eye—or several—on her.

"What are they doing?" she asked, not expecting a response. Humanoids and Chekydran didn't share similar vocal structures. They couldn't reproduce one another's languages.

The Chekydran shifted when Jayleia spoke, jerking her gaze back to it.

She had to force herself to relax when she realized she'd tightened every muscle at the creature's response.

It hummed and chittered at her.

An answer? One she couldn't understand. Frustration broke open in her chest and she huffed out a breath. What she wouldn't give for a translator.

A shrill hum went up not ten meters from where they stood. One of the Chekydran had stopped scurrying. It bobbed and danced in one spot. Two other Chekydran rushed to the scene. The three of them began digging, humming in unison.

Encouragement. Reassurance.

How did she know that?

They stopped digging.

Jayleia realized what was happening as one of them grabbed hold of something with both tentacles and pulled.

Something was emerging from another cocoon.

Damen?

She took a step before realizing it might be a bad idea. The Cheky-dran beside her didn't look concerned, assuming she'd know concern in this species if she saw it.

She had so much to learn.

A spurt of excitement shot into her chest. She shook her head. How stupid was it to get ramped about studying a species that didn't recognize humanoids as sentient beings?

Curiosity overcame fear. She sidled toward the three creatures breaking open the cocoon shell. Nothing stopped her, though the Chekydran shadowed her. The hair on the back of Jay's neck rose at the sound of six legs shuffling in her wake.

Her attendant chortled as they neared the other three Chekydran.

Jayleia jumped.

The three others paused and hummed in their direction, throat pouches vibrating. As one, they stepped back, giving her access to their excavation.

She eyed them. Nothing she'd ever heard about or seen of the Chekydran led her to expect the behaviors she'd so far observed. They weren't allowing her to look. They were inviting her.

Curiosity killed the xenobiologist?

She crept to the edge and peered over. She yelped and staggered back. Her Chekydran caught her.

It was not Damen.

Hand pressed against her chest where her heart tried to beat free, she straightened and went back for another look.

It was a Chekydran, wrapped up tight and glistening with mois-ture. It writhed, straining against the membrane entombing it. Its eyes turned up to the diffuse bluish light.

She swore, voice shaking.

This Chekydran's eyes had pupils that constricted in the light. Those eyes focused on Jayleia. The newborn could see.

The four Chekydran around her intensified their hum as the first tear appeared in the chrysalis membrane.

She watched, fascinated, as the Chekydran emerged a centimeter at a time from the cocoon, then perched on the edge of the hole, waiting for blood flow to straighten crumpled, gossamer wings.

"What a beautiful creature," she breathed, surprised to find it was true. It shifted something inside of her and while fear of these Chekydran didn't drop away, it did diminish.

She'd begun to suspect that whatever portion of the Chekydran made war upon her people, these Chekydran were not the same population. Why hadn't she heard of them before now? This couldn't be first contact. Could it?

She studied the newborn. How could a species that had seemed to be on an evolutionary path away from sight manage to produce an offspring with such advanced visual structures? Did the young Chekydran fanning her wings to dry them and joining in the hum—how did she know the creature's sex?—also exhibit commensurate changes in her brain structure to accommodate those eyes?

Was this mutation? Throwback?

She didn't have time to examine the young female further. Her attendant whipped a tentacle around her neck and yanked her against its throat pouch.

Surprise and terror knifed through Jayleia's gut.

"What are you doing?" she protested, struggling, as another Chekydran brandished a sharp-tipped foreleg. "Wait! No! Don't!"

The Chekydran struck, slicing through shirt, skin, and muscle, laying open her abdomen from belly button to pubic bone. Overwhelming hurt slammed through every nerve, sucking the breath from her lungs.

The sharp, metallic smell of blood spilling hot and heavy down legs that no longer worked filled her head. Her heart labored against panic and shock.

When the creatures began rummaging around in her exposed organs, she screamed until she blacked out.

CHAPTER
31

HE luxuriated in the warmth, the softness, the absence of pain, and in feeling his body becoming whole, or at least as whole as it could be with pieces missing. His brain wouldn't quite answer his every command yet. Nursery attendants hummed outside his cocoon, lulling him, urging him to sink into healing sleep.

Want kept him conscious, aware. He wanted. Wanted his mate. She was part of him. He couldn't heal, wasn't whole without her.

Even through the layers of wyrl-web, he scented her somewhere above him. That alone relaxed him.

Then Jayleia spoke, the words but not the wonder in her tone, got lost in the layers of sound-muffling web. It didn't matter. He knew that voice—had heard it whispering to him in tenderness and desire.

Above his nest, she said something more, confusion climbing to alarm.

He struggled against lethargy.

She needed help. Needed him. She was his. His to protect, to claim.

Then, as if the web realigned to amplify the sound, he heard something tear, a wet, ripping sound that stopped the heart in his chest in terror. The harsh, acrid scent of her blood bit the back of his throat. Her shriek, filled with horror and agony, broke off mid-cry.

He bellowed in rage and protest, fighting the confining wyrl-web, until the queen herself entered the nursery and forced a curtain of unconsciousness over his tortured heart and mind.

Damen woke, aware that he once more controlled his body and his brain. He'd thought he'd understood the price of being someone else's puppet. He'd been wrong.

While entombed within his own skull by whatever illness the Chekydran had given him, he'd betrayed and murdered his mate. The smell of her blood on the web above him was old. The intermittent rain that swept through on the cloud bands of the Chekydran home world hadn't yet arrived to wash away the stinking stain.

Damen's heart shriveled and he squeezed his eye shut. He'd believed he'd known exactly how brutal the Chekydran could be, but until now, he hadn't glimpsed the depths of their cruelty.

They'd infected him, taken over his body and his mind, and used him to find Jayleia. Why allow him to remember the feel of her lips against his when they'd obviously intended to rip her open all along? What more did they want of him?

Did the creatures realize or care that they'd cut out his heart when they'd murdered her?

Damn it. He could still taste her kiss, still smell her all around him.

Above his nest chamber, a Chekydran hummed.

"Queen. Alive," resounded in his head.

Damen frowned and opened his eye. How had the nursery attendants known he'd awakened? He hadn't struggled since Jayleia's scream.

Alive? Which queen? Theirs? Or his?

Thinning his lips, Damen fought his way to the top of the nest chamber, turned, and kicked. The shell fractured. Another kick, powered by rage and despair, shattered the shell. Pieces rained around him.

The towering, glittering Chekydran queen stood above him. Indigo rainbows played over her carapace and oversized wings. Her trill brushed him, washing over his awareness like a mother's reassuring caress.

It loosed the knot of self-loathing roiling around in his stomach, but couldn't soothe the knife-sharp pain in his heart or silence the buzz of rage in his head.

She extended a foreleg.

Damen ignored it and climbed out of the cocoon under his own power. He drew breath to demand Jayleia's location only to find he didn't need guidance.

He followed her scent trail to the nest next to his. Dropping to his knees atop Jay's sealed nest chamber, he glanced at the Chekydran queen.

"Is it safe to open it?"

"Sleeping."

He resisted the urge to swear. He didn't know how the Chekydran queen had managed to implant a translator in his head, but she had. Meaning that no matter how well intentioned the manipulations, he'd been modified by the Chekydran.

Once upon a time, he'd been unable to think of anything worse. Then he'd listened, captive audience, while the Chekydran had killed his mate.

He dropped to his knees beside the nest chamber. Jayleia's grave? No. He caught no sickly, sweet odor of decay. Not her grave. Hope swelled in his chest, crowding his pounding heart, searing the backs of his eyes. He entertained the sudden ache along with the glimmer of belief that she might have somehow survived.

Unable to draw a full breath, Damen began digging.

He needed to see her, to touch her, to feel her warm and breathing. Needed to know he hadn't destroyed her. Yet.

Nursery attendants approached, whether to help him or hinder him in opening Jayleia's chamber, Damen didn't know.

The Chekydran queen warbled, and the attendants stopped, throat pouches quivering in appeasement.

He cleared away the loose wyrl-web. The shell had formed on top of the chamber.

Good.

She'd have emerged on her own within the next several hours.

He glanced at the horrifying stain of her blood on the webbing only a few paces away. Her wound should have been mortal. How long had they been cocooned?

She'd healed quickly. Apparently, her healing trance worked in conjunction with Chekydran medical technique.

Shaking away hesitation, Damen punched the shell. It cracked. Two more careful strikes allowed him to grab pieces and wrest them from the top of the chamber.

Her scent, still tainted by a hint of blood, reached him. He closed his eye and breathed her in. One tiny piece of his heart unclenched.

Opening his eye, he noted that the nursery attendants had set her into a cramped nest chamber and packed healing gel around her. It hadn't been fully absorbed yet, and Jayleia's bowed head gleamed with a coating of the substance.

Damen didn't care. Hooking his hands under her arms, he eased her to the surface and sat back, drawing her into his lap, her back against his chest. Her head tucked beneath his chin, and he folded his arms around her.

She sighed and snuggled closer.

Every nerve in his body lit in response. His heartbeat eased. He smoothed long strands of damp, black hair that had escaped her braid from her face, before subsiding, content to hold her until she woke.

A tendril of sound soothed the ruffle of anxiety at his core. The Chekydran queen sang, urging him to let go of thought, of worry.

Damen resisted for a split second. Then the tension ran out of him and he rocked Jayleia gently in time with the thrum of the queen's wings. His own chest vibrated as he hummed in unison with her. Another voice joined in, off pitch, toneless. Jayleia.

She dreamed the Chekydran hum. She was the hum walking the world. Wings darkened the skies and made the air tremble with the joy of flight. Plain after plain of teeming nests rolled before her. The forests, rivers, and stones resonated with the lives they nurtured. Long ago. It was all gone, now. Only empty nests remained. Sorrow. Loss. Death.

Jay woke humming, surrounded by the scent of sweet, spring rain and new growth. Peace settled deep inside of her. She sighed and opened her eyes.

And stared straight into the huge, iridescent gaze of the biggest Chekydran she'd ever seen. She remembered a tentacle wrapped around her throat. Shock. Pain. Blood.

Her heart jumped. Panic grabbed her in a tight fist. She struggled to back away.

A solid, warm chest and two arms wrapped around her prevented escape.

"They won't hurt you again," Damen rumbled. "Jayleia. They won't hurt you. Not now."

Damen.

Held against him as she was, she felt the words vibrate from his chest into hers.

They wouldn't hurt her, now? Why not? What the Three Hells had happened? Why had it happened at all?

Fear beat at her but she had to look down, to see what ruin remained of her body. Such a vicious abdominal wound should have been fatal.

Nothing.

Jayleia blinked and sat up, pulling out of Damen's embrace. Had she dreamed the attack? No. He'd known. Somehow, he had known what had happened.

The owner of the iridescent eyes trilled.

"Strong." The trill resolved into a whisper in Jay's head.

Frowning, she put a hand on her belly. No wound. No blood. Even her clothes were clean. Only a neat, precise slice remained in her shirt to prove she hadn't imagined the attack.

She shook her head. Smooth, unmarred skin. Something as ferocious as that attack should have left a mark. Her quaking fingers found it then, three narrow scars. She brushed the cut shirt aside and peered at her belly. The wound looked old and long healed, the raised flesh only a shade lighter than the surrounding tissue.

Another trill and burble.

She felt the sound as the brush of a reassuring hand on her cheek. "Daughters. Strong."

Jay looked back into those crystalline eyes.

Daughters?

The creature straightened slowly as if aware of her fragile grip on the terror still beating against the inside of her skin.

It had to be Chekydran. Huge, glittering wings rustled, fragmenting rainbows across their surfaces. This one had no tentacles. An extra set of wings seemed to have taken the place of the appendages, though it still stood on six legs. The dark sheen of its carapace defied color description. It encompassed every color she could identify as well as far more she couldn't.

It was beautiful and graceful for something so large.

"Daughters," it repeated.

Jayleia cocked her head, waiting for the word to make sense beyond the definition. Why were the creature's vocalizations resolving to words inside her head at all?

"She is the Chekydran-ki queen," Damen said.

"Chekydran-ki?" Her voice sounded rusty and raw.

"It's what they call themselves," he replied. "They're a different race than the Chekyrdan-hiin. The Hiin are the ones attacking us."

Jayleia noted and filed the distinction.

"Nothing will hurt you," he assured her. "Go. She wants to show you."

Jayleia blinked. *Go where?* After the last show-and-tell, did she really want to see anything these creatures had to present?

Her damnable curiosity won out over fear. Before her brain could veto the move, she'd climbed to her feet.

The queen led her several meters to a cluster of fresh nest chambers. The fluffy, still-sticky web beneath her feet exuded a faintly sweet, musky odor. Attendants backed out of the queen's path, their throat pouches and tentacles quivering, their chorus of hums soothing.

Adoration? Or fear?

The queen stopped and gently parted the web before turning a burst of barely audible sound at Jayleia.

"Come. See. Daughters."

Awful suspicion rolled through Jay. Eyeing the huge, glittering creature beside her, she sidled closer and looked.

A single pallid egg had been attached to the wall of the nest chamber. Barely perceptible within, the embryo curled in a recognizably fetal position, despite the lack of humanoid form.

"Daughters," the queen had said. Hers? Weren't they all hers? Or did she honestly mean Jayleia's?

Six years of studying Chekydran plagues, six years of asking how the Chekydran had managed to master the humanoid genome to the extent that they routinely modified humanoids for one purpose or another, all the questions, all the bits of data coalesced in her brain.

Jayleia fell to her knees, head spinning. Her daughters.

Slicing her open hadn't been an attack, not intentionally, anyway. It had been the Chekydran harvesting genetic material—eggs—from her.

They'd spliced her DNA into the developing young. The new generation of Chekydran had three parents.

Why?

"Strong," the queen had said.

Diversity. It had to be. If Chekydran biology followed other insectoid hive models then far too few of the adults bred young. The Chekydran suffered from inbreeding.

Jayleia shook her head, staggered. One of the bells still braided into her hair chimed. She shuddered.

Her own mother had woven the trinkets into her hair. They were a request for grandchildren.

Bells for granddaughters.

Gems for grandsons.

What would her mother say to these granddaughters?

Jay grappled with the fact that she was a parent. Like it or not.

The Chekydran had attempted to ensure the survival of their species with a cold-blooded harvest of her genetic material without so much as a by-your-leave?

Her breath came in shallow gasps as she remembered the hatch-

ing Chekydran with eyes that had focused on her. Twelve Gods. She
hadn't been their first bloody harvest.

"How many women have died out here while you robbed them of
such an intimate part of themselves?" she shrilled, climbing to her feet.
"How many survived physically only to be driven insane by the shock?
Did it never even occur to you to ask? For the love of the Gods! I could
have given you half a dozen different ways to retrieve eggs without
drawing so much as a drop of blood!"

"Save us," the queen sang at her.

"I'm not sure I want to!" Jay shouted, her fists clenched. "Had
that cut been one millimeter deeper, you'd have spilled my intestinal
contents. How are your nest chambers at healing peritonitis?"

She glanced at her intact belly.

If the Chekydran had healed such a horrendous wound on her,
what had they done for Damen's wound?

Jayleia spun. He'd been following too close, and she bumped him
and stumbled.

Damen caught her to his chest.

The cut on his face was a thin white scar. His eye had fused shut
and the crooked, jagged scar marred even the eyelid.

Hand shaking, she touched his scarred forehead, not certain she
could trust her senses regarding what was real anymore.

The skin beneath her fingertips remained slack.

Paralyzed.

She frowned and met Damen's gaze.

"I only know you're touching me," he said. "I cannot feel it. Not
there."

Hot tears abruptly flooded her eyes, heating her face.

"What is going on?" she whispered. "And why?"

He met her watery gaze, the gray of his good eye darkening. "It's
clear they're in trouble. What isn't clear is why they seem to believe
we can help."

CHAPTER 32

THE queen chirped. It resolved in Jay's head as, "Called."

Scrubbing her face dry, Jay glanced at the creature who had tipped her head to look skyward.

A noise she'd never expected to hear rent the atmosphere. "A ship? Landing?"

"The Chekydran-ki have ships. They towed us in," Damen said.

She shot a look at the unconcerned queen and tried to shake off the thunder of her pulse. "Would she know if it was another one of the scouts that attacked us?"

He blinked. His gaze turned inward and crinkles appeared at the corner of his eye. "It isn't."

"Called," the queen said again.

"Called?" Jayleia echoed.

Damen smiled. "You understood that?"

The realization that she had indeed understood jolted her. "How did I? Unless . . ."

He lifted his eyebrow. "Unless?"

"The infection. Chekydran favor nanotech delivery mechanisms for altering humanoids to their purposes. At least, our research to date leads us to that conclusion. We have seen immune responses that produced symptoms at the time of initial infection, if you can talk about the introduction of nanotech in terms of infection."

"The illness made it so we can understand the Chekydran?" Damen asked.

She shrugged as the rumble of ship entering atmosphere grew louder. "Until I can get into a lab for tests, it's the only theory I have. My question is why did they use you to infect me? Why couldn't they introduce the nanopak directly?"

"They tried, but you were already in a healing trance and it wouldn't take." Damen looked skyward, then at the queen again. "The ship's getting closer. It's not a Claugh vessel. The pitch is wrong."

Jayleia peered into the blue-and-gray-banded clouds as the shrill of atmospheric engines increased. The craft broke through the haze. Her heart leaped as recognition hit.

She broke free of Damen's grasp and started running, following the arc of the ship.

"It's the *Sen Ekir*!" she shouted.

"What? It can't . . ."

She slowed her pace to conserve energy when it became apparent she'd have a long way to go.

Damen drew even with her, matching his pace to hers.

Should she wonder how they had the stamina for a several kilometer jog so shortly after their respective life-threatening injuries? Shouldn't they have needed recovery time? Time to rebuild strength and endurance?

A wave of familiar dizziness hit. Every question in her head evaporated under a deluge of alarm. She skidded to a halt.

Teleport distortion.

"No!" she shouted. "What the Hells . . ."

Everything vanished.

She found herself staring at the wall of the *Sen Ekir*'s cargo bay.

". . . are you doing?" she finished yelling.

A quick glance to her left assured her Damen had been brought aboard as well.

She spun.

Dr. Idylle and her cousin, Raj, rushed them. The lines of pain in her cousin's face took her breath.

He grabbed her and hugged her hard.

Dr. Idylle gripped her shoulder as if waiting for her cousin to release her so he could embrace her in turn.

"Jay," Raj grated. "Thank the Gods. How the Hells did you get this far out?"

"We were attacked. Damn it, Raj, the biomechs hit Swovjiti."

"I know."

His tone crushed her heart. "Tell me."

"Lania. Her daughter. Uncle Torbuhhal, his son Ochet," her cousin answered, pulling away to meet her gaze. The lines in his face deepened. "Dead. Too many injuries to count, but everyone else will live."

"Mother and Bellin?" she rasped, barely able to breathe.

"Missing," he choked. "They vanished after you left the planet."

Loss knifed through the center of her chest. She held her breath, waiting for the hurt to ease. "Vanished," he'd said, not dead. Had her mother taken advantage of the battle to slip the agents tailing her?

She should have known this would happen. Damn it. She should have foreseen it. Some warrior.

"Twelve Gods, Sindrivik," Raj said, staring at the jagged scar on Damen's face. "Medical. Both of you."

Jayleia gasped at the medical reminder and shoved her cousin away. "We've been modified. We could be infectious!"

"Not according to the readings you've been sending," Dr. Idylle replied.

Jayleia's brain stumbled. She traded a confused look with Damen. "Readings?"

Frowning, Damen shook his head. "We haven't been sending . . ."

"I've lost more family members than I can stand in the past few days," Raj retorted. "Medical. Now."

"But we haven't been sending you data!" Jayleia countered, her fists clenched. "Don't you understand? You were tricked!"

Damen started, but didn't contradict her.

Raj glanced at their boss.

Dr. Idylle blinked. "Let's take this in order of precedence. Deceived or not, we're here. Our scans indicated pockets of abundant wildlife, no settlements, and a marginal population of larger-than-humanoid inhabitants."

"Yes," Damen said.

Jay tossed him a look. Had he meant to forgo mentioning the Chekydran-ki?

"Jayleia, you're my xenobiologist and the most conscientious scientist among us. I trust your judgment," Linnaeus Idylle said. "Are we in immediate danger?"

Dr. Idylle's appraisal hit her broadside. *The most conscientious scientist among them.* Was she really? Did it matter? It hadn't helped save the people of Swovjiti.

She rubbed her forehead.

"You are in no danger from the inhabitants," she replied, then frowned. How could she say that with such assurance? Given that the Chekydran were inside her head in a fashion she didn't understand, could she be sure she'd been the one to say it?

"Then I concur with Dr. Faraheed. Medical," Dr. Idylle said, gesturing them out of cargo. "We'll sort the rest once we're assured you're safe."

"We may have a tactical situation, Dr. Idylle," Damen said. "I'll request a line to Pietre from medical so I can walk him through calibrating his scanners."

"Jayleia said you were attacked," Dr. Idylle said. "By the Chekydran?"

"You were going to mention the Chekydran on this planet, right?" Raj asked as they filed down the corridor.

"They saved our lives," Jayleia retorted.

"The Chekydran on this planet intercepted and destroyed the UMOPG scout ships that were attacking us. The Chekydran then brought us here for treatment," Damen added. "The medical information you've received is intended as a gesture of good faith."

Jayleia stared at him. How did he know that?

Damen scowled. Only one side of his forehead crinkled in response to the gesture.

"I hear the Chekydran-ki queen in my head," he explained. "I'm translating."

"Then we can trust nothing they say," Dr. Idylle said.

Raj grunted as they entered the tiny medical bay. "On the table, Sindrivik. I have your genetic print on file from last year. I can grow a new eye for you, but that will take a little time. We'll get it under way."

"Brief me?" Jayleia queried, looking between Raj and Dr. Idylle.

"If the data we received from these Chekydran can be relied upon, you were infected via a nanotech delivery mechanism," her boss said, folding his hands behind his back. "Initial symptoms were a short-lived immune response to the foreign matter."

"Which survived in our systems long enough to deliver a payload," she concluded. "Do you have a read on what that was?"

"We were hoping you could tell us. There's more," Dr. Idylle said. "You and Major Sindrivik represent two distinct immune profiles. You aren't even the same species, yet the nanotech viral structures were specifically matched to each of you."

Jayleia shook her head. "What are you saying? They knew we were coming and tailored the infection to each of us?"

Dr. Idylle nodded. "It sounds far-fetched, I know, but that is my impression. By wrapping the infectious agent coded to your immune system inside a protein sheath his body would ignore, the Chekydran were able to use Major Sindrivik as a go-between."

"They had your genetic information, Jayleia. You and Major Sindrivik were targeted," Raj said.

Staggered, Jayleia fumbled for a chair, her mind racing. How?

Damen rolled off of the diagnostic bed and crouched before her, his hands resting on her hips. "What are you thinking?"

"They lured us," she said.

He shook his head. "How? Why?"

She wracked her brain, shuffling through her data and rearranging speculation. "Could the crystal . . ."

"Look at this," Raj ordered.

She examined the image he'd brought up on the diagnostic grid.

"Neither of you is manifesting symptoms," he said. "The diagnostic bed read Damen's vital signs as normal."

"We're past the symptoms because the nanopaks broke down under the initial immune assault and released whatever agent the Chekydran-ki used to modify us," Jay concluded. "We're still infected, we're just not reacting anymore, is that it?"

"Maybe." Raj tossed her a sharp look. "Do you know for a fact that you've been successfully modified?"

"We know," Damen replied.

"Tell me," Raj demanded.

"It's a translator," Damen said. "Jayleia and I can understand the Chekydran-ki queen. She understands us."

"Damen can also hear the Chekydran-ki queen telepathically," Jayleia added.

"Now that is interesting," Dr. Idylle said. "Is this a result, do you think, of your training with the telepaths in your ranks, Major?"

"It's the best theory we have, sir," Damen replied. "May I trouble you for a line to Pietre?"

"Dr. Faraheed? Will you release your patient?" Dr. Idylle asked.

Raj waved. "I have no medical reason to confine either of them."

"What is this image I'm looking at, Raj?" Jay asked, nodding at the diag screen as Damen connected to the cockpit via the intraship com and began a rapid-fire exchange with Pietre regarding long-range scanner config.

"Major Sindrivik's brain," Raj replied.

"Does the urge to dissect what you don't understand run in the family?" Damen grumbled over his shoulder before turning back to the wall com.

Raj turned a speculative glance on her, one eyebrow arched.

Jayleia did her best to ignore him and the blush staining her cheeks. "What is it you wanted me to see?"

"This section here," Raj said.

Dr. Idylle closed in behind them, looking between them. "Language centers in the Autken brain, correct?"

Raj nodded. "This is the scan I just took. I'm pulling up one taken last year after the assault on the Chekydran ship holding Ari and Admiral Seaghdh. Highlighting the language center. Executing overlay."

Jayleia gasped.

"What?" Damen demanded, clicking off the intraship and crossing to stand beside her.

"The language center of your brain has been rewired, for lack of a better description," Raj said. "That in itself is disturbing to those of us who learned that brain plasticity is a relative thing and that synaptic growth takes time. Upping the creepy factor is the fact that we're seeing some kind of organism embedded in the tissues."

Jayleia shuddered. "Organism?"

"Can you kill it?" Damen sounded as horrified as she felt.

"Not without killing you, too," Raj said. "I've never seen anything like it. It isn't viral or bacterial or protozoan . . ."

"We assume this is the modification you've been subjected to," Dr. Idylle said. "The question, now, is why."

"The only manifestation we've noticed is the ability to understand the Chekydran-ki," Jayleia said. "Do we assume my scan is similar?"

"Hop on my table and let's find out," Raj said.

She complied.

Dr. Idylle pulled up a scan from her physical not five months ago and readied it for comparison while Raj ran a new image.

"All done," her cousin said.

"The concentration of organisms in your brain is lower than in Major Sindrivik's," Dr. Idylle said.

Jayleia blinked and rose. Was that why Damen heard and understood more than she did?

"I entered a healing trance shortly after being infected," she said. "I wonder if that had any bearing."

Raj shrugged. "You also have proven immunity to Chekydran plagues."

"The one thing the crew of the *Sen Ekir* has in common," Damen said, nodding. "You're all immune to the Chekydran plague that was seeded on Ioccal."

"Are we assuming that is the end of the modification cycle?" Dr. Idylle prodded. "We have evidence that the Chekydran have mastered time-delayed attacks."

Raj stared at Dr. Idylle, the blood draining from his face. "I don't know. I have less than nothing on the organism nestling into their gray matter."

"Perhaps it's time to lift and leave the Chekydran far behind," Dr. Idylle concluded.

"And go where?" Raj asked, the faint echo of bitterness in his hollow tone.

It brought Jayleia's gaze up to Raj's face.

Damen swiveled around to peer at him.

"We've been tossed out on our scientific ears," Raj said.

"Tossed out?" Pain stabbed through her. "TFC banished you and the *Sen Ekir*? Because of me?"

Dr. Idylle sighed and rubbed a hand down his face. "I suspect from a political standpoint that, yes, we were accused of treason as a means of putting pressure on you."

"And by extension, my father," she murmured.

"My actions, however, created a situation whereby the president of Tagreth Federated could make the accusation in the first place," he said.

"You went straight to the *Dagger* after I kidnapped Jayleia," Damen surmised, a glimmer of amusement in his voice, "rather than registering a protest with your political body."

"It seemed the logical course of action at the time," Dr. Idylle said.

"If you were with the *Dagger*." Damen frowned at her crewmates. "Who escorted you here? Admiral Seaghdh wouldn't have allowed you to follow a data signal without armed escort."

"My daughter hardly allowed Admiral Seaghdh a word edgewise between demanding complete copies of our data and barking orders for Captain V'kyrri to follow us," Dr. Idylle grumbled.

Damen started, a smile growing on the mobile half of his face. "The *Queen's Rhapsody*? Will you open a line, Dr. Idylle? I'd like . . ."

"Captain V'kyrri and his crew brought us in, waited until we gave them the all clear, then they turned around to investigate some odd readings at the edge of this sector," Dr. Idylle said.

Jay felt the blood rush from her head. "Hail them! Turn them around!"

"I'll go to the *Kawl Fergus*," Damen said. "Compatible systems have greater reach."

Alarm tightened both Dr. Idylle's and Raj's expressions.

"Teleport?" Dr. Idylle said.

"Faster to open the airlock," Jay said.

Dr. Idylle strode to the com and opened the channel. "Pietre, open main doors, please. Repeat, open main doors."

"Acknowledged," Pietre replied. "Opening main doors. Good to have you back in one relative piece, Jay."

"Let's see how long that's going to last," she grumbled.

"Clear skies at the moment," Pietre said.

"Glad to hear it, but why are the skies clear?" she muttered glancing at Damen.

He shook his head. "Why didn't the ore scouts follow them in?"

Jay looked to her boss. "Dr. Idylle? Do we have an extra com badge for Major Sindrivik? Mine is aboard the *Kawl Fergus*; I'll pick it up."

"Excellent idea," her boss said, nodding. "Pietre? A com badge for Major Sindrivik, if you please. Meet us at the door."

"Acknowledged."

"I recommend powering up your teleporter," Damen said as they strode for the door. "Keep it on hot standby."

"You said these Chekydran aren't a threat. What's out here that we'd have to teleport away from?" Raj demanded.

Jayleia shook her head. "We were on our way from Swovjiti to the *Dagger*. Eluding the biomech soldiers and their ships brought us out to this sector."

"We were attacked by a trio of UMOPG ships," Damen said.

"Com badge," Pietre said, approaching from the cockpit. He started, his dark eyes widening as he surveyed the scar on Damen's face. "Twelve Gods, Damen, what happened to you?"

"The UMOPG happened," Damen said, affixing the badge to his shirt pocket. "They've established a military presence at the edge of this system and altered a trio of ore scouts. V'kyrri's flying right into their sights."

The airlock light flashed and the doors opened.

Damen sprinted off the ship and angled for the *Kawl Fergus*.

"UMOPG?" Pietre sputtered. "They carry rudimentary armaments. They're miners, not military."

"They are now," Jayleia countered, leading the way out of the *Sen Ekir*. "The scouts that hit us had been modified for stealth, speed, and firepower. Have a look at the damage they did to Damen's ship."

Pietre's com badge beeped. He activated it. "Sindrivik?"

"Tell Jayleia I know how we were lured," Damen said, his voice shaking. "And I think I have an ID on the sentient life-forms that altered the crystal."

"What crystal?" Pietre asked.

Alarm shrilled in Jayleia's head. She pounded up the *Kawl Fergus*'s ramp, into the companionway, then froze in the cockpit entrance, staring. The blown-out console above communications had been replaced by a brilliant yellow crystalline structure.

Her heart rose to her throat.

The Chekydran-ki had apparently been repairing the ship, using crystals to fill the voids. Assuming these yellow crystals bore any relation to the rock fused to the *Kawl Fergus*'s engine feed. From the pulse and flow of light and energy through them, she gathered they did.

Damen, seated in what remained of his pilot's chair, met her gaze, and nodded.

"The original crystal was bait," he concluded.

"Okay. We suspected," she said. "Have you heard from V'kyrri?"

"Emergency hail active," he replied. "Awaiting a response."

"Three Hells! Your O$_2$ generator melted!" Pietre exclaimed from the outer doorway. "What is this yellow stuff? Sindrivik, what have you been doing?"

"Is this blood at the outer door?" Raj called. "This is blood. What the . . ."

The com panel trilled. Jayleia nearly jumped out of her skin.

Damen opened the channel.

". . . *se hobhaille no'whyn*," a male voice said.

"*Queen's Rhapsody*! Code Nwylth-Corem-39. Recall. Recall. Recall. This is the *Kawl Fergus*," Damen said. "Major Damen Sindrivik . . ."

"Sindrivik! You were reported missing!" V'kyrri's voice broke over the line.

"Turn around!" Damen demanded. "Now!"

"Glad to have you back, but we've got radioactive debris to check out," V'kyrri countered.

"It's the remains of the attack force that all but destroyed the *Kawl Fergus*," Damen countered. "If the Chekydran-ki hadn't shown up to rescue us, Jayleia and I would have been reduced to free-floating particles. Get out of there!"

"Chekydran?" V'kyrri barked. "Helm! Reverse course! Get us turned! Pour on the speed."

"Aye, Captain!"

"On our way to your location!" V'kyrri said. "*Queen's Rhapsody*, out."

CHAPTER

33

"THE ore scouts were destroyed?" Jayleia frowned, instinct whispering that the data mattered. "Why?"

Damen glanced over his shoulder at her. "What?"

"Why were those ships destroyed? The Chekydran-ki didn't have to burn them down in order to rescue us," Jayleia said. "Why destroy UMOPG ships and not the *Kawl Fergus*? What did they know about you that suggested you might be an ally? What was it about those UMOPG ships that warranted a destroy-on-sight order?"

"We did have the crystal," he said, frowning. "You think that fire-fight indicates prior history between UMOPG and the Chekydran?"

"We know that three Chekydran ships attacked and damaged the *Dagger*," she said.

"Yet rather than destroy the *Dagger*, the Chekydran made a run for it," Dr. Idylle finished from behind her.

Jayleia eased into the cockpit to give the older man space in the doorway.

"Suggesting they had other orders," Damen surmised.

"They attacked Silver City along with a contingent of biomech soldiers," she said.

Interest sparked in Dr. Idylle's face. "Did they?"

"They abandoned a crippled enemy to strike Silver City. That sounds like a grudge," Jayleia said. "The only data the Chekydran-ki had on the *Kawl Fergus* when they rescued rather than destroyed us, was that we weren't UMOPG. The ship configuration is different and three ore scouts were trying to take us apart."

"We did have the crystal in contact with the engine feed," Damen said. "It was broadcasting and our energy output was similar to the ore scouts'."

She considered that. "Then the UMOPG has integrated similar crystals into their weapons and shields?"

Damen nodded. "It would account for the increased energy output. Which means that unless they've found a way to circumvent it, their ships broadcast, too. I'll transfer my files to the *Dagger*. We'll find a way to track it."

"What if the Chekydran-ki already have? Is that how they saw through the cloaks the scouts were using?" Jay said.

"Even if they had, we're still left with more questions than answers," Damen said. "Why rescue us? We could have proven to be anyone or anything."

"Except they recruited you," she said, and once again she'd merely been in the wrong place at the wrong time. The realization hurt. Interesting. What did it mean to want to be part of something so badly that she was willing to be modified by the Chekydran?

"Your theory regarding the Chekydran and UMOPG may have a basis in fact," Damen said. "We pulled first contact information on the Chekydran last year. I noticed a pattern. When offered a choice between two or more ships, they prefer to attack UMOPG flagged vessels."

"Suggesting an acrimonious history between the Mining Guild and the Chekydran that we know nothing about," Dr. Idylle said.

"We have Silver City's data store," Damen replied. "With time, the loan of Pietre, and a few tools, I'll find that history. It might give us something to go on."

"Pietre!" Dr. Idylle shouted down the companionway. "You're with Major Sindrivik."

Damen launched himself out of his chair. "We'll get on data recovery."

"I'll do my job," Jayleia said, an odd swell of contentment settling into her chest at having Damen and her crewmates working in concert while she observed an unknown species. "Dr. Idylle, if you'll join me in the medical bay, I have bloodworm samples you and Raj might find interesting."

She led the way past the open engine compartments, where Pietre already prowled, staring and muttering at the crystalline structures melded to the engine alloys.

Raj stood in medical, his handheld out and active, confusion in his black eyes.

"It's obvious the crystal is meant to repair your systems," he said, "but to what purpose? I can't get a response out of diagnostics."

"The energy signature is wrong," she replied, then scowled. How did she know that? Where had it come from? A surge of displacement washed through her. A hum resonated inside her skull, dumping her out of the pilot's seat of her own body. The buzz in her head stilled and the sensation vanished. She was once again in control of her body and she knew how to alter the handheld's signal to bridge the interface gap.

She cleared her throat to unseat the odd feeling of having another intelligence supplying knowledge to her. "Do you have translation loaded, Raj?"

He nodded and offered her the handheld.

She used it to open the sample stasis chamber, then handed the unit back before gathering sampling equipment and loading into her equipment belt. She finally positioned herself in the doorway where she could catch glimpses of Damen as he collected tools.

"Data chips?" he asked her.

"Cockpit," she said. "My com badge?"

"Same," he said. He retrieved the bag of data chips and brought her badge.

He evaded her attempt to take the badge from him.

"Here," he murmured, stepping closer than necessary and brushing his fingers inside her tunic as he put her badge in place. "Allow me to assist."

Nerve endings lit up all over her body.

Damen grinned and kissed the tip of her nose before spinning away and tossing the bag of chips at Pietre.

"Install them in that array." He pointed a wrench at the backup computer system tucked into the cramped space beneath the deck plates and up against the cockpit bulkhead.

Jayleia cast a glance at Dr. Idylle and Raj. Both men pointedly examined the containers filled with bloodworms, but she mistrusted the crinkles of humor at the corners of her boss's eyes.

"They're from Chemmoxin," she said, damning the rough edge in her voice.

"How long ago did this first pair begin cocooning?" Raj asked.

Jayleia started. *Cocooning?* "I had no idea bloodworms were a pupae form of anything. What do they change into?"

She looked between Dr. Idylle and Raj.

They gaped back.

"You were in the field," Dr. Idylle said. "Did you see an insect form we haven't classified?"

"All kinds!" Jayleia exclaimed. A flash of memory stopped her. The kuorl scout had emerged from the nest tree. He'd snatched something from the trunk and stuffed it in his mouth.

"Beetles!" she gasped. "Itchy, prickly, horrible creatures. They were all over the kuorl trees."

"These are the bloodworms that gorged on your blood and dropped of their own volition?" Dr. Idylle asked.

Jay glanced at the labels and nodded. "Infected blood. Yes. In fact, when they dropped, they were black and stiff. I thought they were dead. The specimens in the other containment dish also gorged and dropped, but the infection appeared to have been drained by the time they fed. When they dropped, they exhibited normal blood coloration and mobility."

"So it wasn't the blood meal that triggered metamorphosis in these specimens," Raj mused.

"Their near-death experience?" Jayleia grumbled.

Dr. Idylle sucked in an audible breath.

She boggled. "I wasn't serious!"

"I am," her boss replied. "Sheer conjecture, but bear with me. Suppose these creatures require a meal of infected blood in order to undergo metamorphosis?"

"They all had infected blood," Jayleia protested. "I manifested symptoms."

Raj studied the two creatures busy wrapping themselves in silk. "Maybe it's a matter of virus load."

"Is it a virus?" Jayleia asked, sudden interest spiking through her. How had they found time to research the disease while trying to recover her?

"Not precisely," Raj hedged. "It shares characteristics in common with most viral structures we know, but there are anomalies. I reverted to 'virus' so I could talk about the damned thing."

"Okay," she said, marshaling her thoughts into order. "If the virus triggers metamorphosis, it would mean that the disease unlocks a chemical cascade inside the bloodworms that initiates chrysalis development. The interesting question would be whether or not the virus itself survives the change and is communicable thereafter."

"Did the beetles bite?" Dr. Idylle queried, frowning.

"No. The kuorls ate them."

Excitement lit through her. She saw it reflected in the faces of her colleagues. Had they just closed the life-cycle loop on the necrotic illness plaguing Chemmoxin?

"Ready!" Pietre's yell sounded hollow coming from beneath the deck plating at the center of the ship. "System off-line?"

"Yes," Damen said from his spot in front of the engines.

"I think I'd better have a look at a blood sample, Jay," her cousin said. "We'll make certain that healing trance completely cleared your system."

She watched Damen taking apart his handheld as Raj applied the leech to her arm. The device beeped.

"Dr. Faraheed, help me secure these specimens," Dr. Idylle said, an avid light in his blue eyes. "We have work to do."

Raj nodded. "Yes, sir."

Her boss paused in the doorway to smile at her. "I need a complete report. Speculation included. If we can isolate the endocrine key or its analogue, we might be able to interrupt the bloodworm life cycle . . ."

"Endocrine keys," she interrupted, her brain shoving a vision of the hatching Chekydran before her mental eye. "What else triggers metamorphosis?"

"Light cycles, right?" Raj said.

"Yes," she murmured, glancing toward the *Sen Ekir*'s open door. "Light, which impacts neurotransmitters."

"What are you thinking?" Dr. Idylle asked standing very still as if afraid to disrupt her train of thought.

"We spoke of interrupting the life cycle of bloodworms," she said.

"By switching off the endocrine key, the bloodworms never cocoon, never mature to a reproductive state, and eventually die," her boss said. His eyes widened and he sucked in a breath. "The Chekydran!"

She nodded, hesitating to condemn the species as a whole, but a good scientist examined every option, whether she liked them or not. "They undergo metamorphosis."

"If we could isolate the trigger, we could end the war!" Raj said.

"We'd be committing genocide based on the actions of one segment of the population," Jayleia countered. "And it wouldn't end the war. Not right away. We have no data on how long the life stages last in this species. We could kill off this population of Chekydran who seem intent on helping us in the war. Could we reverse the trigger?"

Her cousin frowned. "In what way?"

"Forcing metamorphosis?" Dr. Idylle essayed. "Supplementing

the chemical that triggers cocooning, thereby forcing the Chekydran into hibernation?"

"What would that accomplish?" Raj asked, shaking his head. "We'd still have a bunch of aggressive, killer Chekydran on the loose once they emerged."

"I don't know," she replied. "I'm still synthesizing data here."

"Well," Dr. Idylle said, rubbing his hands together, "we have a theory to investigate and a possible means of protecting Chemmoxin's colonists. Excellent work."

"Yes, sir. Thank you . . ." Jay began.

"We're science ship non grata," Raj said. "How are we going to help anyone?"

"We submit results to every government and media outlet that remembers our work on Ioccal," Jay replied. "TFC might refuse the information, but the Claugh and the Citizen's Rights Uprising will use their resources to make the results public."

Raj rolled his eyes, the first hint of a smile on his face. "Sensationalism and claims of conspiracies notwithstanding?"

"We are victims of a conspiracy," Jay protested as her cousin and her boss carried the sample dishes out of the medi-bay, headed for the labs in cargo.

"That's what concerns me," Dr. Idylle admitted. "Everyone we contact will risk accusations of treason, too."

Jayleia stopped short, dismay spilling through her. It hadn't occurred to her. Of course the CRU would help them; they lived to expose the kinds of accusations Jayleia could make against the TFC government, but at what cost?

She'd left a trail of blood and dead bodies in her wake already. Why? What was she that inspired such determination to destroy her and everyone around her?

"Jay."

She found Damen watching her, concern lining his face. It eased the rage threatening to boil over inside her. She couldn't take responsibility for the attack that had injured him. Unless the guild had worked out that Jayleia had both stolen the Silver City data store and been the one to issue the contagion alert for the station. If the guild council had sent the ore scouts after the *Kawl Fergus*, then she was culpable.

Until the thirty-day quarantine period expired or an outbreak-response ship arrived to diagnose and lift the alert, Silver City would be a ghost station. No one would land there. No ships, no customers, no income. How long could Silver City survive that kind of economic siege? Jayleia swallowed a smile of spite-filled glee.

Pietre scooted out from under the deck plates to grab the bag of data chips. "Ready to begin pulling your backup array. How neat a job do you want?"

Damen shook his head. "I don't. It won't matter."

Because they were out of options and wouldn't likely need the backup systems.

Jayleia scowled, but she went to kneel at the edge of the open compartment to examine his handiwork.

He'd wired his handheld to the glowing crystal fused to the engine feed.

"Why do we still have particle flow? The drive is shut down," she said.

"Energy production on a ship of this size relies on the main drive reactor." He crimped another wire to the crystal clamp. "Even with engines off, we need power for ship's systems."

"No room for redundancy." She nodded. "What are you doing, and where did you learn how to redesign handhelds?"

He smiled. "The Ki. This crystal is more than a data store. It's an entire library, the history, art, and literature of a species, save that it was incomplete. It was still being written when I recovered it."

Jay listened to a whisper in her head. "Ah. Confirmation that the Chekydran-ki knew you had it."

"You're hearing them," he said.

"I'm hearing something," she hedged. "I gather the queen is shoving knowledge into my brain but it can't seem to find anywhere to land or settle. Mostly, my mind is full of buzzing."

He tipped his head, considering. "Yes."

"You seem to have an easier time integrating and accessing whatever it is," she noted. "Do you suppose that's biologically based? Or does your experience with telepathy provide your brain with pathways mine lacks?"

"Great."

"What?"

"Now you're going to want to dissect my brain," he said.

"I'd give it back when I was done," she offered.

"You can have it after I'm done using it," Damen countered.

Pietre barked a laugh from beneath the deck plating. "Ready."

"Powering up," Damen said.

The light in the crystal flared, drawing her attention. It changed color from yellow to orange to red, then back again as data flooded the handheld screen.

She gasped. "You're writing the Silver City data store to the crystal!"

"It's a much faster process than stealing it. Stand by to swap out the data chips," he said, satisfaction in his smooth voice.

"Is that safe?" she asked.

He started and stared at her.

"We've never found a way to shield the crystal, have we?" she said. "Everything you dump on that rock will be broadcast."

"The Chekydran will have access to every scrap of data," he mused.

Pietre emerged from beneath the deck plating and glanced between them. "I, personally, have a problem with giving the Chekydran anything, even these Chekydran, but shouldn't we be worrying about the UMOPG military? If they've been using crystal in their ships, it's a good bet they've got a line on reading it."

Damen shook his head. "The Chekydran-ki aren't a danger to us."

"How do you know that?" Pietre demanded. "Because they say so? Damen, they modified you!"

Jayleia shifted, unsettled by Pietre's assessment. His argument made sense, but her gut said to trust the aliens who'd altered her and then sliced her open so they could engineer their species. "They did save our lives when they didn't have to. They healed us and it seems like they've tried to give us reason to trust them. The Chekydran that declared war on humanoids certainly never bothered."

"If my sources are correct," Damen said, "this data directly impacts the war in our favor."

"It's a calculated risk, then?" Pietre mused, peering into Damen's face.

"And the only device with sufficient processing capacity," Damen replied.

Pietre nodded. "All right. Let's do it." He ducked under the deck plating. "Say when."

"Verifying load," Damen called. "Looks good. Go."

"Few minutes!" Pietre replied.

Damen turned and wrapped his warm hands around Jay's. "When all of this is over, whatever it is we're wrapped up in, you tell me where. We'll go. Together."

He surprised a smile from her as her heart melted. "If anyone will have us, you mean? Our only option may be Kebgra."

He shrugged. "You're comfortable with their tradition of taking more than one partner?"

"Depends on the partner," she said. "If you wanted Pietre, we could negotiate."

He blinked, looking stunned.

It made her grin.

"At least the citizens of Kebgra have seen biomechs before," she said.

"They'd know how to handle them," Damen agreed, still smiling.

Jayleia's brain stumbled and froze.

"What?"

"My mother said, 'Seek refuge someplace that knows how to deal with these monsters.'"

"The Citizen's Rights Uprising? Why?" Damen demanded.

"I am an idiot," she breathed. "I didn't put it together until now. Every last one of my bodyguards was CRU. My father is on Kebgra or on a CRU missionary ship."

"You're sure?"

"No, but it stands to reason," she said.

Damen stared at her, his expression unreadable.

"Your father is running the CRU?" He sounded different. Assured. In command.

Shock rippled out from her core slowing both her heart rate and her breath. Her feral Azym, code runner and Silver City sex worker had vanished, transformed into a damnably attractive but far more lethal creature—a Claugh nib Dovvyth spy. In his expression, the predator's pure, uncomplicated drives had been replaced by lines of astute cunning and by the weight of responsibility.

A thrill of desire ran headlong into a new twinge of fear within her. He'd spent years being groomed by the Empire's spymaster. How much choice had she had when she'd surrendered to the spymaster's prodigy? After all, why interrogate when he could seduce her into disclosure?

She choked on a bitter laugh.

She eased her hands out of his grasp and straightened. Ignoring the sudden flexing of the muscles in his jaw, she said, "Not running. Cultivating a series of loyal undercover agents. Their missionaries and CRU fact finders are scattered across Tagreth Federated. They're viewed as harmless crackpots. Dad realized years ago they represented an invaluable source of information. One thing led to another, I gather."

She blew out a slow, steadying breath, trying to ease the sense that she'd maxed out synaptic capacity for sorting and rebuilding data matrices. "I need to send a message to the nearest CRU ship or facility. How long will V'kyrri take to achieve orbit?"

What did Damen see in her face to soften the hard edges in his expression as he moved to a control panel? "A few hours. At least he's in com range. Here. Recording."

Jay nodded. "Jayleia Durante for Augustus Ortechyn. Augie, New Scripture. The Book of the End Times. Chapter, the last. Verse, the last. Judgment. May the Gods bless the righteous."

The muscles in Damen's jaw flexed and thunder threatened in the glint of his eye. "What does that code phrase accomplish?"

"What I presume you've wanted all this time," she said. "Dad had more than IDs on the traitors. He's spent the past decade infiltrating the network. It is the command that will start the takedown."

He rocked back on his heels and growled, "You shared research data with your dad?"

"You never asked what he shared with me," she muttered.

Damen swore. "I am required to notify Admiral Seaghdh of your father's suspected whereabouts."

"Why? I've given you what he would have. Are you going to send the message?" she asked.

"It's away. Anything else I should know?"

She considered as he narrowed his eye at her. "I'm not certain this was the right thing to do. Nothing in my training ever accounted for this circumstance."

"Being marooned on a planet full of Chekydran?"

"Considering you an ally," she corrected. "Common opinion among TFC citizens is that the Claugh covets our territory and our resources."

"I certainly covet your—resources."

A flush burned her cheeks.

His roguish grin died. "You didn't expect to be in enemy hands."

She shook her head and rose. "Not even when I like those hands and what they can do."

The smile returned. "Where are you going?"

"Into the field," she said. "I have a complex, sentient species and no data in the scientific literature about them."

"Chips are in!" Pietre called. "Go!"

Damen glanced at where Pietre crouched, then back at her. "What is the *Sen Ekir*'s standard field op protocol?"

"Depends on the field," she quipped, heading for the door. "Ten-minute check in? *Sen Ekir* coordinating?"

"I will take command at the first sign of threat," he countered.

"Good," she said. "That's worked out well for me so far."

He winked.

She strode down the ramp, aware she'd have to follow her

several-kilometer trail back to the queen and to the nest chamber where her genetic daughter developed. Dr. Idylle would be fascinated. *If* she told him.

"Powering up!" she heard Damen yell as she angled for the *Sen Ekir*.

On board, Dr. Idylle and Raj's voices drifted to her from the labs. Still dealing with the bloodworms, she assumed.

She headed for her cabin, intent on changing to a set of clothes that hadn't been sliced clean through.

"Jayleia," Dr. Idylle said from behind her as she opened her cabin door.

"Sir?"

"I won't have you blaming yourself for the accusations made against the *Sen Ekir* and its crew," he said.

"I don't. I blame my father."

His brow furrowed. "Speaking as a father who has born both his fair and unfair share of blame, I can point out the deficiencies of that strategy."

Jayleia smiled. "The foremost being that it impacts my father not at all?"

"Certainly not at the moment."

"No, sir," she corrected, old sadness stirring behind her breastbone. "Not at all. It's the price of being what he is. Other people's opinions can't matter to him. Not my mother's. Not mine."

"I hope for his sake that isn't true," Dr. Idylle said, leaning one shoulder against the door frame. "If it is, he will be a bitter and lonely man. I would like to think it isn't too late for him."

"I'd like to think it isn't too late for me," Jay breathed, staring at her closed closet door.

"You will always have a family here, aboard this ship," he said. "I apologize if this is inappropriate, my dear, but I have thought of you as an adopted daughter. Perhaps I'm guilty of treating you . . ."

"A-adopted?" Jay choked. Heat flooded the backs of her eyes.

"I didn't mean to distress you," he said, straightening, the lines around his blue eyes deepening in alarm. "My apologies."

She rubbed her eyes with the heels of her hands and barked a laugh. "No. I'm honored and pleased. Ari has so much going for her. Looks, brains, strength of will, a really bad temper, and yet the one thing I most envied her was that she had you for a father."

A delighted smile lit her boss's face. "Does this mean I might succeed in persuading you to use my given name upon occasion?"

She nodded. "Yes, Linnaeus. Thank you."

"Then, if I may go on presuming to treat you as one of my own," he said, still smiling. He left the doorway to put an arm around her shoulder. "About Major Sindrivik. Am I losing yet another of my family to the Claugh nib Dovvyth? Or gaining a new crewmember?"

Jayleia's heart kicked hard. "Neither."

He said nothing for a moment. "Of your possible answers, I admit that was not the one I'd hoped to hear."

She blinked. "My government may have kicked me to the airlock, but I won't give up on TFC. There's too much worth preserving. Damen can't carve away the part of him that belongs to the Claugh, not without cutting away who and what he is. There's a vast expanse of increasingly unfriendly space between our two worlds. I can't bridge that."

"Do you love him?"

She sighed. "I'm running for my life, ruining everyone else's lives, failing to find my father, and now I've been changed in some fundamental way by the Chekydran. I can't even begin to contemplate love."

"It hadn't occurred to me that my xenobiologist would be afraid of love," he said.

"Not of love."

"Loss?"

She nodded.

Dr. Idylle's arm tightened around her shoulders briefly. "My dear, life is a risk in and of itself. Isn't the act of loving someone an enriching enough experience to sustain you through the pain of loss?"

"Not in my experience," she said.

"Ah. Your parents," he said, pulling away and returning to the doorway, his head down and his hands clasped behind his back.

"They were so unhappy, so hurt, using me as a weapon against one another. The gulf between them was so wide," she murmured.

"And you spent your childhood trying to close it?" he asked.

She nodded. "I couldn't, of course. I swore I'd never get into a situation like it. And here I am. I'm not enough to bridge the divide between Damen and me."

"If you will accept unsolicited advice from an old scientist," he said, looking back over his shoulder, "I'll say this—only you can decide if what you feel now is worth the potential for pain."

"Do you regret your wife?" The words were out of Jay's mouth before she could stop them.

He turned, a wistful look in the shine of his eyes. "Not for a moment."

Stillness settled inside her. Even knowing that his wife had broken the law and genetically engineered his youngest daughter, knowing she'd lied to him up to the day she'd died, he had no regrets about having loved her?

Jayleia drew a deep breath as her heart seemed to settle into place inside her. "Thank you."

Dr. Idylle smiled. "Of course. Another unsolicited piece of advice? You might change that shirt before your cousin sees it and realizes you're carrying three new scars."

"Would you be willing to meet the reason for them?" she asked.

His expression darkened.

"These aren't the same creatures that hurt Ari," she said. "They don't look like the Chekydran we're accustomed to seeing. They certainly don't behave the same way. I have assurances that you will not be infected or modified."

Curiosity won past the distrust and remembered rage in his gaze. "I can't see that it will matter at this point whether the Chekydran keep their word in that regard. I'll gather my equipment."

CHAPTER

34

"Fascinating!" Linnaeus Idylle breathed as they stood beside the nest chamber of the Chekydran infant bearing Jay's DNA. He glanced at the nursery attendants working nearby, and then at the queen. "Splicing DNA from three parents indicates a level of sophistication and control that we cannot yet match. Have you been able to determine the purpose of the changes they're making?"

Jayleia shrugged. "Vision is the obvious outward manifestation, but I suspect the primary purpose is to diversify immunity."

Frowning, Dr. Idylle backed away from the nest chamber as the nurses began covering it with fluffed web.

Jay activated her badge. "Damen? Do you have a complete data set?"

"Yes," he replied.

"It's stunning," Pietre said. "With the right hardware, you could walk through the records on this crystal as if you had been there when the files were captured."

"Reliving history?" Jayleia asked. The notion both tickled and repelled her.

"Another non-humanoid species' history," Damen answered, "as experienced by them."

She shared an avid grin with Dr. Idylle, who immediately tapped his badge to join the channel.

"That data may be priceless," he said, "from both a scientific and tactical point of view."

Jayleia gasped. "We could define the progression of Chekydran biological warfare if it's encompassed in the time frame covered."

"I don't have the time for speculative searches through the Chekydran material," Damen said. "We're combing the Silver City data store."

"We already have confirmation that the United Mining and Ore Processing Guild made first contact with the Chekydran long before they admitted they had," Pietre said.

"Any mention of what happened?" Jay demanded.

The Chekydran-ki queen warbled. "Death."

Dr. Idylle jumped and spun to face her.

"She says, 'Death'," Jayleia translated, frowning. "Whose?"

A memory that wasn't hers unfolded inside Jay's mind. Bodies. Blood. Terrible, wracking pain. Everyone and everything she'd ever loved, dead. The music of life dimmed and fell silent over the nest plains.

She staggered.

Dr. Idylle grabbed hold of her arm. "Jayleia?"

"It's okay," she rasped. The sense of loss struck open the memories of her first trip to Ioccal, when an entire ship full of her friends and crewmates had fallen ill and died.

The queen hummed. It registered as a caress of comfort.

Grappling for control, she gasped, "The UMOPG introduced humanoid illnesses into the Chekydran. It devastated them. They're on the brink of extinction."

"Of course," Dr. Idylle said. "The hive model upon which the population appears to be based results in a nearly homozygous genetic profile of the species."

"What?" Damen demanded over the com line.

"Millions of siblings," Jay translated. "They are all one family with only the genetic variation to be had in the process of recombination. Their immune systems were so alike that what harmed one Chekydran harmed them all. We've seen this before in first-contact situations."

"But they survived," Pietre protested. "Didn't survivors breed with other survivors?"

"If the Chekydran reproductive cycle follows other insectoid hive models, the queen and a single male who is her son are the sole breeding pair," Dr. Idylle said.

Jayleia nodded. "That is the case. Under duress, a Chekydran queen can and will create more queens, but they are her daughters and the drones are her sons."

"Inbreeding," Raj finished.

"Outcrossing was their only hope," Jay said.

"It also suits a sense of justice to use the species that precipitated their population crisis in the first place," Dr. Idylle added.

"It is poetic, isn't it," Jay agreed. "I can't know whether that played into the decision or if humanoids were simply the only available, remotely compatible, resource."

"If humanoids transmitted disease to the Chekydran," Raj essayed, "it suggests our species have enough genetics in common for the insectoid/humanoid outcross to work."

"Do you know," Dr. Idylle said, glancing around the nest plain, "I've seen larva and adults. Where are the pupae?"

An alarm wailed over the com.

The shrill of fighter engines drowned out the *Kawl Fergus*'s proximity siren.

The Chekydran-ki queen screamed.

Jayleia started, heart pounding in fright. She and Dr. Idylle stared at the huge creature. She'd risen to her full height, her head thrown back, her iridescent throat pouch shimmering.

"Incoming!" Damen shouted over the line.

"V'kyrri?" she hollered.

"Negative!"

Nursery attendants joined the keening shriek and swarmed as one, scurrying to the left.

Another sound reached Jayleia.

Weapons fire.

Horror knifed into her gut. She stepped toward the sound. What the Three Hells? More important, who and why?

Damen teleported in beside her and Jay started again. He gripped her arm tight enough to wring a cry of protest from her.

"Soldiers. Like Kebgra," he gasped, his expression grim and pale, his eye blazing with rage. "Killing. Nests."

She stared at him. Sensor readings? Or the Chekydran queen speaking directly into his head? What language did he hear when the matriarch bespoke him?

Then his words registered and a chill moved through her.

"Nests? Why?"

A swarm of nursery attendants, wailing a battle cry that made Jay's blood run cold, harassed a group of soldiers. The biomechs had come close enough, firing at the ground as they strode across the plain, that she could count the flashes of their weapons. Twelve.

"Evacuate!" Damen shouted.

Jayleia held her breath as the nursery attendants reached the line of soldiers. The biomechs ignored the adult Chekydran flailing at them.

The attendants weren't coordinating their assault, weren't concentrating on taking the soldiers down one at a time. As a result, they had no appreciable impact.

The misshapen, grotesque soldiers could afford to ignore them in favor of slaying the young in their nest chambers. Why destroy the infants? They were the future.

Was that it?

For the first time, Jayleia noticed the scars lining the carapaces of the Chekydran-ki rushing past her to join the fray. She realized how few of the creatures there were to defend the nest plain.

This queen and her family were under siege.

Fury broke free deep within Jayleia's psyche. She dropped her handheld. No one victimized the innocent. Not of any species. Not while a Swovjiti warrior lived to stop them.

The bastards were killing children.

She'd taste their blood for it.

Damen felt the change in Jayleia, smelled the chemical bite of rage overtaking her scent. He squeezed her arm. It brought her head around to look at him. A stranger stared out of her eyes.

"We don't have weapons," he cautioned.

"I'm the weapon." She pulled out of his grasp. Without a word, she sprinted into danger.

"Jayleia!" Dr. Idylle cried.

Damen swore.

"Teleport back to the ship," he commanded. "I'll get her."

Dr. Idylle gaped at him, then his features tightened with grim lines. He nodded.

Damen tore after her. So much for a coordinated plan.

He surveyed the nest plain. Two of the nursery attendants lay dead or dying. Their assaults on the bio-engineered soldiers had finally drawn fire.

Jayleia reached the retreating front line of defending Chekydran.

A cadre of Chekydran soldiers flew over Damen's head to join the battle. Too few, too late.

Jayleia ran straight up the back of one of the nursery attendants, vaulted over the creature's head, flipped in midair, and came down boot first in a soldier's exposed face.

Pride nearly burst his chest. He couldn't see it through the line of Chekydran, but he smelled the soldier's acrid blood. He grinned as something primitive and bloodthirsty woke within him at the scent.

He crossed the Chekydran defensive line and saw no sign of Jayleia, though he sensed her nearby.

He scanned the advancing enemy. Nine soldiers remained. His fingers itched for a gun and a trigger to pull.

The soldiers were grotesque parodies of various humanoid forms, bio-organic armor covering every bulging, oversized body part. Only their faces remained clear, their milky white eyes fixed on their targets. Every single one of them strode the nest plain, destroying with mindless efficiency.

Damen darted, snarling, to the nearest dead body and grabbed a gun.

Two soldiers responded, raising weapons.

A tentacle whipped around his waist and flung him out of the line of fire. Pulse rifles whined. A Chekydran soldier screamed.

Damen cursed.

Jayleia answered.

Something impacted his chest. He glanced down as want rocketed through his body. A bloody hand shoved a second rifle against his ribs.

Jayleia.

Damen sniffed. Not her blood. Good. He gathered the former owner of the gun she'd given him would no longer need it. His grin widened. Too bad Jay had no idea what an aphrodisiac the hunt was to him. Once they'd killed the soldiers, maybe he could show her.

"Try to miss me," she said before she sprinted away and used another Chekydran as a springboard to launch an attack. Her target dodged and trained its rifle on her. She tumbled, rolling to her feet and then springing head over heels away from the advancing line of soldiers.

Damen's heart clenched hard. He lifted one rifle, knowing he'd fire too late to save her.

Flashes from the soldier's weapon, the stench of wyrl-web burning. No cry of pain from his mate. Her acrobatics kept her ahead of the deadly spray of energy bolts.

He sighted and fired. The shot impacted the soldier's head, but not the exposed flesh of the creature's face. Damen drew a shallow breath, held it, acquired his target, and as the soldier turned to fire upon him, he squeezed the trigger.

The soldier's face disappeared in a sickening burst of energy and flesh.

Eight soldiers.

Damen retreated to keep the line of Chekydran between him and the still-advancing biomechs. They'd slowed, he noted, and focused more firepower on the adult Chekydran.

But something vital had shifted among the Chekydran, too. The nurses and the soldiers concentrated their efforts, focusing on a single target at a time.

Jayleia's doing?

Seven . . . no, six soldiers.

Fierce gratification welled up within Damen as Jayleia bounded out of nowhere to deliver a bone-crushing kick to a soldier's jaw. The soldier's head jerked with such violence that Damen suspected she'd snapped his neck. She'd chosen a target lagging behind the rest as if she'd trained for the hunt her entire life.

Still grinning, Damen picked off another target as Jayleia grabbed up the fallen soldier's rifle and shot him point-blank in the face before she dropped the weapon and vanished.

Five soldiers.

Four. One went down screaming beneath the onslaught of enraged Chekydran.

Again, the tenor of the battle shifted. Damen couldn't single out what alerted him. Scent change? Whatever it was, cold apprehension gripped his innards.

"Jayleia!" he roared.

"The queen!" she shrieked. "Shield the queen!"

The Chekydran picked up the cry as they tore another soldier to messy pieces before turning as one.

Three soldiers barreled through the defense line, guns poised, already aimed. Already firing at the queen.

Damen threw himself in front of the Chekydran-ki queen, spraying suppression fire at the oncoming soldiers.

Laser fire grazed his flank, ripping a bellow of pain and protest from him. Damen landed in a heap, hazing as fire ate at his side.

He saw Jayleia falter. Her lovely cream and chocolate complexion blanched. Then wrath seemed to explode within her. He swore she grew larger as she charged a soldier from behind. The creature spun at the last moment, firing.

She wasn't there to hit. Jayleia had dropped to the ground, sliding in to sweep the soldier's feet out from under her. The soldier went down hard, raising yellow orange filaments of wyrl-web into the air. Jayleia pounced, slamming the heel of her hand into the soldier's face.

They were close enough that Damen heard the sickening crunch when bone broke beneath Jayleia's rage-empowered onslaught.

A com badge beeped.

"Raj," a voice rasped. "Medical emergency. My location. Pietre. Bring weapons."

"No," Damen croaked. "Pietre, stay with ship. Alert *Queen's Rhapsody.*"

"Belay my order, Mr. Ivanovich," Dr. Idylle said. "Major Sindrivik is right. Get that cruiser here."

Dr. Idylle knelt beside Damen. He stared ashen and shaking, as Chekydran tentacles grappled one of the last two soldiers to the ground. The thing went down firing.

A guttural yelp from behind him froze Damen's heart in his chest.

The Chekydran paused, and then caterwauled in one despairing voice.

The assassin had hit the queen.

Jayleia rose covered in blood. Damen heard her gasping, her breath coming in sobs.

Crying. Her sorrow clawed apart his ribcage, but she did not hesitate. Snarling, she stalked the last soldier, terrible, dark liquid dripping from the claws she'd made of her hands.

Damen could feel the gun still in his grip. Locking away hurt, shutting the door on the queen's rasp rattling his brain, Damen sighted the remaining soldier and pulled the trigger.

The last soldier's head exploded as Jayleia closed on him. Blood, brain matter, and bits of biomechanical yuck sprayed out all over her. She'd throw up later.

It was over. Not without cost. The queen was down, probably dying. Damen had been hit. Three Chekydran bodies littered the plain. She couldn't count the number of smoking holes in the ground that had once contained infants.

Jay sprinted for Damen, then stumbled to a halt at the horror-stricken pallor of Dr. Idylle's face as he gaped at her. The rush of adrenaline, which had fired her through the battle, flashed off as terror stabbed through her.

Her crewmates knew about her Temple training. Until today, none of them had ever seen her use it. Raj, believing he understood her capabilities, had tried to explain to Pietre and Dr. Idylle.

She'd hoped to never have to prove to them that the Temple had, in its own way, turned her into as efficient a killer as the biomech soldiers she'd destroyed.

Dr. Idylle's fear cut, severing her from the people she'd believed understood her.

But how could they? They only knew a part of her—the part she'd allowed them to see. She'd never given them the chance to know and accept or reject all of her.

Until now.

It had never occurred to her how much someone else's fear could hurt.

The Chekydran scuttled past her as a huge, glittering creature flew overhead, circled back, fragmenting the light into myriad rainbows full of colors Jayleia couldn't identify. It landed beside the queen.

Its head swung toward Jay, drawing her gaze to his and she knew him. The beautiful, elegant creature with eyes black as bottomless pools was the queen's consort.

"Jayleia," Dr. Idylle gasped, struggling to his feet as Raj teleported in beside him.

"Twelve Gods!" Raj yelped when he spotted her.

"Are you hurt?" Dr. Idylle demanded.

Trembling with dread and reaction, she shook her head and dropped to her knees beside Damen.

Raj swore. The whites of his eyes showing as he tried to keep an eye on the Chekydran gathered around their queen. He rounded Damen and knelt beside her.

Jayleia scrubbed moisture out of her eyes with one filthy forearm.

She tried not to notice that the man who'd claimed her as an adopted daughter an hour ago could no longer meet her eye. "Damen? Raj is here."

"He'll be okay. Burn damage," Raj said. "Blunt-force trauma."

Damen groaned.

Jayleia choked back a curse.

"Easy," Raj said, ripping open his field kit. "We'll get the pain under control and set you up for a few hours of regen."

"Not for me," Damen rasped, shaking his head. "Treat the queen."

The color drained from his face. Pain response. Possibly shock. Damn it. Jayleia rose.

One of the Chekydran, a long sear mark marring her thorax, sidled close, her throat pouch quivering. As she edged past, Jay saw she carried something gelatinous in her tentacles. She began patting the reddish purple substance into Damen's wound.

"Spawn of a . . ." Raj bit out.

"Stop it!" Dr. Idylle protested.

"Leave her!" Jayleia commanded. "She's healing him!"

Her family stared at her as if they'd never seen her before in their lives.

Damen stirred, restless and sweating.

Rubbing her forehead as guilt shot through her, Jay turned away. She should have anticipated the assassination attempt. Regardless of why the soldiers attacked the Chekydran, once it had become clear they were attacking, she should have realized assassination made sense. If your mission is to destroy the young, destroying the source of those young would be even more effective.

Maybe she'd been a scientist too long. Her questions, her desire to analyze had slowed her. If she'd simply reacted, adhered to her training, Damen and the queen would never have been injured.

She shoved her way through the cluster of Chekydran blocking the felled queen from view.

They opened a path.

Jay glanced at Damen. He understood what she'd done, what she'd become in order to protect Chekydran—members of a race bent on destroying her own. If conspiring with them made her a traitor, what had she become by fighting to preserve them?

He clawed his way around to meet her gaze.

She saw approval, even pride, in his eye. It soothed the ache behind her breastbone.

Fortified, she turned and cried out in horror. One of the queen's wings had been severed. Her throat pouch was ripped and charred. Yellow green fluid stained the ground beneath her prone body. The right side of her carapace had cracked. One eye dangled, the iridescent light dying.

But still she lived.

"My handheld," Jayleia breathed, rushing to her side, cold tears sliding unbidden down her face. "Where is it? I need to understand Chekydran biology . . ."

The queen wheezed.

It registered in Jayleia's head as amusement tinged by warmth, as if her desire to treat the queen, despite everything that had happened on the nest plain, had reached past the barriers of their separate species.

"I don't know what I can do, Jay," Raj said, his voice shaking, "but I'll try."

"Field stasis?" she breathed.

"I don't even know that it would work," Raj protested.

"Can we please try?"

She felt her cousin's stare.

When he answered, the sharp edge of tension had left his voice. "I'll get it set up."

She wondered what had shown in her blood-and-gore-smeared face to make him sound like that.

"Major Sindrivik's bleeding has stopped!" Dr. Idylle called, striding to join them. "We need more of that gel they used on him, assuming it's designed for Chekydran physiology rather than humanoid."

"Good. Jay," Raj prodded. "Ask them."

The queen convulsed.

Jay choked on futility. The creature was Chekydran. Even with the *Sen Ekir*, Dr. Idylle, Raj, and equipment in a language Jay could read, their medical gear was calibrated for humanoid biology. Everything she knew—everything she was—wouldn't be enough to save the queen.

"Show me how to help you," Jayleia said.

The creature grunted and, with a trembling foreleg, pressed something into Jay's filthy hand.

She staggered. Images, memories not her own, lineage, and history whirled through her head, seeking to burrow into brain tissue already too crowded. She sucked in a ragged breath and the impression broke apart.

"Queen," the Chekydran queen whistled.

Damen gasped.

Everything but Raj and Dr. Idylle, busy setting up the mobile stasis field, froze.

CHAPTER

35

JAYLEIA'S pulse thundered in her ears as she stared at the wounded matriarch.

A sweet scent filled her head. Jayleia blinked. Her stomach rumbled. She looked at what the queen had given her and frowned, unable to identify the white substance. A sheen moved over the surface of the glob in her hand. The smell emanated from it.

As Jay glanced at the Chekydran queen, then around the group of stock-still Chekydran, awareness burst through her.

Royal jelly, the substance only the queen of a hive could produce that turned a developing larva from worker into a queen.

She'd offered Jayleia the rule of this portion of the Chekydran race. After the complete hash she'd made of trying to protect the hive?

Jay shook her head. Pride had led her to believe she could pick up the mantle of a warrior without consequence. As a result, Vala was dead. The Temple had been attacked and her family shattered. Damen had been injured again, and Jay had cost a species the life of its matriarch.

No. She couldn't lead these beleaguered creatures. They couldn't even understand one another. They needed a queen who shared their biology and their way of life.

Of course they did. And maybe, if she'd checked her ego before coming to this planet, Jay would have seen that she wasn't being offered the rulership of the race, only the opportunity to declare the new ruler because the old one lacked the strength to do so.

She stalked five or six paces away to the nest chamber she'd shown Dr. Idylle. Jay held out the royal jelly to the nearest attendant and pointed at the infant Chekydran.

"Her," she said.

The attendant's momentary hesitation made Jayleia wonder if she'd committed another grave error in information processing.

Then the creature leaped forward, scooped the precious jelly from her grasp, and began feeding it into the chosen nest chamber. Two more attendants rushed to assist. They rubbed their back legs together, scraping their wings in the process. A weird, churring song rose over the plain and Jay realized they were spinning webs. They were enlarging the new queen's chamber.

The old queen's shallow, broken hum of approval caressed her. Jayleia turned to aid Raj and Dr. Idylle.

The shimmering, midnight blue drone intercepted her. He trilled a note that sounded familiar. Bending, so that his face was even with hers, he studied her a moment, or so it seemed to her, as if seeking permission for something. Then he swept delicate, silky-fine antennae over her dirty face.

A flutter of unfamiliar emotion tickled through her body. Hers? Or his? Jay frowned, trying to attach a name to it. Acceptance? Welcome? It felt more complex than that.

A bare thread of sound reached her, charged her with a task.

She nodded. "I'll do all I can."

The sound of her own voice jolted her. Twelve Gods. She was making promises to aliens who'd sliced her open in order to steal genetic material.

"They're cocooning the queen," Damen rasped.

She turned.

Nursery attendants, soldiers, a few workers, and even the drone, began spinning web. A symphony arose from the music of legs rubbing wings.

Longing tugged at Jayleia. Once upon a time, the entire world had resonated with the sound of spinning, humming, and with the song of flight. Now the Chekydran were too few to sustain more than a few trembling strains at a time.

Raj and Dr. Idylle retrieved the stasis equipment, doing their best to give the Chekydran a wide berth.

Jayleia picked up her handheld from beside the two nursery attendants who were still enlarging the new queen's nest.

The device sported a crusting of crystals along the top and back of the unit. Two of the stones were milky, the rest were shades of indigo.

Weary and stiff with blood and gore, she tottered to Damen's side and fell to her knees.

Sweat still beaded Damen's face, but his color looked better. His gaze, dark with pain, met hers.

"What are we?" she whispered.

He frowned. "I don't . . ."

"We hate the Chekydran, with good reason. They're killing us. Our friends, our families," she said. "We've spent the past year working on any means to destroy them as a species. Yet you and I just threw ourselves into harm's way on their behalf."

His eye closed. "I don't know."

"They modified us."

"Yes."

"Did they control us? Make us . . ."

"No." He opened his eye; a glitter of iron will turned his expression to polished Isarrite. "I don't know what made me take a shot for a Chekydran, but I know what it feels like to be under their control. This wasn't it."

Jayleia released a shuddering breath. He was right. She'd had possession of her body. It hadn't been the buzz of Chekydran minds in her head. Her indignation and rage had propelled her into battle. What did you call someone fighting for the enemy because it was the right thing to do?

"I can tell you what I see," he said, "a beautiful, dedicated scientist with a compassionate nature and the soul of a warrior. You don't need to dissect me. You took my heart already."

Jayleia's chest tightened. Longing ripped through her, sending stinging prickles into her eyes.

"Don't you dare die," she choked, wiping dirt from his temple. "Or I swear I will dissect you for real. Stay with me. Promise."

"I promise." His smile looked wan as his fingers twined through hers. "You love me."

Her breath caught in her throat. *Damned predator.* She couldn't hide anything from him. And no longer wanted to. "Yes."

"I know."

The familiar shriek of fighters in atmosphere drew her gaze to the sky. Three biomech fighters streaked overhead, climbing. Leaving.

Jay scowled and tensed. If the soldiers had been sent to assassinate the queen, what had those three been doing elsewhere? She traded a glance with Damen.

His frown deepened.

"Were the twelve we faced a distraction? Or the main attack force?" she asked.

"One thing's for certain," Damen replied. "They know we're here."

Jayleia wiped sweat from her own forehead. "We can expect a visit from the mercenaries Eudal has hired, then."

"And the UMOPG," he said.

She smiled, not in the least amused. "After getting three of their ships handed to them in the form of constituent particles, you think they'd come here?"

"They were trying to reduce us to constituent particles," he protested.

"I didn't say they didn't deserve it," she countered, brushing the hair from Damen's face.

He closed his eye.

"With any luck, they don't have any more ships with crystal fully integrated," she said.

Raj came in behind her and activated his com badge. "Pietre, Major Sindrivik and I need a teleport to the medi-bay. Jayleia and Dr. Idylle will follow."

"Acknowledged," Pietre said.

The two men vanished.

"Jayleia," Dr. Idylle began.

"Linnaeus?" Pietre queried via the open channel. "Ready to initiate teleport."

"We're in place," he said. "Awaiting teleport."

Teleport distortion grabbed Jayleia, flashing a moment of nausea through her. Then she found herself staring at the same cargo-bay wall she and Damen had faced what seemed like an eternity ago.

"I'll get cleaned up," she said, turning and striding for the companionway.

"What happened out there?" Dr. Idylle demanded. "You changed. Someone else looked at me from out of your eyes."

She stopped short outside of medical, schooled her expression to reveal nothing, and met her boss's gaze.

His brows lowered. He looked away.

The hurt in her chest expanded.

Raj's expression clouded when he glanced at her.

"I discovered that it doesn't matter whether the children being murdered are of my own species. I changed because in the second I realized what the soldiers were doing, I became a killing machine no different than they are," she said, pressing her tone flat.

"How?" Pietre asked from the cockpit doorway.

"She's a Swovjiti warrior," Damen said from the diagnostic bed. The ripple of pride in his voice once again proved a balm for the pain clawing her.

"She's not," Raj replied, his tone apologetic as he met her gaze. "You were disavowed by the Temple and sentenced to death for betraying the people to the attackers."

The accusation slammed through her, amping her pulse. "I didn't!"

Her cousin shrugged, sorrow lining his features. "It doesn't matter anymore. Too many people are dead. The cost was too high. The Temple has been disbanded and the training halted."

Clenching her fists against the sense of betrayal slicing her defenses to ribbons, Jayleia brushed past Dr. Idylle and stomped down the ramp.

She couldn't stay aboard the *Sen Ekir*. Not when her boss feared what she'd become and her cousin condemned her in the Temple's voice.

Breath coming in ragged, shallow gasps, she took shelter aboard the *Kawl Fergus*. She went straight to Damen's cabin, shut herself into the cleansing unit, and paid assiduous attention to scrubbing away dead super-soldier.

When the unit cycled off, she put on her uniform. If the Temple had been disbanded, no one remained to tell her she'd once again lost the right to wear it.

The com panel chimed a tri-tone.

She went to the cockpit and sat in the chair she'd come to think of as hers.

Jayleia activated the channel. V'kyrri? "*Kawl Fergus*."

A moment of interstellar static.

"Unknown female on this channel," a young woman's musical voice said. "Please identify."

"Jayleia Durante!" a different female's voice, one Jayleia knew well, shouted. "Where the Three Hells have you been? And what have you done to my officer?"

Not V'kyrri.

Jayleia grinned. "Don't yell at me, Alexandria Rose Idylle. It's been a stellar few days. What possessed you to send Damen to kidnap me?"

"I did have some concern for your life," her friend countered. "I'm heartened to know you're on a first-name basis with my officer."

Jay propped her elbows on the panel in front of her and buried her face in her hands.

"Gods, Ari."

"Jay," Ari said, the good-natured, we're-playing-an-old-game tone noticeably absent. "What's going on? We expected you aboard the *Dagger* days ago. So did my father. He's been clinging to my ship like a starved bloodworm until you began broadcasting that signal."

"Yes. He mentioned that he'd decided to adopt me." *Until I scared him half to death being what I am.*

"It's not all bad," Ari said. "You inherit a couple of stuck-up prigs for siblings, but I'm not bad, as sisters go."

"Yes, but you get my mother's entire family," Jayleia countered. "You'll never have another secret."

"Oh, Hells."

"Speaking of secrets," a male voice Jay recognized as Admiral Cullin Seaghdh cut in, "where is your father?"

His voice rolled around the tiny cockpit, echoing within the confines of her head.

"I don't know," Jayleia replied without consciously choosing to answer the question.

She straightened, frowning. He was Okkarian, a race rumored to possess a voice talent that allowed them to compel other humanoids to do their bidding.

And she'd just had a firsthand demonstration. She didn't know whether to be outraged or captivated.

"That's enough," Ari commanded.

"No!" Jayleia countered, deciding on captivated since Ari seemed to have outrage covered. "That's amazing. Is the ability innate or can it be learned? If it's physiologically based, do you know what that means?"

Jay heard the grin in Ari's voice when she replied, "Anyone who hears and reacts has a physiological basis for responding to compulsion, which indicates an adaptation on the part of the Okkarian race to take advantage of primal brain constructs present throughout a number of species."

"Exactly! Would you be willing to try it again, Admiral? With a different question?"

"Where is Major Sindrivik?" Seaghdh demanded, his voice powered down.

Irked by the suspicion in his tone, Jayleia shot, "I'm a scientist, Admiral. I don't have the time or the inclination to seduce your friend into an allegiance change the way you did mine. I found it more expedient to tie your agent to the bed."

Ari choked on a laugh.

Jayleia cringed and buried her face in her hands, torn between mortification and laughter.

"Congratulations, Admiral," Ari said. She sounded incongruously placid. "You've managed to piss off the most even-tempered person I know. Stellar people skills, Seaghdh. Really."

The tension ran out of Jayleia's taut muscles. She should have known Ari wouldn't blindly pick a side. Not his. Not Jay's.

Where did that leave them?

She heard and recognized Damen's footfalls on the deck plating a moment before he settled a hand on her shoulder.

Tied to the bed, indeed. Jayleia's pulse jumped, but she shot him a frown over her shoulder. He'd been injured. Why was he up? "Shouldn't . . ."

"I'm here, Admiral," Damen said. The laughter in his tone crushed Jayleia's fervent hope that he hadn't heard her sarcastic response to his boss.

Electricity radiated from his touch, catalyzing a potent, debilitating flood of chemicals into her blood.

"Mission objectives, Major?" Admiral Seaghdh rumbled.

Damen slanted an unreadable glance at her, then faced the com panel. He pushed buttons. Verifying a secure line, Jay assumed.

"Two out of three, sir," he said. "Though we have recent data suggesting that Zain Durante has taken refuge with the Citizen's Rights Uprising."

Jayleia pressed her lips tight. The Murbaasch Tu had a well-earned reputation for ruthlessness, something she'd seen firsthand when Seaghdh had hijacked the *Sen Ekir* and its entire crew a year ago merely to get at Ari. She imagined she knew what Damen's mission objectives read. The Silver City data store, the crystal, and her father.

Where did that leave the daughter of TFC's missing director of Intelligence Command?

CHAPTER
36

"WITHOUT the information Director Durante attempted to share with us, we are at an impasse," a melodic, cultured voice observed.

Jayleia opened her eyes. Eilod Saoyrse, the queen of the Claugh nib Dovvyth Empire, would be listening in.

Jay knew she had to represent a political time bomb and, after Silver City and Swovjiti, not just because of her father. Unless being a TFC traitor meant her father was no longer classified as an enemy of the Claugh Empire. How many enemies of their enemies did Jay have to be in order to be counted a friend?

"Are we at the point of no return?" Eilod asked, her tone making Jay's blood run cold. "Have our options dwindled to the point of eliminating the Tagreth Federated Council?"

Shock and dismay rippled through Jay.

"Absolutely not!" She was on her feet, her hands flat on her panel. She clenched her teeth to keep from speaking before she could think, but they had her backed into a corner, whether they realized it or not.

"You can't invade TFC without compromising over a decade

spent unraveling and isolating the network of traitors at the heart of TFC's government," she said.

Damen turned to stare at her. He closed his eye, but that didn't hide the hurt in the white line around his lips or the anger in the set of his jaw.

"Yes, I sent the message to CRU that should have triggered a series of quiet arrests, but I am not a spy," Jay snapped. She needed to make Damen understand she hadn't willfully misled him. "Entirely. If you attack TFC, you'll sacrifice millions of innocent lives on both sides to take out a few hundred corrupt and power-mad individuals. IntCom, in the form of my father, and a few, trusted agents, has known about the network inside TFC's government since the pandemic on Shlovkura."

"You knew?" Damen demanded.

"No one knew for certain, Major," Jay replied. "My father and his people suspected, in part, I think, because of the work done unraveling the epidemic on Ioccal. The crew of the *Sen Ekir* spoke freely about the investigations we conducted. Our science, by its very nature, could not ethically be held in confidence."

"And ideas that aren't aired and given room to breathe and grow are usually bad ones," Ari concluded for her in a muted, rebuilding-my-data-matrix tone of voice.

"The Shlovkura disaster unfolded in too predictable, too encompassing a fashion," Jayleia said. "Pandemics leave refugees, survivors. Yet on Shlovkura, there were neither. Precious few Shlovkurs survived off planet unless they were also outside TFC controlled space."

"It wasn't until long after Shlovkura had been locked and tagged as a plague world that Dad came to believe the people had been the victims of genocide at the hands of traitors within the ranks of the TFC government itself."

"Who ordered it?" Seaghdh demanded, every fiber of his voice vibrating with tension.

"President Durgot," Jayleia said.

"How do you know any of this?" Damen demanded, his expression and his tone cuttingly neutral.

Jayleia shrugged. Should she be pleased or cautioned by the fact that he'd left off the implied "if you aren't a spy"?

"When I was seventeen, my parents made me my father's data backup. At that point, I became an ancillary member of IntCom, under my father's command."

"Jayleia! What the Three Hells are you saying?" Raj grated from behind her.

Jay glanced over her shoulder. "Raj. Dr. Idylle. We have the *Dagger* on the line. I'm confiding TFC state secrets to the enemy. Come on in."

"You're implying your parents implanted something that's gone undetected all this time? For the love of the Gods, it's not possible," her cousin said.

"Assume that it is," Dr. Idylle countered, concern in his voice. "How would it be possible?"

"It isn't!" Raj insisted. "It would have to be a device, wouldn't it? Minds cannot function like computers. One cannot simply upload data to them."

"I'd implant a shielded medical chip," Damen said. From the considering, slow cadence of his words, Jay suspected he was developing his thoughts as he went, reverse-engineering the possibilities in his head.

"The challenge would be anticipating changes in medical technology which might prematurely expose the hiding place, but if you've already programmed the device to receive regular data burst updates, modifying the shield coding as necessary would be a minor inconvenience. You should know, Admiral, that the guild indicated they'd implanted some kind of listening device in me."

"Yes," his commander said. "We removed that when you first joined us so we could feed the guild information we wanted them to have."

Relief stood out in the stark shadows beneath Damen's eyes.

Raj shook his head. "Governments are so twisted. Even if Jay had some kind of shielded device, I'd have seen indications of the energy signature. The shield itself would have shown up on scans as—" He stopped short. Awareness burst over his expression and darkened to anger.

"I take it something has been showing up on your cousin's medical scans?" Admiral Seaghdh ventured into the silence.

"A calcification on a collarbone," Raj said, his tone weary, defeated. He glanced at her. "Your parents said it was surgery to repair the break in your collarbone."

"I agreed to it," she said. "I went in fully informed, Raj. I seemed uniquely qualified to serve."

Her cousin blinked, looking unsettled.

"Now this is interesting," Ari said.

"What?" Seaghdh's tone was bland.

"We're being hailed by Zain Durante," she said.

The bottom dropped out of Jayleia's stomach. "What?"

"*Dagger*," her father's voice said via the open com channels. "If you will authorize a secure location and path, I will transfer information pertinent to the Empire to your ship."

"Stand by to receive data," Ari commanded.

"Standing by. Data received. Flashing files to your specified location," her father said. "May I speak with my daughter?"

"I'm listening," Jay said.

"How long?" her father demanded.

She raised her eyebrows. She'd never heard such anger in his voice. "How long, what?"

"How long have you remembered?" her mother's voice broke in. "You were never meant to recall the implantation."

"Mother?" Jayleia marveled. "What are you—Raj said you and Bellin had disappeared! We thought you were dead!"

"The deception was necessary," her mother replied.

"You're on the same ship as Dad?"

"Yes."

"And neither of you has injured the other? You aren't neuro-locked, are you?" she shrilled, her heart slamming against her ribs.

Silence.

The faint clearing of her father's throat sounded like it covered a chuckle.

Her brain rolled. "Precisely how far does your deception extend?"

"From the moment twenty-two years ago, when your father and I separated," her mother replied, her voice serene. "Don't lose focus."

"Focus?" Jayleia screeched. "You destroyed our family and my childhood! For what?"

"Security," her father said.

"What security? You had me kidnapped!"

"Jayleia," her mother said, "it may be difficult for you to understand what a target you became the moment you were born. I was a warrior. I knew what I'd stepped into. Your father and I . . ."

"All this time?" Jayleia gasped and only then felt the tears on her face. "You've been working together? You couldn't do it while we were a family? Or let me in on the secret?"

"We have always been a family, Jayleia!" her mother snapped. "Perhaps not the one you wanted. But we are a family! When did you remember the implantation surgery?"

"When I reacted to the anesthetic and died shortly after the procedure," Jayleia said, wiping a sleeve across her face. "Didn't they tell you they had to restart my heart? Or that they had to force me into stasis without sedation to ensure I'd survive?"

"What? No! They told us you'd developed aspiration pneumonia!" Raj gritted. "That's—Jayleia, they can't have done what you say. It's unethical and illegal!"

"It's torture," Dr. Idylle said.

"It was necessary," she countered. Her voice sounded foreign to her ear, hard, dead. "The only lasting side effect is that I now have a raging case of claustrophobia."

"No," Raj said, shaking his head. "You've always had that. You were so popular for hide-and-seek games when we were kids because you hid in the open. You were easy to find."

"Raj! That is enough! Why didn't you tell us you remembered, Jayleia?" her mother demanded. "It put you in grave danger . . ."

Jayleia stared at the com panel in disbelief. "What were you going to do? Wipe my memory so I'd go missing another piece of myself? No thanks."

Raj had saved her life and her sanity. He'd come to the hospital every day, exhausted from his medical training courses, and implored her not to die.

"You promised me I could be named father to your first child," he'd finally whispered. "You can't die, Jayleia. You have promises to keep."

She met Damen's eye. He'd wiped his expression clean. The Isarrite mask he'd made of his handsome face chilled her heart. Jayleia saw acceptance in the depth of his eye, but nothing else. He'd closed down and locked her out. Desolation wrung the blood from her head. By doing her duty, she'd shattered his trust.

"Mr. Durante," Ari said. "Data transfer complete, files verified."

"The Empire thanks you for your assistance, Mr. Durante," Eilod said. "Again, we invite you and your family to accept the hospitality of the Claugh nib Dovvyth . . ."

"Your Majesty," Ari interrupted, her tone sharp.

Alarm jerked Jay to attention.

"Developing tactical situation," Ari said. "Mercenaries. My best guess is they're on approach to your location, *Kawl Fergus*. Edge of our sensor range, just leaving the reach of the last marker. Ignoring us."

"Dad? I activated the order to dismantle Eudal's network," Jayleia said.

"Yes. I did wonder what had taken so long," her father said.

"I was under the impression I ought not lead the enemy straight to your door," Jayleia snapped, knowing she was cementing Damen's belief that she'd used him. Maybe she had. "Do you have results for the dragnet?"

"The Claugh aren't our enemies . . ." her father started, his voice rising.

"Results!" she barked. "Tactical situation, Dad. Or have you decided that my crewmates and I are expendable? You've been using the *Sen Ekir* and its crew without their knowledge from the moment you had the ship built!"

"What?" Rage rang in Dr. Idylle's demand.

"Yes, we used you," her father finally said, sounding weary. "Jayleia most of all. You and your ship were in a unique position, Dr. Idylle to benefit . . ."

"In the entire span of my life," she said, "has it escaped you that I'll do anything when you ask and nothing when you order? Captain Idylle, I surrender the debriefing to you and Major Sindrivik. It appears I'm an impediment."

"Understood," Ari said.

From the tone of her voice, Jayleia knew her friend did. She rose.

Damen had to swallow a growl. Snarling at his mate's father fell under the heading of career-limiting moves. Especially when he contemplated dragging Jayleia to his bed, where he'd strip her of every secret she'd kept, every lie, every omission, every defense she'd ever imagined protected her from him.

An ache grew in his chest and in his lower belly.

Looking more alone than he'd ever seen her, Jayleia rose and made for the cockpit door. She glanced at him.

Damen met her guarded gaze, trusting she could detect his desire for retribution.

She sucked in a sharp breath and pressed her lips tight, but she didn't turn away. Holding his gaze, she nodded once as if accepting his judgment. The fire went out in her eyes. She lifted her chin.

The ache in his chest intensified. Damen stomped on the guilt rising within him. He'd asked her for honesty, damn it. She'd handed him a vial of her blood and evasion instead.

Jayleia strode down the companionway.

Bleak and empty, Damen closed his eye.

"Mr. Durante?" Ari prodded.

Damen swung back to piloting, opened his eye, and forced himself to pay attention. Survive first.

"Durgot and Eudal escaped. It was Gerriny Eudal who uncovered the agent assigned to him. Her body has yet to be found," Zain Durante said. "When she missed an assigned check-in, I went underground. Durgot has implicated his religious advisor, Ildri Bynovan. She's been sent to the front lines, accused in his attempted assassination."

Damen did growl. From the information the Murbaasch Tu had amassed on the elegant, statuesque woman, she alone, of all President Durgot's inner circle, might be innocent.

"Can she be cultivated?" Damen asked.

"Durgot's got something on her," Durante said. "Something so compelling, she's unreachable. I've spent the past four years doing my damnedest to find out what it is."

"Wasn't he grooming her for his office?" Raj asked. "She was a sure thing, next election. If she's out of the running, who will he put forward?"

"He won't," Damen said. "He'll use the assassination attempt and the war to declare martial law."

"Yes," Jayleia's father said. "He and Gerriny Eudal have seized control of the government. It is our worst-case scenario defined."

"Exile is sounding better all the time," Dr. Idylle noted, his tone wry.

"It didn't come from Durgot's office," Jayleia's father said. "When he orders someone contained and silenced, it's permanent. Over and above your undisputed value to humanoids the known systems over, Jayleia is happy aboard your ship, sir. She all but worships you. I couldn't let the spawn of a Myallki bitch destroy that. She'd have been annoyed, too, if anything had happened to her cousin."

Raj barked a laugh. "You ordered us exiled so we wouldn't end up in an IntCom black hole? Thanks, Uncle Zain."

"It wasn't a pleasure, Raj, but you're welcome. Our operation was a marginal success," the man went on. "The bulk of Durgot's network fell to my agents. We did arrest some operatives who may yet prove to be of interrogation value. They have vanished into CRU custody. This vessel is in pursuit of another suspect, the former United Mining and Ore Processing Guild Mistress, Kannoi."

"She's built a standing army. There's a base on the edge of this system," Damen said. "They have cloak tech that doesn't register on scanners. Their weapons punch through our shields as if they don't exist."

"Captain V'kyrri indicated he was investigating a hot spot at the edge . . ." Admiral Seaghdh began.

"I issued a recall," Damen interrupted. "Two, three hours ago. He acknowledged but has yet to report in."

"Com, raise the *Rhapsody*," Ari ordered.

"Aye, Captain."

"*Kawl Fergus*," Ari went on. "We're coming to get you off that rock."

"ETA to your location, six hours, Major," Admiral Seaghdh said. "The mercenaries will get there first, but not by much. Don't make it easy for them."

"No, sir."

CHAPTER
37

THE moment she cleared the *Kawl Fergus*'s doorway, Jayleia stopped and pressed the heels of her hands against stinging eyes. From the gorge behind the ship, an animal hooted, the sound carried on the anemic breeze. She lowered her hands and wandered around the aft of the vessel, pausing long enough to slide her pack inside the *Sen Ekir*'s airlock.

Mist blanketed the foliage below and the humid, spice-scented updraft seemed to have died.

She perched on the edge of the cliff, peered into the mist-shrouded foliage below, and tried to breathe around the sore spot where her heart had once been. Numbness settled over her. Was it the same emotionless state she'd cultivated most of her life? Or was it merely confusion over which feeling to allow to rise up and overwhelm her until she broke?

Damen had seduced her out from behind her shields.

Now that she desperately needed solace, she found that her defenses no longer offered shelter. Had they ever?

Maybe what she'd said to her father was true. Maybe she was the wrong tool for the job. Or simply a poorly designed one. If none of what had happened over the past several days had ever been about her, why had so many people died on her behalf? Why did her parents still seem to believe they had the right to use her as a pawn in their game? Why did her boss fear her? Pain expanded in her chest.

Why did Damen hate her?

She knew the answer to that. She'd lied to him. Not outright lied, but omission qualified, didn't it?

And what didn't seem to matter was that she had committed treason for him. And was still doing so.

She sensed his voice inside her head and heard the crystalline music of his wings, before she looked overhead to see the queen's consort dive from the bottom of the cloud layer. He lit in a musical whir of wings.

The wind from his landing buffeted her.

For no good reason, it made her smile.

He brushed her face with one feathery antenna in greeting.

Jayleia sensed it again, the emotion she hadn't been able to identify. Acceptance. Welcome, but more complicated than that. She knew what it was now.

He's accepted her not only as an ally, but also as kin, related to him by the desire to protect the queen and her progeny.

Great.

Acknowledged by the insectoid species, outcast and alienated by her own kind.

She sighed and looked back into the gorge.

A single, winged creature fluttered above the mist layer.

"I can't protect your mate," she said. "I can't even protect mine."

Her com badge beeped.

The drone settled into the soil beside her, his antenna quivering in the faint breath of the wind.

She activated her badge. "Jayleia."

"Jay," Ari said. "I need your take on our situation. What's going on?"

Jay scrubbed her face with her hands. A year ago, even after months in Chekydran captivity, she'd trusted Ari implicitly. Now?

She blew out a measured breath. How far had her friend's allegiance shifted since she'd switched sides? Jay found she couldn't judge the woman's reactions or her thought processes anymore.

And she had no idea where to start.

"We've been modified," she said.

"Raj gave us the files," Ari replied. "I have Dr. Annantra on it."

"You know Damen has the Silver City data store," she said.

"Yes. He told us about the crystal."

"And the UMOPG military."

"Naturally, because what you and I both need is another problem," Ari said.

Jay tried to smile. "The Chekydran attacked Swovjiti."

"Not of their own volition they didn't," Ari countered. "The order came from TFC."

Rage uncurled inside Jayleia. *The traitors.*

Head buzzing, Jayleia sighed, looked up at the pale sky, and said, "Ari, there are two Chekydran cruisers in orbit around this planet. Do not fire upon them. They won't fire on you."

"I don't believe it," her friend breathed. "When TFC accused you of collaborating with the Chekydran, I laughed. But it's true?"

Frustration cut through Jayleia. "Damn it, Ari, we've stumbled into the middle of a civil war. The Chekydran-ki are a different race than the Chekydran you're fighting."

"And as far as I'm concerned, the entire species can take a short orbit into their central star," Ari snapped. "I can't believe you're defending Chekydran to me."

"The Chekydran-ki saved our lives, Ari, Major Sindrivik's and mine."

"They modified you! In fact, how can I trust anything you tell me? They're in your head, Jayleia."

"You're holding an entire species responsible for the actions of a portion of its population?"

"The damned majority of the population," Ari snarled, "which is killing people as we speak."

"And this set of Chekydran want it stopped," Jayleia retorted. "They need our help."

"As if we aren't spread thin enough? No. I can't ignore the possibility that you aren't even Jayleia anymore. You're asking me to bring Her Majesty into a situation that is, by your admission, overwhelmingly hazardous. How do I know that isn't the real aim? To get at Eilod?"

"It is," Jay gritted. "The Chekydran-ki queen requests an alliance with the Claugh nib Dovvyth."

Ari breathed a curse. "Absolutely not."

"They can heal what would normally be mortal wounds, Ari," Jay said.

"Something you found out because they inflicted a mortal wound upon you," she countered, her voice rising. "I saw Raj's medical report."

Jayleia blinked. How had Raj known what had happened? She hadn't told him.

Damen. Damn it.

"It was a misunderstanding! These creatures are the last remaining source of knowledge and information acquired from a unique point of view that could swing the war in our favor! We can't throw that away!"

"You know what I can't throw away?" Ari demanded. "The lives truncated by these monsters, either by death or by modification. I can't throw away the sacrifices made by soldiers from either side of the zone in the pursuit of their duty. I can't throw away the hope we represent to the people cowering in fear on the planets in the path of this damned war."

"No," Jayleia replied, bitterness choking her. "You'd rather throw away a potential ally because of the configuration of their DNA. Is it just insectoid species to whom your prejudice extends? Or does it include the rest of us who aren't like you?"

She cut the connection and buried her face in her hands, her eyes achingly dry while rage and fear and grief carved her apart from within. What had happened? She'd thought she knew Ari.

Yes, Ari had been held prisoner by the Chekydran and tortured for months before they'd finally released her. Jay had naïvely thought her friend had gotten past that.

Maybe it was impossible to get past something like that.

Where had it happened? She thought she'd wanted her life as a scientist back. Yet in order to achieve that goal, she'd had to become something else. As it stood, if she turned her back on being a Swovjiti warrior and her father's fledgling spy, she could still be a scientist, but the Chekydran-ki would die. She'd lose Damen and the war would grind on.

It would be easy. Safe. Cowardly.

Determination stirred to life within her. She couldn't give up. Damen had been right. She was a Swovjiti warrior. She wouldn't give up. Not on the Chekydran-ki. Not on herself. Not on Damen.

Jayleia clamored to her feet.

Grumbling, the drone beside her surged to his feet.

She spun on him. "I'm done being used. By anyone. My parents. My friends. And by you! You most of all!"

He rumbled a hint of placating hum.

She waved it off. "Yes. Yes. Everyone has an excuse for taking without asking, for giving orders and then looking hurt when I balk, yet they're all the while twisting the 'but you love me' knife in my back. No. More."

He chuffed, hooked his foreclaws under her arms, spread his wings, and lifted off the cliff, leaving her stomach behind.

She yelped in surprise. A tendril of icy fear slid through her belly. Did the Chekydran register humanoid anger? Did they deal with it by dropping the irate person from altitude?

In a musical whir of wings, the queen's consort flew her over the surface of his world.

Pride not her own welled up within her. Joy, too, at the complex, subtle fragrances—she wondered at that translation. Should it be chemicals—pheromones?—brushing through his antenna on the wind?

Jayleia relaxed.

He darted into the gorge. Lush forests of bulbous trees, fragrant with exotic spice, spread beneath them. The drone chortled.

She frowned at the impression that unfolded within her. The spice trees were poison to her kind.

Interesting.

"What kind?" she asked. "Contact? Does it have to be ingested?"

Confusion answered her. He either didn't understand her question or didn't know the answer.

The drone hovered as a swarm of tiny, fluttery creatures rose in a cloud from the surface of a yellow stream. He showed her the waterfall tumbling from the black rock partway up the cliff face.

He climbed and flew her over the nest plain.

She saw the mound where the queen lay cocooned. A pang of regret hit Jayleia as she craned her neck to keep the still, web-enshrouded queen in sight.

Was she alive?

Something stirred inside Jay's mind. A faint trill rippled through her skull and she smiled.

Rest, she thought at the trill, not knowing whether it would have any effect at all. *Heal*.

The impression of someone, or something, sharing her brain space diminished. Data and experience suggested the Chekydran were a telepathic race, though data also indicated that insectoid thought patterns couldn't mesh with humanoid thought patterns any more than humanoids could produce Chekydran vocalizations. How had the queen heard her?

The drone carried her over the place where the biomechanical soldiers had landed in a dozen single occupant ships. Chekydran workers were dismantling the little fighters and carting pieces away for use elsewhere, though she couldn't say how she knew that with such surety. What had happened to the bodies?

She shuddered, not certain she wanted to know.

They paused, hovering above a nest chamber, humming encouragement in unison with the nursery attendants as another infant hatched and perched at the edge of her nest, waiting for blood flow to straighten her wings.

And Jayleia remembered Dr. Idylle's question.

Where were the pupae? Every single Chekydran she'd seen outside of a cocoon had been an adult. A Ki. The larvae were called Eyn.

The queen's consort whistled. It resolved to a familiar refrain. "Save us."

She realized he'd taken her on a tour of what the Chekydran were asking her to save.

Jayleia sighed. "Why should we trust you?"

The buzz in her head swelled.

"No," she countered. "Not me. I mean all of the humanoids out there on the front lines fighting and dying. The Chekydran out there are going to such great lengths to destroy us. You've altered me. And Damen. Without our permission. How do we trust you?"

Sorrow and regret overflowed the buzz in her brain. Her throat closed in sympathetic response. Disagreement. Violence. Desperation. He stamped the image of the massive, tentacled, aggressive Chekydran she was familiar with into her mind.

They lived in isolation on this planet.

She shuddered.

The flood of emotions and images dried up. "You're at war with them, too."

Another tidal surge of sorrow.

He was asking her to choose. Two life-forms so alien to one another they couldn't even say each other's names and he understood that by offering her a choice, he'd tipped the scales in his favor.

"Show them to me?" she asked.

Refusal.

"No more using me," she said. "Full disclosure or no more help. I can't choose with incomplete data."

Her head felt too full and she could no longer see. She cried out.

Her eyesight returned and the throb in her skull subsided to vague discomfort.

Gently, the drone shifted the information in her brain, moving a bit there, shifting a piece from this place to that. He drew forth a shard of memory that didn't belong to her and opened it.

She experienced and absorbed the memory as if it had been her own, but she knew full well she'd never walked on six legs or flown with crystalline wings.

The Chekydran pupae were called Hiin. And over a century ago, under the pressure of looming extinction, a clutch of Hiin had found a way to suppress metamorphosis. They'd broken away, warring with the Ki, until the queen and her consort had banished them from the planet.

They still had Hiin. Every larva, save the one destined to become the next queen who underwent her Hiin period inside the nest being fed by her attendants, emerged from the egg as a Hiin.

The drone expressed reluctance when she asked him to fly her over the feeding grounds where the Hiin spent months eating, quarreling, and finally, succumbing either to the chemical pressures of metamorphosis or refusing to do so.

Jayleia blinked. The queen and her consort no longer banished renegades. Sadness stabbed pain through her chest.

If they could not force their children to accept the change to adulthood, they destroyed them rather than allowing them to shore up the Chekydran-hiin war machine.

The drone took her to the mountains. Black, jagged rocks pierced the belly of the clouds. Stinging rain fell against the upper slopes in sulfurous-smelling sheets. At the foot of the mountains, thick, dense mats of purple growth hosted groups of Chekydran in a size and body form she recognized.

Her heart rate skyrocketed.

The drone hummed reassurance.

The adolescents couldn't fly and he would not land.

The wind of their passage had made Jayleia's eyes water, but it had also proven therapeutic.

She listened to the Chekydran-hiin humming as they swept their tentacles over the violet foliage below, obviously foraging.

Calm settled over her.

Some things were worth dying to preserve.

Family. Knowledge. Discovery. Peace, even when the price was gut-wrenchingly high.

She'd thought she wanted her life aboard the *Sen Ekir* back, so she could return to making a difference in the lives and health of people of Tagreth Federated.

Damen had shattered her myopic loyalty. She did love him. A feeling of power and of possibility swelled within her. How had he known?

No matter. She could no longer think in terms of protecting just her people. Didn't her work in science better all humanoids? Could she let go of her prejudices and consider working for all life-forms? Chekydran included?

As the drone turned to leave the mountains behind, she laughed. She'd accused Ari of prejudice. Looked like that blade cut both ways. Fine. The Temple had taught her that a deficiency known was a deficiency defeated.

She'd overcome terror and prejudice to defend the Chekydran. All of them. She could do it again.

Confidence flooded her. She was a Swovjiti warrior. It didn't matter what accusations were leveled at her. It didn't matter that the Temple had been disbanded. The law of the Temple said that so long as one Swovjiti lived, so too, did the Temple.

The thunder of a ship entering atmosphere startled them both, and they slide sideways in the sky until the drone recovered.

Her companion hissed.

Jayleia followed the bright arc of the vessel through atmosphere. It looked like a Chekydran cruiser. She frowned. Two of their cruisers had rescued Damen and her from the UMOPG. Why shouldn't one land?

The drone's agitation resolved into something grim and resolute inside her head.

Of course. This wasn't one of the Ki's two cruisers. This was a Chekydran-hiin vessel. The biomech assassins had been the advance guard. They'd injured the queen. The Hiin were landing and massing to finish the job.

Rage pressed against the confines of her body. She'd made her choice.

"If you give me the weapon to fight the Hiin, I can help you protect your mate!" she shouted at the drone. "Take me back to the *Sen Ekir*!"

CHAPTER

38

HE spun and flew. The ground was a blur. Atmospheric resistance and speed pushed her legs back, up under the drone's body to the point that she felt like she was the one flying.

The ships zipped past beneath them. The dark maw of the gorge yawned.

They circled, slowing.

Jay's feet touched down.

The drone let go and lit behind her.

She sprinted for the *Sen Ekir*.

Pietre gaped from the ramp. "What is that?"

"The queen's consort," she replied.

She yanked her handheld from her belt, activated it, pulled the data the buzz in her head told her was there, and thrust it at a confused Pietre.

"The Chekydran-hiin—they're the bad ones—have landed for an assault. This is a chemical weapon that may help us stop them. Make as much as you can. We'll be dosing Chekydran-hiin," she said.

"What is it?"

"Their metamorphosis key," she said.

He stared. "You're going to use the *Sen Ekir* to bomb the Cheky-dran into hibernation? That guy gave you this?"

"They are very knowledgeable about their own biological pro-cesses," she said. "They've broken down every aspect of themselves, looking for possible points of modification. Because the adults can't manufacture this chemical once they've been through their change, it hadn't occurred to them to attempt to use it as a weapon."

He stared at her, excitement lighting in his brown eyes. "Wait. So, okay, this helps win battles, but what happens when they emerge? Aren't murderous, violent Chekydran that go into a cocoon going to come back still murderous and violent?"

"Sometimes," Jayleia allowed, "but it's rare. The Chekydran-ki actually control when and how the cocoons break open. The queen exudes a pheromone . . ."

"Of course!" Pietre exclaimed. "When food resources were scarce she had to stagger emergence. I'll recall the team and get to work."

She gripped his arm. "Thanks. Where's Damen?"

"In surgery."

"What?"

Pietre waved off her panic. "Repair work. Raj had the downtime. He'll be done by the time the *Dagger* lands."

Meaning she'd have to do without his tactical ability. She'd have to do without attempting to patch up the damage she'd done to his faith in her.

Jayleia's breath hissed between her clenched teeth. She needed him. And she couldn't have him. What she felt for him would have to be enough. Her faltering courage steadied and her heart rate nor-malized.

Dr. Idylle was right.

Love *was* enough.

She grabbed her pack and sprinted into the ship, gathering laser triggers and spare power cartridges from the weapons locker. She even found two ancient plasma grenades Ari had tucked into the locker prior to the ship's original Ioccal mission.

She donned the face mask and gloves that completed her uniform.

Dressed in black, she'd be nearly invisible against the midnight-hued drone. And when it came to close quarters fighting, the Skeppanda silk would confer protection her lab clothes couldn't. She shoved her equipment and tools into the bag, sealed in, hefted it over her head and one shoulder, then returned to the drone.

Pietre boggled when she headed down the ramp. "Jay. Where are you going? Aren't you going to help?"

"I'm going to buy us time."

"You?" He shook his head. "You're too valuable to risk! We need you."

A sore place in Jayleia's heart unraveled. Pietre thought they needed her? Maybe she'd had a solid family template, just like Damen had in his family of sex slaves, all along.

"I'll be back," she promised before turning to the drone.

"Ready," she said. "Let's go protect your queens."

He picked her up. They raced to the nest plain.

"I need some of the toxin from the spice trees," she told him when they touched down. "We'll make our anti-personnel traps multi-purpose."

He hummed confusion.

A tendril of exploratory thought filtered into her awareness. She peeled off a glove and extended her hand.

He stroked an antenna across her palm.

Eyesight dimmed. Her head pounded. Rather than shifting patterns inside her brain this time, the drone seemed to page through her plans.

He left, but a tinge of amusement remained behind.

Jayleia's vision cleared and the pressure in her head subsided.

As she divested herself of the pack and began rummaging around inside, he bugled a complex, layered sound.

It wouldn't translate.

The creatures had obviously had to reduce themselves to what amounted to Chekydran baby talk to make themselves understood to her.

Evidence that the translator virus frustrated the Chekydran-ki as much as it did her?

Workers answered the drone's call.

He issued instructions while Jayleia assembled modified kuorl traps and snuck a few soil and web samples.

The workers launched, raising a pall of web and grit.

Jay swiped a hand over her face to clear the yellow web tendrils from her eyelashes and went back to work.

She'd finished assembling her traps moments before the workers returned with gobs of brown, pungent-sweet scented goo.

Jayleia demonstrated what she wanted the workers to do, packing her modified traps with the substance, then closing the doors on the six units.

They caught on instantly, chortling and whistling in apparent pleasure as they worked. One of the workers even provided a sample of the toxin when Jayleia extended a sterile swab. She stuffed the sample into a container and activated the stasis seal.

She gathered that the workers were rarely called upon to protect their queen. Their soldier-sisters, converging on the cocooned queen for guard duty, did that job.

"These are reverse traps," Jay told the drone. "I put the laser trigger on the outside and a charge on the inside. When someone activates it, the charge is going to hurt, but it will also spray this toxin into the surrounding air. We need to keep your people away from these without giving their location away to our bad guys."

The queen's consort offered reassurance. He had it covered.

She nodded. "Let's get this done."

They planted her six anti-personnel-reverse-kuorl traps around a perimeter dictated by the drone.

"It isn't much," Jay admitted, "but unless we're hit with another set of biomech soldiers, even one of these going off will give an attack force pause."

She surveyed the nest plain, her gaze coming to rest on the contingent of soldiers surrounding both the mound where the old queen slept and the enlarged nest where the new queen gestated.

"Never put all your soldiers in one formation," she murmured, quoting Temple teaching.

The drone chirped a question.

Pressure built at her temples. She held a picture in her head as long as she could.

He trilled agreement, warbled orders she felt more than she heard.

A multivoiced warble of confusion washed over her from the soldiers, but they began digging in as she'd intended.

She planted the plasma grenades. Plasma burns weren't a kind death by any means. But if the Chekydran-hiin reached the nest plain, they'd lay waste to everything in their path. Unless she made them think twice.

As they returned to the queens' mounds, she prayed her crewmates were making bucketfuls of the sleeping formula she'd given them and that they'd arrive in time to prevent that kind of slaughter she'd prepared for.

The queen's consort uttered a piercing cry. The song of his flight faltered.

They fell.

He banked hard, the noise of his wings sharp and labored. He set down hard.

Jay dropped from his grasp into the wyrl-web and dirt.

"*Oof!*" She rolled to her feet and stared at him.

"What?" she cried. "What happened?"

He settled to the ground, raising a cloud of green and yellow dust. His antenna waved.

She stepped closer. He touched her face.

Her world collapsed beneath her. Incomprehensible thought patterns assailed her. Physical sensation vanished as if cut off. Perception of up, down, depth, breadth, and width twisted around her.

She gasped.

And fell out of confusion into terror and soul-killing pain.

She recognized the source.

"Damen!"

An image played through his mind, resounding through the drone's brain and into hers.

The *Queen's Rhapsody* had been destroyed.

It arced into a death dive over a seared, rocky world. Pursued by UMOPG scouts.

Rage and panic slashed her gut.

V'kyrri. It had to be V'kyrri in telepathic connection with Damen, even as Damen lay on Raj's surgical table.

She was seeing what V'kyrri saw. On his way to death.

Please, Twelve Gods, she shrilled mentally, fighting for breath that didn't rasp in her burning throat. *Not V'kyrri. Not easygoing, good-natured V'kyrri.*

A blinding flash. Searing pain.

She screamed.

Horror ripped her out of the strange, relayed contact. Dumped her into her sorrow-wracked body, huddled and sobbing on the ground between the drone's front legs. Tears wet her face.

She knew what she'd seen.

The engine core had detonated.

They'd lost the *Queen's Rhapsody*. And everyone on board.

Helpless rage rocked her, followed swiftly by terror. If V'kyrri died while in contact with Damen . . .

"Damen!" she shrilled, anguish ripping her heart.

The queen's consort stirred, but didn't rise.

"Is Damen alive?" she pleaded. "Did he . . ."

The drone lowered one feathery antenna. It trembled.

Jayleia choked on a sob, fear squeezing her heart. She pushed herself to sitting, resting her back against the drone's carapace. Fingers shaking, she shed her glove and touched the antenna.

The drone swept his senses across the world as if they were still flying. There. Her mate was alive, but not conscious. Like the queen.

Jayleia dropped her hand to the soil and let the tears run down her face.

V'kyrri must have broken contact at the last second, right

before . . . she caught in a shallow breath and screwed her eyes shut. He hadn't taken Damen with him into death, but that didn't mean V'k hadn't done irreparable harm on his way out of Damen's mind.

How easy V'kyrri had made it to forget that telepathy had a dark and deadly aspect. Ari's telepathic attack on the TFC admiral who'd given her to the Chekydran had left the man a permanent resident of the Armada psychiatric ward.

Jayleia shuddered and closed her eyes.

"You can't be gone," she murmured aloud. "V'kyrri wouldn't want that. Damen, I need you. I know you think I lied to you. It's fair. I suspect you only seduced me because I was your assignment. I don't care."

She paused, sniffed, and scrubbed her face dry with her sleeve before leaning back again. "It doesn't make any sense. Knowing you want to hurt me for not telling you everything, and knowing you only care about your mission, how is it that I fell in love with you, anyway? It's not rational."

"I'm not rational.

"You promised to teach me."

Color. She heard it. *Cascading, swirling, humming.*

She joined in. The sound soothed her aching heart. Adrift in the play of color and hum, Jay lost track of time. At some point, another, deeper voice augmented the sound.

Damen.

Her eyes blinked open. No. Not Damen. She and the drone were alone, disabled on the edge of the nest plain.

But she'd heard Damen's voice, *felt* his presence so clearly. She frowned. She wasn't telepathic, not by a long shot. But the Chekydran were. Were they acting as a connecter, putting her in contact with her mate?

Her mate. Heart expanding, she smiled, closed her eyes, and leaned back against the drone.

She dropped into the play of color and hum.

And collided with him instantly, the gold and green glow of his mind recognizable in the sea of alien colors and minds.

Jayleia ignored her trembling heart. She swallowed against the lump in her throat at the desolate tone of Damen's wan hum.

"I'm sorry," she choked in a mental whisper.

His hum and the sense of his presence winked out.

She'd surprised him.

It took only a few seconds for him to return.

"Jayleia." He sounded ragged. "Where are you?"

"On the nest plain," she said. Grief pierced her, her own and Damen's. "V'kyrri . . ."

"He was my friend," Damen murmured. "Before I knew how to have or be a friend, he was mine."

"I'm sorry," she whispered again.

"I dreamed," he said, his voice relaxed, wistful as if he hadn't quite returned to full consciousness. "Dreamed you said you love me."

Shock rippled through her. How had he heard that? She'd spoken that aloud in the middle of nowhere, before the Chekydran hum had brought them together in a way she couldn't comprehend.

"It wasn't a dream. Do you want me to say it again?"

"Yes."

"I fell in love with you," she said, her mental voice breaking. "Some things are worth dying for. You're one."

A locked-up, frightened place inside Jayleia's heart tore free. She gasped at the initial twist of pain, but then light and heat suffused her. A sense of liberation welled within her.

Via the drone at her back, she flashed Damen a snapshot of the Chekydran-hiin landing and of the traps she'd laid.

His pride, approval, love, all underpinned by the sorrow of lost friends, encompassed her.

"I love you," he said. "I prefer you not die for me. Live, instead."

"That complicates things."

"It usually does."

CHAPTER

39

JAYLEIA opened her eyes and sat up.

"Jay?" Ari's voice on the com badge channel. "We've received data from the Chekydran cruisers you didn't want us to fire on."

"Yes?"

"They tweaked our sensors," her friend said. "I've got new targets entering system. Cloaked, but carrying a distinctive energy signature."

"UMOPG military."

"That's my guess," Ari said. "They're decloaking! Scan! I want to know what those Carozziel slime-bats ate for breakfast!"

"The lead ship's singed, Captain," a young man's voice called. "Residual energy readings match the *Queen's Rhapsody*'s main guns."

"They're making a run for the planet!" Ari yelled. "Damn it, where'd they get that speed? Weapons! Get me a shot at them!"

"Working, Captain!"

Behind Jayleia, the drone coughed out a curse.

A ship, then another and another, entered atmosphere, angling for the queen.

"Stand down, *Dagger*. I've got them." Jay watched the craft slant across the horizon and smiled in spite and satisfaction. UMOPG. The scavengers come to pick the carcass clean. Save this one wasn't dead. Not by a long shot. And regardless of Temple teaching that vengeance killed more warriors than it avenged, she intended to exact terrible retribution for V'kyrri's death.

The drone's hum strengthened. He rose, hooked his forelimbs under her arms, and lifted off.

The UMOPG scouts had set down in a tight triangle formation within sight of the queen's cocoon. A group of ten people clustered in the defensible center of the triangle.

Jayleia frowned. So many factions seemed to want the queen dead. The Chekydran-hiin she understood. What did the UMOPG get out of genocide? She studied the group, not buying for an instant that they were the sole attack force. She surveyed the plain.

Half the Chekydran-ki soldiers stood guard over the two queens. The other half were invisible.

The drone chortled approval of their preparations.

A humanoid shout sounded. Laser fire sizzled past. They'd flushed a cluster of soldiers between forty and fifty meters south of the queen's mound. The men and women sprayed weapons fire into the air.

The drone dodged, sliding one way, changing altitude, canting his body first one way, then another.

He made it look so effortless, Jayleia couldn't help but laugh. She pulled her knees up, creating a surface for her pack. It took effort and concentration to unseal it without the full use of her arms. If the drone intended to continue flying her around, they'd have to develop a harness system of some kind.

As the queen's consort circled the squad, Jay managed to extract a handful of poppers. They were little more than toys, noisemakers with a time-delay fuse, useful for flushing specimens toward a trap in the field.

She activated five fuses and dropped the tiny toys behind the entrenched group of miners wasting their power cartridges on a creature who owned this world's skies.

Pressure built in her head.

Jay showed him what she'd done.

The first popper string fired. *Blam. Blamblamblam.* Screams sounded from below.

The drone peeled east, away from the troop, as the next four strings blew.

Figures scrambled out onto the nest plain, and sprinted for their ships, dodging nests as they went.

The drone zipped sideways to watch.

Something flashed.

An innocuous-sounding pop reached Jayleia's ear over the music of the drone's wings and she realized what had happened.

The lead runner had passed within six meters of one of her modified traps.

He threw himself to one side, trying to avoid the detonation, too late. His comrades, fleeing on his heels, plowed into him from behind.

What looked like a fine spray of dark powder exploded into the air before settling to the ground. Wind currents carried it in whorls and eddies, something Jayleia hadn't calculated for.

The lead runner had suffered concussion injury and sprawled, dazed, in the webbing. His squad members shouted, then finally picked him up and ran.

Straight through the cloud of spice tree toxin.

Nothing happened.

Jayleia cursed. Now or never. Once the squad reached the ships, her chance to pick off the soldiers diminished.

"Drop me on them," she said.

Refusal. The drone clicked. It resolved as a request for patience. He dropped a meter and slid sideways, keeping the limping squad in view.

They dropped their stunned friend.

At first, she thought he'd recovered and demanded to be put on his feet. The screaming started.

One by one, the squad of eight fell into the webbing, thrashing, rolling, and shrieking in agony.

Blanching, Jayleia gathered the toxin had taken effect. But what effect?

The drone slipped upwind of the downed miners and hovered closer.

Huge, angry, red blisters covered the soldiers' faces. Where the toxin had touched clothing and armor, it had burned through and attacked the exposed skin beneath.

An attractively scented, powerful acid? Jayleia blanched. What the Three Hells did those spice trees eat?

When the first blisters began bursting and the soldiers' screams dwindled to wet, gargling noises, nausea surged within her.

Her companion spun and flew her directly into the wind. It cleared the dizziness and settled her.

This was war. She hadn't started it, but by all Twelve Gods, she'd end it.

They circled the queen's mound.

The guard trumpeted a challenge.

"There!" Jayleia shouted as movement on the plain caught her eye.

The Chekydran-hiin.

Wave after wave.

Her resolve faltered.

Where was the *Sen Ekir*?

The drone flushed another squad of twelve UMOPG soldiers advancing on the young queen's nest. They'd eluded Jay's traps and the margin for error was dwindling.

She drew her knees up again, rummaged in her nearly empty pack, and pulled out five more poppers.

Pressure built in her head.

She showed him her intent. Exultation flushed her. Hers? Or his? Did it matter?

He agreed.

Two Chekydran-ki soldiers sprang from false nest chambers as the first wave of miners crept over them. The Ki grabbed two miners apiece, one in each tentacle and began using them as clubs on their companions.

Jay activated the popper fuses all at once.

The drone darted straight at the second wave of UMOPG soldiers, standing in mute horror as the Chekydran decimated their companions.

Jay dropped the toys at their feet.

Staring at the mess that remained of their fellows, faced with an enormous, oncoming Chekydran, the squad panicked and fled when the poppers fired in unison. They scattered.

Jayleia picked the two who'd fled together.

The drone swooped in and dropped her on their heads.

Almost.

Warned by the sound of his wings and by the increase in air pressure, the two men flung themselves to the ground.

She landed a scant half a meter ahead of them and tumbled to one side to evade potential gunfire.

They did shoot, just not at her.

It gave her plenty of time to bound in, disable one man with a lethal blow to the head, flip over his body, and land on the second trooper's gun hand.

He bellowed, and yanked backward to his knees, leaving his weapon and his trigger finger beneath her boot. Gnashing his teeth, he swung at her.

An alarm shrilled inside her head, nearly blinding her. She dropped.

The deafening, crystalline noise of wings, the beat of wind against her back, and the dull sound of an overripe stripe fruit impacting a solid object rolled over her. She rose on one elbow and peeked at the man whose weapon she'd taken.

He still knelt in the webbing, but his head and the upper quarter of his torso were missing. The corpse wavered and fell, spraying her with blood.

Jayleia managed to get her knees under her before she threw up. She was eternally grateful she'd opted not to wear her mask.

The queen's consort lit beside her.

More screams reached her ears and she assumed the Chekydran-ki soldiers were mopping up the stragglers.

After a few moments of gasping and wiping the sweat from her forehead, she climbed to her feet, fished a hydration packet from her equipment belt, rinsed out her mouth, then forced herself to drink what remained of the doctored water.

It helped.

"More attackers?" she asked, tottering to the drone.

He hummed.

She nodded. "Take me to the queens then. They won't give up. And we still have the Chekydran-hiin to fend off."

His antenna drooped.

She nodded. They were both tired.

"The enemy doesn't care," she said.

He whistled agreement, hooked her under the arms, and took off. They didn't have far to fly.

She spotted the group of ten leaving the cover of their ships as the drone circled the queen's mound.

He lit atop the web sheltering his mate and set Jayleia on her feet.

She shed her pack. Empty though it was, it had thrown her off in the last fight. She couldn't afford the distraction. Had the drone not intervened, the last miner might have landed his blow.

The standing guard trilled in greeting and in exultation.

Two more UMOPG squads had been cut down. One Chekydran-ki soldier had given her life protecting her queens.

The loss cut, but without the preparations Jay and the Ki had made, far more of the fighters would have perished.

"Jayleia Durante!"

She started. After a day spent learning to hear and understand the people she'd pledged to protect, a humanoid voice sounded odd to her. Still. A part of her insisted that she should recognize the voice.

"This is Guild Mistress Kannoi! We know you're colluding with the Chekydran," the woman called.

The guild mistress? What would drag her so far away from Silver City? Unless Jayleia's quarantine flag had turned the political tide on station against the woman.

"Surrender to custody and you will not be harmed!"

Jayleia blinked. Surrender? Not be harmed? She grinned and turned her back.

"IntCom and a ship full of Ykktyryk mercenaries have your ships, your companions, and your mate," the woman yelled.

Shock jolted the smile from Jayleia's face. Fear ate at her.

"Damen," she breathed, stripping a glove from her hand and reaching for the drone.

Refusal.

She gaped in disbelief.

He called out an order.

A soldier lifted off and raced away to assess the situation, skimming low to the ground to avoid being seen by Kannoi's party.

Jayleia nodded in understanding. Talking to her drained the queen's consort. It made sense to conserve resources, regardless of how little she liked it.

Too bad she couldn't recruit the Chekydran-hiin to fight the United Mining and Ore Processing Guild Army.

"Surrender! Or I tell those bloodthirsty reptiles to start shooting!" the guild mistress bellowed.

"You want me dead!" Jayleia countered. "Why pretend?"

"On the contrary, my dear!" Kannoi returned. "I am being offered an exorbitant amount of credit to deliver you to IntCom alive. Maybe not whole. But alive."

"Baxt'k," Jayleia muttered.

The Chekydran-ki soldiers bugled in concert.

Jayleia's heart rate climbed and she stared at the drone. Anguish rang the blood from her head. Her knees gave way.

It was true.

Mercenaries had the *Sen Ekir* and the *Kawl Fergus*.

She had a choice. One she'd never wanted. She could protect the Chekydran-ki or she could save her friends.

Ironic.

She choked on a broken laugh as moisture burned her eyes. How often she'd railed about not being offered options. She'd counted choice a luxury, one the people she'd loved most had dangled just out of her reach.

The Chekydran-ki soldier circled high above the mound, the song of her flight a gorgeous soundtrack to the siege shattering Jayleia's heart.

She closed her eyes and dropped her chin to her chest, knowing what choice she had to make. Despair wrapped tight bands of pain around her chest.

"I'm sorry, Damen," she whispered. "Dr. Idylle. Raj. Pietre. If the Chekydran-ki live, they will stop the war. They have so much to give our kind.

"I have to become my parents. I have to choose to sacrifice you without even pretending to ask your permission."

Something soft and feathery trailed through the moisture tracking her face. Antenna. The tendril jerked and stiffened. Another antenna joined the first. Then another. And another.

What did her grief taste or feel like to the Chekydran that so many of them came to sample it?

"Time . . ." Kannoi began, shouting.

"Baxt'k you!" Jayleia shrieked.

She opened her eyes.

Soldiers and the drone backpedaled, peeling damp antennae from her face.

They hummed and trilled a clumsy cascade of sound that rendered as embarrassment.

Why?

Their vocalizations dwindled to a mutter as Jayleia studied them. They seemed—unsettled. She looked at the drone.

His presence in her head grew heavier and she understood.

They'd never seen tears, but in tasting them, they'd recognized an emotion analogous to their own experience of loss. Of grief.

She climbed to her feet, shoving torment to one side, and glared around the plain. The Temple taught that everyone lost loved ones. When a Swovjiti warrior lost a loved one, she honored the fallen by taking four enemy lives for each loved one she could name.

The sixteen lives Kannoi owed her wouldn't be enough. Ever.

"Get these soldiers back on guard!"

The drone chortled and Jayleia realized the soldier he'd sent to scout the *Sen Ekir* hadn't returned to her post. He touched her bare hand.

She gasped. The bands of sorrow around her ribcage loosened slightly. Her loved ones were still alive.

The drone straightened, warbling a battle cry.

Jay dove for her glove, pulled it on. Cursing, she slid down the side of the mound, rounded the Chekydran defensive line, and crouched behind a nest cap.

Jay spotted the guild mistress and her troop. Her muscle-bound bodyguards stood out. Jayleia tracked Kannoi's position by their movements. They flanked her. The seven other soldiers formed a loose semicircle around the trio, ready to close ranks at a moment's notice.

They'd stopped short of another pair of concealed Chekydran-ki soldiers.

Jayleia chewed her bottom lip, considering showing herself to see if she couldn't bait the group into the trap.

Then she heard the sound of wings. The missing Ki soldier flew high overhead.

She drove straight for Kannoi.

Jayleia shouted, jumped to her feet, and broke into a run.

The UMOPG personnel opened fire.

CHAPTER

40

SWINGING and dodging, the soldier shrilled a battle cry. She banked hard.

The dull color of the soldier's carapace flashed and changed color in the light coming through the blue and gray clouds. Her flight was a dance, an expression of devotion that couldn't last.

The fire laser bolt seared her thorax.

She screamed.

Jayleia screamed with her and stumbled to a horrified halt.

Another shot hit. Then another.

The soldier spiraled up above the formation of humanoid soldiers, burbling a death song.

The final shot tore through her wings. She tumbled out of the sky.

The guild mistress screamed. The men shouted and the formation of UMOPG personnel broke apart.

The soldier impacted directly behind them.

The sound and vibration drove a shard of agony into Jayleia's heart. She found herself on her hands and knees, fists pounding the soil as tears she didn't know she still had to cry turned the dust to mud.

A tentacle wrapped around her waist and yanked her backward.

Jayleia yelped as her tailbone hit the ground.

The drone snagged her under the arms and lifted off, backpedaling, drawing her away from the cloud of dust . . .

"Twelve Gods!" Jayleia choked.

The soldier had been carrying a payload of spice tree toxin.

Three of the UMOPG soldiers stumbled into range.

The Chekydran-ki soldiers burst forth from hiding and ripped the three men limb from limb while the remaining men realized they had a problem.

Kannoi's bodyguards hustled her out of range of the toxin cloud, whether by instinct or because their people had called in a warning before they'd died, Jayleia didn't know.

The four guildsmen from the back of the formation fell into the wyrl-web. The screaming started.

"Kill the hostages! Kill them!" she heard Kannoi shrieking.

Jayleia snarled.

The drone did, too. He launched them into the sky.

The speed blinded her. So did the pressure in her head. She understood what the queen's consort wanted, a merger of sorts. No matter how badly she wanted to, she didn't know how to give it.

He seemed to understand the dilemma. He mentally nudged something in her head.

Something shifted in her brain. Pain laced her body, but he was there, in one particular spot inside her mind. The hurt dwindled.

They slowed, circled three ships where there should only be two.

The mercenaries had her family lined up in front of the *Sen Ekir*.

Dr. Idylle, Raj, and Pietre knelt in the dirt. Two Ykktyryk mercenaries and one humanoid male stood behind them, holding guns to their heads.

The man, dressed in a navy uniform with no insignia, watched the drone carrying Jayleia, his posture relaxed, as if he'd been expecting them. Eudal.

She'd played into their hands.

Where was Damen?

The drone hummed a query. It went unanswered.

Jayleia's heart clenched tight in fear.

"Sleeping," whispered through her head. She had no way of knowing what that meant.

"Come down, Ms. Durante," the man called. "Before my friends here decide to disobey orders and avenge their shipmates."

Avenge? Jay raised her eyebrows. What had her friends and family been up to?

The drone hummed. "Attack. Who?"

"Take out the reptilian mercenaries," she said. "The tall, scaled creatures. Sufficient blunt-force trauma to the spiny ridge of their backs will incapacitate them. I'm on the third."

Because he's the most dangerous of the trio, she didn't add.

The drone dove and dropped her on top of Gerriny Eudal.

She landed a kick to the man's face with one foot, bloodying his nose and landed, clasping his pistol. She spun, wrenching the gun from his hand.

He yelped and struck her lead shoulder with his free hand.

It was exactly what he should have done. The blow augmented her momentum.

She stumbled, lost control, and tripped over Dr. Idylle's legs. Jayleia pitched the gun under the *Sen Ekir* as she fell.

Gerriny leaped to keep pace with her as she rolled away. He landed a devastating kick to the small of her back.

Searing agony rocketed head to toe. She wheezed. Her legs went dead.

The queen's consort warbled.

Desperate, heart-pounding euphoria burst through her. Not hers, the drone's. The queen was emerging from her cocoon.

The dwindling song of the drone's wings spoke volumes.

She was alone.

Eudal hauled her upright.

Her legs wouldn't hold her, would barely respond at all. Her brain registered the picture: her crewmates, kneeling in the dust, two mercenaries at their backs.

But there weren't.

Where there had been two, she saw only one. And he looked mighty uncertain. Confusion felt like another closed-fisted blow.

Eudal chortled, snapping her attention back to her predicament. His laugh was a high-pitched, unhinged sound that matched the overly bright glitter of his brown eyes.

"Did you really think I hadn't spent your entire life learning how to fight a Swovjiti?" he said. "I want your thrice-damned father. Where is he? He crippled my agency! My work! Work that would put an end to the Claugh nib Dovvyth Empire. Tagreth Federated would dominate this sector."

With trembling breath, Jay sneered and spat in his eye.

"Where." He slapped her.

She landed in a heap, tasting blood.

"Is." A kick meant to shatter her ribs, but she rolled and the Skeppanda silk absorbed most of the force.

"Your." Another kick, to her belly this time.

"Father!"

Her breath whooshed from her lungs, but the armor spread out the impact.

Once more, he grabbed her hair, yanked her to face him, and laughed his high, scratchy titter.

A memory, dislodged by the hair-raising sound, burst open in her brain.

Four years old.

Hands tied. Feet tied. Gagged. Folded up, cramped, hungry, thirsty, and scared to death. She'd cried until she'd had no more tears. She'd wet her pants. Twice.

She'd lived simply because her nightmare-ridden child's body didn't know how to give up.

She'd been kidnapped at her father's behest. Not content to allow the legal system to decide the custody battle he'd waged with her mother, he'd sent agents to abduct her.

To smuggle her off-world, the men had shoved her into an old leather valise and left her there. Once they'd lifted, two of the agents had told the third to let her out and to look after her.

He hadn't.

She'd screamed herself hoarse.

Only the young man's high-pitched, hysterical-sounding laugh had answered.

Awareness jolted her. Gerriny Eudal. He'd been the one who'd tortured her when she was a defenseless child. He'd betrayed the people she'd sworn to protect.

He'd killed innocents.

Raw, primitive fury slashed through her bloodstream. It must have shown in her face.

"Don't be stupid, little girl," he sneered. "This isn't about you. It was never about you. You're nothing but a pawn."

Wasn't about her? Never had been? She'd said it herself more than once. Yet this time, something broke free within her psyche. If all of the death and all of the pain and all of the striving hadn't been about her, that left her . . . free.

She could think and act in ways no one expected.

And sensed an echo of the drone's presence in her head. Through him, she caught something that shot exultation through every nerve and fiber.

Damen.

Awake. Furious. Bloodthirsty.

Gods, she adored him.

Jayleia spat blood and grinned.

Eudal's eyes narrowed and he stilled, his grip on her tightening.

"You studied all that time to defeat a Swovjiti? Did you never work it out?" she whispered, finally getting her feet under her. "Or didn't it occur to you to ask why the high priestess hated me so much?"

It didn't take much of a weight shift to jab a fist beneath Gerriny's diaphragm. His breath went out in a rush. He didn't quite double over, but he did release her.

She got her balance and planted a fist in Eudal's nose as he flailed, trying to catch hold of her again.

She danced in close and planted the heel of her heavy expedition boot on his instep.

The man winced.

"They hate me because I refused to fight by rote as the training program dictated," she explained, slamming her elbow into his face.

He staggered.

"I think. I adapt." She followed him, snapping a kick to one of his knees.

With a grunt, he fell.

"Once I find out a man knows how to fight a Swovjiti, I don't have to fight like one anymore."

"I should have killed you," he spat.

"When I was four?" Jayleia clarified. "You tried that."

Jayleia spun away intent on taking down the remaining mercenary.

Someone had beaten her to it.

The creature had a smoking hole in his back where his spiny dorsal ridge should have been. He'd fallen across Pietre and Raj, pinning them to the ground. Dr. Idylle was rolling to his knees.

Damen woke knowing Jayleia was in grave danger.

The hum of the entire Chekydran-ki population filled his head as, out on the nest plain, the queen emerged from her cocoon, healed. The mental noise of greeting, joy, summary, and warning drowned his initiative for a moment. Then the cacophony dwindled.

He sensed her, the Chekydran-ki queen. She'd taken up residence in a portion of his head.

She mentally nudged him.

He opened his eye and felt the patch covering the right eye socket. Relief left him shaky. He recalled Raj taking him to surgery to repair the paralysis in his face and to implant the still-growing eye that would restore Damen's sight. It would take a few days for the nerve grafts to take and for the eye to finish developing. When it did, he'd see as if nothing had ever happened.

Damen glanced around.

Raj wasn't in the medi-bay. Neither was Dr. Idylle. Nor Pietre.

He sat up.

An Ykktyryk mercenary lay slumped in the medi-bay doorway. Adrenaline dumped into his system. His senses expanded, went on high alert.

The queen flashed a picture of the *Sen Ekir*'s crew, bound, and lined up for execution outside the ship. Through her, Damen caught a faint whisper of Jayleia.

Anticipation shot into his chest.

Damen rolled to his feet, cased the corridor to the ramp, and found four Ykktyryk rifles inside the main hatchway. He grabbed one as he surveyed the situation.

Jayleia, dressed in her black Swovjiti uniform, bloody, and bruised, slammed her elbow into a man's face before taking one of his legs out from under him.

Pride and love welled up within Damen. He grinned. Gods his mate was beautiful when she was taking someone apart.

The man dropped into the yellow green dirt. It turned his navy uniform a distressing color, almost the same color as the sole mercenary's scaly hide.

Damen shot the reptilian holding a gun to Raj's head.

It took the creature several seconds to realize it had died. The corpse fell, knocking Pietre, Raj, and Dr. Idylle to the ground.

Dr. Idylle rolled to his knees.

Damen glanced at the man his mate had felled. He was down.

Jayleia leaped to tug the mercenary off her cousin and her friend. It wouldn't budge.

Damen slung the rifle over one shoulder and descended the ramp. He grabbed the dead reptilian's legs.

She started and stared at him, elation leaping into her beautiful eyes as she studied his face as if memorizing it.

"Get it off!" Pietre croaked.

She grinned.

They heaved.

Over Jay's shoulder, Damen saw the man in the navy uniform

climb to his feet, loathing in his bloody face as he cocked back to strike at her back.

Damen didn't even have time to growl.

Something alerted her.

Jayleia let go of the corpse and sidestepped the man's intended blow. She turned on her heel, coming in close to the man's hip. She landed a lightning-fast strike into the side of his head.

He screamed and went down.

Jayleia returned to drag the mercenary off her crewmates.

Damen found the neuro-cuff control and freed the men.

"Did you get it?" Jayleia demanded as the crew of the *Sen Ekir* beat the dust from their clothes.

"The formula?" Dr. Idylle asked. "Yes. I don't know that it will be enough and I pray it works."

"What formula?" Damen demanded, frowning.

"I'll explain," Pietre answered. "Help us clear the ship?"

"What did you do in there?" Damen asked, nodding at the *Sen Ekir*.

"Tranquilizers are mightier than the laser pistol," Raj replied as the three men climbed the ramp.

Jay tottered to his side, a tremulous smile on her face and tears in her eyes.

Damen wrapped his arms around her. "I appreciate you saving Eudal for me to arrest."

"Cheaper than psychotherapy," she said into his chest. "What did you do with the other mercenary?"

His pulse faltered. "What other mercenary?"

"There were two."

Instinct put Damen's hackles up before he smelled the sharp, bitter poison of the man's hatred.

Snarling, he shoved Jayleia to one side.

Blood oozing from his right ear, Gerriny Eudal tottered on his feet, his gaze locked on Damen's mate, an Isarrite knife in his hand.

Damen pounced. He bowled Gerriny from his feet, twisting away. The spawn of a Myallki bitch wanted to kill his mate?

The man smiled. The cunning behind the twist of lips chilled Damen's blood.

"Your bitch is dead."

Something cold and deadly took possession of Damen. Some things were worth dying for. She was one.

Humming in time with the Chekydran song of reunion resounding inside his skull, he attacked.

His first strike dumped Gerriny to the dirt. The knife skittered away.

The agent scrambled to his hands and knees then dove after it.

Damen followed, aiming a kick at Gerriny's ribcage. He connected. At least two ribs snapped.

Gerriny grunted and stabbed for Damen's leg.

He missed.

Damen didn't. He caught Gerriny's knife hand, planted a knee in the man's diaphragm, crushing his ability to draw breath. Damen bared his teeth and pressed Gerriny's knife toward the agent's chest.

Impotent rage stood out in the man's crimson face.

Good.

For all the pain and suffering he'd caused. For V'kyrri's death. For trying to murder the woman Damen adored.

The blade contacted with Gerriny's shirt.

A thready plea escaped the man's lips.

Damen drove the blade into his heart.

CHAPTER
41

"ARE you hit?" Jayleia rasped. Her hands landed on his shoulders. "Damen! The blade was poisoned! Are you hit?"

"No," he said. "But he won't be getting up again."

"Come on," she urged. "The Chekydran-hiin are advancing on the nest plain."

He rose, turned, touched her cheek, heard the queen's consort humming, and nodded. "Time to keep your promise to protect the queen."

She looked startled.

He grinned. "I don't understand how we're all locked together, you, me, the queen, and her consort. I only know we are."

Her smile looked wistful as they climbed the ramp.

"Sometimes you don't get to choose your family?" she asked.

"It chooses you," he finished for her, smiling in return. "Even when it doesn't share the same branch of the species divide."

It took Damen and Pietre less time to clear the ship by heaving mercenaries out the airlock than it took Jay and Raj to round up a pair of anti-grav units.

Dr. Idylle ended their argument over who had failed to stow the units properly the last time by ordering Raj to help Pietre load the sleeping formula into wide dispersion bombs as the com panel chimed.

While Raj was occupied, Jayleia grabbed a couple of stimulant medications from the medi-bay. He'd protest her taking them, but the drugs were no more a danger to her than the forces gathering for an attack. She trotted to the cockpit to bring the atmospherics online.

The com beeped.

She tabbed open the channel. "*Sen Ekir*."

"*Sen Ekir*!" Captain Ari Idylle's voice rolled across the cockpit, forced good cheer in her voice. "I have an agitated and delusional Ykktyryk mercenary in my brig who swears he and his crew were attacked by a woman falling from the sky. Care to explain?"

Jayleia's smile grew. "I'd love to, *Dagger*, but I'm late for a war. I gather you teleported him out? Good timing. Thanks. I leave you to our esteemed leader, Dr. Idylle. Sir? Your youngest."

"Prepare to lift," Dr. Idylle said, a twinkle in his blue eyes as he looked between Damen and Jay.

"Negative, sir," Damen said. "Jayleia and I aren't going with you. We have an alternate means of transportation. We're needed on the ground. Don't worry. Your bombs won't hurt anyone but their intended targets."

Dr. Idylle blinked as Jayleia joined Damen in the doorway. "I'd hope not. It distresses me to consider what kind of web you'd weave in the process of building yourself a cocoon."

"I'd worry more about what we'd turn into," she muttered as they trotted down the ramp.

Damen's chuckle sounded pained.

The queen and the drone waited beside the *Kawl Fergus*.

Jayleia tugged out of Damen's grasp, rushed to the queen, and gingerly traced the scar on the queen's throat pouch.

The queen hummed assurance and hooked her claws under Jayleia's arms.

The drone did the same to Damen.

They flew into the center of a maelstrom of Chekydran-ki soldiers, workers, and nursery attendants fighting Chekydran-hiin.

The drone set Damen on his feet, beside the new queen's nest chamber.

Jayleia touched down a moment later.

The queen stretched out, lifted her head, and began to sing. The drone fanned his wings. A *chur* arose, resonating across the battlefield.

Damen swayed, buffeted by the sleeping song. The queen and her consort were ordering their Chekydran-hiin children into metamorphosis.

Jayleia closed with him and offered him a wry smile. "I love you."

His blood beat loud in his ears, suffusing him with heat.

"You knew I was planning a bit of revenge, didn't you?" he teased. "For not telling me everything."

Jayleia stiffened, but he sensed the thrill rippling along her nerves. "Revenge? Centered on a pair of neural cuffs?"

"How did you guess?"

She scowled like someone trying not to smile. "How much blood do you require to sate your thirst for vengeance?"

A rush of electricity shot through his veins. "It isn't blood I crave and I will never have my fill of you."

Her heart swelling at the promise in his tone, she prodded, "Still not safe from you?"

"Never."

"Good."

She turned and sprinted to intercept a Chekydran-hiin bearing down on the queen and her consort.

Damen dropped to one knee, shouldered the mercenary rifle he'd brought, and began picking off targets. He wouldn't shoot to kill, only to disable. If their plan worked, there'd be no need to destroy the Chekydran-hiin.

Jayleia ran into the midst of battle with the drone and queen sharing her brain. She knew where to strike, and how hard, in order to

disable her opponents. That was the goal; disable the Chekydran
young until the *Sen Ekir* could arrive and force them into metamorphosis.

She had no desire to kill more of the queen's children than she
had to.

From scout reports, Jayleia gathered some of the young had already succumbed to the queen's song, Chekydran-hiin who'd never
left the planet, who were conditioned to their parents' voices. It
wasn't enough, but at least a few of the innocent ones were safe.

The rumble of approaching atmospherics heartened her as she did
a handspring from a soldier's back to plant her boot right between a
Chekydran-hiin's eye rows. The creature collapsed.

Two more took its place, the pitch of their hum hitching up a
notch, their attacks frenzied.

"Damn," she muttered.

"Damen?" she hollered. "Something's changed! I can't hold
them!"

"The engines!" he yelled. "They're interfering with the song."

She grimaced. They needed the *Sen Ekir*. If there was the remotest
chance that her crazy plan might work, they had to take it. She'd
sworn to protect the queens and she would. But weariness and pain
were her additional enemies now.

Nearby, a bomb detonated in midair.

She turned to look and frowned. Too far away to assess results.

With stress-heightened senses, Jayleia heard a Chekydran-hiin
rush her from behind.

Jay threw her body left. Flinging her feet over her head, she flipped
a half a meter away, touching down on the balls of her feet and one
hand, knees folding to absorb impact.

The Chekydran missed. It sounded heavy and slow.

Jay rolled, dodging the creature's kick. She fetched up against the
remnants of the queen's mound and had to use it to boost herself to
her feet.

Muscles aching, her body weary, and her thinking increasingly muddled, Jayleia caught sight of Damen. Pride swelled in her breast. And love. She loved him. That was enough. Regardless of whether she lived or died.

She still had promises to keep.

One, she desperately wanted to keep: to live for him.

The Chekydran-hiin closed, and swung one tentacle right after the other.

One caught her chin. Jay saw stars. The other tentacle impacted her chest and swept her over the edge into the queen's empty cocoon. When she hit bottom, it knocked the breath from her.

Gasping, she crawled for the opening.

A tentacle grabbed her around the waist and flung her out of the hole, and into the dirt. A rib cracked and she found herself blinking at the striped cloud layer.

The chortling, burbling Chekydran-hiin closed for the kill.

A huge matte black chunk of spaceship hull, bristling with guns and communications arrays blocked out the clouds.

A dot fell from the ship, coming directly for her.

She wondered what it was. Rain? The first Chekydran snow?

A burst of alarm rolled Jay away. The broken ribs shifted. Pain exploded through her torso.

A boom sounded above her.

Her adversary slashed with one leg and laid open Jayleia's arm.

A concussion wave and a spray of odorless liquid pelted her.

Hurt fired up her arm. Training gathered Jayleia in its hands. She mouthed the pain suppression chant in a singsong that followed the queen's melody.

A hum filled her head.

Damen.

The drone.

The infant queen, singing from her cradle.

Bleeding badly from the cut that had rendered her left arm useless, Jayleia smiled and joined in.

Her pulse steadied, strengthened. Pain receded and energy seeped into her limbs.

Her tormentor screamed in triumph.

Instinct brought Jay's hands up.

A razor-sharp claw struck, aiming for her face. She caught it.

It sliced deep into her left hand, ripping a cry of anguish from her abused throat. Blood poured down her arm, but she had the creature's leg. Embedded in the bone of her left thumb.

She wrenched the thing free with her right hand and twisted.

The Chekydran-hiin coughed a ragged protest, fell to its side, and convulsed.

Jayleia frowned.

Another convulsion wracked the insectoid body thrashing in the wyrl-web.

Web.

That was it.

The Chekydran was succumbing to metamorphosis.

She smiled as belated recognition told her she hadn't recognized it as a ship blocking the clouds from view because it hadn't been the *Sen Ekir* dropping the dispersion bomb right on top of her.

It had been the *Dagger*.

Ari had come through.

As if from far away, panic and horror murmured through the space inside her mind.

Damen.

The queens.

The drone.

A wounded nursery attendant limped into Jay's blurring line of sight and shrilled in alarm.

"Come on," she wanted to say, but couldn't. "I'm not that bad off."

Damen fell to his knees beside her, his lips lined white with terror. Sighing, Jayleia closed her eyes, hummed, and welcomed the Swovjiti Healing Trance.

CHAPTER
42

JAYLEIA came awake, humming, knowing that Damen, the queen, and her consort hadn't left her nest chamber since the nursery attendants had packed her in healing gel and wyrl-web. She fell silent. Awareness returned, along with memory. War. Blood. Death.

The light increased. She could guess Damen had sensed her waking and was clearing the web from the top of her shell. She sighed, ridiculously afraid to open her eyes to see the terrible damage that had been done to her body.

A shard of fright stabbed into her system. Her pulse rate rose and she gasped for a breath.

Stop, she instructed.

She'd lived through this before. Besides. What sense did it make from a scientific perspective to allow panic to take over her body chemistry when overwhelming evidence indicated she'd been healed so thoroughly she'd hardly bear scars?

Her heart rate slowed. Good. She recalled one of the major tenets of her Temple training. What could be survived could be endured.

She had promises left to keep.

Opening her eyes, she stirred.

The web released her.

"Open it," she said aloud.

His exultation reached her as he broke the shell and wrenched pieces out of the way.

Her blood quickened and she couldn't keep the grin from her face.

Damen peered in, wearing a matching smile, and drew a deep breath as if by scenting her he assured himself of her well-being. He grabbed her outstretched hands and pulled her to the surface.

Her mate gathered her into his arms, sank until they were both seated on the ground, and tucked her head beneath his chin.

"I heard what you said to your father about choice," he murmured against her ear.

A shiver of awareness went through her.

"You're my mate. I can't change that. But I won't have you coerced," he said, "or manipulated."

Jayleia shook her head, fear spiking through her.

"You don't understand," she said. "I've complained about choice because all my life, I've never earned anything. I'm a xenobiologist whose only claim to a coveted spot on the best science ship in the known systems is that I survived a plague. That was an accident of genetics. I didn't earn my place. My mother was the high priestess of the Temple; they *had* to train me. You had my blood forced on you. I can't even earn your love."

He pulled away.

Missing the warmth and security of his arms around her, she forced herself to meet his gaze regardless of what she might see there.

"I don't know what to say," he finally admitted, his voice mute and hurt. "I love your curiosity and your ability to ask questions about the most mundane things.

"I love your ability to rush headlong into danger to protect the young of any species. You deserve my admiration, my respect, and my love, and not because you gave me your blood."

In the nest they rested against, the young occupant trilled.

The sound resolved in her head. "Parent."

Jay sucked in a sharp breath. One of her genetic daughters.

"Had you intended to declare your daughter queen?" Damen asked, his voice lazy.

"What?" she breathed. It hit her. She'd been so distraught over the injuries Damen and the old queen had sustained, she hadn't paid attention. The new queen, the one she'd chosen, was her genetic daughter.

The young queen hummed in greeting, and acknowledgment, then her hum dwindled as she sank back into sleep.

"It'll take a year or more for her to mature in there. Do you feel anything for her?" he asked. "She's got a piece of you in her makeup."

She stirred the confused tangle of emotions running through her. "As for feeling, I don't know, parental? Is it telling that I think she's going to be beautiful?"

"So do I," he confided, his gray eyes lighting. When he smiled, both sides of his face moved.

She'd lifted a hand to trace the scar before she'd realized. She paused.

He wrapped her hand in his and brought her fingers to his lips. "Raj did surgery. He finished just before the mercenaries arrived."

"You were under sedation when they took the ship," she surmised.

He nodded, suppressed laughter rippling in his voice when he said, "Dr. Idylle, Raj, and Pietre managed to arm themselves with tranquilizer injections. They took out more than half of the mercenaries before Eudal put two and two together."

"Where are my inestimable crewmates?"

"With the Chekydran," he said. "Doing research. Monitoring the progression of the Chekydran-hiin while they're cocooned."

She shuddered.

Damen tugged her back into his arms.

She settled her back against his chest and closed her eyes as he smoothed her hair.

"There are three UMOPG ships . . ." she began.

"Two," he corrected.

She stiffened. "There were three. I'd intended to hand one to Admiral Seaghdh and one to my father and the Citizen's Rights Uprising. The third one I'd intended to use in defense of this planet. Damn it. Someone escaped. I'm sorry."

"What for?"

She shrugged. "I wanted revenge."

"For V'kyrri."

"And for you."

He sighed. "How can you believe you haven't earned my love? But damn it, I don't want love to be conditional or to have to be earned. Am I not allowed to simply love you? I think there comes a time in every life when you have to look inside yourself and become more than you've been up to that point.

"You pull together bits and pieces of information from wildly disparate sources and combine them in ways that boggle my mind."

She frowned, listening to the words rumbling through his chest. "I have to pull all the bits and pieces of me together now?"

"Would it be so bad to claim all of you? To be whole?"

"You make it sound so easy," she said, "and you haven't even let me up to face my family and debriefing."

He chuckled. "The queens threw Ari and your father off planet so you could heal."

Jay sucked in a sharp breath and choked on a laugh.

"They wanted you in the *Dagger*'s medi-bay," he said. "As much to have you in a healing system they trusted as to have immediate debriefing access. You'll be called on to fill in a few holes in the narrative, but between my debriefing and input from the queen's consort, we managed a chillingly clear picture. Your parents are offering to take you and the entire crew of the *Sen Ekir* into the CRU network."

"I'm not leaving," she blurted, "I have an opportunity here, to make a difference. To . . ."

"You committed to help the Chekydran?"

"Yes." She sighed. "I'm glad I could live down everyone's worst expectations of me."

Damen's chuckle vibrated through her bones. "Not mine."

She lifted an eyebrow. "When you have a career and duty? To the family we got out of Silver City? To your Claugh family?"

"You left two out," he noted, resting his cheek against her hair. "I'm a part of the Chekydran, now, like you are. I also have a standing invitation to join the crew of the *Sen Ekir*."

"I have an embarrassment of riches when it comes to families," he said, his voice breaking. "Yet none of them will be home to me unless you're beside me."

Loss ripped her breath from her chest. "One year," she choked, "maybe two. I'll find you wherever . . ."

"Her Majesty, by which I mean Eilod, has requested that I establish and command a Claugh outpost on this world."

Hope slammed her heart into rhythm again. Her eyes burned.

"Our primary aim is establishing diplomatic ties between the Chekydran-ki and the Claugh nib Dovvyth, but the scientific mission runs a close second. Offers have been extended to the entire crew of the *Sen Ekir*, you included, I believe. If you decide to stay, I'll be right here beside you," he promised.

"Threatening to lock me in neural cuffs?" she finished for him, smiling.

He growled deep in his throat and tightened his arms around her. "That hasn't stopped you so far. And there are advantages to being properly motivated."

Jayleia laughed as heat flooded her body. "Tahem said, 'Don't let the past define what you could become.' I don't want to become anything that doesn't include you."

"Is that your choice?" Hope, mingled with elation rang in his question.

She detected the erratic beat of his heart, and smiled. "You're my mate. I can't be whole without you. You're already a part of me. Even if you manipulated me into a trap of your making."

He stilled.

Her smile widened and her heart took wing. "I promised to protect you until the day I died, so you turned around and extorted a promise from me to live for you. A very neat snare, Damen Sindrivik."

Damen laughed, hope and exultation in the sound.